VETERINARY
PARTNER

Visit us at www.boldstrokesbooks.com

VETERINARY PARTNER

by

Nancy Wheelton

2020

VETERINARY PARTNER

ISBN 13: 978-1-63555-666-7

This Trade Paperback Original Is Published By
Bold Strokes Books, Inc.
P.O. Box 249
Valley Falls, NY 12185

First Edition: June 2020

Credits
Editors: Victoria Villasenor and Cindy Cresap
Production Design: Susan Ramundo
Cover Design By Tammy Seidick

Chapter One

Dr. Lauren Cornish slung her equipment into the back of her pickup truck and, without washing the blood and manure off her boots, jumped into the cab. She slammed the door and revved the engine. She wanted to roar down Callie's driveway spitting gravel, but that would be unprofessional, and she would hear about it from her bosses. Instead, she squeezed the life out of her steering wheel, her fingers turning white. *Deep breaths. That woman is frustrating. You only tried to help.* A timid tap on her window caused her to jump in her seat. She straightened, and with one eyebrow raised studied tall, blond Callie Anderson.

Contrite blue eyes, brilliant in the first light of sunrise, regarded Lauren through the passenger window of the cab. Callie mouthed, "Please wait. I'm sorry."

Lauren pried her hands off the steering wheel and rolled her shoulders. She'd been at Callie's farm, Poplarcreek, for the last three hours and she was cold and tired. She climbed out and strode toward the back of her truck. She couldn't show up at the next farm with dirty boots, however much she wanted to escape from Callie's farm. But if Callie wasn't going to listen to her, she'd just wash her boots and go. "Please excuse me, Mrs. Anderson. I thought my suggestions did *not* interest you. I was *not* aware you had questions. Sorry, please go ahead. I'm at your disposal."

Lauren grabbed the hose attached to the twenty-gallon water tank in her truck and sprayed water into a red bucket, followed by disinfectant. She snatched a long-handled brush from her truck and washed the blood and manure off her boots.

Callie cleared her throat. "Thanks for your help this morning."

While she scrubbed her boots, Lauren struggled to regain her composure, taking deep breaths.

"I'm sorry I snapped at you," Callie said. "So many people have been telling me I made a bunch of wrong decisions for the farm. People are trying to be helpful, I know, but sometimes it's annoying."

"Like me?" Lauren snorted and poured the dirty water on the ground. She fought the urge to dump the pail at Callie's feet. Though it was tempting, she banished the childish impulse.

She tossed her empty pail and brush into the back of the Bowie unit housed in the bed of her silver four-door pickup truck. The Bowie had been expensive, but mobile veterinary units were a godsend, and it meant she didn't have to ask Callie for water, since she had her own supply. She took another breath and swiveled to face her.

Callie raised her arms as if she might cross them over her chest but appeared to change her mind and let them drop instead. "I'm tired of being reminded I'm a novice. I agreed the heifer was too young to be calving, but why did you say it three times? Once was enough, and I didn't appreciate being told it was inhumane. What's done is done and I have to cope with it, as do my poor animals."

Lauren pretended to rearrange the equipment in the back of her truck and tried to relax the muscles in her neck. "Don't you pay your veterinarian for advice?"

"Advice and suggestions are great, but I've been up all night, and I resented the lecture."

Lauren gripped the edge of the truck and hung her head. She *had* been lecturing, and Callie's irritation was justified. "I was only trying to help."

"It's difficult to tell these days who is helping and who is judging, and I felt like a stupid little woman, again."

Ouch. I was a patronizing jerk. Welcome back, Dr. Lauren Cornish, you snarky cow. "I'm sorry. Did I overstep?" Lauren turned to face Callie.

"Perhaps."

"Who thinks you're a little woman?" Lauren grinned, figuring Callie was at least three inches taller than her five seven. "Sorry. It's a state of mind. I get it."

Callie's shoulders relaxed as the tension between her and Lauren dissipated. "You do understand."

"I offered advice, but I should've worded it differently and I shouldn't have stomped off when you told me to stop lecturing you. Sorry, again." Lauren chuckled. "Wow, how many times have we said sorry? How Canadian of us."

"I apologized to the barn door for hitting it with my elbow yesterday. How weird is that?" Callie smiled at Lauren for the first time all morning.

Callie's smile made it to her eyes this time. Lauren swallowed, startled by the stab of attraction. Even in bulky insulated coveralls with more patches than a quilt, and an ugly orange wool cap, Callie was exquisite. Lauren shook her head. Those thoughts did not belong at work. "I guess that's it for now."

"Thanks. You know I'll be calling if there's another problem." Callie gave a little wave and headed back to the barn.

Lauren watched Callie for a moment and then climbed into her truck. How could one beautiful woman unsettle her so much? Especially a woman who was too inexperienced to be in charge of animals. Callie was nice and all, but under her management, Poplarcreek was a disaster waiting to happen, and she wanted no part of that.

After finishing at Poplarcreek, Lauren drove home for a quick shower and hurried to the clinic. As the newest veterinarian at Prairie Veterinary Services, it was her job to check on the patients before morning appointments started. She arrived at PVS at eight thirty a.m. The harsh wind of a snowy Saskatchewan morning pushed at her as she struggled to close the back door.

PVS was a mixed animal veterinary practice in Thresherton, Saskatchewan, a one-hour drive southeast of Saskatoon. The clinic saw pet animals such as dogs, cats, birds, and small rodents. PVS had many large animal clients with pigs, cattle, sheep, horses, and goats. The veterinarians drove to the farms when the large animals required treatment, but often farmers transported livestock to PVS for surgery.

Lauren dropped her coat and boots at her locker and slipped on the shoes she kept there. "Morning, Val. How's Rufus today?"

"He's brighter and ate his breakfast." Valerie Connor, the head veterinary technician, stood beside Lauren and they studied the dog. "I was about to take him for a short walk."

"Great." Lauren placed her lunch in the staff room refrigerator, greeted Janice, the full-time receptionist, and scanned the waiting room for clients. PVS was a serviceable facility, but the walls of the waiting area were a dull gray. The sole attempt at decorating was the yellowing horse and dog prints her boss, Dr. Ian Wilson, had hung thirty years ago. PVS could use some redecorating. It didn't have to look like a palace, but an updated appearance would bring in more small animal clients, and these days people expected a comfortable waiting room.

Lauren had built a small animal practice in Toronto, Ontario, with her ex-wife, Dr. Tanya Jenkins. She and T.J. had paid their professional decorator thousands of dollars. They had painted the walls in soft blue tones to accent the colorful paintings of pets. Cushioned chairs matched the walls and were organized around a coffee table with books on animals and leaflets on pet care. The built-in electric fireplace and a fish tank gave their waiting room the feel of a cozy living room.

PVS's blandness didn't mean the animals were any less cared for in Thresherton, but as the only veterinary practice within eighty kilometers, it could dispense with the glitz without losing customers. The PVS building began life as an automotive repair business and still had the wide-open cement feel of the shop. It couldn't get much further from her past experience, and that was exactly what she needed. That said, it could still use a little updating.

Lauren strolled into the cavernous waiting area toward Val's eight-year-old daughter. Gwendolyn sat on one of the plastic chairs in the row against the outer wall. The girl's head was bent over her schoolbooks. "Morning, Gwen."

Gwen raised her head and beamed at Lauren. "Hi, Lauren. Rufus ate his breakfast this morning. Mom and I came back before bed last night, but he wouldn't eat canned food even when I fed him from my hand."

Lauren dropped into a chair beside Gwen and slung an arm over her shoulders. Gwen was waiting for her grandfather to pick her up and drop her at school. Val was a single mom and started work at seven thirty a.m. Thresherton was a small, rural town of six thousand, and Gwen might have walked to school in the warmer weather. But today it was minus thirty degrees Celsius. Not exactly the kind of weather to skip to school in.

"Thanks for trying. The drugs we gave him yesterday upset his stomach, and he needed time to get his appetite back."

"That's what Mom said."

"Have a good day at school." Lauren dropped a kiss on the top of Gwen's head and walked back to reception.

At one end of the waiting area, the receptionists sat at a long counter. Beside them, the cabinets housed the medical records of patients and clients. On the other side of reception there were individual doors leading to two exam rooms used for appointments with small animals. The exam rooms opened into the treatment room. Behind reception were the offices for veterinarians and the clinic office manager.

Lauren headed into her office to drop her briefcase and unpack the patient files she took home to review. She studied her reflection in the mirror behind her door. Her eyes looked tired and dull. T.J, at least at the beginning of their relationship, had described them as warm and animated. That was when she and T.J. had been young and full of excitement about the future. All Lauren did now was work to live and pay off student loans. No wonder her green eyes looked more like pond scum than spring grass.

Lauren sighed as she fought with her hair that had been sticking out at odd angles since she pulled her wool hat off. *Perhaps I should have dried it after my shower?* Lauren preferred her hair short and practical. When it was tidy, it was a flattering cut. It curled around her ears and onto her neck but stopped short of her shoulders. Too bad it was seldom tidy. Now she just tried to cultivate the messy look. Hair product was too fussy.

As per the schedule, Lauren started the day taking care of the small animals. She donned a fresh white lab coat and buttoned it closed. She smiled, pleased it was looser in the belly and tighter through the biceps. Regular trips to the gym and her hard, rewarding job at PVS had helped her shed forty pounds since she arrived in Thresherton eight months ago. She pinched the roll of fat at her waist. She still had weight to lose, but at one hundred and fifty pounds of muscle wrapped in softness, she was proud of how far she'd come.

Lauren headed into the treatment room. When Val returned with Rufus, Lauren lifted him onto the table and examined him. She gave him his medication and placed him in his kennel. Then she and Val looked after the other small animals in the clinic. When they were done, Lauren played with a litter of stray kittens. She had perfected the technique of cuddling two at a time and pretended the contact was to get the kittens used to people. A few minutes later, she returned the rowdy kittens to their kennel and headed to Ian's office. She admired her boss, and her goal was to emulate him by getting fit, working hard, and being well-liked in the community.

"Morning, Ian, anything special for today?" Lauren asked. "We have a full schedule of annual dog and cat vaccinations. What's happening on the large animal side?"

"Callie Anderson called. She has another dystocia in her Charolais heifers."

"Another one? Already? I did a C-section for her this morning." Charolais were a large breed of beef cow, and a dystocia, or difficult calving, was uncommon unless you had Callie's luck.

"It's not been an easy calving season for her."

"Because she has twenty, sixteen-month-old heifers calving right now. It's not too early for mature cows to be calving, but these are immature heifers. Practically babies. This spring is the earliest time to breed such young heifers for the first time. Why would she have bred them so young they're calving in February?" Lauren was horrified by the stress on the young animals, but she was ranting and took a deep steadying breath.

"A valid point. And I have no idea."

"When I asked her this morning, she yelled at me and accused me of lecturing her. I'm afraid my comments *were* pretty brusque. I thought she was going to cry when I'd finished. But I couldn't help it. It's irresponsible." Fear of Callie's weeping, not her angry words, had been Lauren's cue to bolt from the barn. She had to leave before Callie's tears slipped through the cracks in Lauren's defenses and triggered her protective side. Then the instinct to look after Callie would follow, and she was determined not to go there again.

"Callie's been raising her daughter alone since her wife died five years ago, and she's been running the farm by herself since her father-in-law, Doug Anderson, died last year. Poplarcreek is a huge responsibility, and Doug didn't teach her much about cattle before he died."

"She's gay? Did you know Callie's wife?" Callie was beautiful and a lesbian and needed a ton of help. The best place for Lauren was far away from Poplarcreek.

"I'd known Liz since she was a kid. She joined the police department and was killed on the job. She was only thirty-five. Such a damn waste."

"How horrible for them."

"I'm keeping an eye on Callie and her daughter, Becky. Callie's making mistakes, but she's learning quickly. At least she has help in the house. Her older sister, Martha, is visiting from British Columbia. Anyway, I've done two C-sections and a calving there in the last week. I know you were just there, but it's your turn again."

Ian scratched his chin. "While you're there, check the new calves for scour and see if Callie understands how to take care of them. Just give her a hand, will you?"

"No problem." Lauren left to change into coveralls and pack her gear. Ian's daughter and business partner, Dr. Fiona Wilson, would do the small animal appointments in the morning when Lauren left. Lauren's job today was more handholding at Poplarcreek. She entered the pharmacy and collected antibiotics and electrolytes for Callie's calves.

Val was tidying the pharmacy shelves and glanced over her shoulder at Lauren. "Heading out already?"

"Back to Poplarcreek."

Val winced. "Poor Callie. Another C-section?"

"Hope not." Lauren packed her gear. "Ian asked me to check on the calves. How will I explain to Callie, without upsetting her this time, that scour is dangerous in young calves because they could dehydrate and die? I didn't realize how little she knows about cattle, and I need to teach her without lecturing. But it's not my forte."

"You can do it. Callie's probably in over her head, but she's tough. I think with enough time, she's got a chance."

Lauren seriously doubted it. "Callie needs more help with her cattle than the vet showing up every ten minutes. Why not hire somebody? Surely it would be cheaper than calling a veterinarian for every calving?" But then Callie wasn't the most sensible of women and it was Lauren's job to help clean up Callie's mess.

Val laughed. "Why not ask her?"

Lauren gave a comical shudder. "And get my head bitten off again? Not a chance. Wish me luck with my new pupil."

Val patted Lauren's shoulder. "You'll think of something, L.C."

Val had become Lauren's good friend, even though Val was eight years younger. They hung out at lunch and sometimes she agreed to have dinner at Val's house with her and Gwen. In her Toronto veterinary clinic there had been a distinct social separation between veterinarians and staff. Nobody would have called her L.C., and there was little socializing beyond the obligatory Christmas dinner. She preferred the relaxed atmosphere at PVS, as long as everyone kept their distance and stayed in the colleague or friend zone.

Lauren gave a little wave as she left. "Thanks, V.C."

CHAPTER TWO

Thirty minutes later, Lauren rolled into the yard at Poplarcreek and parked by the cattle barn. The property had several buildings. A large cattle barn capable of housing a hundred head of cattle protected Callie's herd of sixty from the worst of the winter weather. An empty horse barn with six stalls stood beside the cattle barn. It wasn't decrepit but could use a cleaning.

The small utility building, west of the house, would house a generator. A huge machine shed held tractors, a cultivator, a planter, and a combine. Callie's house appeared to be an old farmhouse the same age as the wooden barns and would have at least six bedrooms. It had a wraparound porch encrusted with faded, peeling green paint. It was a solid house, but the porch made it look shabby. The porch probably wasn't a high priority to Callie, but a few dollars and a couple of high school kids would have sorted that out. How could she stand to have people see it that way?

Most farmers brought their cattle into PVS for C-sections. They didn't want to stand in a cold barn any more than Lauren wanted to work in one. But Callie couldn't transport her animals. She had a stock trailer and a truck with a hitch, but towing the trailer scared her, especially with snow on the roads. And even if she got it to the clinic, Callie hadn't learned how to back it up to the loading chute. When Lauren had moved to Saskatchewan, she'd towed a trailer of her belongings from Ontario and only stopped where she didn't have to back up, so she understood, to some extent. *But if you're going to own cattle...* Lauren shrugged. She'd do her job and go.

Lauren jumped from her truck and yanked on her rubber boots. She grabbed her calving kit and squared her shoulders before striding into the barn toward the calving pens, figuring Callie would probably be with the heifer in trouble. The cattle barn housed livestock on the ground floor while the upper floor was storage for hay and straw. As she passed pens of cows and calves, the air was hazy with their breath and the steam that rose from their bodies. The water system would have supplemental heating to keep it from freezing, but the animals' body heat warmed the barn. It was warmer inside than outside, and the barn protected Lauren from the wind, but she would need to work quickly to stay warm.

She peeked inside each calving pen until she found a heifer flat on its side on a thick bed of fresh straw. The animal emitted feeble groans with each pitiful contraction. The heifer was a healthy Charolais, well-muscled, but much too young to be calving. Crouched by the beast's shoulder and stroking its neck was Callie.

"Mrs. Anderson? Callie?"

Callie glanced at Lauren and nodded before turning away. "Hi, Lauren." Callie wiped at her eyes with the sleeve of her jacket and tugged her wool cap firmly over her ears.

Callie's dejected state almost made her feel sorry for her. But her past had taught Lauren to keep her head down and her eyes on the job. There was no room for emotions here. She advanced into the calving pen. "What's been happening?"

"She's been pushing for at least an hour, but I don't know when she started."

Poor creature. The thought leaped into Lauren's head, but she wasn't sure if she meant Callie or the heifer. She set her kit down and slipped off her heavy parka. She shivered in the chilly barn and wished she could keep the coat on, but it was too bulky to work in. She hung it on a handy nail.

Callie rose and stepped out of the way. "I'll get the water." Callie disappeared and a few minutes later, returned with a bucket. The steam rose off the hot water and mingled with their breath.

Lauren pulled on a rubber calving suit over her coveralls to keep her dry while she worked. She opened her calving kit, snagged a bottle of liquid soap, and shot two squirts into the bucket. "Let's see what's happening." Using the side of her boot, she pushed a pile of fresh, dry straw behind the animal and kneeled.

Lauren washed the heifer with warm soapy water around the vulva and below her tail. Then she tugged on a shoulder-high disposable OB glove and reached inside. "The calf's too big for the heifer's pelvis. Another C-section. Sorry." Lauren stood and stripped off the OB sleeve.

Callie's shoulders drooped and she groaned. "Of course, it'll be a C-section." Callie sighed in one loud puff. She fetched a long extension cord, two more buckets of hot water, and a ten-foot length of baling twine. "Let's do it."

Nearly an hour later, they managed to get the calf out and the mother sewn up. The sight of the calf wobbling toward its mother for its first drink was sweet.

"She's a nice heifer calf and will cover the cost of the C-section if you sell her in the fall." Lauren was impressed by Callie's calm demeanor throughout the ordeal, and she thought of what Val had said. Maybe she would succeed after all. But probably not.

Callie grimaced. "I'm relieved I have a healthy calf, but please, don't mention my huge vet bill."

Lauren grinned. "Every tenth C-section or calving should be free. I'll suggest to Fiona and Ian we enroll you in our frequent heifer-surgery reward program." As she spoke, Lauren started gathering up her tools.

Callie nodded, but had no smile for Lauren's joke as she watched her work. "I know my heifers are much too young to be calving. They were in the paddock by the creek. I'd planned to leave them there to grow and play all summer and fall, then bring them in for the winter. My neighbor's bull busted into the paddock and bred them. You know Heinz Kruger and his sons, Tommy and Kyle? Anyway, they searched for the bull and when they found him, they roped him and towed him out with a tractor. Then they patched my fence. But obviously the damage was already done." Callie counted on her fingers. "There've been six C-sections and four calvings and I still have ten heifers left to calve. Not a good start to this calving season. The only upside is I have amazing calves because my heifers and the bull are purebred Charolais. At least that's lucky."

Lauren busied herself with her task to avoid eye contact with Callie. "Yes, lucky." She doubted the bull breaking into the heifer paddock was an accident. *Callie's too naive to spot whatever scheme Heinz Kruger is up to.* And how long was the bull in with the heifers? Lauren tossed her dirty instruments in a bucket of water and scrubbed the debris off them.

Callie untied the heifer mom, rinsed her hands in the bucket, and helped Lauren carry her equipment out of the pen. A healthy calf seemed to have improved Callie's mood. She grasped Lauren's forearm and held it for a few beats. "Thanks, Lauren."

Startled by the contact, Lauren's cheeks burned as she grinned back. She would have recoiled if any other stranger had touched her. She preferred to keep her distance until she got to know a person.

When Callie released her arm, Lauren collected her gear and stowed it in her calving kit. Callie handed Lauren her parka, and she pulled it on. "Let's look at the other calves while I'm here. It might save you the cost of calling us out again." Lauren had no intention of spending all day driving back and forth to Poplarcreek.

They strolled to the other pens to inspect the new crop of youngsters. "Have you seen any scour? Ian asked me to check."

Callie nodded. "Possibly the little one, or maybe he's the littler one. He's in the corner pen by the door with his mother. I'm not sure I know how to treat calves for scour."

Lauren gazed into warm blue eyes framed by strands of white-blond hair escaping from a wool cap. Callie was strong and beautiful. Lauren sucked in her breath, amazed that Callie could still smile. She marveled that Callie stayed optimistic with so much responsibility and after being widowed young. Lauren would have been ranting, swearing, and mad at the world. Hell, she was like that anyway, and her ex was alive and well. Callie must have a core of steel and determination that helped her stay positive.

"No problem. It's good you're willing to say when you don't know how to do something. Heifers don't supply as much immunity to their calves as mature cows do. Calves without immunity are more prone to developing scour. Calves with scour may dehydrate and die. Electrolytes replace the minerals lost because of the diarrhea." Lauren stopped, conscious of their argument that morning. "Was that a lecture? It wasn't meant to be."

Callie shook her head. "Thanks for the information."

Lauren examined the calf and noted its elevated temperature and the wet, yellowed fur under its tail. She observed mild lethargy and drooping ears. "Watch the abnormal way its skin tents when I pull it. He has scour for sure. He's dehydrated, but not at the dangerous stage yet. I have antibiotics and electrolytes in the truck. Bottle-feed the electrolytes if he'll drink them. If he won't drink them or it takes much longer for his skin to smooth out, you'll need to bring him to the clinic for IV fluids."

Lauren jotted the calf's ear tag number on her PVS record pad of NCR paper and noted the animal's clinical signs. At the bottom of the page she wrote the dose of antibiotic to give and instructions on how often to administer the electrolytes. When she finished the note, she handed the original to Callie and kept the copy for the clinic records. "Do you want help to get started?"

"I can do it, thanks." Callie rolled her shoulders and sighed. Then she raised her hand as if reaching for something. Then she lowered it. A second later, she raised it again.

Lauren frowned. "Is there something else?"

"You have a streak of something on your face." Callie tried to wipe it off Lauren's cheek. "Yikes, now I've smeared it. Come to the house for coffee and you can clean off my artwork."

It wasn't a busy day, but Lauren had other farms to visit. She could wipe her face clean using her truck rearview mirror and probably should. As a rule, she turned down all offers of a cup of coffee or something else from clients. Going into their houses invited unwanted confidences and often made it necessary for her to fake appreciation of the new couch, a child's art project, or the latest recipe for muffins.

Lauren spoke, not sure where her words came from. "Thanks. It would be nice to wash my face. And a hot drink sounds amazing."

After stowing her gear in the truck, Lauren retrieved the antibiotics and electrolytes from her front seat and gave them to Callie. Then she snagged her flashing phone off the dash and listened to a message from Janice.

Calving at Myrondale. Call the clinic if you're too busy and Ian will go. Lauren smiled with relief as her excuse to linger evaporated. "Sorry. I wish I could come in, but I have another calving. Thanks anyway."

Lauren had her escape, but she wished her next calving wasn't Myrondale. Barry Myronuk didn't bring his cattle to PVS for C-sections or calvings, because he was lazy. He made his son stay in the cold barn with the veterinarian, unwilling to brave the cold himself. Lauren shuddered. There would be no buckets of hot water at Myrondale. Their animal would be in a squeeze chute or lying on a cold cement floor cushioned by only a few wisps of dirty straw.

Callie shook Lauren's hand and Lauren was sure she held it a few seconds longer than necessary.

"Maybe next time." Callie shrugged and a slight grin floated across her face a second before she returned to the barn.

Flattered by the disappointment in Callie's eyes, Lauren smiled. Then warning bells blared in her head. *Put those thoughts out of your head, Lauren Louise Cornish. You're in Saskatchewan to do a job, not to make friends.* Besides, Callie had a farm to look after and a kid to raise. Lauren cleared her mind of all things blond and beautiful and switched her thoughts to another calving.

Chapter Three

Callie mixed the electrolytes for the scouring calf. He was a sweet calf with appealing deep brown eyes and an innocent face. She poured the liquid into a calf nursing bottle. "Here you go. The sexy vet says electrolytes will stop the scour, so drink up, honey."

Doug had taught her how to lean over the calf and hold the bottle. It drank when something above its head mimicked a cow's body. Callie chuckled as the tiny calf butted her with its head while it drank.

Callie spoke to the calf as he suckled. "Becky is nine years old and old enough to feed calves. You and I'll give her lesson number one after school today."

Callie's morning had been horrendous, but the tension had drained from her body with Lauren's arrival. Lauren was an attractive blend of confidence and compassion, for the animals and inexperienced farmers, both. Callie was grateful there were no sharp words or hurt feelings, this time. Whoever said women looked beautiful when they were angry had never met Lauren Cornish. When angry, she was scary, but she could cause a girl to melt inside with one bright smile.

Callie shook her head to dispel the image. She had no time for melting around Lauren. She laughed. Who had time for all that romantic nonsense? It was too bad Lauren had rushed off, though. A cup of coffee would have been nice, and she had no objection to making a friend. A friend who understood agriculture and what she was up against.

When the calf finished his electrolytes, Callie gave him an injection of antibiotics using the dose Lauren prescribed. "Sorry, honey." Callie winced as he kicked out with the leg she injected. "The needle's done, sweetie. That's the good drugs working." Callie had flinched the first few times she gave injections. She wrapped an arm around the calf and held him against her body. Then she rubbed his leg where she had injected him, to help clear away the sting of the needle. Baby animals liked touch as much as baby humans, and she was good at that.

She closed the barn and fetched her small tractor from the drive shed. She grabbed a large round bale of hay and drove into the paddock where she placed the hay in the feeder for the cows. When she finished her chores, she headed to the house. It was only ten a.m. and she was tired already.

In the mudroom, Callie hung her coat on a hook, kicked off her boots, and dropped her gloves on the heater to dry. She used the bathroom and then shuffled downstairs to feed the washing machine. "How do two people create such a mountain of laundry?"

She emptied the dryer and folded the laundry. She held one of Liz's old RCMP sweatshirts to her chest and buried her nose in it, hoping to find Liz's scent. Callie had worn it to bed for five years. The collar was in tatters and she could no longer read all the letters spread over the chest. When it was new, the shirt had said, Royal Canadian Mounted Police. She folded the sweatshirt and put it in a bin with Liz's other clothes. It was time to stop wearing them.

Her sister, Martha, was visiting for three weeks and helping her sort through Liz's belongings. She had saved one box of items for Becky, one box for herself, and the rest she would let go. Liz had died five years ago. She still missed her, but not with the deep, crushing grief she'd had in the beginning.

The first two years after Liz died, Callie and Becky had lived with Callie's parents. Callie had spent hours hiding in bed or staring at the wall. Then she'd moved from British Columbia to Poplarcreek to be near Liz's father, who needed some help and company. The change had also been good for Becky, who loved the animals and the adventure of riding the school bus.

Callie sighed. Liz had been gorgeous and strong, and her deep brown eyes were always full of laughter. But things hadn't been perfect. Liz had always been in charge and Callie had let her make most of the decisions. When Liz was gone, Callie realized just how much she didn't know how to do, how naive she was, and how much she had to learn. Now that she was older, Callie would insist on an equal relationship. If and when that time came.

Callie extracted her sheets from the washer and added them to the dryer. She loved the subtle shades of peach and the flower pattern on her sheets. When they moved in, Doug had insisted she have the largest bedroom. She'd brought little from the house she'd shared with Liz. So, after painting the room, she had forced herself to pick new curtains, sheets, bedspread, and carpet. Her pillows had soaked up many tears over Liz in those early years. Her bedroom was a bright, cheery room with a view of the small backyard and garden.

Callie carried the basket of clean laundry upstairs and set it on the kitchen table. Breakfast was the next task. While the coffee perked, she put two slices of bread in the toaster and dug through the refrigerator to find the egg salad Martha had made. As she leaned against the counter waiting for the coffee and toast, she flashed to Lauren's smiling eyes and curvy body. It was a shame Lauren had vanished in such a hurry. One minute, she'd appeared eager to stay, but after the call about the other calving, she'd looked relieved to go.

"Oh well, she wasn't interested in visiting with me. Lauren is smart, educated, and a doctor. I only have two years of technical college. I'd bore her straight. Well, not straight." Callie chuckled at her conversation with the coffeepot. "Talking to small appliances? Time for a break from the farm."

Callie sifted through three days' worth of mail. She got tired of the all the bills, many overdue. She peeled open the intriguing red envelope and removed the Valentine's Day card. She gagged when she read the saccharine sentiment, then she tore the card in eight and stuffed it in the trash. A card from Kyle Kruger, her irritating and revolting neighbor. The man didn't take no for an answer. She bet she could yell at him and he'd see it as encouragement. He was creepy, but not scary like his father. Heinz Kruger's last letter had been a list of how old all her farm machinery was. How did he even know that? Then he'd included the cost to replace it if there were a fire. That letter she had kept for the police just in case her drive shed mysteriously caught fire.

Callie spread egg salad on her toast and set it on the table with her coffee. She dropped into a chair and surveyed her kitchen with satisfaction. After calving season and before seeding, she would tackle the kitchen cupboards or the front porch. But then the porch looked pleasantly rustic and it was days of work. "Cupboards first." Callie nodded, pleased with her decision. It was more important to be comfortable inside, and the kitchen cupboards screamed for sanding and repainting. Callie sighed. Her three-story house was almost one hundred years old, but still sturdy. After she and Becky had moved in with Doug, he'd suggested redecorating. Callie had agreed because the house needed it, but she knew Doug had sensed she needed a project to keep her busy.

First, she'd painted most of the rooms, beginning with Liz's old room, the one Becky picked for herself. Then she and Doug had removed the torn and scuffed linoleum from the kitchen floor and laid new tile. The basement remained unfinished, but the main floor held a big country kitchen, an office, a utility room, and a small living room with a fireplace. This time of the year she loved to stack logs in the fireplace and watch the flames. She often shut the living room door, and she and Becky snuggled on the couch and read books or watched television.

Still, it was a house begging for a large family. There were full bathrooms on each floor and the top floor had six bedrooms. Becky's room, her room, Doug's room, and three guest rooms. The guest bedrooms were sparsely furnished, with peeling wallpaper and scratched and worn wood floors. Still, her family and friends used the guest rooms when they visited. Callie had made an excellent start with the decorating but hadn't done any for a year. She told herself she was watching expenses, but the truth was that she'd had no heart for decorating since Doug died.

Callie rolled her shoulders. Forget the porch. Her next job, after she finished the kitchen, would be the spare rooms. Martha would have decorating ideas, but farm work was never ending, and decorating would be the last thing to happen. After Doug died, Callie became responsible for the entire farm. One thousand acres of wheat fields and sixty head of cattle and their calves. The days were long and hard, and fixing up the house was the last thing she wanted to do when she fell into bed at night.

Callie sipped her coffee. Martha was also helping her sort through Doug's belongings. She'd donate the clothes. Personal items she would save for Becky or box and ship to Liz's brothers. It was a painful slog sorting through all the keepsakes and memories of people's lives. Callie sniffled and reached for a tissue. She wanted to give Becky a sense of stability, so she hadn't removed any photographs from the walls or shelves. There were still reminders of Liz everywhere. Callie looked up as Martha entered the kitchen.

"Is that fresh coffee I smell?" Martha asked.

"Yes."

"How did the calving go?"

Callie moved to the sink and washed her hands. "A C-section, but I have another heifer calf." Callie pointed to her breakfast. "Do you want a sandwich?"

"No, thanks. I ate breakfast with Becky and then drove her to school."

"Sorry she missed the bus again. It takes a small explosion to get my kid out of bed unless it's a weekend. Thanks, Mar."

Martha poured herself a coffee and settled on a chair beside Callie. "It was fun, and she loves telling me about the farm."

"This place is in her blood. She's flourishing here. Happier than I've seen her in years. And she loves the cattle."

"I got that. I received a thorough accounting of all the new calves."

Callie smiled. "Did you get to see pictures? Becky loves her camera."

Martha laughed. "I did, but I have to admit each beige-white calf looked pretty much like the rest except for the boy-girl difference. She was disappointed that you couldn't weigh them at birth so she could chart their growth."

"Yeah, maybe." Callie stared at the wall and nibbled her sandwich.

Martha slid her chair closer and laid her hand on Callie's shoulder. "Where are you? You look sad."

"Hard to believe Liz died almost five years ago."

"You still miss her."

Callie straightened. No more pity party. "Yeah, I still miss Liz, but I'm ready to live again." A twinge of guilt poked at her as she imagined kissing someone else. *Could I miss Liz and still be ready to love again?* She had love to give and Liz no longer needed it. Not that she had time for that kind of thing. But it was nice to daydream, and the vet was a good, safe option in that regard.

Callie sighed. How soft would Lauren's full breasts be? Callie loved breasts. Not her own. They were too small, but other women's were amazing. She loved the feel and taste. She enjoyed the way a woman's nipple would grow taut under her tongue. "Enough. I'm not ogling the vet's breasts." Callie's hand flew to cover her mouth. She couldn't believe she'd spoken out loud.

"Excuse me?" Martha's eyebrows winged up. "I see the new vet has caught your attention."

Callie groaned and pillowed her head on her arms. "But I'm making a poor impression. I'm either yelling at her or crying in front of her."

Martha rubbed Callie's back. "Are you sure she's a lesbian?"

Callie shifted to face Martha. "I saw her in the grocery store once. She was wearing a pair of expensive black slacks and a dark-blue shirt that fit her curves to perfection. She was gorgeous. Maybe I was staring, I'm not sure, but the woman nearest me winked at me. She told me Lauren was a lesbian and didn't hide it. I almost asked why she should hide, but I let it go."

"Some random woman in the grocery store said that? That's kind of weird."

"I knew her slightly from some activity at Becky's school." Callie shrugged. "I guess I'm getting used to small town life where everybody knows everything about everybody. It's no secret that I'm gay."

"Perhaps she told you because she was trying to be kind." Martha nudged Callie with an elbow. "Are people trying to fix you up?"

Callie pushed her plate aside, propped her elbow on the table, and rested her chin in her hand. "The cashier told me Lauren was picking up a dessert for a party at one of the veterinarian's homes. She wore no makeup, but it's not like that's some big indication. Some women just don't. Lauren's wavy short hair, bright green eyes, and masses of freckles are something makeup wouldn't improve anyway." Callie sighed. "The natural look suits her perfectly."

"You've got it bad."

Callie shook her head. "No, I don't. I just need a night out. My friend Rachel's been bugging me to come to Saskatoon for a visit." Callie longed to have some fun. No dating, though. That was a mistake she wouldn't repeat. She'd dated a woman for three months the previous year, but their relationship had fizzled out because the woman hated Poplarcreek and Callie refused to meet up four nights a week in Saskatoon. She'd struggled to find time to get away on Saturday nights. Hell, she'd barely had the interest or energy to pay attention to the woman's conversation. After that Callie had tried to have a one-night stand, but she couldn't follow through. Sex without connection was meaningless.

"Mar, how about a night out while you're here? Let's go to the city on Saturday. A tasty dinner and then dancing, maybe? Rainbow's a straight-friendly club. It'll be a riot. There's no shortage of babysitters around here."

"No thanks. I'll stay with my niece, but you have fun. Maybe you'll meet somebody."

"Whoa, hang on. I'm talking about a little fun." She wasn't sure why she felt the need to justify herself, but she did anyway. "I'll always love Liz, but I need a break from the farm, and Rachel's a lot of laughs."

"So, no dating?"

"An active nine-year-old to raise and a farm to run are a lot to handle. Fitting a relationship into my life would be beyond tricky. Now come and help me pick out a dress."

Chapter Four

Callie stuffed toiletries and a spare set of clothes into a small suitcase. She wasn't planning on staying in Saskatoon overnight, but it was good to be prepared if the weather changed and she was stuck. Although, given the calving problems at Poplarcreek, being away from the farm overnight wasn't a good idea. She glanced at the clock. It was Saturday afternoon, and she was headed into the city to meet Rachel for lunch and then they planned to shop. She had no money for new clothes, but it was fun trying on the latest dresses.

Callie looked up and smiled as Becky bounced into the room. Becky was bursting with energy. She opened her arms and Becky ran in and hugged her around the waist. She hugged Becky back and kissed her on the top of the head. "Hello, you. Will you be okay with Aunt Martha for the evening? I'll stay if you want."

"No, Mommy. You have fun. Aunt Martha says you're going to a party for big girls."

Callie laughed. "I am." It was women's night at the Rainbow Club. Some men still came, but it would be mostly women. And most of them would be lesbians. There'd be laugher, dancing, and light conversation, which was just what she needed to help her cope with a frigid winter and a truckload of worry. "What're you doing tonight?"

"We're having spaghetti and we're making brownies. Your recipe."

"Yum. Save me some." Her sister sure liked to bake. Baking was comfort food, and Martha was nothing if not a comfort to have around.

"Then we're going to sort my pictures and Aunt Martha's going to show me how to make a slide show. I'll be able to push a button and all the pictures of the calves will scroll by. Then we can put it on Facebook."

"No pictures of me, I hope. Or you."

"Not our faces. Maybe some of your back or your hands holding a calf. Is that okay?"

Unable to resist the joy in Becky's face, she pulled her in for another hug, followed by more kisses on the top of her head. "That's fine. You have fun."

"You too." Becky kissed her cheek and then bounced back out of her room.

Callie picked up her suitcase and the garment bag with her dress and almost bounced downstairs the way Becky had.

"Hey, Callie. Missed you, girlfriend," Rachel said. "About time you escaped from the farm." They hugged and kissed each other on the cheek. Callie had met Rachel at their favorite bistro in Saskatoon, and it felt a little like a homecoming.

"I'm not trapped, Rach. I love Poplarcreek."

"If you say so. I'll never live in a small town again or let anyone bury me on a farm surrounded by manure."

"You're awesome. I wish you lived closer."

"Thresherton? No, *thank you*. I wish you could visit every weekend, but why don't you make some more Thresherton friends?"

"I would if I had time. I need more friends and fewer enemies."

Rachel leaned back in her seat and crossed her arms over her chest. "What did Kruger do this time?"

"Another letter with a list of money I owe around town. I don't know where he gets this information."

"Computer hackers?"

Callie shrugged.

"Why not ask your parents for a loan? You said they helped your brother."

"They did, and they're very kind, but then they started asking for progress reports on his business. They said they wanted to help, and they probably did, but then they started giving him directions."

"But they helped him."

Callie shook her head. "I don't need my parents' help, and even their well-meaning suggestions would drive me batty."

"Poplarcreek is a lot of work and worry. Why do you stay? Move to Saskatoon. You were happy enough in the city when you first moved to Saskatchewan."

"I came to Saskatoon to take computer courses and if I hadn't, we'd never have met." The waiter arrived, and they ordered a second coffee.

Rachel shook her head. "Those classes were boring, but you made it fun. I lusted after you."

"You were good for my ego, but Liz was all I wanted. I wasn't ready."

"I know, sweetie, and anyway I had a boyfriend." Rachel patted Callie's hand. "Remember the night we went drinking after our last exam?"

"I had to call Doug and explain I was too drunk to drive. I thought he might disapprove, but he told me to have fun."

"Well, I was hoping for a fun night, but you spoiled it by passing out."

"I'm ready to have fun tonight. Dinner and dancing. Are you dating a man or woman right now?" Callie asked.

"Oh, you know me. I'm chasing a surgeon, but she's working tonight. Let's go to the Rainbow Club and find somebody for you. Maybe Mitch is there."

Callie groaned. "Don't go there, please. Mitch and I are friends."

"And have been for years."

"Mitch was Liz's good friend and part of the honor guard at our wedding. It would be way too weird."

"Does Mitch think you're just friends?"

"Yes, of course, and anyway, I'll never date another police officer. Too bossy. I loved Liz, but she made all our decisions and I just followed."

"I would resent that."

"Funny, I didn't. It felt natural at the time and I didn't mind. But that was then, and I want a more equal relationship this time."

At ten p.m., Callie and Rachel joined Rachel's friends at the club. It was a mix of gay, straight, and bisexuals of both sexes. The common denominator was a desire to drink, dance, and have fun. Callie felt as if she were the matron of the group. She was the only one with a child and was a few years older than Rachel's other friends. But after two drinks, she relaxed and no longer cared.

An American friend of Rachel's teased her about Canada, and in honor of Callie's rare visit to the club, she told her favorite Canadian joke. "I love Canadians. You guys are a riot. What does Canada mean? Wait, it has no meaning. Your forefathers were sitting around drinking beer and trying to name the country. One said how about we start with a *C*, eh? The next guy said maybe an *N*, eh, and the third guy said we should end it with a *D*, eh. Get it? C-A-N-A-D-A."

There was plenty of laughter at that, and thanks to the amount of alcohol flowing, the joke probably got more laughs than it deserved. Callie was soberer than most. Earlier, she had switched to sparkling water to ensure she was sober enough to drive home.

Callie was chatting with Rachel when Rachel leaped to her feet. Rachel smoothed her dress over her hips. "Who's that? She's new and cute."

Callie grinned. Somebody had sparked Rachel's interest, and Rachel often got the woman or man she wanted.

Callie peered in the direction Rachel was staring and her stomach flipped when she saw who it was. Lauren walked through the club and settled at a table with a group of women.

While Callie sipped her drink and tried not to stare, Lauren's eyes swept the room until they locked on hers. She grinned when Lauren froze with her glass halfway to her mouth. Callie straightened in her chair, smiled, and nodded at her. Callie glanced at Rachel, who posed seductively, leaning one hip on their table. She didn't have Rachel's killer figure, but she hoped Lauren had noticed her instead.

Rachel tipped her head and studied Callie. "What's with that expression? Why are you pushing your breasts out?"

Callie turned her back to Lauren. "I wasn't sticking my breasts out. They're too tiny to attract attention even if I did. Don't laugh at me. Anyway, the cute woman is Lauren Cornish, and she's my veterinarian. She's been at Poplarcreek a bunch of times. Yesterday she did two C-sections for me. She's saving my sanity."

"Hey, your yummy doctor is staring at us. Introduce me."

Callie hesitated and tucked a loose strand of hair behind one ear. "I guess. I suppose I could."

Rachel grinned. "Or don't introduce me."

Callie tore her eyes away from Lauren. "You're my friend, Rach, but, well, if Lauren is looking for company..." Callie shrugged.

"You want it to be you? Aren't doctors bossy, though? They are where I work." Rachel worked in the records department at the large city hospital.

Callie grinned. "I'm not sure, but I'd like to find out. At least temporarily."

Rachel spoke out of the corner of her mouth. "She's on her way over."

"Hi, Callie."

Callie swiveled on her seat and found herself face-to-face with Lauren. "Hi, Lauren." Callie paused for a beat. "Are you having a nice evening?"

"I am. I don't get here that often." Lauren glanced at the table of women she had been sitting with. "I'm with Val Connor and her girlfriend, Christine, and their other friends. You know Val, right?"

"Sure, she works at PVS." Callie turned. "This is my friend Rachel." She introduced Lauren to her friends. She suppressed the urge to do a little dance when Lauren didn't give Rachel a second glance.

After introductions they made polite but uncomfortable conversation until Callie took control. "Would you like to dance, Lauren?"

They squeezed their way into the crowd and danced to a fast song. Next to Lauren, Callie felt like a clumsy farmer in sexy heels that made it awkward to dance. Sexy wasn't what she was feeling.

The next song was slow. Lauren tilted her head in question.

Callie slipped into the proffered embrace and settled in against Lauren. She wrapped her arms around Lauren's neck and gave in to her desire to caress Lauren's shoulders. She bit her lip when Lauren shivered in response. They swayed to the slow rhythm with Callie's cheek pressed against the side of Lauren's head. She brushed her cheek against Lauren's soft, silky hair and breathed in the delightful scent of rosewood shampoo.

Lauren wore black jeans and a long-sleeved, dark green shirt that hugged her body in all the best places. A few buttons undone gave Callie, from her higher vantage point, a glimpse of tantalizing cleavage. Heat emanated from Lauren where only the thin fabric of the shirt separated Callie's hand from warm skin. After two slow songs had come and gone too soon, Lauren said, "Can I buy you a drink?"

"Maybe later? Dance some more with me?" The next song was romantic with a midrange tempo, and the dance floor emptied. Callie liked the extra room but preferred to be close to Lauren. "The beat and pace of this song is perfect for a rumba."

Lauren blinked. "You rumba?"

"It's been a while. What about you?"

Lauren answered by taking Callie's right hand in her left. Then she circled her right arm around Callie's waist, her hand coming to rest in the middle of Callie's back. Lauren led them with the slow-quick-quick series of steps of the rumba. They danced well, as if they had been partners for years. They were rusty, but only tangled up once. While they danced, Lauren shifted to caress the bare skin of Callie's lower back with her thumb.

Callie attempted to pay attention to her feet, but the gentle caresses distracted her. *Does she know it makes me crazy?*

When the song finished, Callie grinned at Lauren. "Wonderful. Thanks for the dance."

"You're a great dancer. Thanks for letting me lead. I never learned to follow."

They drifted to the bar for a drink. "Where did you learn to rumba?" Callie asked.

"My mother taught me, but it didn't make my father happy. He said she made me gay because she taught me to lead." They laughed at the ridiculous logic, but Callie saw the hint of sadness flash in Lauren's eyes.

Callie said, "I took lessons with a group of friends when I was in high school. They tried to pair us up boy-girl, which was annoying, but since there weren't enough boys interested, my partner was another girl. She was very sweet."

"You had things figured out early."

"I did. Probably from birth. You?"

"Let's just say that the undercurrent of homophobia in my family didn't make being gay an option."

"That sounds tough."

"Not really. It never occurred to me to do anything about it." Lauren shrugged. "I learned to fill the gaps in my day. I studied and had part-time jobs. Dating wasn't an issue."

Callie felt a stab of compassion. Lauren shrugged it off, but how hard had it really been?

Callie said, "I never got to work at McDonald's with my friends. My parents always had work for me at home on the farm. Did you work on a farm?"

"I did for a couple of summers in college, but in high school I worked at Baskin-Robbins."

"You served ice cream?"

"Yeah, and there was never a job I was less suited for. I'm a bit of an ice cream addict. I was always sneaking samples."

Callie laughed. "I'd take a bag of chips or popcorn first."

"Salt, eh? Not into sugar?"

Callie didn't see anything odd in the comment until Lauren blushed. Then she grinned. She was into a certain kind of sugar. She debated teasing Lauren further, but an instant later, a pair of skinny arms with scary long red nails snaked around Lauren's waist from behind. Lauren jumped and then pivoted, but Red Nails hung on tight and followed Lauren until the interloper ended up between Callie and Lauren.

Lauren sputtered. "What're you doing, Tina?"

Tina turned and scanned Callie's body. Callie returned the favor. Tina was in her mid-twenties and short. Borderline scrawny, with shiny brown hair piled high. Her red strapless dress clung to her petite frame and left nothing to the imagination.

Tina gave her a final dismissive glance before she grasped Lauren's arms and wrapped them around her waist. "Hey, L.C., are you going for older women now?"

"Pardon? Lauren's older than I am," Callie said.

"Stealing my vet, stretch?" Tina slurred her words and would have fallen if Lauren hadn't supported her.

"We were dancing." Callie frowned at Tina and waited for Lauren to say something. To tell Tina to go away.

"I like my vet. She screws like an animal. Get it? Vets screw like animals." Tina giggled inanely at her own joke. Then she followed it with a sloppy pirouette and latched her arms around Lauren's neck. After a quick kiss on Lauren's chin Tina rested her head against Lauren's breasts.

Lauren's face burned, and she held her arms out to her sides as though unsure what to do with Tina using her as a leaning post.

Callie searched Lauren's eyes for an explanation and willed her to say something. When she didn't, she stepped back and shrugged. "Okay then, good night, Lauren."

Callie marched over to her table, plopped into a chair, and crossed her arms. From her table, she watched Lauren tow a staggering Tina across the crowded dance floor toward the restrooms. "Seems Lauren had a date. Perhaps her style is drunken little girls."

Rachel glanced from Lauren to Callie and raised an eyebrow. "You're kidding?"

"Funny. I can't picture Lauren interested in such a child. But I guess I don't know her, really."

"Lauren should appreciate maturity and class."

"Yes, she should." The sharp pain in her chest told Callie that she no longer wished to be at the club. Tina was attractive in a cute, tiny, perfect, I-was-a-cheerleader-in-high-school way. In heels, Callie towered over most women and made some uncomfortable. She had what her sister called a sporty build, tall, lean, and fit, but never cute and petite. What she wouldn't give to make a quick exit, go home, and crawl into bed.

Fifteen minutes later, Callie spotted Lauren and Tina crossing the dance floor. Lauren had her arm wrapped around Tina's waist and escorted her to a seat beside Valerie. As hard as she tried, Callie couldn't look away, and the fun vibe of the night disappeared completely.

"I'm going now, Rach. I'm not having fun anymore."

"What? Don't let Lauren chase you away. Those women at the table by the bar were watching you dance and they're still watching you. There are plenty of other women to choose from."

Callie shook her head. "Thanks for inviting me, but I think I'm done for the night. I came here ready to have fun and all I feel is annoyed." If she couldn't keep one woman's attention for more than five minutes, it was a sign she should stay at Poplarcreek and concentrate on being a better farmer. She was having a shitty calving season and the Krugers were circling her like vultures. Enough playing. Women were a luxury she couldn't afford. With a determined shake of her head, Callie jumped to her feet. "Time for me to go. Thanks, Rach." She hugged Rachel, slipped on her coat, and bolted from the club.

CHAPTER FIVE

Lauren dragged herself out of bed on Sunday morning after five hours of sleep. It had been fun at the club and marvelous dancing with Callie. Just as well that Tina had crashed their conversation and stopped Lauren from suggesting a meal or something equally ridiculous. It had only taken two drinks for her to forget to steer clear of women.

She tossed on her robe, made herself a coffee, and settled in the living room with the phone. She had a ten a.m. phone call with Sam, and she couldn't be late.

"Here goes nothing." She dialed.

"Hello?"

The bored sound of her daughter's voice wasn't encouraging so Lauren poured on the perky. "Hi, Sammy. How are you?"

"Sammy is a *baby* name."

"Sorry, Sam. How are you?"

"You abandoned me. My friends tell me stepparents always ditch the kids after a divorce."

Sam wasn't wasting any time on small talk. Lauren's face burned and her chin sank to her chest as shame consumed her. "I'm more than a stepparent, Sam. I caught you when you were born and helped raise you."

"You still left me."

Lauren knew in her heart she had been in the wrong. Sam was only twelve, but she tried to explain. "After the divorce, you wouldn't see me, and I didn't blame you. I was deep into a cycle of self-loathing and despair and figured you'd have a better life without me. I'm so sorry."

"You still left."

"I'm so sorry, Sammy. I love you and I shouldn't have gone so far away. But I'm around now, and we can talk whenever you want to. I'm still here for you."

"Then come home."

"Toronto's not home anymore. Saskatchewan is my home now, but you're welcome to visit as often as you want. My job at PVS, working with farm animals, is great and I prefer the slower pace of life in Saskatchewan. I still work hard, but I'm under less pressure, so I'd have plenty of time for us to have fun. Does that make sense, Sammy?"

"You're not coming back." Sam sobbed. "You don't want me anymore."

"Please, Sammy, don't cry. I'll visit you and you can visit me. I love you. I'm your mother as long as you want me as a parent." She was the adult, and it was her job to mend their relationship. "I'm sorry I stayed away so long. I love you."

"You left."

Lauren paced her living room. Sam was nearly three thousand kilometers away. She was too far away to do anything, and Sam was sobbing as if she might shatter. "I love you, Sam. I'm so sorry."

"I got to go."

"Can we talk again? Sam? Can I call you again?"

"Lauren, it's T.J. What did you *say*? Sam's terribly upset."

"I told her I loved her and that I'm sorry."

T.J. sighed deeply. Her exasperation was clear. "Okay. That's enough *fun* for today. She needs time."

"Sorry," she said but her ex-wife had already hung up.

Lauren dropped into a chair and cradled her head in her hands. Was there a shittier mother in the world? She didn't think so.

❖

On Monday morning, Fiona came into Lauren's office. "Lauren, can you please make a house call to Mrs. Wilma Lawson today? She lives in town."

"No problem. What's happening?"

"Her cat, Smokey, is due for her annual vaccinations and Mrs. Lawson's unable to bring her to the clinic. She seldom leaves the house since her husband died two years ago and she doesn't drive anymore. Smokey's almost two years old, so please talk to Mrs. Lawson about spaying."

"Does Mrs. Lawson have family?"

"Her daughter comes from Saskatoon several times a month to help. She's allowed time off work to take her mother to the doctor, but not her mother's cat. We've been considering your idea of opening one Saturday a month. If we were open, they could have brought Smokey to us."

"Saturdays or Thursday evenings. To catch the folks who work Monday to Friday. It worked for us in Toronto." She hated referencing her old life, but there were definitely positives from it she could use now. It was time to drag PVS into the modern age.

Fiona nodded and gave her a little wave, already turned to focus on something the receptionist said. Lauren shrugged. Fiona was pulled in seventeen directions at once. She remembered those days back in Toronto and was happy to be away from it.

She left her office and entered the pharmacy. She tossed a multipack of vaccine in a cooler and grabbed her medical kit. She always packed extra vaccine in case the cat jumped and she shot the vaccine onto the floor. It was embarrassing, but not as ridiculous as having to return to the clinic to fetch more. She also often vaccinated barn cats for farmers, and she never knew how many cats they would find when she arrived.

Lauren drove across town, taking Val with her to hold the cat.

"How'd the phone call go yesterday?" Val asked.

"It was nice to hear Samantha's voice. But unfortunately, William wasn't home." She had the urge to tell Val more, but she was too full of shame, too tortured by how upset Sam had been.

"Sweet. And how was the conversation?"

"Awkward."

Val winced. "How so?"

"It's been ages since I last talked to her. I feel like I don't know what's going on in her life. I'm out of the loop." It was her fault for moving so far away after the divorce. She liked living in Thresherton, but it had a cost.

"But you found common ground, right? She *is* your daughter."

"Maybe next time. I was going to tell her about doing a C-section on a cow. She's watched me do one on a dog before."

"Perfect. And?"

"I wanted to set up a time for another call, but she wasn't sure when." Lauren shrugged. It was a half-truth, but it would do.

"It's a step in the right direction."

"I suppose. A tiny one." Lauren tried to smile. She held tightly to the nugget of hope that she could repair her relationship with Sam. She loved her daughter and wouldn't give up. Sam hadn't called her Mom, but she would again, one day. And that hope was something she would hang on to tightly.

When they arrived, Mrs. Lawson ushered them into her home. "Oh, hello, dears. You're here to vaccinate my Smokey. She's my sweet kitten and I don't know what I'd do without her." The delightful old woman rattled on as they looked for Smokey, moving from room to room.

Lauren found a sleek, solid gray cat basking in the sun in the living room. Val captured it with ease and set it on a table. Lauren examined the animal and administered the vaccine. "Your cat is very healthy."

"I hate to tell you this, Mrs. Lawson, but Smokey's a boy," Val said.

"Is she? Odd. Smokey was a girl last year."

It was difficult, but Lauren kept a straight face. "Oh?"

"I'm sure Dr. Ian told me she was a girl cat. Oh well, thank you, girls. Please stay for tea and cake." They headed into the kitchen. "There you are, Smokey. You believed I would come in here and you expect milk now. My Smokey loves me and follows me everywhere. Sometimes she appears in a room before I do. Don't you, Smokey?" Mrs. Lawson set a saucer of milk on the floor.

Smokey ignored the milk and remained perched on the windowsill. Val peered at Lauren behind Mrs. Lawson's back and crossed her eyes. Lauren gave a slight shrug in response and walked to the window. This couldn't be the same cat as the one in the living room; it looked similar, but its build was more slender. She scooped up Smokey and examined the cat. "Smokey is definitely a female. We made a mistake earlier. Sorry, Mrs. Lawson." Lauren put Smokey on the floor and the cat darted out of the room.

"That's all right, girls."

While Mrs. Lawson was filling the kettle, Val caught Lauren's eye and mouthed, "No way." Twenty minutes later, after light surface chatter, they got up to leave. At the front door, Lauren discovered Smokey sniffing their boots, and this one, too, looked somewhat different.

Val plucked the cat off the floor and peeked under his tail. "Um, Dr. Cornish, based on his equipment, Smokey's a boy."

Mrs. Lawson leaned close to the cat. She settled her glasses on her nose and squinted at him. "How did you do that? You were in the kitchen."

Lauren watched Mrs. Lawson peer in confusion at her cat. Then she frowned and studied the ceiling for a few seconds. Lauren jogged to the kitchen and glanced inside before running into the living room and then the parlor. She returned and winked at Val. "Mrs. Lawson, how many Smokeys do you have?"

"What do you mean, dear? I have one Smokey, and she's magic."

"I found two more gray cats in your house."

"Oh no, that can't be." The elderly woman touched one hand to her cheek.

"Is it okay if we search your house for cats?"

Mrs. Lawson leaned on Val as Val escorted her to the couch. "Of course."

A gray cat jumped onto the couch and Val petted him. "I'm sure this boy is the one we vaccinated because he has a nick in his ear. I'll shut you in the living room with him while we hunt for more."

Twenty minutes later, Lauren opened the living room door. "We found three females and a male, which means you have three girls and two boys. They're all solid gray which happens when both parents are gray. It's a recessive gene for—" Lauren stopped when she caught Val rolling her eyes at the irrelevant explanation. "I have extra vaccine with me. Shall I vaccinate the rest?"

Mrs. Lawson nodded. "Thank you, girls."

"I'll put a strip of gauze around your first boy's neck as a collar, so we know who he is," Val said.

Lauren vaccinated the cats and Val wrote a number, from one to four, with indelible marker in their left ears so she could tell them apart. When Lauren was done, she smiled at Mrs. Lawson. "Mrs. Lawson, please consider spaying and neutering your cats before you have an army of Smokeys."

"Okay, Doctor. Goodness. It explains why Smokey was always underfoot, doesn't it?"

"I'll bring cat collars by after work if you'd like," Val said. "That way you'll know which one is which."

"Thank you, Valerie, but what will I do with five cats?"

A gray cat rolled on her back at Val's feet and she tickled its stomach. "You'll have fun thinking up more names."

On the drive back to the clinic, they laughed with affection at Mrs. Lawson's magic cat Smokey who was lightning fast and everywhere at once.

"Didn't she notice how much cat food they ate?" Lauren shook her head, still puzzled.

"Well, since Smokey's a magic cat, she eats for five and never gains an ounce." Val squeaked as Lauren poked her in the ribs with a sharp finger. "Hey, quit it." Val poked Lauren back. "Don't you think five cats is an army already?"

"I was being diplomatic. My guess is Smokey had a litter. But how could Mrs. Lawson miss kittens?"

"I know her daughter, and she told me they installed a washer and dryer beside the kitchen so her mom didn't have to go downstairs anymore. Maybe the kittens were in the basement? Her neighbors take her grocery shopping and she has a cleaning service. I'll bet nobody noticed how much cat food she bought or how much dirty cat litter there was."

"I'll ask Fiona to give Mrs. Lawson a group deal on spays and neuters."

"Good idea. So enough about work." Val nudged Lauren. "How are you and the delectable Callie Anderson these days?"

"Do you think she's too young for me?" Something about the baggy coveralls and goofy cap Callie wore in the barn made her look like a kid.

"Well, you *are* an old woman of thirty-three."

Lauren poked her. "Almost thirty-four."

"Stop poking. The answer's no. Callie's only about four years younger than you." Val's attempt to look innocent didn't work. "You two looked awesome dancing together last weekend."

Lauren sighed. "The evening was wonderful for a while. Until Tina."

"Sorry Tina mauled you. Does Callie know Tina was out of her head with wine, and you never slept with her?"

"I wanted to tell Callie that Tina was drunk and I'd just met her, but I never got the chance. I was so stunned I couldn't speak. Just gaped at Callie like a mute fool." It had been exciting and a little scary holding Callie that night. Lauren had been hoping for more conversation and another dance, but Tina spoiled it. "Did you see Callie leave? I tried to shake Tina off, but she hung on like a dog to his favorite chew toy."

"Nope, sorry."

"I'm sure Callie saw me dragging Tina to the restroom." Lauren had cursed to herself in frustration as she half carried Tina across the dance floor. She had found a line of women out the door of the restroom and said, "Look out, we're next." She'd hauled Tina into the first empty stall and positioned her above the bowl just in time. Tina had vomited and retched until she was dry. She couldn't leave her, but she certainly didn't want to be there, either.

"And it's not like I owe her an explanation, right? And how would that even go? Picture the conversation." She put fake perkiness in her voice. "Hey, Callie, your cows look great today and I never slept with Tina, the little drunk from the club. Just saying because I thought you might want to know, for no apparent reason."

Val laughed. "Awkward, but it's what you need to do. Tell her. You don't need any misunderstandings."

"Tell her? Are you kidding? It was a miracle I even spoke to her that night." Lauren's mouth had dried up as she approached Callie. She wasn't sure where she found the courage, but her legs had carried her to Callie's table. "Did you see how breathtaking she was?"

Lauren sighed. Callie had worn a black dress with thin spaghetti straps and a hemline that stopped mid-thigh. The dress showed off Callie's long legs and finely muscled arms and shoulders. Lauren's breath hitched at the memory. Callie's dress had displayed a large expanse of her gorgeous back. She had never seen Callie dressed in anything but insulated coveralls or jeans and a parka, and even in those she'd been attractive. Lauren had imagined Callie's figure was marvelous and now she was sure.

Did Callie like to party? Lauren didn't. She was a homebody and didn't enjoy dressing up and going out. After they moved to Toronto, T.J. had mixed with the young and trendy professional crowd. Often, Lauren had used work to avoid parties and dinners. She preferred quiet evenings at home. Eventually, T.J. gave up pressuring Lauren and went out without her. It had been another sign she and T.J. didn't fit. It was also a good reminder why she wasn't looking for another relationship. Finding someone who truly matched you was something from the movies. It didn't happen in real life.

When Val and Lauren arrived at PVS, they unloaded and tramped into the clinic. Lauren said, "I'll consider your suggestion, but there's really no reason to bring it up again. I'm not looking to get involved with anyone, especially someone with kids." Lauren had learned that to be in a relationship with a woman with children was heartbreaking. She loved Sam and William, but it had taken months of coaxing to get Sam on the phone for more than a few minutes. And that had been a disaster. Nope, her next girlfriend, if that day ever arrived, wouldn't have kids.

Chapter Six

Callie stretched and smiled up at the blue sky. There were few clouds, and the sun was bright. She snugged the earflaps of her bomber hat over her ears. She was enjoying the heat, but it was still winter in Saskatchewan. A quick peek along the side of the house showed abundant animal tracks. Becky had asked to put a bale of hay outside for the deer and they had found it. Callie had placed the bale so Becky could see it from her bedroom window and photograph the animals. She grinned at the many small footprints that told her other creatures had also discovered the free meal.

Callie shoveled snow off her front walkway. It was a waste of energy because she and Becky used the side door at the mudroom. The few visitors to Poplarcreek also used the mudroom door, but the house appeared more welcoming with the path to her front door shoveled. She smiled with satisfaction as her walkway emerged from the snow and ice.

It was peaceful in the barn with no calving problems for two days. Only Fiona and Ian had been out to help her recently. It had been a week and a half since she'd last seen Lauren at the club. It had gotten weird at the end of the dance, but she focused on how nice it was to be held by an attractive woman. Callie shrugged. It wasn't something she should get used to, but it was nice all the same.

The tranquility of Callie's morning vanished as a white four-door pickup truck rolled up her drive and parked two wheels on her front walkway. It stopped eight feet from where she was shoveling.

There was enough parking beside her house for six vehicles. There was no reason to park on her walkway. Callie's stomach clenched when she recognized the bully behind the wheel. Heinz Kruger bullied everyone, including his sons, Kyle and Tommy. They were grown men and had turned into bullies too.

Heinz was one of the first people Callie had learned about when she and Becky arrived in Thresherton. People warned her the police had never charged him with a serious crime, but that was probably only because there wasn't enough evidence. She was warned not to get in his way. Heinz got what he wanted. It was cold outside, but a trickle of sweat skittered down her back as she became conscious of her isolation at Poplarcreek.

He exited the truck. He was six-foot-four, with greasy, gray, thinning hair, and a belly straining at his worn leather belt. His predatory, cold eyes sliced into her.

Heinz scratched his scruffy chin. "Hello, Catherine, nice morning."

He never called her Callie. He preferred to use her full first name the way a teacher or parent might. She kept shoveling to avoid focusing on him. "Morning, Heinz."

"Need to talk to you, Catherine."

Callie continued shoveling the walkway. "Sure, go ahead." She shuddered inside. Heinz was after something.

He zipped his coat and stomped his feet. "Any chance of a cup of coffee and a sit-down? Too cold to stand outside today."

Callie's heart pounded and her stomach rebelled at having the man in her house. He was in worn dirty jeans and his coat sported old food stains. Ever since his wife deserted him four years ago, Heinz resembled a hobo. It was better for a while when Heinz's younger son, Tommy, returned to Kruger Farm with his wife. But tired of feeding and cleaning up after three men and her three children, Heather left a year later. Callie didn't blame her. She wouldn't live with that family either.

"Come in then." Callie dropped the shovel, and with feet dragging, led the way into her house. She had the fleeting idea she should run inside and shut the door in his face. But that wouldn't be neighborly, and she wasn't rude. Besides, Kyle owed her four thousand dollars and she hoped Heinz planned to pay today.

Once inside the house Heinz parked himself in a chair at the kitchen table. He leaned back and stretched his legs in front of him. He didn't remove his dirty boots and left a puddle of mud and melting snow on her floor.

Callie struggled against a wish to escape and willed herself to ignore his mess.

"Awful quiet. Where's that pretty sister of yours, Marsha?"

"Her name's Martha." As the skin on the back of her neck prickled, Callie lied. "She's shopping in town but should be home soon." Martha had shopping and errands and might be another hour, at least.

When the coffee was ready, Callie plopped a cup in front of Heinz and placed cream and sugar near him. The fresh blueberry muffins Martha had made still cooled on the counter, but Callie's hospitality was grudging, and she didn't share them.

Callie eased into a chair across from Heinz and perched on the edge. She preferred her coffee with sugar and cream but feared he would hear the spoon rattle against her cup as her hands trembled. All the men in her life had been kind and gentle. She wasn't used to men like Heinz.

Heinz surveyed his surroundings. "Big kitchen. You keep it nice. Bet you wish you had a man to take care of and feed in here."

"What do you want, Heinz?" Callie hoped he would make his point quickly and then take his dark energy and leave.

He regarded her with a fake smile and small, sly eyes. "My boy Kyle would be good for you. He'd take charge of the farm and you. No more decisions to worry you and lots of kids to keep you busy."

Callie cringed at the repulsive idea. "What do you *want*, Heinz?"

Heinz sneered. "Payment for my big bull, Bulldozer. You have nice calves because of him."

"Payment? How do you figure?" Callie's insides churned, and she swallowed her nausea. She had no money to pay him. Every dollar Poplarcreek earned she reinvested in the farm or transferred to the bank.

"My bull bred 'em."

"It wasn't my idea. Your bull broke my fence."

Heinz snorted. "It wasn't much of a fence. Doug never built a decent fence. My bull busting in is Doug's fault. That short wimp would have given me something in compensation." He followed the dig with an ugly, mean laugh.

"Well, I don't owe you anything. Your bull tore through my fence."

Callie ignored the comment about Doug because Heinz said it to goad her, but her thoughts spun. Doug died the day they were fixing fences. Did they fix the fence of the heifer paddock? She'd never finished the repairs because she'd been busy planning a funeral and caring for Becky, who refused to eat. *Were the breedings my fault because I forgot to check on the heifers for a few weeks?* She wasn't about to bring up that nugget of self-doubt.

"And besides, Kyle owes me four thousand dollars for my two cows," Callie said.

"Four thousand dollars?"

"Kyle borrowed my truck and trailer a week ago. He said his trailer was broken and he needed my truck to tow my trailer. I forget why he couldn't use his own truck. In turn, he said he'd take two of mine and sell them for me. Anyway, he took eight cows to a sale in Montana. Dr. Lauren Cornish is an accredited vet with CFIA. She inspected the cattle and signed the export health certificates. You know all this. Six of yours went and I helped him load two of my best."

"Eight cows?" Heinz scratched his chin and his eyes went colder. "And you think yours were worth two thousand?"

Callie had the impression that Heinz was surprised. Maybe Kyle took cattle without asking? Never mind, it wasn't her problem. "Yes." Callie cleared her throat. "Yes, two thousand *each*," she said more loudly. "Perhaps I should talk to a lawyer."

"Each, eh? Must have been nice cows. Well, no reason to make the lawyers rich," Heinz said.

Callie scrutinized him, one eyebrow raised.

"Well, you think about my offer." Heinz slurped the last of his coffee and belched. Then he heaved himself to his feet and hitched up his pants. "I expect two of your new calves as payment. It was my bull. But maybe I'll just deduct them from the four thousand, if that's the *real* amount."

"You think I owe *you* for the calves? If I deduct the cost of my veterinary bills, you might owe me *more* than four thousand, Heinz." Callie leaned back in her chair and clasped her hands to keep them from shaking. She refused to let him see how much he had rattled her.

Her friend Mark told her Heinz always bullied his boys. He bragged that he treated them harshly to toughen them up. As adults, they were still under Heinz's control. They followed Heinz's orders. She would not.

"Why don't you make it easy? Sell me Poplarcreek and go back to that chicken farm you came from. I could use the extra land, and Heather told Tommy she would move back, if she has her own house." Heinz looked around. "She'd like this kitchen. How many bedrooms do you have?"

"I told you, I'm not selling, and my parents own a berry farm." Callie stared into her coffee cup and fiddled with the handle to avoid his cold eyes. "Poplarcreek is Becky's inheritance, and the Andersons have lived here for a hundred years."

"Berry farm." He scoffed. "Blueberries aren't cattle, Catherine. You don't know what you're doing, and one day soon you'll lose the farm to the bank. Better to sell to me now."

"Please go, Heinz." Callie raised her voice to disguise the tremor in it. The thought of losing Poplarcreek was more terrifying than ten Krugers.

He moved into her personal space and glowered down at her. His lips stretched into a snarl. "You better not play it tough with me, girlie. I'll win. You should leave and take that pervert's kid with you."

Callie leaned back and gripped the arms of the chair. She longed for the strength to leap to her feet and yell at him, but her legs refused to cooperate. All she managed was a hoarse whisper. "Get out now or I'll call the RCMP."

"If you're a smart girl, you'll consider my offer. I'll get my payment, one way or another." He tossed the comment over his shoulder as he swaggered through her front door and left without closing it.

In rural Saskatchewan, nobody locked their doors, but Callie shut and locked her door and leaned against it on legs of rubber. When her legs gave out, she slumped into a chair. She buried her head in her arms and cried. Maybe he was right and she should sell. She rarely had any idea what she was doing.

Callie indulged in several minutes of crying mixed with self-doubt and self-pity. Then she straightened and dried her eyes. No one would take this place from her, and she'd be dammed if she'd let someone like Heinz make her feel inept. Poplarcreek belonged to Becky and she'd do everything she could to keep it running.

Callie cleaned up the mess from Heinz's boots, pitched her mop into the closet, and slammed the door. When the closet door bounced open, she slammed it again. "That creep would never have dared to call Liz a girlie. What an asshole." Callie flashed to the chilling expression in his eyes and felt nauseated. Maybe if she just ignored him, he'd go away.

Callie dropped into a chair. She regretted not telling him to shut up about Becky and Liz. Liz wasn't a pervert. She was amazing. Liz's funeral was still a blur. Becky had been old enough to know her mama wasn't coming home, but too young to understand why.

There'd been a large funeral procession, and police officers had come from all over Canada to honor Liz. Three hundred RCMP officers, dressed in their red serge jackets, had marched behind the hearse. Callie and Becky rode in a limousine behind the hearse, but Doug and his sons walked beside the hearse with a select group of RCMP officers. Mitch had followed the hearse carrying Liz's Stetson, which was a great honor. Another of Liz's friends led the rider-less RCMP horse with Liz's boots reversed in the stirrups, heels to the front, to symbolize the loss of a comrade-in-arms.

Doug and Callie had buried Liz in the Thresherton cemetery. The funeral had been an important event in Thresherton, and many businesses had closed for the day. As the funeral procession passed through town, led by the RCMP pipe band, people had removed their hats and solemnly lined the main street. Many people wore red that day to support the officers. When Callie moved to Thresherton a few years after the funeral, most people remembered her as the widow of the slain RCMP officer.

Callie squared her shoulders. She was tired of people feeling sorry for her. One day, when she had Poplarcreek running well, she hoped the town would see her as a successful, independent farmer. Most of all, she wanted Becky to be proud of her.

Callie's phone rang a minute later. A surge of warmth spread through her when the PVS number appeared.

"Hi, Callie. I'm calling...I just wanted to...How are the scouring calves?" Lauren asked. "Are they better? Have you seen any more scour? I should drive out and look at them."

Callie took a deep steadying breath. "It's okay. I've got it covered. Those calves recovered ages ago. But now three others are scouring."

"Same treatment for the new ones."

"Okay, and if you're in the area, I'd like it if you dropped in, but don't make a special trip for me." Was Lauren planning to visit her, or the calves?

"I'll do that. How's everything else?"

"Okay, I guess."

"Callie?"

"Nothing. Thanks again for checking in. Bye."

"Okay, bye."

Callie hung up. It was the right call she needed at the right time. The brief exchange with Lauren calmed Callie and made her feel more competent, and she didn't need to extend the call into a woe-is-me saga. She could handle life on her own. She rolled her shoulders and straightened. She was learning about her cattle and she would manage. Callie sighed. Heinz Kruger was her problem to solve. Callie's shoulders slumped. It would be nice to have someone around to talk to about things like this, but Callie was tough. She'd be just fine.

She shoved the loneliness aside and went to work.

Chapter Seven

Lauren hung up. What was going on? Callie's voice had trembled. Had something frightened her? She hoped if Callie needed help, she would ask. She wasn't sure what had possessed her to call, and now she was worried. She sighed and pushed the thoughts aside.

She had a full morning and day of patients ahead. She strove to school her thoughts and quit worrying about Callie. It was ten thirty in the morning. She had two cats spayed and a neuter done. She had another two spays to do, but postponed them because there was an emergency coming in. The owner told Val that she didn't see the car hit her dog but thought it was the dog's right front leg that was damaged.

Val dug a surgery kit out of the cupboard by the autoclave. "When you lived in Toronto did people bring you their injured animals or take them to an emergency clinic? Thresherton is too small to have an emergency clinic."

Val pronounced Toronto like someone not from the area, by pronouncing every syllable To-ron-to. Locals pronounced it Tron-no. Lauren had only moved there because T.J. had insisted on living in the big city. The ready access to restaurants, shopping, and theater excited T.J. Lauren enjoyed those activities too, but in smaller doses.

Lauren shuddered. "I saw too many injured dogs and cats in our practice. Our clients only went to the emergency clinic after we closed for the day. On Saturdays I usually had Sam with me to help with emergencies. I built her a wooden bench to stand on so she could see the animals on the surgery table. She was getting really good at assisting." Lauren laughed. "And she looked very cute in a gown and mask." She missed her children. Ontario was too far away.

"Next time you call, tell her about this emergency."

"I will, if there is a next time," Lauren mumbled. Minnie, the other PVS veterinary technician, jogged into the treatment room. "They're here."

Lauren snapped out of her reverie.

Val and Minnie wheeled the dog into the treatment room on the stretcher and Val laid a hand on the animal's head. "Poor Max."

Lauren studied the dog. Max was a medium-sized black and white border collie with gentle, intelligent eyes. The tip of his muzzle was white and blended into a white band that stretched up his nose and forehead, ending between his eyes. Under a layer of filth, his chest, belly, and paws were white. Minnie and Val hooked him up to an IV. Then Lauren helped Val take X-rays.

Lauren examined the X-rays. "He's bright and alert, and in decent shape considering." Lauren wrinkled her nose. "It's a horrible fracture and several days old." She seethed with indignation. Max had a mangled right front leg and his paw drooped. "An unsupported compound fracture would be excruciating."

Tears slid down Val's cheeks. "Why do people do this? I don't understand. The poor puppy." Val petted Max on the head and ran a soft ear through her fingers. Max responded by carefully licking tears off Val's cheek. "What a good boy he is. We should call the SPCA."

"Maybe." Lauren strode into the waiting room. She almost tripped when she spotted Callie sitting two chairs away from Roberta Macpherson. Callie was bent at the waist talking to Roberta's small son, Nelson, who stood in front of Callie with his hands on her knees. An instant later, Callie glanced up, and they shared a warm smile.

"Doctor?" Roberta said.

Lauren shifted her focus to the other woman. "Hello, Mrs. Macpherson." Lauren approached Roberta. "Would you like to go into an exam room to discuss Max's condition?"

Roberta glanced at Callie and shrugged. "It's okay with me if Callie hears," Roberta said.

"Max's injuries are not as bad as they could be. His chest, abdomen, spine, and other legs are normal. But he has multiple fractures of his right front leg. He requires extensive orthopedic surgery with pins and plates to hold the bones while they heal. We'll stabilize the fracture and refer you to the WCVM."

"That's the veterinary college in Saskatoon. I heard they're expensive. Can't you do the bone pinning?"

"Orthopedics is a complicated specialty and we don't have the right surgical instruments to do that surgery. It'll cost about three thousand dollars at the college, but it's the best chance of recovery for Max. How long ago was his leg injured?"

"On Sunday. We hoped he'd improve, but now he reeks."

Lauren felt an angry rant building. She dug her fingernails into her palms and concentrated on keeping her tone neutral. "After three days there may be too much tissue damage and injury to the nerves and blood vessels to save the leg."

Roberta frowned at Lauren. "I won't spend three thousand dollars on a pet. The kids love him, but he's only a dog. I'll get them a puppy from my cousin." Roberta waved her hands in front of her as though done with the matter. "I better just take him home."

Callie's gasp at the lack of compassion was quiet, but Lauren heard it. Roberta might have heard it, but she didn't react. Lauren swallowed and kept smiling at Roberta, but her jaw throbbed from clenching it. "He's not in any shape to move and it would be agonizing. It would be kinder if I euthanized him before you took him home."

Lauren had the urge to say it was more *humane* to euthanize the poor dog, but that would imply Roberta had been inhumane and piss her off. A pissed-off Roberta might snatch her dog and leave. There was always the SPCA, but Max required rescuing now. Lauren took a deep breath and spoke. "It costs eighty dollars for a euthanasia."

Roberta scratched her head. "I'll check with Colin." She walked away to phone her husband and Nelson trailed after her. Lauren plopped into a chair beside Callie

Callie was perched on the edge of a chair, her fingers white where they gripped the plastic edge. Her eyes sparked with anger. "What's this? What's she thinking?" she asked softly.

Lauren frowned. This was nothing new. She had seen this before in Ontario and Saskatchewan. "To some people a sick dog is a dead dog. Harsh, but you heard her. She can get a new puppy for free, so why spend money on Max?"

Callie glared in Roberta's direction as if she wanted to hit something or somebody.

Lauren sensed Callie was on the verge of exploding. "Give me a minute to speak with her. I've not given up on Max." Lauren loved that Callie felt the injustice of the situation, but her approach would have to be more professional and diplomatic. Unlike her first interaction with Callie, which had been anything but. Besides, if Callie yelled at Roberta, she might stomp out of the clinic and take Max. Her priority was to save Max any more suffering.

Callie gave a sharp nod, and with another horrified glance at Roberta, she slid back into her chair. She crossed her legs and then crossed her arms, the very picture of a woman keeping herself from whacking someone over the head.

Lauren strode to within several feet of Roberta and waited for the call to finish.

Roberta lowered her phone. "I talked to Colin. We're not spending a fortune on a dog." She laughed as if it was a crazy idea.

Lauren stepped toward Roberta and struggled to control her irritation. "Amputation at PVS is an option. Most dogs learn to walk on three legs." She spoke in clipped tones. "He's a light dog and should walk well with one front leg. The infection already in the wound is a concern, but it's worth giving him a chance. I'll take care of him for eight hundred dollars."

"Still too much money, Dr. Cornish."

Lauren was aware she had negotiated for the dog's life and lost. Eight hundred dollars was as low as she should go, and when she factored in the supplies, surgery costs, and nursing care the clinic would only break even. Frustration built. She couldn't go any lower unless she paid for it herself.

"And we won't pay you to put him to sleep. We have a twenty-two at home." Roberta's voice lacked emotion.

Lauren looked away so Roberta couldn't see how disgusted she was. Roberta Macpherson had pushed her patience too far. It was a strain to hang on to her professionalism. Val was right. They should call the SPCA.

Callie jumped to her feet. "I'll take him."

Roberta stared at Callie. "What?"

Callie crossed her arms and shifted her weight to one hip. "Give me Max and I'll pay his bills."

"Callie, you're crazy, but he's all yours." Roberta cackled as she walked to the counter and completed the forms to sign Max over to Callie. Clearly, she wasn't going to reject the easy solution. "Thanks, Callie." Roberta gave a little wave as she and Nelson exited the clinic.

Callie faced Lauren. "He was her pet. How could she be so cold and unfeeling?"

Lauren shook her head. "On some farms, animals are a tool, and when a tool breaks people do a cost-benefit analysis and decide whether to fix the tool. To Roberta, Max is just a tool for herding cattle or guarding the farm."

Callie looked incredulous. "Do you believe that, Lauren?"

"Not as it pertains to Max, but could you keep a cow that couldn't give you a calf?"

Callie's arms dropped to her sides. "Max is a pet, not livestock, and he suffered for three days with a broken leg."

"Abandoning any animal to suffer is unconscionable."

"I agree." Callie squeezed Lauren's forearm. "Well, now I have a dog. I met Max before when I dropped Becky off to play with Lisa Macpherson. He's a sweet dog, and I'd like to save him."

"Shall we review your options?"

Callie shook her head. "I can find three thousand dollars for the veterinary college." She didn't look totally confident in her statement. "But if the WCVM can't save his leg, I'll go with the amputation option for eight hundred. I'd prefer you do it because I trust you to look after my dog."

"He'll do well on three legs. We have a veterinary saying; 'Dogs have three legs and a spare.' I'll call you at home when the surgery is over and let you know how he's doing." Lauren turned to go but stopped. "Oh, did you need something else? We weren't expecting you."

Callie shuffled her feet and stuck her hands in the pockets of her coat. "I was in town for more electrolytes for the calves and I thought I'd invite you to a late lunch, but now you have surgery."

"I'd love to have lunch, but we have to take care of Max. Then I have two other surgeries to do and an afternoon of vaccinations. I'll be lucky to escape by nine." For an instant, she warmed at the idea of a meal with Callie, but then balked at the idea of being seen by the whole town having lunch with a woman. A woman who was single, pretty…and a client.

"Another time?"

Lauren nodded, and they smiled at each other. Callie clasped Lauren's hands, and Lauren gave Callie's a confident squeeze before she jogged to the surgery room. Callie's visit was a nice surprise, and it left her slightly breathless.

Val and Minnie had Max anesthetized. Lauren stroked the sleeping dog's head. "You have a new owner, Max. It'll be amputation for ole Max. Not the ideal solution, but with his leg in this shape, amputation is his best chance of survival."

Val frowned. "I heard it all. It's been a while since I wanted to punch a client."

"Almost two days." Minnie laughed and scampered away as Val reached for her.

"Let me know when you're ready." Lauren headed to her office to review the anatomy for the surgery in one of her medical textbooks.

Later, Val tapped on Lauren's office door. "We've prepped Max for surgery and Callie left a down payment of three hundred dollars." Val waggled her eyebrows. "Oh, and Callie forgot her electrolytes.

Wasn't that her reason for dropping in? Looks like she'll have to come back."

Lauren shook her head as she followed Val to the surgery room. "Stop meddling. I'm single and happy."

Val shrugged and gave her a knowing look before they got to work. And as Lauren pulled on her gloves, she decided it was almost true. She wasn't happy but she was content. Callie would be a nice friend to have, but that was it. Romantic entanglements were just a heartbreak waiting to happen. She would concentrate on her work. When she was in medical mode, life made sense.

CHAPTER EIGHT

Callie flung open the door of her house and set the bags of groceries on the floor. She kicked off her boots and tossed her coat on a hook. Then she bounded into her kitchen, snagged Martha around the waist, and lifted her as she spun in a circle. Callie was four inches taller than Martha and her sister's feet didn't touch the floor.

"Let me go. Put me down." They were laughing when Callie lowered Martha to the floor. Martha narrowed her eyes. "Why so happy, little sister? Nice lunch? Get all your errands done?"

"All done and I've already unloaded the bags of feed and the new equipment." Luckily, she'd remembered to pick up electrolytes at the feed store.

Callie talked as she put the groceries away. "I had an amazing day. I bought a three-legged dog for eight hundred dollars."

Martha nudged Callie. "Did you have too many glasses of wine at lunch or are you drunk on fantasies of the sexy vet?"

"She didn't have time for lunch. Lauren had patients waiting after Max's surgery." Callie told Martha the story of Max's injury and abandonment.

"I'm not sure it was financially sensible, but I'm glad you helped that poor dog."

"Lauren's wonderful and promised me she'd look after my dog." Callie spun in a circle in the kitchen. "You should've seen her face while she talked to Roberta Macpherson. You've got to love a woman in green scrubs and a white lab coat."

"Uniforms again? What is it with lesbians?"

"What a cliché I am." In her dress uniform with her red serge jacket, Liz had been breathtaking. Callie hugged Martha and then held her hands. "The attraction isn't the uniform, but the air of confidence and strength that goes with the uniform. Confidence is S-E-X-Y, big sister." But in her experience, too much confidence made the other person think they should be in charge. A confident friend was okay, though.

Callie's musings were put on hold as Becky bounded through the mudroom door and tossed her backpack on the floor.

"Hi, Mommy, hi, Aunt Martha." Becky hugged each of them and then peeked in the pot on the stove.

Callie grabbed Becky and gave her a big squeeze. "Dinner is almost ready." She looked at Martha.

Martha nodded. "Thirty minutes."

"Can you wait, or do you need a snack?" Callie kissed the top of Becky's head. She was five-ten and Becky was getting closer to her chin every day. Her kid was growing like a weed.

"I can wait, thanks. Gwen posted some new pictures online and I want to look at them." Becky slid from Callie's arms and loped upstairs.

Callie snagged the backpack off the floor, winked at Martha, and followed Becky.

Callie sat on Becky's bed and watched her fiddle with the computer. She leaned closer to look at Gwen's pictures. They were all of animals, some taken at the clinic. Val and Lauren were smiling at the camera in some. "Gwen must spend a lot of time at work with her mother." Val was a redhead, pretty and petite. Lauren said Val had a girlfriend, but Callie had never picked up a gay vibe from her. So much for gaydar.

Becky laughed. "Look at the puppies. They're so cute. Look, there's a link to a video. Gwen said Lauren and her mom delivered them. Gwen said Lauren let her watch. Gwen said Lauren let her hold them right after they were born. Gwen said Lauren let her rub them dry, but that she had to be careful. Gwen said Lauren is really nice and lets her help all the time."

Callie grinned. Gwen was right. Lauren was nice. "Would you like a puppy?"

Becky swiveled in her chair and focused on Callie. "Can we, please? I would love a puppy and I would take care of him always." Becky pointed at the computer screen. "Can I have one of those?"

Callie squinted at the tiny animals. "They're small, even for puppies. Are they poodles? Wouldn't you like a farm dog? Maybe a collie? One that can run down to the creek with you?" Callie grinned. Every farm kid wanted a dog and she had the perfect one.

Becky clapped her hands. "Yes please, Mommy."

Callie couldn't resist hugging Becky and dropping several kisses on the top of her head. "Good. Well, here's your backpack, which you left in the kitchen, again."

"Sorry, Mommy."

Callie headed to the door. "That's okay. Please wash up and come down and help me set the table."

"Wait, Mommy. I have something to show you."

Callie turned and watched Becky dig through her backpack and then dump the contents on her bed.

"Here it is." Becky handed a brochure to Callie.

Callie opened the cover and studied the pictures of a large Charolais bull. It listed his pedigree and the performance of his progeny. Then it listed the cost of having one cow bred. The cost was astronomical.

"He said that bull's called Bulldozer."

Callie froze as she read the caption under the bull. *Bulldozer. Owner: Kruger Farms.* "Who said?" she snapped.

"Mr. Kruger. He stopped at school while I was waiting for the bus and asked me to give it to you." Becky sat on her bed and slowly placed her schoolbooks into her backpack. "Did I do something wrong?"

Callie crumpled the brochure and jammed it into her pocket. Then she dropped onto the bed and pulled Becky into her lap. "No, you didn't do anything wrong." She rocked Becky while fear and anger flowed through her. "Was it Mr. Heinz Kruger?"

"Yes." Becky touched Callie's cheek. "Are you okay?"

"Mr. Kruger scares me, and I would like it if you didn't talk to him again. Or his sons. Can you do that for me?"

"Yes, Mommy. I didn't like him either. His breath smelled like floor cleaner."

The hair on her neck stood up. Heinz Kruger had been drinking and then approached her daughter at school. She would call the principal in the morning.

"Hey, you two, dinner's ready," Martha called from the kitchen.

Callie sat Becky on the bed and kissed her cheeks. "Let's eat." She stifled the strange urge to count all Becky's fingers and toes. The Krugers were sharks. They had been circling her, but now they were approaching her daughter. It was time to grow a backbone and do something about it. If only she knew what to do about it.

After dinner, Callie washed the dishes and set them in the strainer to dry. Becky had run upstairs, hopefully to do her homework.

"You're quiet," Martha said. "You hardly said two words all through dinner."

"Sorry, I was thinking."

"About a certain veterinarian?" Martha waggled her eyebrows as she spooned the leftover dinner into several plastic containers.

Callie blinked. She'd been worrying about Kruger and was about to tell Martha about the brochure, but thoughts of Lauren were more pleasant. "Sure, yeah." She glanced at her watch. "She's probably still at work. Mar, there's lots of leftovers, what if I take her some?"

Martha grinned and handed Callie one of the plastic containers.

At eight in the evening, Lauren closed the last of the patient files. She stretched her shoulders and rubbed her eyes. Her first calving had been at five a.m. Max's surgery had gone well and she'd stayed to administer pain medication to keep him comfortable, and to ensure he left his IV alone. Dogs often fidgeted and pinched off or tore out IV lines. Some pets chewed them off, so she had to watch him. A cone over his head prevented him from reaching his sutures, but he could still reach the IV line.

Lauren allowed herself a minute to daydream about Callie. Callie cared about her cattle, but her fire and her sense of justice showed she also had compassion for a dog she didn't even own. A woman who cared about animals was a woman Lauren could admire. She pictured Callie's badass pose as she squared off with Roberta. She wouldn't want Callie's fierce expression focused on her. Glowering, Callie had looked dangerous.

Lauren's stomach growled and she groaned with it. It had been eight hours since lunch. With resignation, she opened the drawer of her desk. She stocked cans of beans for emergencies. The ones with the pull tops. She removed a can and studied it. How long had it been there? Was it still safe to eat? If she had the energy, she'd take it to the staff room and toss it in the microwave. Tonight, it would be cold beans in congealed brown sauce straight from the can. Just as she was about to open the can, the front doorbell rang.

The sound in the quiet clinic startled her and she dropped the can and watched it bounce under the desk. It was gone for good now, lost in the inevitable balls of dog and cat hair that collected in the corners of a veterinary clinic. With a sigh, she walked to the front door and looked out. In the dim light she spotted Callie glowing in the moonlight. Lauren rubbed her eyes at the illusion. Then looked again. Callie was really there. She held up a red lunch bag and mouthed something. Lauren unlocked the door and ushered her in.

"Hi, Callie. This is a surprise. Did you want to see Max?"

"Well, okay, sure, if you think it's okay." She held up a red bag. "I actually brought you dinner. I hope that's not weird."

"Dinner?"

Callie grimaced. "Goofy, eh? It's just that you said you'd be working late, and I thought…" She shrugged.

"Would you like a coffee or a soda?"

"A soda would be nice."

Lauren locked the door behind Callie and led the way to the staff room. She pulled a selection of sodas out of the refrigerator and set them on the table. "Glass?"

Callie shook her head. Then she sat and pushed the red bag toward Lauren.

Lauren slowly unzipped the bag and then lifted the container out. She peeled back the lid and inhaled deeply. "Oh, wow. Smells amazing. I'm starving."

"Stew. Martha made it. I won't take credit."

Lauren's tired brain tried to work out why Callie was really there, but it was too much and she abandoned the task. "Do you want some?"

Callie sipped her soda. "It's for you. I already ate. How's Max?"

Lauren set the spoon aside and opened her mouth "He's—"

Callie held up her hand. "Wait. You eat. I'll talk." Callie rested her elbows on the table and watched Lauren eat.

Lauren took several spoonfuls and smiled back. After the sixth she put the spoon down and giggled.

Callie sat back. "What?"

"You were going to talk."

Callie sat up. "Right, yeah."

"What did you do after you left here?"

"Errands, groceries, dropped by the feed store for a bag of calf pellets."

"Spoiling your calves?"

"They're just so sweet."

"Wonder if Heinz Kruger calls his cattle sweet?"

"No cattle and no Krugers, please. Not tonight. Tell me, what would you be doing if you weren't working? Wait, I was going to talk while you eat. What do I do in the evening, you might ask? When I've done the farm work, have fed Becky, helped her with homework, and cleaned up the kitchen, I end the day with a shower and bed. I'm very boring."

Lauren shook her head. Callie wasn't boring at all. She was a farmer who worked hard.

"I am. I do nothing but work. You saw me at the club, but it had been months since I was there last." Callie shrugged. "That's agriculture."

"What do you want to do?"

"There's a community basketball league in the winter. I'd love to play."

"Ah, so you were a jock in high school. I thought so."

"Why?"

Lauren blushed. "It's well, obvious." Exhaustion and hypoglycemia had lowered her inhibitions. In ten seconds, she would tell Callie she was beautiful and then the evening would be weird.

"You're embarrassed." Callie slapped her playfully on the shoulder. "Now I absolutely must know what you meant. Spill."

Lauren stuffed a huge spoonful of stew in her mouth and chewed slowly, willing it to last a week. "You're tall and fit. And, well, you move like an athlete."

"I'll take that as a compliment. Do you play any sports?"

Lauren grimaced. "I made sub on the volleyball team in grade six. I'm afraid that was the peak of my athletic career."

"I wish we had the scholarship thing in Canada like they have in the USA. I played basketball and it would've helped pay for my college diploma."

Lauren laughed. "What about Becky? Does she play basketball? Hockey?" She wanted to slap herself. Now she was asking about Becky like Callie was a pal. Like she had any right to ask. She'd never even met the child.

"No hockey for her. She had the choice, but she's not into all the rough stuff."

"But there's no contact in women's hockey."

"Tell them that. We play a little basketball at home and she loves running. She's a quiet kid and into her art." Callie rested an elbow on the table and smiled at Lauren. "You look relaxed. Or is it exhaustion?"

Lauren felt the heat in her face. She pushed the container of stew away. "Enough. The rest is lunch tomorrow. I'm stuffed. Thanks, and please tell Martha thanks. It's not often I get a home cooked meal."

"Not at Val's?"

Lauren gave a half shrug. "Sometimes, but she has her family and I don't like to impose."

"You should come to Poplarcreek for dinner. Before Martha leaves. I can cook, but my sister is way better. She has a sense of adventure in the kitchen. Becky and I have been her guinea pigs these few weeks to mixed results."

"Is Martha older?"

"Four years, but we're close. I love having her visit, but I'm afraid I put her to work helping me sort out my junk and clean the house." Callie hesitated, like she wasn't sure what else to say. "Well, I should probably head home. Long day tomorrow and I'll bet you want to go home."

Lauren hadn't responded to the dinner invitation, but Callie hadn't noticed. There was something about Callie that made her nervous. A sense that Callie wanted more than friendship.

Lauren said, "I'll check on Max again and head out. Do you want to see him? He's probably sleeping, but you're welcome to."

They tiptoed into the treatment room and studied the sleeping dog, then tiptoed out again. "Thanks," Callie whispered.

Lauren walked Callie to the front door. She unlocked it and Callie stepped out. They stared at each other for a beat until Callie said, "Night, Lauren."

"Night."

There was another moment of hesitation before Callie turned and walked to her truck.

Lauren stood with the door open and let the cold air wash over her. She needed cooling. It had been a nice visit. A bit awkward, but they were still practically strangers. At least even in her exhausted state she hadn't revealed anything really personal. It would help keep some distance between them, which was a good thing. She still wasn't certain what had made Callie come by with dinner, but she wasn't about to analyze it too closely.

Lauren returned to the staff room to put the remaining stew in the refrigerator. She searched the zippered pocket of the red bag and found an excellent drawing. It was of a cow and tiny calf with one line of childish printing: *Dr. Cornish, thank you for taking care of our calves. Becky.*

She studied the picture and hoped she wouldn't have to disappoint Callie. Callie's heifers had done well after surgery, but Max might be different. He was alive, but in rough shape. They still had to worry about infection, and he had to learn to walk again. A dog might refuse to move even if tempted with treats. He was an awesome dog with a great new owner, and Lauren refused to let him die. She wanted to do this for Callie.

Why was it so important to please Callie? It was as if she wanted to protect her. "No, no, no." She was *not* going there. Callie was a client and possibly a friend, but the air was charged when they were together. Not like when she was with Val. Life had just become more dangerous.

Lauren folded the drawing carefully and carried it to her desk. Instead of posting the drawing on her bulletin board with the pictures from her clients' children, she slid it into the back of the drawer. It was best not to have reminders of Callie near her.

As she was withdrawing her hand from the drawer, her fingers found the small photo album she kept there. Lauren opened the small book and flipped through the pages. They were old photographs of her family...when she'd had a family. She sniffled and studied the pictures of Sam and William. This was the wrong time of day for this. When she was sitting alone in a dark clinic, three thousand kilometers from her heart, with nobody waiting in her dark house, it was a mistake to look at pictures that made her sadder.

Lauren blew her nose and switched on her computer. She opened her email and started to type. *Dear Sam and William, I love you and I'm sorry.* Her thoughts began to flow as she gradually saw her heart laid out in words. She wouldn't send it tonight, not when she was over-the-top emotional. She might not send it at all, or maybe not this version, but just putting the words down helped ease the pain.

CHAPTER NINE

"Hi, Lauren, how's my dog doing?" It was the morning after Max's surgery. Callie wanted to know how Max was, and she jumped at the chance to speak with Lauren. Taking Lauren dinner at the clinic had been fun, but she was curious about Lauren and the only thing she'd learned was that Lauren didn't play sports.

"Max is doing well. It's too soon for him to walk, but he's eating a little. I need to keep him at least a week until he's walking."

"Okay, I trust you to decide what's best for him."

"It shouldn't add much to your bill."

"The bill doesn't worry me, but I'm surprised how little it'll cost." Callie gulped. The suggestion that Lauren might add more to her bill was worrisome. She trusted Lauren and had no doubt it was a fair price. Surgery and a week's nursing care was the same price as two C-sections. Maybe it was fair, but she didn't have eight dollars to spare, let alone eight hundred. Callie squared her shoulders. Max deserved saving and she would do it. Somehow.

"The big expense was the surgery, but he should heal more before I send him home. Also, given the state his leg was in, serious infection is still a high risk."

"I'd like to thank you by taking you to lunch sometime?"

"You brought me dinner, and besides there's no need to thank me. All part of my job."

"But I'd like to thank you for taking care of him." This wasn't going the way Callie had hoped it would. It was as if Lauren were deliberately misunderstanding her offer.

"I enjoyed it. Max is a great dog."

Callie snorted and shook her head in exasperation. "Dr. Lauren Cornish, will you please have lunch with me sometime? Just because we should have lunch together?"

Lauren hesitated for a moment. "That would be nice. When?"

Callie suppressed the urge to dance when Lauren accepted. "Do you have time today? I'll be in town. Or we could meet another day?"

"Today I can meet at twelve, but I have to be back for my first afternoon appointment at one. Shall I meet you somewhere?"

An hour would feel rushed compared to dinner, but she'd take it. "Meet me at the Thresherton Diner. Don't worry if you're late. I'll wait."

"I'm looking forward to it. See you then."

"Me too." Callie hung up the phone. *I did it. I asked Lauren out. Good for me.* Callie danced her way upstairs to change into something pretty. She didn't want a relationship, but friendship with an attractive woman wasn't the end of the world. And if they developed something casual that didn't require a lot of time, well...

At eleven forty-five, Callie arrived at the diner. She was early but planned to find an empty table and collect herself before Lauren appeared. She waited at the counter for five minutes, and when a table for two became available, she snagged it. At lunch, diners occupied every table in the restaurant. Doug told her you could always tell the best places to eat in town because at breakfast and lunch there would be a row of pickup trucks parked in front. And sure enough, there was a row of them outside.

Callie ordered coffee with cream on the side. The fancy coffee craze hadn't arrived at the Thresherton Diner, but the coffee was excellent, and the cups were bottomless. She would have ordered coffee for Lauren, but it would probably be cold before Lauren arrived. And she didn't want to appear presumptuous, either. Maybe Lauren didn't even like coffee?

Callie fidgeted in her seat. It had been a good idea to invite Lauren to lunch, but she hadn't counted on the entire town having front row seats to their lunch. Maybe she should have stuck to dropping in at PVS in the evening, but she had nothing to hide. They were two friends having a meal. No big deal.

Callie sipped her coffee and scanned the diner. She nodded to a few people and said hello to others. When she reached the far corner, her eyes darted away from the person staring at her. She studied the menu as if there were a test later.

"Hey, Callie girl," a greasy voice said, too close to her ear.

Callie winced. His breath was foul and reeked of cigarettes, coffee, and she wasn't sure what else. "Hello, Kyle." She struggled not to gag as Kyle Kruger sat uninvited at her table.

Kyle snuck an arm along the back of Callie's chair. "Whatcha' doin' in town today? I'll buy you lunch."

Callie moved her chair to force his arm to drop. He was a slightly built man, several inches shorter than her, but it still felt threatening to have him that close. If he didn't repulse her so much, she might almost feel sorry for him. She imagined he had been bullied all his life by his father. "No, thanks. I'm meeting someone." Kyle bent toward her and she leaned away from him.

"Is it Mark Renfield?"

"Why would I meet Mark?"

The man shrugged. "I seen his truck at your place a few times."

Callie almost answered, but it was none of Kyle's business. Mark Renfield was Becky's cousin. He often helped Callie with repairs on her farm machinery. And it was creepy to know any of the Krugers were paying attention to who came and went on her farm. "I'm meeting somebody, so maybe—"

"You look nice today. I never seen you look this pretty."

"Thanks. Now please, go back to your table."

"I gotta wonder what fella made you want to dress up." Kyle reached for her hand.

Callie could no longer hide her irritation. "Do you remember the part where I had a wife? Why would I wait for a man? Why would I want a man?" A second later, she regretted engaging.

"Maybe you just need the right man." Kyle played with the little scruffy bit of hair below his bottom lip. He was a cartoonish buffoon, a repulsive lowlife, much like the rest of his family.

Callie's stomach clenched, and she felt queasy.

"Hello, Callie. I hope I'm not late. Hi, Kyle."

Callie hadn't noticed Lauren enter the diner because she was too busy attempting to dislodge Kyle from her table. Her soft, deep voice was music to Callie's ears. She grinned at Lauren. "You're just in time."

Lauren replied with a warm smile and a quick wink.

Kyle looked from Lauren to Callie and back. "Well, now I get it." Kyle scowled at Callie. Then he leered at Lauren, taking his time to ogle her chest "Hey, Doc." Kyle stood and swaggered to his table.

Lauren slipped into the chair vacated by Kyle.

"Thank you, thank you, thank you. Perfect timing." Callie laid her hand on top of Lauren's and gave it a slight squeeze.

"At first, I didn't want to interrupt, but if you'd leaned any farther away from him, you'd have fallen off your chair. I decided you needed rescuing."

"I did. Kyle was telling me how lesbians just need to find the right man."

"Oh, yuck." Lauren grimaced. "Do men still think that way?"

Callie shook her head. "Maybe just Kyle. He's extra creepy. Although his dad and brother are pretty gross too."

"True." Lauren leaned toward Callie. "Kyle's always talking to my chest. And he always stands too close behind me when I'm at their farm. Every time I step back, my butt hits him below the belt."

Callie rolled her eyes. "Yuck. Perhaps he thinks you only need the right man." As they laughed, Callie glanced Kyle's way. His lips curled into a sneer and his nostrils flared as he stared back at them. She read the hate in his eyes. She recoiled from the expression and focused on Lauren.

"Are you all right, Callie? You've gone pale."

"I was thinking about Kyle. Forget him." Callie shoved thoughts of the Krugers away and let her good humor return. "How are you settling in? How do you like Thresherton?"

"It's nice and I'm renting a great little house." Lauren shook her head. "I've never lived in such a small town, but I'm adjusting."

"To what?"

"I'm growing accustomed to being stared at. When I first moved to Thresherton, it shocked me when people I didn't know greeted me by name. Then I discovered that a single female veterinarian, over thirty, was somebody everybody recognized."

"Your picture was in the paper." *Single. I like the sound of that.* "Really?"

"It said, 'Prairie Veterinary Services welcomes their new veterinarian, Dr. Lauren Cornish.' There was a sweet picture of you cuddling a kitten."

"No kidding."

The waitress appeared, and they ordered. Lauren handed her menu to the waitress. "Thanks."

Callie rested her elbows on the table and stared at Lauren. What to talk about? "Tell me how your day's going."

"Well, Max is healing well, but I'm worried about coaxing him to walk. He has to try tomorrow. Border collies are an upbeat breed, but Max is too quiet even when you consider the surgery. I swear he knows his family has abandoned him. We know so little about the subtleties of how dogs in a pack communicate. The Macphersons were his pack, and they discarded him. Is that a crazy theory?"

"No." Callie tapped her bottom lip with her index finger. "Why don't I visit him and let him know he has a new pack?"

Lauren nodded. "Perfect. But don't bring Becky until you've seen him. He's healing well but has a long row of sutures that might frighten a child."

The comment felt like an order, but Callie tamped down her annoyance. "Becky's seen plenty of sutures. Or are you forgetting all the C-sections?"

"Sorry, yes. Whatever you think is best."

"Can I bring Becky to see the animals another time? She'd like to meet you, too."

Lauren leaned back and her eyes shifted from side to side. She didn't answer.

Callie filled in the awkward silence. "We'd like to visit, but only if it's okay. My sister Martha's here for a few weeks. Can I bring her too?" Maybe that would take the pressure off, make it more like a field trip. Though what made Lauren uncomfortable about it she wasn't certain.

"Sure. I'll let you know when we have something to see."

Wasn't there always something to see at a veterinary clinic? Callie ignored the evasive answer and motioned at her clothing. "I'm not dressed for visiting Max today, but I'll visit tomorrow. Shall I call first?"

Callie watched Lauren's eyes slide over her body. It was a warm look, caressing. She had dressed in tight blue jeans, a lavender V-neck sweater, and matching earrings. She'd piled her hair high on her head and she wore a little mascara. Lauren leaned in to catch the subtle scent of her perfume and Callie grinned. The dreamy expression on Lauren's face was inviting, and she longed to crawl across the table toward her. Fantasies were always better than reality, though, and that's where this one would stay. Even if she did like Lauren's attention.

"Can I visit him tomorrow? Should I call first?" she asked again. Callie suppressed the urge to laugh when Lauren blushed. *Busted, Dr. Cornish.*

"Sure. Val will help you with him if I'm not there. If you coaxed him to walk a few steps that would be great. He needs to believe he can still walk."

"Okay. I'll call tomorrow." The conversation stalled, and when their lunches arrived, they concentrated on their food and talked about surface things like Callie's cattle until she stopped them. "Let's not talk anymore about my animals or calvings, please."

"What do we talk about?"

"Why did you become a vet?"

Lauren picked at her salad. "Don't remember. I just always knew. Since I was little. Years ago, when my mother sold her house, I packed up my stuff from when I was a kid. I found a stuffed dog with an ink mark on his leg, where I'd taken blood or given a vaccination or something. I picked my career a long time ago and I don't recall why." Lauren blushed again.

"Ah, sweet. Are your parents veterinarians?" Lauren was extra cute when she blushed. Callie had imagined Lauren was too experienced and confident to blush, given that she was from a big city and all. She wasn't sorry to be wrong. Lauren's vulnerability was compelling.

"My mother has a university degree in English, but she was a stay-at-home mom. My father was a university professor. He taught physiology at the veterinary college in Guelph, Ontario, but he wasn't a veterinarian."

"Is he gone?"

"He died the year before I graduated from vet school. He never saw me graduate and I still miss him." She gave a small, brief smile.

"I'm sorry." Callie rested her hand over Lauren's. "I'm sure he was proud of you."

"Thanks. How about your parents?"

"My parents own a berry farm in Surrey, British Columbia. I did a two-year agribusiness course at college and planned to work with them."

"You didn't intend to run a farm at all, then?"

"Oh, I've always loved farming. I'm a country girl at heart. I just never imagined I'd be running a farm with livestock and cash crops, but now I can't imagine doing anything else."

"So, no plans to return to British Columbia?"

"Only every time the temperature dips below minus twenty here."

"I hear that. It must be hard to find the time to visit your folks. From what I've seen, farming is more than a full-time job."

"It is, but I also work for the RCMP part-time. It's nice getting off the farm and interacting with adults." The extra cash helped too. Many farmers had two jobs.

"Is it interesting?"

"Sometimes, but I'm not solving crimes. I type and file and sometimes cover reception." Callie shrugged. "Six months after Becky and I settled in Thresherton I went looking for part-time work. I practically pick my hours and the detachment budget even paid for a couple of computer classes in Saskatoon." Believing he was responsible for assisting the widow of a fellow RCMP officer, the detachment commander had driven out to Poplarcreek and offered her the job. He was a generous man and she was grateful.

"I can't imagine how you fit it in."

"I usually only work about eight hours a week, but not this calving season. Not when I'm all by myself and have heifers calving." Callie shook her head. "How does every conversation manage to circle back to my cattle?"

"That's agriculture."

"Becky's at the police station almost more often than me so she can visit Mitch. Officer Mitchell is our good friend from British Columbia. I don't know if you've met? It was a gift to move to Thresherton and find her here. The first year I was here Mitch was at the farm all the time helping with whatever I needed. On her weekends off she took Becky for a day. She said it was to give me a break, but she always made it fun for Becky."

"That's a good friend."

"She is. She visits less often, but still steals Becky away for the odd day of fun."

They chatted for a while longer about school, traveling, and life in Saskatchewan. Then Lauren peered at her phone. "Twelve fifty already. I feel as if I sat down ten minutes ago. I wish I could stay longer."

Callie dropped cash and a generous tip on the table. She liked that Lauren didn't insist on paying. Liz would have.

Lauren accompanied Callie to her truck. "Here's the insulated bag and container from last night. Thanks for dinner. That was really considerate."

"I'm glad you enjoyed it."

"Tell Martha I said thank you too, please. My mother told me never to return a dish empty, but I'm not brave enough to cook for you." Lauren scratched the nape of her neck. "Fiona was at Kingsway Farm this morning and picked up eggs for me. I put a dozen in your bag in lieu of my cooking."

"Thanks. I love Kingsway eggs."

"Thanks for lunch."

"You're welcome." Lauren started to turn away just as Callie leaned in for quick hug. It was awkward and Callie ended up hugging Lauren's shoulder. She stepped back inexplicably dissatisfied and slightly embarrassed.

Callie waved at Lauren, then she climbed into her truck and drove away. She circled the block to drive by Lauren and wave one more time. But Lauren was strolling along the sidewalk and didn't notice her drive past. Callie turned on the radio and sang along as she headed home.

Lauren had checked her out, and it generated a wave of warmth that flowed through Callie, making her wonder... She slammed on the brakes and skidded, stopping with one front tire hanging over the ditch. Callie backed onto the road and straightened her truck. She wasn't interested in Lauren in that way and she'd just been looking at her clothes. "We're friends. Yes, friends with similar interests. Nothing more."

As she drove on, Callie pondered their conversation. She'd done most of the talking, and once again, she'd learned very little about Dr. Lauren Cornish.

CHAPTER TEN

That was an amazing class, Becky," Callie said. "You've worked hard and I'm proud of you." It was Monday night, and Callie and Becky were in town for Becky's painting class. "Would you like to go to PVS and visit the animals? Dr. Cornish invited us." It was four days since their lunch date, and she was pleased that Lauren had called. She hadn't forgotten about her request to visit PVS.

"Yes, please." Becky bounced in her seat.

Callie drove into the PVS parking lot. She spotted Lauren's truck and another car. She didn't want to get in the way. What if Lauren was dealing with an emergency? Callie parked behind the clinic and they climbed out.

As they approached the door, laugher floated from the building. It was a sweet, musical woman's voice, but not Lauren's. She loved Lauren's laugh, but it was deeper and not as loud. Callie froze. Becky was there to see the animals, but Callie was at PVS to see Lauren. Hopefully, she wasn't interrupting anything. Becky tugged on her hand and hopped in excitement until she moved forward.

"Come on, Mommy. Let's go."

Callie squared her shoulders and knocked. An instant later, the door flew open and Val grinned at them.

"Hey, Becky, hey, Callie. Come and join the party."

"V.C., come here, quick." Lauren called from somewhere deep in the clinic.

Val pointed to hooks by the door. "Hang up your coats but keep your boots on. On my way, L.C." Val jogged from sight.

They removed their coats, hats, and gloves, and headed into the treatment room. Lauren and Val stood shoulder to shoulder, with their backs to Callie as they struggled with something on the table. Lauren and Val were laughing hard, with their mouths inches apart. Callie couldn't help the jolt of jealousy at their easy banter.

Callie followed Becky into the room. "What're you doing?" Becky's voice rose to end on a squeak. "Why're you putting clothes on that kitten?"

Lauren looked at her with a wide smile. "You must be Becky. You're very observant, my friend. We are indeed dressing Mr. Paws, but he's a grouchy kitten." The kitten was hissing and scratching, but he was so small his tantrum was cute.

Becky fired off questions. "How old is he? Is he soft? Where's his mom? Is he hurt? May I hold Mr. Paws, please?"

"Just a second." Lauren focused on the struggling kitten. "There we are." Lauren raised the little cat in triumph. It was a brown tabby kitten sporting a bright red shirt. "Hi, Callie. Did you bring Martha?"

"I invited her, but she's taking an online accounting course and wanted to catch up on her homework. She's been helping me so much she's fallen behind."

"What about this one, Mommy?" Gwen entered from the next room with another kitten in her arms. "Hi, Mrs. Anderson. Hi, Becky."

Callie grinned at Gwen. It was impossible not to like her. She was a tiny eight-year-old, with the same red hair and blue eyes as her mother. "Hello, Gwen."

Callie had met Gwen on Becky's first day of school in Thresherton. She and Becky had been waiting for the school bell. Becky was toeing the ground with her boot and clutching her knapsack against her chest as if it were a shield. Gwen had jogged toward them full of big smiles and announced, "We both have lesbian moms so we should be friends." Callie could have hugged Gwen. As accepting as society was becoming, it still helped kids with same-sex parents to have peers who understood the challenges of their nontraditional families.

Becky glanced at Gwen and then at Lauren and then back at Gwen. Callie watched Becky waver between petting the kitten Gwen held and waiting for Lauren's answers.

"His name's not Mr. Paws, but it could be. I name all the kittens Mr. or Ms. Paws until they have a real name." Lauren blushed. "He needs a little shirt to cover the sore on his back to keep him from licking it." Lauren lifted the little cat's red shirt to show Becky and Callie the quarter-sized area of red, raw skin. "He has to quit licking the sore or it won't heal. I prefer shirts instead of cone collars on tiny kittens because they have problems walking with the cones on and it keeps them from cuddling with the other kittens."

Gwen crinkled her nose. "And they get gross and yucky when they eat wearing a cone collar."

Lauren nodded. "That's true. He's six weeks old and you may hold him, but don't touch his back, please."

Becky held out her hands for the kitten and peered up at Callie. At Callie's nod, Becky accepted the little cat and at once cuddled him to her chest. Becky's reward was a tiny motor. "He's purring." Becky squealed, delighted.

Callie looked away from Becky to find Lauren's green eyes and bright smile focused on her.

Val opened the door that led from the treatment room. "Come on, girls. Let's take those kittens into the next room where the others are."

Callie glanced at Val, and Val winked. After they departed, Callie wanted to swallow her words, but they escaped. "Val is nice. And attractive, too." *Subtle.*

Lauren shrugged slightly. "Val is outgoing, and I admire her for the way she interacts with clients. She knows when to help them and cajole or shame them into taking care of their pets. She's even better with the animals." Lauren looked at Callie thoughtfully.

Callie stuffed her hands into her pockets and poked at a piece of crumpled paper on the floor with the toe of her boot. "I see."

"No, you don't see." Lauren stepped closer. "Number one, I work with Val. Number two, she's way younger than I am, and number three," Lauren counted on her fingers, "she's dating somebody in the city. Number four, we're great friends, and number five, I'm—" She stopped as two giggling girls bounced into the room with arms full of kittens. Lauren swiveled to face Becky, and Gwen and inspect the kittens.

I'm what? Callie screamed in her head. *What was Lauren going to say?*

Val followed the girls into the room. She caught Callie's eye and mouthed, "I'm sorry" above the bent heads of the girls.

Those few unspoken words combined with the sympathetic expression on Val's face told Callie everything she needed to know. She smiled in gratitude, a little embarrassed she was so transparent. "You two are working late."

Val grinned. "PVS has become the unofficial local SPCA and rescue shelter. Ian and Fiona support the rescue project as much as they can afford to with housing and medical supplies. The community donates bags of food."

Callie nodded. "That's generous."

"The deal is whichever veterinarian I get to help me has to see the rescue patients on their own time. In the evenings, Lauren and I spay or neuter stray animals and some nights we treat sick kittens." Val poked Lauren in the side. "I had no trouble convincing you to join me when you moved to Thresherton."

Bent over a kitten, Lauren twisted to stick her tongue out at Val. Then she gazed up at Callie. "It's true. I am a willing accomplice."

Callie felt special for being included in the camaraderie of the circle. She had never seen Lauren playful and unguarded before. Gwen chatted nonstop to Lauren, and Lauren smiled fondly as she answered the girls' many questions. Gwen all but hung off Lauren's arm, and Becky crowded close, making it more difficult for Lauren to treat the kittens.

It was another thirty minutes before they finished. They had cleaned sores and medicated the kittens. Two now sported little shirts. Becky cuddled a kitten that had brown ears with black, hairless tips.

"The kitten had frostbite and the top halves of its ears froze." Lauren shifted like she was going to put her arm around Becky's shoulders, but then paused and let her arm drop instead. "Now the tips of his ears are black because they're dead."

"Will his ears heal?" Becky asked.

Lauren shook her head. "When he's stronger and has eaten lots of good dinners, we'll do surgery on him to remove the black bits. Mr. Paws will look different with short ears, but he'll be a happier kitten afterward."

A few minutes later, the kittens lay curled together in their fleece bed. Lauren and Val cleaned the treatment room and then everyone traipsed to the back door.

Val and Gwen tugged on their coats. "Night, Callie. Night, Becky. See you tomorrow, L.C." After a quick wave from Val and after Lauren hugged Gwen, the Connors exited the clinic.

Lauren grimaced. "Sorry the kittens took so long."

Callie gazed into Becky's happy face. "They were fun, but is it too late for us to visit with Max?" She'd been by twice to see Max. It was unfortunate Lauren had been out of the clinic on both her visits, but this morning when she visited, Val told her Max was going to survive, so there were no worries about Becky becoming attached to an animal that might die.

"Not at all. Follow me." Lauren led them to the room with the dog runs. At five feet by twelve feet, the runs weren't large enough for a dog to go far, but they could jump and stretch their legs.

Max's tail thumped when he saw Lauren, but he didn't move. He lay on a thick fleece blanket with his head in a cone collar resting beside his remaining front leg. Sad, anxious eyes flitted between Callie and Lauren. When Max spotted Becky, he lifted his head and glanced from Lauren to Becky and back. Callie imagined he was asking if Lauren had brought him a playmate.

Lauren opened the door to Max's run and removed the cone collar. Max slowly got to his feet and hobbled on three legs toward

Becky. "Wow! We always have to lift him or coax him to stand. He walked right over to you," Lauren said to Becky.

After receiving permission from Callie, Becky petted the dog with small, tentative strokes to his head. "Max is Lisa's dog."

"Not anymore. He lives here now," Lauren said.

Actually, Max belonged to Callie and therefore Becky, but she hadn't told her and she'd requested Lauren not tell her yet, either. She hadn't wanted to get her hopes up, but it was time to start the process.

"Becky, Max mopes in his bed all day and only nibbles at his meals. If I fixed him a snack, would you try to coax him to eat, please?" Lauren asked.

When Becky nodded without taking her eyes off Max, Lauren left and returned with a bowl of canned dog food with a handful of dry kibble mixed into it. She gave Becky a mat to sit on and Becky sat beside Max. She petted Max and talked to him while he ate.

Callie studied Lauren, who had tears in her eyes.

When Lauren caught Callie studying her, she turned her back to Max and Becky. She dug a tissue from her pocket, blotted her tears, and blew her nose. "That's embarrassing."

"Max is walking better." Callie wasn't sure what else to say. It was a moving moment with Max, but she didn't think it explained Lauren's tears.

"Max?" Lauren swallowed with difficulty and turned. "Yes, right, Max. He's doing great." She looked down at Becky and the dog. "He's been reluctant to eat, and then Becky appears and in two seconds he has the appetite of a wolfhound. He doesn't eat that much for Val and me." Lauren blew her nose. "There really is a special relationship between children and dogs."

Moved by Lauren's emotion, Callie stroked her arm. Callie whispered, "Maybe he knows he's part of Becky's pack."

"There's so much we don't know about animals. Scientists tell us instinct and learned behaviors drive dogs to act the way they do. There has to be more to it." Lauren looked everywhere but at Callie.

Callie gazed at Becky with pride. "I'm sure you're right."

Lauren collected Max's empty bowl. "Becky, can you please walk around the clinic and see if Max will follow you? He needs to practice walking on three legs." The dog followed Becky for a few steps and then sat. When she petted him and encouraged him to keep trying, he stood and followed her again. After Max walked for fifteen minutes, he dropped to his belly and refused to follow her anymore.

Lauren scooped up Max and cradled him in her arms as she carried him to his run. She carefully lowered him onto his bed, where she kneeled beside him and stroked his head. "Thanks, Becky. Max needed the exercise, but he's tired now." She shifted to make room for Becky to push in beside her.

Becky surprised Callie by sitting in Lauren's lap while she petted Max. Lauren hesitated and then put her arm around Becky, and it made Callie smile. Lauren had a comfortable manner with children and had made friends with Gwen. Callie wasn't afraid of Becky becoming any more attached to Lauren than Gwen was. It wasn't as if Lauren were Liz. No, she and Becky could both use more friends.

"Would you like to know what's been happening with Max?" Lauren asked.

"He has no leg," Becky said.

"That's true, but there's a little more to it than that." Lauren described Max's injury, omitting the part about his leg being left to rot for three days before his last owners abandoned him at the clinic. She explained the surgery and the stages of Max's recovery.

"Why isn't he Lisa's dog anymore?"

Lauren shrugged. "The Macpherson family doesn't want him. Sometimes it's hard for families to care for an animal with special needs."

When Max settled in for the night, Lauren fastened the cone collar on him and closed the door to the run. Then she escorted Callie and Becky to the back door where they slipped on coats, hats, and gloves.

Callie hugged Lauren and gave her a kiss on the cheek. "Thanks."

Becky bounced on her toes. "Thank you, Dr. Cornish, for showing me the kittens and Max and telling me about them. It was fun."

"I enjoyed having you here, Becky, and thanks for your help with the animals."

Callie smiled when Becky raised her arms and Lauren squatted to hug her.

But when Lauren straightened and stepped back, Callie's smile slipped. Lauren's eyes glistened with tears again. What had happened to make her so sad? Callie wanted to know so much more about Lauren. But that was okay, right? Friends learned about each other. It didn't have to be anything more…

CHAPTER ELEVEN

While Callie waited in the dentist's office for Becky, she flipped to an article in her magazine about rearing calves. She tried to concentrate on the vaccine options, but there were so many. Raising her calves would be her next big project after the calvings were done, and she couldn't expect the veterinarians at PVS to continue to hold her hand. But it would be fair to ask them to suggest a vaccination program.

Callie smoothed the well-worn magazine. She liked *Cattle Rancher*. The publisher was in Alberta, but the articles were still applicable to Saskatchewan. The first issue had shown up right after Christmas, but none of her family would admit to buying it for her. Callie smiled. Probably her big brother being a thoughtful goof.

After repeatedly reading the same two sentences, she gave up. With a sigh, she folded the magazine and slid it into her purse. Her head was full of thoughts about Lauren. It was two nights since she and Becky had visited PVS and Becky was still talking about it. She wanted to help after school like Gwen did. Callie was happy Becky had new interests, but could becoming better friends with Lauren lead to disaster? What if Lauren moved away or something happened to her? She couldn't stand the thought of Becky losing someone else she'd gotten close to.

"It's been two weeks and nothing," the young man said. "Poor Kev."

"Yeah, the RCMP have found nothing. It's not fair. When Kev went to bed, he had forty cows, when he woke, he had thirty-four. Each one was worth at least two thousand dollars," the older man said.

Intrigued by the conversation, Callie studied a poster about flossing and pretended not to listen.

"Kev didn't see nothing, but the RCMP has a print of the truck and trailer tires."

"What? Is the RCMP going to check hundreds of trucks and trailers?"

"Listen, old man. Tires have sizes and patterns and they also have a unique series of cuts or damage to the tires."

"Still, can't go checking everyone's tires." The man scoffed.

"True, but if they have a suspect, they check their tires."

Callie pulled out her phone and scanned the calendar. It was two weeks ago that Kyle had borrowed her truck and trailer and taken two of her cows to Montana. She still hadn't been paid for them. "Was that on February twenty-fourth?" she asked the men. Where had she been? How had she missed hearing about this? Callie worked at the RCMP detachment part-time but hadn't made it to work since the heifers started calving.

The young man nodded. "Yup. Exactly two week ago. You okay? You've gone pale."

Callie's stomach clenched and her vision blurred for a second. "No, I'm okay." There had been six other Charolais cows on the trailer. Was it a coincidence? She needed to know, and it was time to toughen up and press Kyle for the four thousand dollars for her two cows. If Heinz was really going to make her get a lawyer to recover her money, then she needed to know now.

After Becky's dental appointment, Callie drove her to school. Then she phoned Kyle and left a message. "Kyle, we need to talk. Can you drop by the diner at two? For coffee?"

Kyle appeared at the front door of her house at lunchtime. Callie opened her door four inches. "Kyle, I said two, at the diner."

"I'm here now. Gotta be in the city by two. You wanna talk or what?" Kyle waited. "Suit yourself." He turned to go.

"Okay." Why, oh why, was Martha always out when the Krugers dropped by? Did Kyle watch her laneway and wait for Martha to leave? Did Heinz? Martha had left ten minutes ago and would shoot Callie for letting Kyle in. Callie opened the door, and he swaggered in and sat at her table. He tipped his chair back on two legs and smirked at her. He continued to smoke his cigarette and flicked the ash on her floor.

Callie fetched an ashtray and set it near him with a clunk.

Kyle leaned forward and grabbed the magazine Callie had open on the table. "*Cattle Rancher*. You like it?"

"It's good. Informative."

Kyle flipped through the magazine and set it on the table. "You gonna thank me?"

"Pardon?"

"I paid for it."

Callie had been reading while she ate lunch and could barely resist the urge to push the magazine into the trash. She mustered a weak smile. "Thanks."

Kyle extracted several sheets of crumbled paper from his pocket and set them on the table. "That's a copy of last month's article on calvings. My dad put some comments or something on it for you."

Callie stared at the crumpled sheets. After a few seconds, Kyle smoothed out the pages and pushed it closer. She glanced down. Heinz had highlighted certain sections and provided a list titled: *Catherine's Foolish Mistakes.* She pushed the papers aside. "How very thoughtful of Heinz. He's such a *good* neighbor. *So* helpful."

"He is and you should listen to him." Kyle set an envelope on the table and tapped it with a finger. "Dad wants to buy you out. You could go home." He winked. "Or stay with me."

Kyle reached for her hand and Callie pulled back so quickly she smacked her elbow on the edge of her chair. "That's never going to happen." She'd had enough of these games. Callie rubbed her stinging elbow. "Do you have my money from the sale in Montana? It's been two weeks."

Kyle settled his chair on four legs and helped himself to half her sandwich, smacking his lips as he ate. She cringed and slid her plate toward him.

"My dad does the accounting and he says you owe him money."

Kyle snatched Callie's coffee cup and slurped, making a sound like a cow pulling its foot from thick mud. He placed the half-empty cup by Callie. Grimacing as her stomach roiled, she pushed it to the side. "I spoke with your father about the money from my cows."

Kyle's chair rocked forward, and he sat up straight. "You told my father?"

"I did, and he seemed surprised."

"No, he didn't, and I'm in charge of Kruger cattle sales. He just handles the money."

Callie saw the sweat on his forehead, and he appeared less sure. She wanted him gone and was done being subtle. "Kyle, where did the six cows come from that you trucked to Montana? Were they Kevin Bradley's? The ear tag numbers on Kevin's cattle are different than yours."

"They are."

"But Lauren tested and inspected the cattle for export. She signed the certificates. She would have read the ear tags of the six cattle she inspected at your farm and written their numbers on the export health certificate."

Kyle leaned back in the chair and clasped his hands behind his head, his eyes narrowed. "She did."

The renewed cockiness in Kyle was disconcerting. "But USDA veterinarians would have unloaded Kevin's cows at the border. They would have seen the tag numbers didn't match the health certificate and refused to let you enter Montana."

"Would have, if the tags didn't match." His grin was sly and slimy.

"Kyle, did you steal Kevin Bradley's cattle, switch their identification tags, and truck them, along with my cattle, across the border?" It wasn't hard guesswork but saying it out loud made her stomach turn.

"You're not only pretty, but smart too." Kyle leaned forward and leered at her. His gaze made her skin crawl.

Callie said, "Forget this shit. I'm calling the RCMP."

As Callie rose from her chair, Kyle lunged toward her. He grabbed both of her hands and slammed them on the top of the table. He pinned her in place and brought his face close to hers. "Shut your fucking mouth."

Her palms stinging with pain, she shrank away from him but maintained eye contact.

"Better think before you call the Mounties." He released her slowly.

Callie collapsed into her chair. She crossed her arms over her chest and pinned her hands to keep them from shaking.

He leaned back and stuck his legs out. "I used *your* truck and trailer when I stole Bradley's cattle. Then I came over here and you helped me load two of yours." Kyle's laugh was mean. "I found the coat, hat, and boots you keep in your truck. I wore them, made sure to leave footprints at Bradley's. There's video of me at the border in your hat and that stupid ugly coat with the name of your college on the back. We're the same size and I kept my head down." Kyle smirked. "Nobody will suspect me. You were the one with two cattle on the same trailer as the six stolen cattle. If you don't keep your mouth shut, I'll call the RCMP tip line and they'll arrest you. It'll be your word against mine."

"I work for the RCMP. They'll believe me."

Kyle shrugged. "But there's no evidence. And you're overdrawn at the bank. Maybe the cops will think two pervert dykes lied to make extra cash. Cornish's name is on the health certificate. The Mounties will say she faked them. Who'd want her for a vet after that?"

How did he know she was overdrawn? Did everyone in Thresherton cringe in front of the Krugers? Even staff at the bank? "People saw you at the sale, not me."

Kyle snorted. "Didn't go to the sale, you dumb bitch. Got a buddy wanted some nice cows and a good deal. Easy enough to pop your tags out once we crossed the border."

Callie desperately searched his comments for an escape. "I was home all day. How could I have driven to Montana?"

"Who saw you? You go to Thresherton? I know you didn't drive my truck." Kyle snickered. "Kinda smelly, huh? I put rotting trash under the front seat, figuring a stuck-up bitch like you wouldn't drive it." He cleared his throat and nose with a disgusting snort and spit a glob of green mucus on her kitchen floor. "You better shut up, or you and your girlfriend will be in trouble." Kyle sneered. "Who'd look after Becky if you ended up in jail?"

Callie slumped. If she went to jail, Liz's brother would claim Becky and she might not ever get her back. That was a risk she wouldn't take. But she wasn't about to prolong the argument with him now. She'd come up with a plan after he left. "I want you to leave."

"Suit yourself. See ya later, girlie." Kyle swaggered through her front door, leaving it open.

Trembling, Callie got to her feet and shut and locked her door. She cleaned the table and mopped Kyle's mess off her floor. Leaving a mess on her floor was a challenge, a way to intimidate her. It gave Heinz and Kyle power over her. Ever since she'd lost Liz she'd been struggling for control over her life and fending off well-meaning friends and family. Now criminals were out to hurt her.

How had she let this happen? How had the most dangerous family in the province gotten ultimate control over her? They had her money and had forced her silence by threatening her with arrest, and more importantly, the loss of Becky. They knew she'd do anything to prevent that. Callie shuddered. What else would she be forced to do?

Callie went upstairs to her bedroom and crawled into bed. Her life was a mess and it was her fault for loaning Kyle her truck and trailer. She would never get the money she desperately needed. She'd sacrificed two of her best cows for nothing. Kyle had stolen twelve thousand dollars from Kevin Bradley and four thousand from her. Now she would lose Poplarcreek. Lose Becky's inheritance.

She held a pillow over her face and cried. She *was* incompetent. No woman would ever want a relationship with a destitute, incompetent fuckup. Luckily, she wasn't looking. Or was she? "Concentrate on the farm, you stupid woman," she yelled into the room.

Callie sobbed until her chest ached. Heinz was right. She had no business running a farm. Every time she tried to get ahead, she fell further behind. What was the point? Maybe Becky would be better off if Callie sold Poplarcreek and they moved in with her parents.

Chapter Twelve

L auren had been lying awake since six a.m., with her cat curled on her chest while she tried to convince herself to get out of bed. She had to be at the office by half past seven. While she weighed the pros and cons of crawling from bed, she stroked Digit.

Digit was eight pounds of purring orange tabby, and he was only seven months old. Judging by his thin body and long legs, he would be a big cat. When he was sixteen pounds and sleeping on top of her, it would be an effort to breathe. It was her fault for letting him develop the habit when he was a tiny kitten. But he'd been sad and pathetic, and she'd been lonely. Her clingy cat insisted on being with her every second she was home and that was okay with her. Elsa, her other cat, wasn't as clingy and slept tucked in a corner of the couch.

If Lauren had dragged herself from bed at six a.m., there would've been time for a freshly cooked, leisurely breakfast. If she stayed in bed until seven a.m., she would have to settle for a protein bar. It was always a difficult choice in the cold weather to choose between her warm bed and a hot breakfast. A second after she determined a protein bar for breakfast would be perfect, the insistent ringing of her phone decided for her.

Maybe Sam was calling. Their last phone call had been chatty, and thirty minutes had flown by. Damn it, she missed Sam. Missed seeing her smiling face when she came home from school excited to talk about what she'd learned. Last week Sam had even forced William to talk to her, and the five minutes of one-word answers from her son had been heaven.

"Hello, Dr. Lauren Cornish speaking," she said after the answering service transferred the call to her. Her voice sounded clear, professional, and wide-awake, but she wished her brain were awake. She focused on the clock and saw it was six thirty.

"Um, Lauren?" The voice was hesitant.

"Yes, how may I help you? Who is this, please?" The voice was faint and almost impossible to hear.

"It's Callie, again. One of my heifers is calving, but she's not progressing, and I don't know what to do." Callie sounded defeated.

"No problem, Callie." Lauren nudged Digit off her chest and crawled from bed. She should've been grumpy in the early morning of another frigid day, but she was lighthearted about the prospect of seeing Callie.

"Thanks. Sorry that I can't bring her to the clinic. I've never towed a trailer and the driving would be dangerous in this storm."

Lauren glanced through the window at her outdoor thermometer. Minus twenty-three and she could barely see the house next door. It would be hell driving through forty kilometers of blowing snow, but worth it to be able to help Callie. "I understand. I should go get ready. The weather's bad so expect me in about forty or fifty minutes."

Lauren washed her face, brushed her teeth, and took a moment to pet Elsa. The little cat was waiting patiently for attention.

Lauren dressed in thermal layers with loose jeans over long johns. She slipped on a fleece vest followed by a parka, wool hat, and boots. On her way out, she snatched a protein bar. Outside, she collided with a blast of frigid air and blowing snow that pushed her back a step. "Just another day in balmy Saskatchewan." She grinned and pushed on. There were bigger struggles in life than a little snow. Snow she could handle.

Lauren waded through the snow to her garage. She unplugged her truck from the wall where the interior cab heater and engine block heaters plugged into receptacles. It was difficult to start a vehicle at this temperature if she left it parked for three hours without plugging it in. She'd never heard of block heaters until she moved to Saskatchewan, but the province was full of surprises. Lauren rubbed her hands together, pleased her interior heater worked. The cab was cold but not freezing. She resisted the urge to crank the heat. The last time she had done that the temperature difference between the outside and inside caused a small windshield chip to become a large crack. The crack had inched across her windshield as if somebody slowly sliced along the glass. It never got that cold in Toronto.

Lauren applied several thorough swipes of moisturizing lip balm and winked at herself in the rearview mirror. Then she headed out into the storm, pleased that the plows had been through once already and the roads were partly plowed.

It had been three days since Callie and Becky had visited PVS, and she'd missed seeing them. But then, that also meant she and Callie weren't spending too much time together, and Lauren wasn't tempted to do something rash, like ask her to lunch. Distance was a good thing when attraction was involved.

Lauren arrived at Poplarcreek an hour later. Late was better than stuck. A local dairy farmer still teased her about the time she'd gotten stuck. He said, "I had to rescue the vet from the snowdrift and drive her to my farm so she could rescue my calf." When she got stuck in Toronto, cars would squeeze past her on the road, but eventually someone would stop to help out. Here, people wouldn't drive by. You could count on someone stopping for you. It was a nice difference.

Lauren parked at the cattle barn, angling her truck to block the wind. As she jumped to the ground, she crossed her fingers and prayed. *Please, be a calving, not another C-section.* She collected her equipment and arrived at the barn door as Callie opened it. "Morning, Callie."

"Hi, Lauren. She's this way."

Lauren followed Callie inside. Callie looked exhausted and there were dark circles under her eyes. Her back was bent, and she shuffled along, the picture of despair. Lauren frowned, determined to do what she could to help put the sparkle back in Callie's eyes

She set her gear on top of a bale of straw and entered the calving pen. It was another generous twelve foot by twelve foot pen, bedded with a foot of fresh straw. Callie had everything ready. There was lots of light, but Lauren wished for a warmer barn. The heifer stood in the corner with her head tied and one foot of the calf protruding. Callie stood against the wall holding Becky by the shoulders as the little girl leaned toward the animal for a better view. Becky's brow was creased with worry, identical to her mother's. Lauren prayed for a simple calving. Callie deserved a break.

Becky wrung her hands. "Is Daisy's baby all right?"

"We'll do our best." Lauren injected as much perkiness into her voice as possible on a freezing morning. *Please, be a calving, not another C-section.* "See, Becky, there should be two legs sticking out by now. Calves are most often born as if they're diving out with two front legs first, followed by their head and the rest of the body. I'll check and see what's happening."

Lauren stripped off her winter parka and hung it on a nail in the calving pen. Lauren groaned. She had forgotten her rubber calving suit. She could picture it in the basement where she'd hung it after she'd washed it. All she had on over her clothes were cloth coveralls. So be it. She'd be a soaking mess when the calf was out. She slid on a glove and reached in.

"Ah, here we go, Becky. I have the left leg and the head and now I'm touching the right leg. The right leg is bent and caught on the pelvis. That's why the calf's stuck." Lauren looked at Callie and gave her a reassuring smile. "Calf's small enough. He only needs organizing before we pull him out."

Callie sighed, her breath expelling in a loud whoosh. Her shoulders dropped and she gave Lauren a grateful smile. "Thanks."

Stunned by her smile, Lauren aimed to do everything possible to make it appear again. "When I pull the right leg out the calf will come. I'll put one calving chain on its right ankle. Next, I'll push its head farther inside to create space. Callie, please, move behind me and hold the chain. Pull when I tell you. I'll guide the leg and you'll be the power that pulls it out. Here we go." Lauren twisted her head to the side and gritted her teeth.

"Are you all right?" Callie asked.

Lauren grunted. "Yup, it was only a contraction, and she squashed me." Lauren would have a collection of bruises on her arm when she finished. With the chain in place, Lauren handed it over her shoulder to Callie's waiting hands. "Grab the metal handle and hook it to the chain. Pull slow and steady. Slower." When the right foot appeared, Lauren removed the calving chain and dropped it in the bucket. She peeled off her OB glove and watched the heifer.

When Lauren glanced at Callie, her relief was unmistakable, and the sparkle was back. *She's as happy as I am that there's no C-section.*

But it wasn't long before it was clear the heifer still needed help. "We have to pull the calf out. She can't push it out. She's too tired. Callie, you take one leg and I'll take the other. Pull when I tell you. Grab a handful of straw to help your grip." With a layer of straw in each hand, they each latched on to a leg and heaved. "Come closer. Beside me," Lauren said.

Becky edged closer until she almost stood on Lauren's feet. Lauren tipped her head to the side of the pen. "Hey, Becky, you should probably stay over there, please. We don't want to drop the calf on top of you or for you to get slimed." Lauren made a wacky grimace as she said the word slimed to take any sting out of her words. Becky giggled and stepped back. Lauren glanced at Callie and her reward was another bright smile.

They pulled for twenty seconds. Then stopped for five seconds. Then they pulled for another twenty seconds, but the calf didn't budge. This could be a problem after all. Lauren hoped for Callie's sake they could work it out.

An instant later, a woman ran into the barn. "Hey, Becky, you missed the school bus."

Lauren looked Becky over when Callie groaned. Becky was wearing pajamas under a dirty barn coat, and boots covered in manure. And there was a brown smear on her forehead. Lauren coughed to disguise her smile and returned to the calving.

"Ah, darn. Mar, can you please clean Becky up and drive her to school? Um, there might be odder places for introductions, but, Lauren, meet my sister, Martha."

Martha nodded. "Hello. Nice to meet you, finally."

"Hi, yes." Lauren glanced at Martha and looked away quickly. She had caught Martha waggling her eyebrows at Callie and making a blowing motion with her lips as she fanned her face with her hand. Lauren suppressed the urge to giggle when Callie mouthed, "Go away."

Lauren observed the small family. Becky jumped up and down and swung her fists. "No, no, Mommy, Mommy, please. I want to see Daisy's calf born."

Callie sighed. "Go inside and dress for school. Grab toast and your lunch, and then before you go, you may return to the barn to see the new calf. It should be out by then." One eyebrow raised, Callie frowned at Becky, and she scampered away, followed by Martha who winked at Callie and smiled at Lauren.

"It'll come soon, right?" Callie directed a pleading expression at Lauren.

"I've shifted it. Let's try again." They scooped up handfuls of fresh straw, gripped the calf's legs, and pulled. The calf didn't come. They tried again, but no calf. Lauren pulled on a glove and checked inside. "That's got it." She slipped off the sleeve. They grabbed handfuls of straw, braced their feet, and hauled hard on the legs. With a whoosh, the calf slid out. Lauren and Callie lost their balance and flopped in the straw on their butts.

"Sorry. Forgot to warn you to look away while we pulled the calf out."

Callie groped under the front of her coat and gripped her T-shirt. She wrenched the bottom of her shirt up to wipe fluid off her face. The shirt stretched and Lauren glimpsed a flat stomach and the bottom edge of an incongruous, lacy pink bra. She pretended to study the calf as Callie lowered her shirt.

"You forgot to share that little gem of useful advice." Callie squinted at her. "Go ahead and laugh. I don't want you to injure yourself." Callie's words emerged as a good-natured grumble.

Lauren laughed, but stopped when Callie plucked a piece of straw from Lauren's hair. Startled by the gentle intimacy of Callie's action, Lauren blushed. Their eyes locked, and the air vibrated between them. Callie tilted her head and leaned toward Lauren.

"Yahoo, the baby's here." Becky bounded into the barn and yelled into the stillness.

Callie jumped up from the straw and didn't meet Lauren's eyes. Butterflies swarmed in Lauren's stomach at the almost-moment, and she tried to shake off the disappointment. Lauren and Callie dried the calf off and lifted it to its feet.

"Off to school, please," Callie said after Becky had stroked the calf's nose for a moment.

"Do we have time for one picture?" Becky asked.

"Aunt Martha's waiting for you."

"One, please."

Callie sighed. "Yes, one. You're already late, so what's another ten minutes. I'll call your teacher. She's used to us by now."

Becky pulled out her camera. "Mommy, you and Dr. Cornish and the baby."

Lauren blushed and stood awkwardly beside Callie with the calf in front of them. "How about you, your mom, and the calf?"

"Yes, please."

"Let me." Lauren accepted the simple digital camera. "You two stand beside the baby. Kneeling is better for you, Callie. Perfect." Lauren took several shots of mother and daughter with the calf and several sneaky shots of Callie giving Becky a final kiss and pushing her out the door. Becky made Callie's eyes sparkle more than ten new calves. Lauren missed being a parent. Missed her children.

Lauren stepped out of the way and took several more shots as Callie guided the newborn to its mother's udder. The heifer mom stretched her neck to lick her calf, but her aim was poor. Callie squeaked and jumped as the heifer mom's long tongue swiped once between Callie's legs. Lauren whirled around and kneeled in the straw to clean her gear. She struggled to remain silent, but suppressing laughter caused her body to shake.

"Mocking me again, Dr. Cornish?" On her way out of the barn, Callie ran her hand in one sweep from Lauren's left shoulder, across her neck to her right shoulder. "Come to the house and have breakfast when you're ready. You're welcome to shower and change."

Lauren, electrified by the touch, lost the ability to speak and nodded as Callie sashayed away. The swing of Callie's hips showed she knew exactly where Lauren's eyes were.

Lauren stowed her gear in her truck and grabbed the bag of clean clothes she always carried. She shook her head as she walked to Callie's house for a shower and breakfast. Was this a good idea or not? It was a little daring. She scanned the road to see if there were people who might see her. Then she nipped into Callie's house.

CHAPTER THIRTEEN

Callie jogged to the house. She felt like skipping or dancing or both. There would be no C-section. No extra risk to calf or heifer and no giant veterinary bill. By the time she was standing in her kitchen, she was stressing. *What have I done? First, I tried to kiss her. Then I invited her to the house to get naked. What was I thinking?* Callie pressed on her temples. She hoped the pressure would help clear her brain.

Lauren stomped her feet in the mudroom, then removed her coat and boots and entered the kitchen. She set Becky's camera on the table and held a knapsack up in question.

Callie pointed. "The downstairs shower and bathroom are there. I'll run upstairs and shower and then make breakfast."

Lauren nodded and darted into the bathroom.

Callie grinned and bounded upstairs. She wasn't the only one who was nervous. When she returned Lauren was waiting for her in the kitchen. She wore loose jeans, with a tight green turtleneck that hugged her curves and made her green eyes pop. How was she supposed to concentrate when Lauren was this alluring? "What's your preference for breakfast? I have eggs, bacon, sausage, ham, yogurt, cereal, fruit, and instant porridge, or I can make pancakes or French toast." Callie groaned inwardly. Next, she'd be offering Lauren an omelet or eggs Benedict. *Try hard much?*

"A mixture of the cereal, fruit, and yogurt sounds perfect."

Callie fetched the ingredients and placed them on the breakfast bar. They climbed onto barstools facing each other and mixed their breakfasts. "Thanks for helping with the calving. Sorry I bothered you so early in the morning, but at least the storm's done." Callie took a mouthful of breakfast, chewed, and swallowed.

"I'm happy to help and to see you in better spirits. You seemed very down this morning. I'm not prying, just an observation."

Callie pushed her bowl aside. "It's Heinz and Kyle Kruger. They keep hassling us."

"Hassling you?"

"Heinz sends letters and dropped by once. He even approached Becky at school and gave her a paper to bring home."

"No way. He talked to Becky without your permission?" Lauren looked horrified.

"Yes, I called the principal and he called Heinz. Heinz played all innocent and promised not to do it again."

"What's his game?"

"His personal mission is to get me to sell him Poplarcreek."

"You should go to the police." Lauren stood. "Come on. I'll take you now."

"Whoa there." Callie frowned, then sighed and shook her head. She liked Lauren, but she was one of those friends who couldn't listen to a problem without trying to solve it. Callie would solve it her own way; it was her responsibility. "Don't worry. I've got a plan." She had no plan, but it sounded strong and competent to say so.

Lauren sat again. "Okay."

"Heinz says I'm going to lose Poplarcreek to the bank. He had Kyle deliver an article on raising cattle and a list of all the mistakes I've made." Callie chuckled. "And the list is long." It was a relief to confide in Lauren, and she should tell her about the cattle smuggled to the USA, but that would be a mood killer and she couldn't deal with that right now.

"I bet it's not that long a list, and look at how much you're learning about calving. Most people would be grossed out, but nothing stops you. You're amazing."

"Thanks." Callie grinned and sat straighter. Maybe she could take care of her farm. "Becky enjoyed the explanations you gave at each step today, but I suspect they were for me. Would it be crazy for me to try those steps on my own the next time a calf's stuck?"

Lauren grinned. "Hmm, yes."

Callie frowned. Lauren was looking at her but wasn't paying attention to the conversation. "Yes? You mean it would be crazy for me to try that? I'm sure you're right. I don't know what I'm doing."

Lauren blushed. "No, I meant yes, try. You can do it. Dive in next time. I'll leave a few OB gloves for you. We sell them by the box at the clinic."

Warmth spread through Callie's body and she beamed at the honest praise. "As long as you're sure I can do it."

"I am. Five years from now I'll be calling you for help with calvings."

Callie laughed. "I doubt that very much. Do you still plan to be here in five years?"

"What about you?"

"I hope so." Callie grimaced. "Unless Heinz Kruger is right in which case, I won't last a year."

"Forget Heinz. Do you *want* to be here in five years?"

"Some days no, but most days I want to live here forever, or until Becky has a family and I retire."

"I didn't think farmers retired, or not really. Don't you just switch from sixty hours a week to thirty?"

"Maybe." Callie laughed. "What's your plan?"

"To survive this winter with all my fingers and toes and no frostbite. Long term, I don't know."

"What about your own practice?"

Lauren shrugged. "Ian will retire one day, but I don't know. I haven't thought about it."

"People like you here. Everyone says how great you are, and I agree. You're nice."

Lauren blushed while Callie studied her. "You're very nice too."

After the exchange of simple compliments, Callie couldn't think of anything else to say, and she had much to think about. They bent their heads to their breakfasts in an awkward silence. After the bowls were empty, Lauren handed hers to Callie and their fingers brushed as she accepted it. An instant later, Lauren leaped to her feet and backed away as if the breakfast bar had caught fire. "Um, thanks, Callie. I should go now."

"Are you in a hurry?" Callie searched Lauren's expression for an explanation.

Lauren's head drooped, and she scrutinized the floor tile. "I guess not."

Callie reached across the breakfast bar and touched Lauren's arm. "Stay. The coffee's ready. Please?"

Lauren swallowed and returned to her seat.

Callie enjoyed making Lauren nervous. It meant she had an effect on her. She brought two cups of coffee, cream, and sugar, and sat across from her once more. They mixed their drinks and sipped, alternating between studying each other and studying their coffee. Twice, Lauren opened her mouth to say something but closed it without speaking.

Callie remained quiet and curious. Callie was nervous, but in a good way. Lauren, however, looked conflicted and wary. Could she do something to help? She sauntered around the breakfast bar and stopped beside Lauren.

The blush on Lauren's face expanded and deepened. She swiveled to face Callie. Callie leaned in and pressed her lips against Lauren's. After the kiss, she stepped back. When she read the invitation in Lauren's eyes, she snuck in for a second, deeper kiss. This kiss flew from warm to volcanic at the speed of light. She slid her arms around Lauren's neck and scooted in until she stood between Lauren's knees.

Lauren laid her hands on Callie's hips, slipped her thumbs under the edge of her blue Henley, and caressed the skin of her lower back. Callie gasped at the intimate contact as Lauren enfolded her in strong arms.

Lauren opened her mouth when Callie sought entrance. As she explored Lauren's mouth she trembled in her arms. Callie nuzzled Lauren's neck. The nuzzle turned into kisses and small bites as

Lauren angled her head to give Callie better access. Lauren's phone rang, and they jumped apart like teenagers caught making out. Callie snorted and laughed while Lauren answered her phone. "Dr. Lauren Cornish. Yes, I can. I'm on my way."

Lauren slid the phone into her pocket. "Thanks for breakfast. I'm sorry, I have to go now." Lauren took her knapsack off a chair and headed toward the mudroom. Then she stopped and turned around. In two strides, Callie was in front of her. She waited, hoping for another kiss.

"Thanks for breakfast." Then, with a grin and a wave, Lauren jogged to her truck and headed out.

As Lauren's truck drove away, Callie caressed her swollen lips, still thrumming from Lauren's kiss. Why didn't she kiss her again? She could have.

Callie gathered the dishes and set them in the sink. Next time they kissed that way there would be no interrupting phones. If there was a next time. Maybe Lauren would run away and keep running? Maybe it was a mistake? Whatever it was, Callie wanted more, but did Lauren?

Callie was sitting at the table when Martha arrived home from dropping Becky at school. She'd been sitting there since Lauren left thinking about the kiss.

Martha entered the kitchen and squeezed Callie's shoulder. "Well, there's your kid off to school, again. The bell was ringing when we arrived, so she wasn't too late." Martha poured herself a coffee. "We wouldn't have been late at all if she hadn't stopped to take pictures. She said you let her?" Martha laughed. "Pictures of you and Lauren covered in grossness will now be plastered all over the internet. I hope you're ready for all the modeling offers. You're pretty enough to model for a living. Maybe the cover of *Cattle Rancher*." Martha giggled and opened the refrigerator door. "Any egg salad left? I haven't had breakfast. Have you?" She looked at

Callie for a second and then rummaged in the cupboard, emerging with a fresh loaf of bread. "Of course, you haven't eaten. You've been in the barn for hours."

She worked quickly and placed a sandwich in front of Callie. Then she set her coffee and sandwich on the table, sat, and continued to eat. "Are you ever going to say anything? You look stunned." Martha dropped her sandwich and looked around. "You get another letter from Kruger or a shitty phone call? He drop by?"

"No." Callie shook her head, finally compelled to speak. She pointed to a stack of mail. "Just another written offer to purchase Poplarcreek."

"At least they didn't show up. Every time I leave you alone, I think Heinz or Kyle is going to appear. It's like they watch and wait for me to leave. I like Max, but you should consider getting another dog. A big mean one, with four legs. Something to run around outside and make them think twice. Remember the big shepherd Mom and Dad had when we were kids?"

"Duchess."

"Right. She was gentle as a kitten, but big and scary. We had to put her in the house when the market store was open. People wouldn't get out of their cars to buy any berries if Duchess was around. That's the kind of dog you need." Martha wiped her mouth with a napkin. "That was a good sandwich. Amazing that I had time to eat since I've been doing all the talking." She pointed to the untouched sandwich in front of Callie. "You going to eat that?"

Callie shook her head.

"You can have it for lunch." Martha took the plate, wrapped it, and slid it into the refrigerator. Then she topped up her coffee cup and Callie's and sat down again. She sipped her coffee and stared at Callie.

"What?" Callie asked. Martha had a penetrating stare that could bore into her brain and almost read her thoughts. That's the way it had felt ever since they were kids.

"I just noticed two bowls in the sink. You have a guest?" Martha sipped her coffee.

"I kissed her. I kissed Lauren."

Martha set down her coffee cup and coughed into her napkin. She spoke when she had control again. "Wow. That's big. How'd it feel?"

"I'm trying to decide, but I think I've settled on confusing and terrifying."

"Confusing how?"

"I don't know why I kissed her and I'm not sure if it was a one-sided kiss."

"Come on, woman of the world. You know if she was into it."

Callie grinned. "She was into it. Full on."

Martha patted Callie's hand. "That's my sister."

"But then she ran away without a second kiss. I mean she had to go, but she could have had another kiss and didn't take it. And that might be a good thing. I'm not sure if she's the one for me." Callie cradled her head in her hands. "Or if there's anyone for me, ever again. Am I making sense?"

"Sure, keep talking."

"She's bossy, Mar. Wants to be in charge and tells me what to do. Even today she was insisting on taking me to the police."

"It's not a bad idea," Martha mumbled.

"I have no proof of anything except a few letters that could be construed as legitimate purchase offers or helpful suggestions. I have no witness to their threats. I have no proof they took my cows. And a squabble over who owes who how much would just end in civil court. The Krugers basically have to attack me in public before the RCMP can do anything. Or, I need a video."

"What about the assault? Kyle slammed your hands onto the table."

"No proof, and I let him into the house. Willingly."

"And that was stupid, by the way. Letting him in."

Callie sighed. "It was, but I really needed an answer. I need my money."

"Okay, I get that, but what did Mitch say when you told her about Kyle's visit?"

Callie winced. "I never told her."

"What? Why not? You should tell her."

Callie dropped her head into her hands. "You're right. She'll want to rip his head off, but legally there's nothing she can do." She should also tell Mitch about the stolen cattle, but she was afraid to implicate herself. She wanted control over her life, but it was rapidly disappearing.

"I'm worried about you and Becky. This is getting scary. Please tell Mitch. If she talks to Kruger at least he'll know he's being watched."

"You're right. I guess I just got caught up in my finances. And I was hoping if I ignored the Krugers they would leave me alone."

"That's not likely to happen." Martha squeezed her hand. "How bad are your finances?"

Callie shook her head. "My vet bill is terrifying, as is my overdraft."

"Mom and Dad?"

"No, not yet and you can't tell them, or they'll worry about Becky and me."

"Sure, Callie. But that's their job. Is it the money that's most terrifying? Or the Krugers?"

Callie laughed. "It should be, eh? No, the scariest thing is letting a woman into my life, into Becky's life. I think they're already friends. What if she loses Lauren? Not the way we lost Liz, but Lauren could move away. She only rents a house and she's an employee. She could pack up and move anywhere."

Callie stood and began to pace from one end of her kitchen to the other. "I've been caught up in a new friendship and not considering what happens if it progresses. And I'm so not ready for that. I tried last year and you know…"

"Disaster."

"Disaster. She hated Poplarcreek and everything about Thresherton. Not sure she was that keen on Becky, and Becky thought she was boring." Callie dropped into a chair. "Help me. Tell me what to do."

Martha held up her hands. "I'm not falling for that one. You do *not* like to be told what to do anymore."

"Anymore?"

"Liz loved you and she was good to you, but yeah, you took orders and didn't seem to mind. She wasn't crazy possessive or weird about it, she just wanted to do everything her way and usually that suited you."

"You're right, and I'll own that, but that's not me, not anymore." She sighed. "Why would I kiss Lauren? Why start something that won't work and that I have no intention of finishing?" Tears welled up in her eyes, but she didn't bother to brush them away. "But some nights I just want to curl up with somebody. Most of the time I like running the show, but occasionally I get tired of being alone. Sometimes I even wish somebody would take care of me." She pointed at Martha. "You're not allowed to repeat that. Ever." Callie cradled her head in her hands. "What am I going to do? I'm all over the place. I need you to do an intervention."

Martha looked at her folded hands in her lap. "The timing of this sucks. I want to be here for you. Here at Poplarcreek..."

"But?"

"It's been a month."

"And you want to go home? But it's too early to do much in the greenhouses. Spring on the berry farm is a long way off."

Martha tipped her head from side to side. "Yeah, but there's this guy. I feel like a bad sister for bringing it up, especially now."

"A guy? You've been here a month and never said. Tell me about him."

Martha shrugged. "It's early days for us. Not much to tell."

"That's evasive." Callie dug a tissue from her pocket and blew her nose. "Your visit's been all about what Becky and I need, hasn't it? I'm the bad sister for trapping you here."

"I was never trapped, you moron. I like it here and I love Becky. And you too, I guess." Martha swatted Callie's shoulder. "I love you and you can call me anytime. I'll come back in the spring, before we get busy on the farm, and maybe you and Becky can come home in the summer between seeding and harvest. You don't need to sit here and watch your hundred acres of wheat grow."

"It's five hundred and the other half I rent to my friends Mark and Tracey."

Martha laughed. "Can you imagine how many blueberries we could grow on five hundred acres? We'd be picking until our fingers fell off."

Callie smiled. "There'd be plenty of ammo."

Martha laughed. "Remember how mad Mom used to get when we'd turn up with stains all over our clothes? She knew we were pitching berries at each other. You need to bring Becky home. Teach her how to pick the best berries for a fight."

"Soft enough to splat on impact, but hard enough to throw without squishing them between your fingers." Callie leaned over and hugged her. "I'm going to miss you so much. I love you too." Callie squeezed harder. Martha had been supporting her since Liz died. Martha would stay longer if she asked, but she wouldn't ask. It was time to stand on her own.

Callie said, "You were an amazing help. I can't believe we finished sorting Liz's and Doug's boxes. I've got seven bags for charity and two boxes are already wending their way to the coast to Liz's brothers." Martha was taking Liz's RCMP Stetson with her to have it cleaned and packaged to preserve it. Callie would save it for Becky.

Callie dried her eyes. It was time to take on life on her own. She was alone and that was fine. She was comfortable with her own decisions and she'd survive the Krugers and a shitty calving season without help from anyone. But would her heart survive Lauren Cornish, if she opened it up to her? It was best not to take the chance.

Chapter Fourteen

"Here I am again. Feels like I was only here yesterday." Lauren paused at the door to the Poplarcreek cattle barn.

Callie sighed. "You *were* here yesterday, unfortunately."

"Um, okay."

"I'm happy to see you, but your visit will mean another vet bill and I have enough, thanks." Callie had considered calling Mark for help with the calving, but he'd been over twice in the last week to help with machinery. He had a large farm to run, and she had to stop bugging him.

Callie smiled as she squeezed Lauren's forearm. Their contact was electric, and she flashed back to her kitchen and the heat of Lauren pressed against her. When her brain was functioning again, she registered Lauren staring at her. Lauren's expression was expectant. Had she asked her something? Not wanting to look silly, she just headed into the barn.

Another of her poor heifers stood in the calving pen straining to calve. Two legs of the calf were visible, but the birth had stalled. Lauren carried one bucket of water into the pen and washed the heifer around the back end. "What's been happening?"

"I reached my hand in the way you showed me. One leg was out when I found her, and I pulled out the other one. The nose is there, but when I pull on the legs, I get no..." The sight of Lauren removing her jacket distracted her, and she forgot where she was in her sentence.

Today Lauren wore loose blue work pants, a long-sleeved black T-shirt, and a dark green thermal vest. She looked fabulous, and Callie wanted more clothing to come off.

Lauren pulled on her calving suit and an OB glove and reached into the young heifer. Then she pulled out and said something.

With difficulty, Callie refocused her attention on the calving.

Her head tilted to one side, Lauren gazed at her.

Callie shook her head. "Did you say something?"

The sides of Lauren's mouth twitched. "I asked if you wanted to do this calving? I'll coach you through it."

"Yes, please, but stop me if I'm about to mess up," Callie said as she pulled an OB glove on.

"Put your hand where the leg meets the body. You have perfect arms for this. They're long, strong, and slender. Just what she needs. Slide your hand along the leg and describe what's happening with the joints. Do it with both legs," Lauren said.

Callie frowned. "The joint on this leg is smooth and rounded. Ouch, ouch."

"Stop moving when you feel a contraction. Wait until she's done."

Callie gasped when the heifer relaxed. "I have the second leg, but this joint is sharp." Callie's eyes widened as she focused on Lauren. "Is it broken?"

"Feel along the leg. If two joints on a leg bend the same way, it's a front leg. If the two joints bend in opposite directions, you have a back leg."

"Two legs are sticking out, but I have a front one and a back one, don't I? I can tell by the shape of the joint."

"Correct.

"Can I fix it?"

"Why don't you try? We don't know how long this heifer was pushing, so we should get the calf out soon."

Nervous and unsure, Callie wavered. "I'm not sure. Maybe you'd better do it."

"Your calf, your decision."

Determination replaced nervousness and Callie returned to the heifer. She tugged on a fresh OB glove, reached inside, and manipulated the legs for a few minutes. "I can't do it."

"Let me try." Lauren pulled on a sleeve, repositioned the calf, and pulled it out.

"Thanks, Lauren." Callie grimaced. "This dumb farmer should've realized she was pulling on a front leg and a back leg."

"You're welcome for the help and you're not dumb. You've learned a lot this winter and I'm impressed."

"Nice of you to say, Dr. Cornish." Callie did a goofy curtsey. "Can I give you breakfast?" She stepped into Lauren's personal space.

"Please," Lauren whispered,

They cleaned Lauren's equipment and carried it to her truck. They entered the mudroom and removed outer clothing. After washing their hands, they met in the kitchen.

"Is Martha still visiting?"

"No, she left at five this morning. We loved having her here, but she has a life at home." It had been a tearful departure, and Callie and Becky hadn't gone back to bed afterward. They'd curled together in front of the television and watched cartoons until it was time to get ready for school. She missed her sister, but once Martha had asked to go home there seemed no reason to delay.

"Does she live in British Columbia?"

Callie nodded and prepared fresh coffee. *If I tell Lauren about my past, will she tell me about hers?* "You must wonder why I know nothing about cattle?" She glanced at Lauren and she shrugged. "I grew up on a berry farm, as I mentioned before. No livestock. The year after they married, my parents bought Wilkins Berry Farm from my grandparents. Most of the farm is blueberries, but we have a few raspberry bushes and strawberry fields. My brother and Martha run it with them now."

"Wilkins? So, you took your wife's name when you married?" Lauren settled at the breakfast bar.

"Same-sex marriage had just become legal. It felt like a way to show we were a family. A family with two parents and a child, and all with the same last name. Did somebody tell you how I ended up at Poplarcreek? I'm sure *somebody* in Thresherton told you." Callie placed a cup of coffee in front of Lauren and returned to her stove.

"Ian told me you inherited the farm from your father-in-law, Doug Anderson."

Callie nodded and started to whisk the eggs. "Liz Anderson was an RCMP officer and posted to Surrey, British Columbia, my hometown. When I was twenty-one, I met her at a barbecue." Callie shook her head. "She was trying to juggle a plate of food and hold a baby. Becky was eight months old, and I think she was trying to stick her foot in Liz's salad. I offered to hold Becky so Liz could eat in peace. I fell for the woman and I fell for her cute baby." Callie focused on her task while she struggled to maintain her composure. Her heart squeezed at the memories.

"How sweet."

Callie fumbled with the breakfast dishes and dropped the eggs in a pan. "Liz was ten years older than me, but we fell in love. Two years after we met, we were married and I legally adopted Becky. Then two years later, Liz was murdered. She pulled over a speeder, and when she reached the driver's door window, he shot her in the face."

Lauren gasped. "Jesus."

"Paramedics rushed Liz to the hospital. They stopped the bleeding, but there was too much damage and she died thirty minutes later."

"Oh, Callie, I'm so sorry. How devastating."

"I didn't make it to the hospital in time." Callie brushed a tear off her cheek. "The piece of shit who murdered her ditched their stolen car and escaped on foot. The police have never caught them and that was five years ago." Callie shoved bread into the toaster, angry at the injustice.

"You were so young to go through something like that."

"I was twenty-five." Callie sniffled. "Liz and I only had four years together, but it was long enough to understand deep in our bones we belonged together." Callie blew her nose and then washed her hands. "Becky and I lived with my parents for a while until

Doug invited us to live with him. Before I lost Liz, we visited Doug twice a year. He was a sweet man and accepted me at once as part of the family. I wanted Becky to know him and he needed us in a way my own family didn't and couldn't understand. I mourned Liz, but I can't imagine losing a child. Her death broke his heart."

"It would destroy me," Lauren said.

"Doug was strong, or at least I thought he was. One and a half years after we moved to Poplarcreek, he died of a massive stroke. I learned afterward he'd had many small heart attacks no one knew about."

"How very sad."

"Neither of Liz's brothers wanted to live in Saskatchewan and didn't challenge the will when Doug left Poplarcreek to Becky and me. I think he knew his health was failing when he invited us to live with him. I think he wanted to teach us what he could before he died." Hindsight was always clear, and the pain it brought with it, sharp. "He taught me about crops and combines, but we didn't get to the cattle."

"I'm sorry about Liz and Doug."

Callie rested her hip against the counter and regarded Lauren, whose expression was sympathetic. "It's been five years, but sometimes it feels as if Liz died five seconds ago. We were only a family for such a short time."

"Is Becky's father around?"

"He was a donor and never in the picture. But Becky had two parents, although she's nothing like me."

"I wouldn't say that. Becky's a sweet kid. She's dark where you're fair, but there's something in the polite, calm way she speaks and the confident way she carries herself that reminds me of you."

"Thanks." Callie stared at Lauren as she assimilated the insightful comment. Lauren thought Becky was sweet, and more importantly, she paid attention to her, understood her. "She's quiet too. I've seen Gwen rattle off ten sentences to my kid's one."

Lauren laughed. "Gwen's an awesome kid and a talker."

"You like her."

"I do. In an auntie kind of a way, or as an older friend. She's talked me into letting Becky visit after school."

"That okay? Will she be in the way?"

"It's fine. I like kids, but she'll get put to work walking dogs and cleaning kennels."

"She can manage that." Callie's chest tightened. This was the attachment between Becky and Lauren she was afraid of. But she'd introduced them and there was no way to rewind without upsetting Becky. But Lauren was nice and could be trusted. "Tell me about your family."

"Long, boring story."

"We've got time and I'm interested."

Lauren dug her phone out of her pocket. "Sorry, I should answer this email." She typed away and then her phone rang. Lauren stepped away to answer the call and returned. "I should probably go. I have to check on a horse with a cough."

"Where?"

"Starview Farm."

"They're only ten minutes away. Sit. You can stay for breakfast." Callie set the food on the counter and waited.

Lauren sat like a child ordered back to the table to finish her vegetables.

Callie plated her food and winked at Lauren, hoping to lighten the moment and then changed the topic to their childhoods. They enjoyed a leisurely breakfast while they shared happier stories about British Columbia and Ontario. After their plates were empty, they swiveled in their seats until their knees touched.

Callie said, "Are there ethical rules that say you shouldn't kiss a client?"

"No, but it's unadvisable. It could lead to complications." Lauren looked thoughtful, and there was only a hint of the earlier sadness in her eyes.

Callie traced the rim of her coffee cup with a finger. "So, it was a mistake and we shouldn't do it again?"

"Probably not."

Callie studied Lauren. "You're serious."

Lauren nodded. "I am."

Just as they were leaning forward to do what they both seemed to know they shouldn't, Callie's door banged open and Kyle Kruger swaggered in as if he owned the place. They jumped apart and Callie stepped forward, placing herself between Kyle and Lauren. "What do you want? And how dare you barge in here uninvited?" She'd have to start locking her front door. Callie crossed her arms over her chest and her weight shifted to one hip. She glowered at him, willing him to burst into flames.

"Relax, girlie." Kyle slunk to the breakfast bar and leaned over until he could see Lauren's face. "Hello, Doc. Having breakfast?"

Callie's hands balled into fists as Kyle sneered at Lauren and directed his comments to her chest. "Kyle, what do you want?"

Kyle shifted and slid his arm across Callie's shoulders. "Any breakfast for me, girlie? On Wednesday you made me lunch. I know how well you like to feed me." He smirked at Lauren.

Callie shrugged his arm off and walked toward the refrigerator. She hadn't made him lunch. He'd stolen her sandwich and then slammed her hands on the table and threatened her. Now she knew what he wanted. Free run of her house for meals whenever he wanted.

She yanked the refrigerator door open and snatched the eggs. She hovered over the stove, dropped two eggs into the frying pan, and fetched the maggot a cup of coffee. His threat was clear, and she wasn't about to have him drag Lauren into the illegal crap he'd mired her in. If she fed him, maybe he'd go away and leave them in peace. But every bone in her body ached with fury at being so unable to control the situation.

Kyle made an exaggerated scan of the kitchen, even standing to peer over the breakfast bar near Callie's feet. "Are you done, Doc? No cattle in here. Are you often alone with your woman clients? What would people say?"

"Mind your own business, Kyle," Lauren snapped.

Callie cringed inside. Lauren *was* worried about kissing a client, and Kyle was threatening to make her the topic of town gossip. She directed her next words to the frying pan. Lauren was safer away from Poplarcreek. "She's going now. Thanks, Lauren."

There was a moment of awkward silence. "Thanks for breakfast, Callie."

Callie's shoulders slumped as she heard the scrape of a chair and the click of her front door closing. She could only imagine how hurt Lauren would be. To be chucked out of the house in favor of Kyle, but even as attracted as they were to one another, she and Lauren weren't in a relationship and it was better that way. Lauren didn't know that she was being sent away to protect her, to keep her out of Kyle's way. The man was a buffoon, but still dangerous. Maybe she should have told Lauren the full story of the stolen cattle, but then she'd leave for good and never come back. Besides, the less Lauren knew, the safer she was. Callie had no idea how to crawl out from under Heinz Kruger's thumb, and she wouldn't risk taking Lauren down with her.

Once again, she was unquestionably alone.

CHAPTER FIFTEEN

K yle shouted at her, his face red.
"What's going on, Callie? What were you doing with
the doc? I liked watching, it was hot, but we have a deal."

Callie's skin crawled as she pictured Kyle spying on them
through the window before he came in. "What deal? There's no
deal." She dropped the plate of overcooked eggs and burnt toast in
front of him.

"The deal is that as long as we're friends, I don't go to the cops
and tell them you stole cattle."

Callie ground her teeth. "We're not friends."

"We're not? I told my dad we were. Told him I'd been eating
more meals at Poplarcreek with my girlfriend. He thinks you and
Poplarcreek are in the family now. He said he was proud of me for
the first time in my life." Kyle moved in and stood toe to toe with
Callie. "And you're not going to fuck that up."

Callie shrank back. She was alone in her house with him again
and she'd promised Martha to be smarter in the future and not let
Kyle inside the house. And now unbelievably, Kyle thought they
were dating? A few meals she could handle, but what more did he
want?

Callie fed Kyle breakfast and pushed him from her house with
a minimum of pawing.

What must Lauren think of me? Callie moaned as she sat
slumped at the table with her head in her hands. *How did I let my*

fight with the Krugers get this bad? Now Kyle thinks he owns me because of six stupid stolen cows. She wiped tears from her eyes.

Martha wanted her to go to the RCMP and tell them how Heinz and Kyle were hassling her, and she was right. If she ever wanted to get a restraining order, she'd need to get everything on the record. She thought about just telling Mitch as a friend, but she'd want to help. She bet Mitch would be on Krugers' doorstep ten minutes after she told her. But if she told on Heinz and Kyle would they just get worse? More violent?

It was a milder day, for winter, so Callie spent most of it cleaning the barn even though intense emotions overwhelmed her. She was drawn to Lauren but uncertain about Lauren's feelings. Lauren was attractive, smart, and a wonderful kisser, but was clearly conflicted about getting close to her. Even while they were kissing the other day, she had felt Lauren pulling away. And today she'd made it clear she didn't think they should go there. But the look in her eyes didn't match her words.

And then there was the Kruger mess, and she wasn't sure she could do anything to stop it. It was as if they had her in a vice and were slowly squeezing. Lauren told her she was learning fast about her cattle, but it wasn't fast enough to avoid more vet bills, and she couldn't turn back the clock and unbreed the juvenile heifers. She owed money and needed to get back to work at the RCMP detachment, but first she had to pry the time out of her day. Everything had seemed so much more manageable when Martha was there to help with Becky and the house.

Callie drilled her shovel at the wall, and it hit with a satisfying clang. What had she done? Was there no end to her stupidity? She was convinced she probably had no future with Lauren and now she'd tossed Becky into the mix. What hurt had she set her daughter up for?

Callie felt her stomach heave as she bent to grab the shovel. She scraped the calving pens and shoveled the manure and dirty straw into the bucket of her loader. She drove the loader to the manure pile, dumped it, and studied the steaming pile. This was her life. It began the day as fresh straw, but always ended as a pile of shit and there'd be more tomorrow. It was time to grow a backbone, focus, and try to come up with some kind of plan.

When the barn was clean and the animals fed, Callie trudged to the house. She rolled her shoulders and stretched her back. She had overexerted, but her path was clear. The Krugers *must* keep away from her and her house, and she needed to speak with Lauren and then Mitch. Keeping Kyle's secret meant he had power over her, and she'd sworn that kind of thing would never happen again. Perhaps Lauren would help her deal with Kyle? After all, he was threatening to implicate her, too, and she should know that.

After a shower, fresh clothes, and lunch, Callie toiled away on the farm accounts for two hours and then returned to the barn to feed the calves. When she heard the school bus, she wiped her hands and headed out to greet Becky to learn how her day had gone. She saw Becky waving to her friends as the bus drove away. Becky had fit into Thresherton and made friends faster than Callie had. She was happy for Becky, and she'd made a few good friends herself. Not friends who would stand up to the Krugers, though. Callie laughed. Lauren had told Kyle to "Mind his own business." He'd had no response. Probably not used to strong women. Callie sighed. Kyle hadn't chased Lauren away, she had.

After the bus drove away, a black pickup truck stopped beside Becky. The window opened and Becky walked closer to speak with someone inside. A cold knot formed in Callie's chest. "No!" she screamed and sprinted down the laneway toward her. Becky waved at her before climbing into the truck. "Wait, come back," she yelled. When Callie arrived at the road, the truck was driving away and accelerating, but she read KRUGER2 on the license plate. "Kyle fucking Kruger. What the hell!" Every muscle in her body tensed and her hands balled into fists.

Callie raced to her house. She snatched her keys off the hook in the mudroom, unplugged her truck, and jumped into the cab. She roared from her laneway, skidded at the corner, and shot down the road after Kyle. On a hunch, she drove toward Kruger Farm. She didn't have Kyle's cell number, but she had Tommy's.

Cellular service in the rural areas near Thresherton was spotty at best. She cheered when she found a strong enough cell signal to call Tommy. Their voices cutting in and out, she explained. "Is Kyle there? He took Becky. Snatched her when she got off the bus. Tell him to bring her home, now." Callie was yelling at the wrong Kruger, but she couldn't help it.

"Sorry, Callie. He's not here, but I'll find him. My brother genuinely likes Becky," Tommy said.

"I don't care. He needs to bring her home, now." Callie jammed her phone in her pocket and turned south away from Kruger Farm. *Kyle didn't go home, so where did he go?* She yanked the steering wheel to take the next turn and her tires skidded on the ice. She fishtailed around the corner and slid into the ditch. "Shit, shit, shit!" She crushed the pedal against the floor. Her tires spun, but the truck didn't move. Too much of the truck was in the ditch and they were old tires with too little tread.

Callie snatched her cell phone off the floor where it had fallen. No signal. There had been one five minutes ago. She rested her forehead on the steering wheel and struggled not to cry. He'd taken her daughter, and here she was in a ditch. She barely kept from sobbing.

Callie jumped when someone tapped on the window and found Lauren peering in at her. She powered down her side window. "Lauren, thank God. Kyle—"

"I was helping Tommy at the farm. He told me. Kyle didn't pass me."

Wild with fear, Callie stared out her windows in all directions, hoping for a clue about where the man was who'd taken her daughter. "Where did he go?" Callie growled her words. "He's a dead man."

"We should call the RCMP, but I have no cell signal."

She had no problem calling the police, but she wanted to see if she could get Becky back first. "Let's go to Poplarcreek and call Tommy for Kyle's phone number."

"I have Kyle's number. Want me to pull you out?"

"There's no time." Callie jumped from her truck, jogged across the road, and climbed behind the steering wheel of Lauren's truck.

Lauren followed. "Hey, Callie, should I drive? It won't help Becky if you drive into another ditch and injure yourself this time."

Callie growled. "Get your ass in or stay behind."

Lauren blinked, bolted around the truck to the passenger side door, and jumped inside. Callie spun Lauren's truck in a circle, fishtailing on the snowy road as she drove away. When they neared Poplarcreek, Callie saw what she'd been hoping to see. "There's Kyle's truck!" She plowed into a pile of snow at the door of her house and leaped out.

Callie ran into her kitchen, Lauren not far behind, and skidded to a stop. Becky and Kyle were at the kitchen table playing cards. Callie breathed in loud, painful gasps and her heart thudded in her ears.

"Snap." Becky slammed the six of spades on the pile of cards resting in the center of the table.

Kyle grinned at Callie and winked.

"Mommy, I'm winning." Becky bounced in her chair.

Callie gathered Becky in her arms and collapsed into a chair with Becky in her lap. "Where did you go, Becky?" She rocked her while kissing the top of Becky's head, her cheeks, and forehead.

Becky laid a hand on Callie's wet cheek, her expression worried. "Uncle Kyle took me to see the new foal at Starview. The one Lauren helped birth." Becky glanced at Kyle and whispered, "He promised I had permission."

"Uncle Kyle." He gloated as he looked at Lauren.

Lauren frowned at Kyle. "Callie, if you don't need me anymore, I should probably go."

"Please stay. Please, Lauren," Callie said.

Lauren's answer was brusque. "Sure."

"Hey, Becky, let's get you changed into play clothes." Callie clutched her hand and led her upstairs.

"Bye, Uncle Kyle. Thank you."

"Bye, girlie."

Five minutes later, Callie returned to the kitchen, alone. She glanced at Lauren, who was still frowning at Kyle as if she were contemplating murder. "She's all right."

Lauren glanced at Callie and nodded. "I'm glad."

Kyle sneered at Lauren. "Why are you staying, Doc? To protect them?"

Lauren snorted and Kyle blinked at her in surprise. "I'm staying to save your life, Kyle."

Kyle rubbed the palms of his hands on his pant legs. "Bullshit."

Lauren leaned over Kyle and sneered back at him. "I'll stay as long as Callie wants me to. I'd never come between a mother and her child, so I plan to help her with whatever she decides to do."

"Like what? What's she gonna do?"

"She may want help digging a man-sized hole, excuse me, weasel-sized hole, in the wheat field." Lauren's eyes were hard. "I admire Callie's restraint. If you'd snatched my daughter, you'd already be missing sensitive body parts." She glanced at his crotch. "Although I suspect an insect like you has none."

Kyle crossed his legs and angled his body away from Lauren. He scoffed at Callie. "What a bad mom you are, leaving a kid that young by herself. You should tell her not to get into trucks with people."

Callie glowered at him as she stalked toward him. Every muscle in her body screamed for her to pummel him.

Kyle had been walking toward her, but he scuttled backward and fell into a chair.

Callie towered over him and clenched her fists. "Lauren has a good idea. I own a thousand acres and two shovels. Nobody would miss you." The ground was still frozen, but she'd tear through it with her bare hands to get Kyle out of their lives.

Kyle raised his hands above his head. "Hey, don't kill me, girlie. It was only a bit of fun."

Lauren remained beside her and Callie absorbed her strength. It gave her the power to fight him. "What the hell, Kyle. It wasn't funny, and you damn well know it." Callie's voice dropped to a growl. "Leave and never return. Never speak to Becky again, ever, anywhere."

"Hey, girlie, aren't we friends? Given our business ventures and all."

Callie snorted. "We're not friends, never have been, and I don't care if you talk to the RCMP. But if you do, I'll tell them about this little stunt. And stand up to your father for once in your life, you gutless jerk. You'll never bring him Poplarcreek on a platter and I'll make damn sure he knows you've been lying to him." He'd messed with her child, and no threats or secrets were going to keep her under his thumb anymore. If he wanted a war, she was ready.

Kyle paled and stuttered. "I took Becky to see some horses. Don't make it into anything. I wouldn't hurt Becky."

"Why are you so scared, Kyle?" Lauren asked.

"I'm not scared. I'll go. Shit, Callie. No need for that." His words emerged in a pathetic whine as he scurried through the door.

As the sound of his truck faded, Callie let out a big sigh. "Thanks for staying."

"How will you get your truck?" Lauren asked.

"I'll run over with the tractor and tow it home."

"Why would Kyle call the RCMP on you? Is there something you want to talk about?"

Callie shrugged and turned away, unable to meet Lauren's eyes. The power drained from her body and she slumped into a chair at the table. She wanted to tell her, she did. But what if Lauren didn't believe her? What if—

Callie rubbed wearily at her eyes. She needed to catch her breath and organize her thoughts for that difficult conversation with Lauren. That conversation would happen when she was ready. She was tired of being backed into corners. Besides, she was drained, and she desperately needed to speak with Becky. She'd told Becky to stay away from the Krugers, yet she'd gone with Kyle. That could never be allowed to happen again. Becky's safety came first, before anything with Lauren.

Becky bounced down the stairs into the kitchen. "Lauren, are you staying for dinner?"

"I have to return to Kruger Farm and help Tommy with some sick calves."

Callie followed Lauren outside and grabbed her by the front of her jacket. "Please, come to dinner. Please come back."

"Why?"

Callie put her hand over her mouth and shook her head. She looked away, unable to make eye contact, but she hung on to Lauren with the other hand. She was afraid if Lauren left, she'd never come back and then Callie would never get a chance to explain. She admired Lauren and couldn't stand the idea of Lauren thinking poorly of her.

Lauren softened. "I'll come back when I'm done with Tommy's calves. Maybe then you can tell me what's going on?"

"I will. Thank you." Callie let go of Lauren's coat and smoothed the lapels flat. They stared at each other for several seconds and then Callie returned to the house. A sinking, painful feeling started between her eyes and spread until she couldn't move her neck and shoulders. Hell, but she was tired of all the stress. Life had been simpler back in Surrey with Becky and Liz. Sure, there had been moments of worry when Liz was late coming home from work. But it was nothing compared to the constant worry of saving the farm, protecting Becky, watching out for the Krugers, and now navigating whatever this was with Lauren. She'd told Martha she had no time for a relationship. What if she let go and took Lauren in? Would that be so bad? But what would she have to give up to make it happen?

CHAPTER SIXTEEN

It was early evening when Lauren finished at Kruger Farm. Tommy had disappeared and left their farmhand to help and there hadn't been a Kruger in sight. She briefly toyed with the idea of heading home, but she'd promised Callie and Becky to return and she needed to know what was going on. Why was Callie acting weird? One minute Callie was tough and calling her out for making a few suggestions. The next minute Callie was being ordered around by the Krugers and practically crawling under the table to hide.

Lauren grinned. There'd been no hiding earlier. Callie had yelled at Kyle and joined in the joke about digging a hole for Kyle. She gripped the steering wheel to choke it. Was Kyle a thoughtless ass or a manipulative monster? Why take Becky? Just to torture Callie? Harass her? He'd succeeded. She'd never seen Callie so scared or angry. She shook her head. The anger made sense but not the evasive answers and tears ten seconds after Kyle left.

Lauren pulled over and considered turning her truck around. She wasn't sure Callie's friendship or kisses were worth this kind of agitation. She had leftover pizza, a good book, and uncomplicated feline companions at home. It was tempting. Lauren sighed, pulled out, and drove toward Poplarcreek, but she wouldn't spend all evening pulling the answers out of Callie. If Callie continued the evasive nonsense, she would go home. Enough was enough.

Lauren walked into Callie's house, slid out of her boots, and hung her coat up. Callie was sitting at the kitchen table with her head hanging. She barely raised it to focus on Lauren for a moment. "Thought you were locking doors these days." Lauren sat at the table, and when Callie said nothing, she launched in. "Why were you polite to Kyle this morning? He and his father have harassed you, bullied you, and threatened you. Then Kyle kidnapped Becky. Please, help me understand."

"More is going on than you realize." Callie reached for Lauren's hand.

Lauren recoiled and jammed her hands in her pockets. If Callie touched her, she would crumble and do whatever Callie wanted. She needed to keep her distance to keep her head clear. "Trust me, please. I can help."

Callie squared her shoulders. "I hate asking for help. But sometimes..."

"Maybe I'm being pushy, but Kyle's a jerk. What's happening?" Lauren couldn't fathom the connection between Callie and Kyle. Lauren had returned for dinner because she promised, but her gut was telling her to run far and run fast.

Callie's shoulders sagged. "He's a jerk, but he..."

Lauren prodded gently. "He what? Does he scare you?"

Callie turned her back. "I didn't tell you, to protect you."

Lauren spoke louder than she intended to, but the bizarre situation was annoying, and she had difficulty controlling her frustration. "Protect me? How? Now I'm more confused. I don't want protecting. What I need is honesty."

Callie frowned at Lauren. "What're you saying?"

"I don't like games, Callie. I've had enough of them to last me a lifetime. Can't you just be straight with me?"

Callie sighed and rubbed at her temples. "It's just complicated, that's all."

Lauren closed her eyes and sighed, exhaling in one long breath. Here it was. Evasion and twenty questions. "It's okay if you're not ready to talk. But I'm tired, so maybe I'll just go home."

"So, the first time you don't get an answer you're leaving?"

Lauren sighed. "It's been a long day and I'm tired." She pulled the sleeve of her shirt to her nose. "And I smell like manure. I just want a shower." And she wanted a peaceful evening. She stood. "No pressure. We'll talk when you're ready. I'll get out of your way. I need to get off this merry-go-round anyway."

"Please, don't go. You promised you'd have dinner and visit with Becky and me." Callie's lower lip trembled.

Lauren's back was rigid, and the pressure of a growing headache built behind her eyes. It would be heartless to abandon her in this state. "I'll stay because I won't disappoint Becky, but you and I have to talk this through. And I'd rather do it now than later."

Callie nodded, looking defeated. "I'm not sure what to do, but I'll tell you what Kyle did."

They sat at the kitchen table. Callie clasped Lauren's hand and, in a monotone, told her about the borrowed truck and trailer, the stolen cattle, and the trip to Montana. She described the faked identification tags and the phony health certificate and told her about him saying he'd implicate Callie and Lauren both.

Lauren dropped Callie's hand and gaped at her. "This is serious. Why didn't you call the RCMP?"

Callie shot to her feet and paced. "Because I'll look guilty." She spread her arms wide. "He used *my* truck and trailer. *My* cattle were on the trailer. When he crossed into the USA, he wore *my* coat and hat. He's the same size as me and if he kept his head down, in the border surveillance video, they might mistake him for me. And I have no alibi except that I was here alone, like I always am." Callie dropped into her chair and shook her head. "I don't know what to do."

"I signed those export health certificates." Lauren scowled. "I'll look guilty, as well. If CFIA decides I'm responsible, they may suspend my accreditation. No more working on exports of animals to the USA." Lauren's hands had gone white because she pressed them hard on the table as she leaned toward Callie. "And if the Saskatchewan Veterinary Medical Association convicts me of professional misconduct, they have the power to suspend my license or require me to do remedial training." Lauren's hands dropped to her lap as she hunched her shoulders. "Everyone will think I'm a criminal. How humiliating. Nobody can fake those identification tags or move them. Once you fasten them on, they break into pieces if you remove them."

Callie buried her face in her hands. "Kyle said he removed them from one animal and fastened them through the ear of another. I don't know how, but he found a way. It will be his word against ours."

"There must be something we can do. Is there any evidence? Can we locate the cattle? Do you have witnesses? Are Heinz and Tommy in on it?" Lauren released her rapid-fire questions and watched Callie wince as each sentence slammed into her. "I have a copy of the export health certificate. I'll call CFIA and have them speak with USDA. There must be records somewhere. He delivered them to a sale, and he received the money. That in itself should be a trail to follow."

Lauren struggled to stay calm. She'd known better than to get involved with someone, and now she was in the thick of something potentially career ending. "It will be more awkward with the RCMP and CFIA because we didn't report the incident earlier." And if Callie had trusted her sooner, that could have happened.

"He sold them privately to a friend in Montana. To avoid a paper trail," Callie said. "There'll be no records anywhere, or not ones that'll help us. No witnesses either. I don't think Tommy's involved, but Heinz knows. Maybe not before, but he knows now and is refusing to pay me for my cattle. I'm sorry you're caught in this. They're harassing me because Heinz wants my farm," Callie said in a despondent tone, with her head pillowed on her arms. "I let you down. I'm so sorry."

Callie made no eye contact and the abject misery she exuded compelled Lauren to stay at Poplarcreek. That evening they made no plans and solved nothing. Everything they talked about brought them back to a brick wall. Lauren didn't want her professional name smeared, and Callie didn't want to hand over control and take the risk that things wouldn't go their way. And most importantly, Callie had a child to protect. Lauren understood that part.

Callie dug leftovers from her refrigerator and heated them for dinner. Lauren and Becky discussed Becky's school and classes while they ate. It was the only safe subject there was to talk about. Becky was interesting and enthusiastic, and Lauren enjoyed the chat, but not so much she could forget Callie sitting as if her life had gone up in smoke.

"Mommy, after dinner, want to see the drawing I did in art class?" Becky asked.

Callie didn't respond. She stared into space and stirred her food into mush on her plate.

Lauren smiled to reassure Becky, who looked worried. "I'd like to see it." After that, she and Becky followed Callie's example and ate in silence.

The silence vanished as Callie exploded to her feet, causing her chair to crash to the floor. She slammed her hands flat on the table. "It's not just the cattle." She bolted to the door, yanked on a coat, and disappeared into the night.

Lauren stared at the open door. "What the heck?" She regained her composure after a few seconds. "Becky, it'll be all right. Stay in the house, okay? I'm going to help your mom."

Becky nodded, her eyes wide, and didn't say anything.

Lauren threw on her coat and boots and jogged to catch up to Callie. Callie emerged from the barn with a shovel and sprinted to her trailer. Lauren skidded to a stop. "What's happening now?" Lauren found Callie in her stock trailer. "Callie?"

"Hold the light."

Lauren clutched the flashlight to her chest as Callie thrust it at her. She shone the light, following Callie as she scanned the inside walls and floor of her trailer. While sweat streamed down her face, Callie shoveled the straw and manure from her trailer at a frantic pace. Soon Callie had the trailer scraped clean to the wooden floor.

Lauren remained quiet. The best plan was to stay to one side and observe the manic behavior. Callie was acting crazy and muttering to herself as she worked.

"It never had a wooden floor." Callie dropped her shovel and snatched the flashlight from Lauren. She moved carefully through the trailer, shining the light on the floor and tapping with her foot. She stopped when she heard a hollow sound. Callie tossed the flashlight to Lauren and picked up her shovel. "Shine it here." Callie pointed to a subtle two foot by two foot square cut into the wooden floor.

After two failed attempts, Callie pried up the loose panel with the tip of her shovel. She tossed the wooden panel and her shovel to one side and kneeled beside the hole. Lauren handed her the flashlight, and Callie shone it into the hole. Callie shoved her arm inside. "It's got a bottom and four sides. I can touch the edges, but the box is empty." When she withdrew, there was a dusting of white powder on her sleeve.

They stood for a beat and stared at Callie's sleeve and at each other.

Lauren stared at the hole. "He built a secret compartment for smuggling drugs across the border. I read an article in the paper about this kind of thing. After Kyle drops the cattle in Montana, he can return to Canada without an inspection, because the trailer's empty. Canada Border Services would question Kyle the same as they do other people when they enter Canada. If CBSA suspected something illegal, they have detector or sniffer dogs to inspect the trailer. But if he's just delivered cattle, they'd barely give him a glance."

"Would the dogs catch him?"

"There are many border points between Saskatchewan and Montana. Sonny Bishop, you remember she's a CFIA veterinarian, told me most of these crossings are low volume and don't have dogs. Even if there were a detector dog where Kyle crossed, assuming they'd look twice at him, the dog would have a difficult time smelling drug residue through a layer of fresh cow manure. I wonder if Kyle smuggled drugs for a gang, or if he's doing it for himself?"

Callie wilted at the suggestion. "I should take it to the car wash and rinse it clean. Better yet, I'll remove the floor and burn it."

Lauren yanked off her wool cap and ran her fingers through her hair. "Don't do that. The floor is evidence. Maybe it has Kyle's fingerprints." Lauren sighed. Even Kyle would have remembered to wear gloves. "I'm not sure if the RCMP can lift fingerprints from plywood anyway."

Callie leaped from the trailer. She loped to the barn and returned with an ax.

Lauren stood to one side and struggled to sound calm. "Destroying evidence isn't smart."

Callie held the ax flat against her chest as tears slipped down her face. "This nightmare has to end. I hate these games and threats. They're trying to chase me off my land so Heinz can buy it. I won't let them win. Poplarcreek is Becky's inheritance." Callie's sobs shook her whole body as she staggered against the wall of the trailer.

"I understand, Callie." Lauren lifted the ax from her drooping arms and placed it on the floor. She gathered Callie against her and she rested her head on Lauren's shoulder. Callie was desperate and vulnerable, and her tears slipped through Lauren's defenses.

Callie sobbed for a minute. Then she straightened, yanked off a glove, and ran a hand across her face, smearing her tears with dirt. "Tomorrow morning after chores, I'll call Doug's lawyer and arrange for him to go with me to speak with the police."

"Well done, Callie." Lauren nodded in agreement. Maybe her professional credit would be in tatters, but smuggling drugs was a huge deal. Bigger than stolen cattle and fake identification tags. They had no choice. It was time to go to the police. She was pleased Callie had made the decision first, because she didn't want to have to force the issue.

Callie groaned. "Everything's falling apart."

Lauren's heart ached for Callie. "I'll be there for you and Becky. Whatever you want. Come on." She slipped an arm around Callie's waist and propelled her toward the house. "Let's go inside. It's freezing out here."

Callie tugged on her glove. They linked hands and trudged to the house. Lauren was worried more for Callie than she was for herself. What was the point of involving Callie in cattle rustling and drug smuggling? It was clear Heinz intended to link Poplarcreek with Kruger Farm to give him control of one enormous farm. Greed wasn't an original motive, but an obvious one. At veterinary college the motto had been "When you hear hooves, think horses not zebras." It meant if you saw a sick animal to consider the most common causes first.

When they arrived at the house, Lauren led Callie upstairs. Callie dragged off her jeans and outer sweater and Lauren tucked her into bed. Lauren glimpsed long legs and pale blue panties, and she wished their lives were different. But things were way too tangled for anything more between them now.

Lauren walked downstairs. She cleaned the kitchen and then joined Becky for a movie. She could have left, and Becky would have been just fine, but somehow it didn't feel right.

"Is Mommy watching with us?" Becky asked.

"She's tired, kiddo. I put her to bed. What movie did you pick? I hope it's a funny one." Lauren had difficulty concentrating on the movie. Becky picked one of Sam's favorites, and Lauren could practically recite the lines. It wasn't fair. Becky tucked in against her side and she wrapped her arm around her. *This house is a dangerous place for me.*

After the movie they headed upstairs. "Here's a bag of my new books. You pick," Becky said.

Lauren waited in the hall while Becky changed. She examined the books. Against all good sense, she had promised to read Becky a bedtime story.

Becky returned. "What did you pick?"

"Has to be *The Black Stallion.*" It made sense Becky would like the same books Sam did. Lauren and William and then Lauren and Sam had read their way through the whole series together. She could have selected another novel to read, but she clutched *The Black Stallion* as if she could reach through it and connect with her children. Connect to a simpler and happier time.

In her pajamas, Becky tiptoed into Callie's room to say good night. Callie emerged from her room wrapped in a robe and holding Becky's hand. They walked to Becky's room and Lauren followed. A bedtime story wasn't necessary now, and she ignored the flare of disappointment. She should just go, really. Instead, she waited in the doorway of Becky's room.

Callie tucked Becky in and perched on the edge of her bed. She spoke in her ear and Becky giggled. Callie kissed her, and with one hand flat on the bedside table, pushed to her feet.

Lauren reached out to Callie as she swayed beside the bed. Callie shook her head and squeezed Lauren's forearm. "I'm just tired. Thank you." The blue eyes that glanced at Lauren were dull and gray, not their usual vibrant sky blue.

"Do you want to sit in my comfy chair or on the bed? Mom calls it my comfy chair," Becky said.

Lauren smiled. Becky still wanted a story. Becky was grinning and her eyes were untroubled by all the adult crap swirling around. Lauren could go if she wanted, but her home no longer appealed to her. She smiled and it felt real, not forced. She'd shove all her worries away for the rest of night. "I'll take the comfy chair, thanks."

CHAPTER SEVENTEEN

The house was cold and silent when Callie woke in the middle of the night. She wandered her house, closing curtains and admiring family photographs along the way. Her heart warmed as she studied the new pictures of her and Becky, several of which Lauren took for them with Becky's camera. She contemplated the old photographs of her parents and siblings, and the photographs of Liz and her brothers while they were growing up on the farm.

Callie studied the photographs of herself and Liz. On stressful or scary days, she missed Liz's strong, broad shoulders and her tendency to fix everything. Liz would have known what to do with the trailer and would have taken care of them.

Lauren hadn't tried to take care of Callie, but she had helped her make the smart decision. It was scary, yes, and it could backfire. But keeping secrets and playing the games of monsters wouldn't keep Becky safe. It was a risk she had to take, and maybe it would mean getting the Krugers off her back entirely. She had to admit to a certain amount of pride in having made the decision on her own. Liz would have taken care of things, but without her, Callie found she could manage on her own. At least that's how she felt now. Tomorrow she might get shaky again. But for the moment, she could lift her chin and think it might be okay.

In her journey through the house, she found a drawing of Lauren fastened to the refrigerator with several magnets. Becky had drawn her delivering a calf. Callie kissed the tips of her fingers and brushed them against Lauren's face in the picture.

"Want to kiss the original?" a soft, husky voice whispered behind her.

Callie jumped and whirled, heart pounding, as her lips parted in surprise. "Where were you?"

"Sitting in your living room reading."

"You didn't leave me?" It sounded weak and desperate, and she winced.

"Not tonight."

It was a far cry from a vow of forever, but it was just what she needed. Callie looped her arms around Lauren's neck. She stared with wonder into Lauren's eyes and kissed her. Lauren's arms tightened around her waist. The kiss began gentle and sweet but changed in a heartbeat as they pressed together.

When they stepped apart to breathe Callie held on to Lauren's shoulders and stared into Lauren's eyes. "Will you stay with me tonight? Please? I can't—not tonight—but I don't want to be alone." Somehow, she knew Lauren would take it the way she meant it. She wouldn't think less of Callie for needing comfort, and Callie wouldn't let it become a habit. She could stand on her own, and she would. Just…not tonight.

They linked hands and walked upstairs to Callie's room. Lauren showered and dressed in the pajamas Callie left for her in the bathroom. The top was snug and the pants too long, but she managed.

She climbed into Callie's bed and Callie turned her back to her. She drew Lauren's hand to her lips and kissed it. She held Lauren's palm against her cheek for a few moments before snugging it across her waist. "Thank you, Lauren."

Lauren slid in tight behind Callie, wrapping her body around her, and dropped light kisses onto her soft blond hair. A few minutes later, regular breathing and soft breaths announced that Callie had fallen into an exhausted sleep.

Lauren was tired, but sleep eluded her. The proximity to Callie's strong, sensual body was making her crazy. Callie's heady scent of vanilla and fresh soap overwhelmed her. Given the chance, she would have stripped off their clothes and made love to Callie. She longed to kiss Callie, moving from one end of her body to the other.

Lauren disappeared into a fantasy and envisioned long legs wrapped around her waist, or better yet, draped over her shoulders. *Stop, stop, stop. Your last relationship was a disaster. She had children too. You could never make this work.*

She forced herself to focus on the contents of Callie's bedroom until the fantasies dimmed. The room was a pleasant collection of soft colors, very feminine, but the furnishings were practical, strong, and solid. Then her eyes landed on a picture hanging beside the bed. It had to be Callie on her wedding day. She studied the ten-by-twelve-inch wedding photograph of Callie and Liz. Callie was in a white wedding dress, wearing Liz's red serge jacket. In the picture, Liz stood grinning with Callie cradled in her arms. Callie laughed toward the camera, waving Liz's RCMP Stetson above her head.

They looked so happy. Callie's eyes were bright and full of light. Not weighted with the stress and worry they carried now. Callie's marriage was cut short by tragedy. Lauren's, because she'd walked away from her family. Liz had to have been a better wife. How could she compete with that? And hell, Liz was big. She held Callie like she was nothing. Lauren would need a fire at her heels to find the strength to carry Callie.

She abandoned the happy couple to study a photograph of Callie, Becky, and a calf. She'd taken that picture and remembered each step of the calving. She went through the details in her head as she drifted to sleep. It was better than counting sheep and guaranteed to calm her libido. What was left of it.

Lauren woke when Callie's ass ground against her. Callie tugged Lauren's hand to cover her breast. Lauren was unsure for a second but slid closer and kissed Callie's nape and caressed her breast. She'd been wet and ready for hours, and every inch of her skin buzzed and urged her forward.

Callie moaned. "Oh, Liz."

Everything sexy died. Lauren's body froze. She was a stand-in for Liz. She almost shook Callie awake to shout at her, but it wasn't exactly Callie's fault, was it? It wasn't as though she hadn't told Lauren about her past. What did she think would happen with this? Callie wasn't over Liz. How could she be?

Without waking Callie, Lauren snuck out of bed. She gathered her clothes and marched downstairs. She dressed and stalked from Callie's house. Bolting without saying good-bye or leaving a note was unkind, but she needed to escape. Her eyes blurred with unshed tears as she drove home. This was what happened when you let yourself get close to someone, when you forgot the cost of emotional connection. Would she never learn?

After lunch, Lauren entered the RCMP detachment office and perched on the edge of a chair in the waiting room. The text she'd received from Callie that morning confirming they'd meet at the police station had been their only contact, and she was both glad and depressed by that. She'd intentionally gotten there a little late so she wouldn't have to face her. Twenty minutes later, Callie and a man in a suit and tie exited an interview room. She guessed the man was Callie's lawyer.

Callie approached her, her expression showing her confusion. "Hi, Lauren."

Lauren stood but couldn't make eye contact. "I'm here to give my statement." She stepped back when Callie stepped closer.

"Lauren?"

Lauren studied her shoes.

"I see. You've reconsidered and want nothing to do with me? Do I deserve this? Kyle conned me. I know it's a mess and I'm sorry."

"No problem." She should have said that it wasn't about this mess. That it had nothing to do with it, but she wasn't prepared to discuss her feelings in a public waiting room. Besides, letting Callie think it was that simple was easier. Cowardly, yeah, but easier.

"Will you come for lunch on Sunday?"

"No, thank you."

"Dinner?"

Lauren shook her head.

"Dinner, ever?"

Lauren shrugged.

"Please, don't let this destroy us. Don't let them win. Please, have dinner with us at Poplarcreek." Callie waited a beat before continuing and her voice cracked. "What is wrong with you? Why're you doing this?"

Lauren raised her eyes to Callie's. *Well done. Why not kick her while she's down? Way to be there for her. You chicken.* Wounded, confused blue eyes stared at her. Callie might be attracted to her, but Liz's whispered name on Callie's lips told her where Callie's heart was. "We're not in the right place to take this," she gestured back and forth between them, "any further right now."

"Take what? Aren't we friends? Or more?"

"I don't know."

"Well, when you figure it out, you know where to find me."

Lauren watched Callie stride away. She recognized that angry walk. Why did she always seem to provoke her?

"Dr. Cornish?"

Lauren focused on the police officer. She looked up into critical hazel eyes and registered the frown. Mitch was about the same height as Callie but wider through the shoulders. Her skin was tan, and with her high cheekbones and black hair, her Métis heritage was evident. Just when she thought her day couldn't get shittier here was another cop that made her feel small, weak, and fat. "Officer Mitchell. Hello."

"Dr. Cornish, please follow me."

Lauren followed Mitchell to a room. The room had a water cooler, a table with magazines, comfortable chairs, and several posters on the wall. It wasn't the stark room of the television shows.

"Dr. Cornish. This is Officer Scott. We will be conducting this interview."

"Sure." Lauren scanned the other woman. She had light brown hair and was shorter and stockier than Mitch, but pretty where Mitchell was just intimidating.

"Mrs. Anderson told us her full story and gave us permission to tell you anything about her circumstances that would aid in our investigation." Mitch leaned forward. "Her life is private, and all details must remain here."

Val had told her Mitchell and Callie were friends. Lauren wasn't sure if she was being interviewed or warned off by a big sister. She bristled under the cop's intense stare. "I understand. I'm here to help, not to invade Callie's privacy."

"Good. Our investigation centers on the Kruger family and their interactions with the Anderson family." She flipped through her notes. "Callie said you're aware of the various letters, threats, phone calls, and visits by Heinz and Kyle Kruger to Callie's house."

"I remember some details, but I only witnessed two visits by Kyle. One at breakfast and the second later in the day after he took Becky." Mitchell's knuckles turned white as she clenched her pen. How could Mitchell conduct this investigation and remain impartial? The mention of any harm to Becky made her look like she wanted to kill somebody.

"Yes, we need to discuss that incident as well as stolen cattle and possible drug smuggling. Were you aware of his earlier visit when Kyle assaulted Callie?"

"Assault? What assault?"

"Callie told us she confronted Kyle about the stolen cattle, and he grabbed her hands and slammed them on the table. She said it hurt, but he stopped there."

"She never told me. If I'd known, I'd have never left her alone with him." Lauren wanted to punch herself. "I left her with him at breakfast that day and later I almost left her with him again. I had no idea."

"Neither did I. Callie has kept a lot to herself. I don't understand why, but she's promised to come to me if there are more incidents. I need you to as well."

Lauren nodded. Kyle had hurt Callie and she hadn't told her, hadn't trusted her with the details. Why not? Weren't they friends?

There was an hour of questions and Lauren stuck to the facts as she knew them. At the end she was sure she'd learned more from Mitchell than she'd had to offer. At least the police were satisfied, and she was able to back up Callie's stories.

"Dr. Cornish, you should know that we also interviewed Mr. Heinz Kruger and Mr. Kyle Kruger, but had to let them go, pending concrete evidence." She pushed her business card across the table. "So, if you remember anything more, please contact me."

At the end of the interview Mitchell showed her to the waiting room and followed her to her truck. Lauren paused by her door. Mitch had followed her for a private conversation. "Dr. Cornish, it's important to warn you that the Krugers were very angry when they left here earlier. They didn't make any threats, not in front of us, but I'm worried about Mrs. Anderson."

"Is she safe, Mitch?" There was real worry in Mitch's voice and Lauren naturally used the name everyone called her.

Mitch's jaw tightened. "No, I don't think Callie or Becky *are* safe. I'm worried about what comes next, now that the Krugers are really pissed. And there may be others involved with the drug smuggling. I doubt Kyle Kruger is capable of organizing the smuggling on his own."

Lauren shuddered. "You mean gangs?"

Mitch nodded. "Drugs means real criminals. Dangerous men with guns who wouldn't hesitate to hurt Callie and Becky if it suited them. I offered to move in and sleep in Callie's spare room, but…" Mitch shrugged.

"I get it. She's very independent."

"She is, but she needs someone to watch her back. Maybe you should stay with her."

Lauren blinked. "She's unlikely to accept my offer, either."

"You need to try and watch your own back. You're not on the Krugers' Christmas list either. I don't think they chose you to verify the cattle because of Callie. I think it could have been any one of the vets, and you got lucky. Or they could have picked you because you're an outsider. Either way it puts you in the middle of this shit storm together."

Lauren flinched at the word outsider. Was Mitch reminding her that she didn't belong in Saskatchewan, or in Callie's life? Mitch was just looking out for Callie and Becky, but what would people think if Lauren stayed at Poplarcreek? In the interest of doing what was best for Callie, she accepted the suggestion. "I'll try, and thanks for the heads up."

"Call me if you need anything at all." Mitch shook Lauren's hand and headed inside.

Lauren stepped into her truck and sat staring at the police detachment. Was is possible coming to the police had put Callie in more danger? What was the point if the Krugers were still free? She should move into Callie's spare room. Callie and Becky needed protection, or at least another witness. She wasn't a bossy police officer, but she could help.

Lauren groaned. She'd just refused multiple invitations to Poplarcreek. She'd made a difficult conversation nearly impossible. How would she casually suggest relocating to Poplarcreek without annoying Callie? But she had to find a way to protect Becky and Callie. Somehow, they all had to stay safe.

Chapter Eighteen

L auren cleared her throat before she answered the phone. "Dr. Lauren Cornish." She worried for a second that it might be Callie calling because the Krugers were at her house again. The interview with the police the day before had shaken her and made her reexamine her priorities. Callie and Becky needed protection and it was irrelevant what other people thought of her staying with Callie. After lunch she'd pack a bag and drive out to Poplarcreek and try to wheedle an invitation to stay in the spare room.

"Dr. Cornish? Are you there?"

"Yes, sorry."

"A man is on his way to Prairie Veterinary Services with a cow requiring surgery. He didn't give his name."

"Thank you." Lauren hung up and groaned when she read the clock. It was two a.m. on Sunday morning, and she'd been hoping to sleep in until ten and then phone Sam. It had been three weeks since the first phone call and they were speaking a couple of times a week. Sometimes William even joined for a few minutes. She didn't want to mess that up.

"Well, kitten. Another long night for me." Digit jumped off the bed when Lauren stirred. While she dressed, he wove between her legs and meowed. "Somewhere in your little cat brain you think you're helping. Too early for breakfast, sir. We'll eat when I return." Lauren dressed and kissed Digit on the top of the head. Attracted by the commotion, Elsa padded over for a kiss too.

Lauren pulled on her coat and stumbled into the frigid night air. After a short drive, she arrived at PVS, coded off the alarm, and jogged through the clinic. She pushed the button to open the ten foot by ten foot door through which large animals entered. Lauren stepped outside and, in the semidarkness, observed a man getting out of the truck. "Hey, cold night. Sorry the main floodlights are out. We need to get them fixed. Please straighten your trailer and back up to the lower chute. Then we'll run her inside."

The man didn't respond, just continued to walk in her direction. Hair prickling on the nape of her neck, she walked to the trailer and peered in. It was empty.

Lauren backed toward the clinic, but the man swaggered closer. He lurked in the shadows and she couldn't see his face. He wasn't a big man, but he was bigger than she was. He seemed to be waiting, but his eyes never left her. She jumped when a second truck tore into the parking lot spraying gravel. She couldn't see who was behind the wheel.

"Who are you?" When the man didn't answer, Lauren whirled, sprinted into the clinic, and slammed the button to power the automatic door closed. Adrenaline pumping and struggling not to panic, she wasted time deciding whether to race through the building outside to her truck or hunt for a weapon to defend herself. Her self-defense training taught her to flee, but she balked. Criminals tackling her from behind and dragging her to the floor wasn't an option. She would meet them face-to-face and if they wanted a fight, they would get one.

Lauren snatched a covered scalpel from the surgery tray and jammed it in her pocket. Then grabbed a shovel and raised it to shoulder height as she hid against the wall beside the door. "You'd better stay out or explain why your trailer's empty," she yelled.

The door crept closed, and she almost screamed at it with impatience. When it was two feet from the floor, an arm poked underneath. The door hit the arm hard, and the impact triggered the door's safety mechanism. It reversed direction and opened again. Then the first man entered the clinic with the second man close behind.

"Kyle and Tommy Kruger." Lauren struggled to keep her voice steady. Mitch had warned her she was in danger, but she hadn't thought they'd make a move so soon.

"Hang on, Doc." Kyle sneered, holding his arms high. "What ya gonna do with the shovel? You gonna dig a hole? Or are you scared of us? We scare you?" Kyle focused on the larger man. "Tommy bro, we scared the doc." Tommy remained quiet, his eyes locked on Lauren and an inscrutable expression on his face.

Still clutching her weapon, Lauren glared at Kyle. "What do you want? Your trailer's empty."

Kyle crept toward her. He had one hand in his pocket and the other scratched his chin. "We got no animal with us, Doc." The cigarette hanging from his mouth, combined with his scruffy beard and slimy demeanor caused Lauren to go cold.

When Kyle was six feet from her Tommy laid his huge hand on Kyle's shoulder and stopped him. Kyle glanced at Tommy. "S'kay, bro, I only wanna talk to the doc."

Kyle faced Lauren, his expression cunning. "We had a stuck calf, but right after we called the answering service, we winched it out. Thought I'd slide over and let you know so you weren't waiting."

Bullshit, but I'll play. Lauren kept the shovel against her chest. "Good to know. Thanks."

"Sorry we scared you. Guess you're alone tonight." Kyle scratched his chest and smirked. "What you need is a man at home to notice when you go missing. If something happened to you, like a broken leg, nobody'd find you until morning."

"I'm okay the way I am, thanks."

"You know, maybe you'd be better off back in Ontario with your own people where it's safe. Not sure you fit in around here. In Thresherton, people have learned to mind their own business and keep out of our way. They've learned not to go running their mouths."

Tommy grabbed Kyle by the shoulders and started to pull him out of the clinic.

"See ya, Doc. Hope you enjoyed the lesson," Kyle said. He brushed Tommy's hands off and looked at Lauren. His cold gaze landed at her chest again. Lauren recognized the tactic as an attempt at intimidation. It was designed to prey on a woman's insecurities and zap her confidence. Kyle had tried this trick one too many times, and she was unaffected.

"Well, night, Doc. You should watch out, you know. There are lots of dangerous criminals in the dark." Kyle laughed. "Let's go, Tommy."

Lauren watched them exit through the automatic door and she punched the button the moment they were past it. After the door closed, she lowered the shovel to the floor and returned the scalpel to the surgery tray. She staggered backward until her back hit the wall. Her legs buckled and she slid down, landing on her butt on the cold cement floor. She buried her head in her arms as she hugged her knees to her chest with shaking hands.

The threat was clear. Stay out of the Krugers' way or move back to Ontario. And if she did neither? An attack in the dark? Assault? A broken leg or worse?

Light-headed and nauseated, Lauren remained there for several minutes, listening to a dog bark. "Enough cowering, Cornish, and your butt is freezing." Lauren took a deep breath and dragged her feet under her. She crawled up the wall and teetered on wobbly legs. Still dizzy, she staggered for a step, before walking into the small animal wing of PVS.

Taking care of animals calmed her, and right now that's exactly what she needed. Lauren opened a can of dog food and grabbed an antibiotic pill. She entered the dog run and dropped to sit beside Max. "Hey, Max. You're a good boy." Lauren fed him the pill wrapped in a ball of canned food and he wolfed it down without chewing. She stroked his head while he ate the rest.

After he finished eating, Max crawled toward Lauren and laid his head on her thigh. "Everything's okay, Max. Nothing to fear, big guy. The snakes have slithered away." As she cuddled the dog, Lauren pretended she was reassuring Max, but anybody who saw them would have realized it was Max comforting her.

What was she going to do? Callie and Becky needed protecting, but Lauren could hardly protect herself. She was a weepy mess from one threatening interaction. Suddenly, showing up at Poplarcreek as Callie's knight protector seemed like a dumb idea. All she wanted to do was go home and crawl into bed with Digit. She should get Callie to reconsider Mitch's offer. Mitch would protect Callie and Becky, just as Liz would have. The best thing she could do right now for Callie and Becky was to leave protecting them to Mitch. She'd never felt so useless.

After a cuddle and a kiss on the top of his head, Lauren left Max. She closed up the clinic and headed home. She parked in her driveway for a few seconds and then with a deep sigh, backed out and drove to the RCMP detachment. Lauren waited at the front counter not sure if she wanted Mitch to be working or not.

"Dr. Cornish?" Mitch said, coming out from behind the counter.

"Can I speak with you?"

"Are you okay? Are Callie and Becky?"

Mitch's mask slipped and Lauren spotted real warmth and affection for Callie and Becky. The cop wasn't a block of granite after all. "Everyone's fine, but there was an incident at the vet clinic tonight."

"Follow me."

Mitch led her into an interview room and set a bottle of water in front of her. Then she fished a pen from her pocket and opened her notebook.

"Kyle Kruger lured me to the clinic tonight." Lauren told the story and resisted the urge to downplay how scared she'd been. Now wasn't the time for ego, and any woman would have been frightened.

When Lauren finished, Mitch wrote for another minute, then closed her notebook. "The threat is clear. Time for me to have another talk with Kyle. What will you do?"

"Do?"

"Are you going to move away?"

"No, well, at least not now, and not because of Kyle."

"And Callie? She needs someone to stay with her."

Lauren drew circles in the condensation left by her bottle of water.

"Are you going to stay at Poplarcreek?"

"You should do it." The meekness in her voice made Lauren shudder, but she couldn't protect Callie and Becky. One slightly threatening visit from Kyle and she was a mess.

Mitch planted her hands flat on the table and leaned forward. "She said no to me. I already told you that."

Lauren shrugged and looked up. Mitch was studying her as if she were something unpleasant that needed to be scraped off the bottom of her shoe.

"I'm sorry," Lauren whispered.

Without another word, Mitch showed her out. At home, Lauren turned on all the lights, stripped off her jeans and jacket and crawled into bed. She pulled the pillow over her eyes to block the light. "Digit. Here, Digi." When the soft furry body crawled into her arms, she pulled him close. She loosened her grip when he squirmed and meowed. "Sorry, Digi. I'm a big suck." She kissed the top of his head.

Callie and Becky needed protection and she should be doing it. She should be staying at Poplarcreek, but instead she was hiding. Hiding in bed with her cat. Next, she'd be sucking her thumb like when she was three. Lauren groaned, thoroughly disgusted with herself.

Maybe she should go back to Ontario. Tuck her tail between her legs and run. Her feelings for Callie were confusing enough, and now there was a real threat from the town bullies. Why not leave? It was the sensible thing to do...or was it cowardly? She wasn't a coward, but this was about self-preservation.

CHAPTER NINETEEN

Callie jumped when the phone rang and grabbed it on the second ring. She'd been hoping to hear from Lauren. It had been three days since she'd last seen her, during an awkward exchange at the police station, and she hadn't even had a text since then. Maybe all her crap with the Krugers had scared Lauren off?

"Hello? Lauren?"

"Hi, Callie."

"Oh, hey, Mitch." Callie struggled to contain her disappointment. "How are you? Everything good?"

"We're fine, Mitch. How are you?" Callie smiled. Mitch was a good friend.

"Callie, you need to let me stay with you for a while. You need an extra person in the house to dissuade visits from the Krugers."

"No, thanks. We're fine." It would be too much like having Liz in the house again, and although she was afraid of the Krugers, she wasn't about to give up control again.

"Just for a few days."

"How about I call you if I change my mind? Okay?" Callie listened until Mitch ran out of reasons for her to stay at Poplarcreek. Then she hung up after promising to think about it. Mitch made some good points. Maybe she should get a big dog like Martha suggested? The ringing phone pulled her back to the present.

"Hello? Lauren?"

"Hello, Catherine. Were you expecting Dr. Cornish?"

Callie went cold as she recognized the mean little laugh. She should have looked at her call display. Everyone was calling except the person she most wanted to speak with. "What do you want, Heinz?" Forget any semblance of polite. He was a criminal and he was going to jail.

"Why so hostile, Catherine? I'm just being neighborly. Calling to chat."

"Do you have the money for my two cows?"

"Ah, women. You're too impatient to be in business."

"Should I talk to a lawyer? I can prove how much my two cows were worth."

"These things take time, Catherine."

He was a patronizing asshole and she was two seconds away from telling him that. Callie took a deep breath. "Heinz, what do you want?"

"Have you gotten your big tractor out for the spring? It's never too early to check that it's working properly."

"Did you mess with my tractor?"

Heinz laughed. "No, but I know it's *very* old. I doubt you'll get another season out of it. And have you looked at how much they cost?"

"Go away, Heinz."

"Let us know if you need help this spring. You've been telling lies at the police station, but I'll forgive you. Women are so emotional."

"They're not lies. Bye, Heinz." Callie hung up and stared at the phone. Now she was worried about getting her big tractor going. Without it she couldn't plant any seed. How did Heinz know it was old and failing? She'd had Mark over every week to tinker with it and help her nurse it through last season. Now, given her finances, she'd have to do it again. Heinz was an asshole and knew just what buttons to push.

Callie slammed out of the house and grabbed her snow shovel. She violently shoveled her walkway and watched for a truck. Callie leaned her shovel against the porch and approached the truck that pulled into her yard. She rolled her shoulders to shake off the bad mood and find her smile.

"Hi, Mark. Thanks for helping me today. How's Tracey doing?" Mark and Tracey Renfield were Callie's neighbors on the other side of her from the Kruger Farm. Mark was always willing to help her when she broke something, and any other time she needed help.

"Trace is doing well, thanks. The C-section zapped her energy, but she's healing. Amanda and Sally are old enough to help after school, and Hughie is behaving himself. We've decided Jenny will be our last baby."

As they walked to Callie's drive shed, she said, "Four children are a decent number."

"Yeah, four is enough. Six was the plan, but we'll stay at four."

Callie pointed. "The small tractor's broken, again. I tried to fix it myself but no luck. And wouldn't you know, it's the one with the snowblower so I need to get it going. Sorry to bother you, again."

"I don't mind. I'll come over anytime I'm asked." They lifted the cover and Mark inspected the engine. He adjusted items as Callie handed him tools.

"Four kids," Callie said. "You know you have to put your children through university or technical college, if they want?"

"We're already saving money, and it helps that you're renting land to us."

"I have my hands full with five hundred acres, the house, the cattle, and Becky. I have no time to cultivate all my land and I'm too slow at it anyway."

"Slow?"

Callie laughed. "I have to keep the tractor speed to a crawl if I want the rows straight. Doug wouldn't let me plant the rows along the highway because I didn't make them straight enough."

"Hilarious. He wouldn't have wanted the neighbors to think he couldn't drive straight. Hey, but what did he expect? Straight is not you." He winked at her.

"Ha, ha. Ladies and gentlemen, we have our first joke of the day."

Mark laughed and then became serious. "You know Tracey and I like you and are cool with you being a lesbian? We grew up with Liz and she was my cousin. Doug was like my second father. If you ever need to talk or whatever, we're here."

When he was fifteen, Mark's parents and little sister had died in a house fire while he camped with friends one weekend. There was talk of sending him east to live with an aunt or putting him in foster care. Instead, Doug had offered Mark a home. Mark's help on the farm became indispensable because Liz and her brothers were living in British Columbia by then. Staying in Thresherton had allowed Mark to continue to date his girlfriend, Tracey, now his wife, and remain as part of the community he knew. His history with Doug had transferred over to Callie, and she'd never been more grateful. It was an easy decision to rent a large portion of her land to them so they could farm it and make some extra money.

Callie lightly slapped Mark on the shoulder. "You two are good friends."

"You too, Callie." Mark set down his pliers. "That should do it. Try to start it."

Callie jumped into the tractor, twisted the key, and it roared to life. She gave Mark two thumbs-up and he made a cutting motion. She shut the engine off and jumped down. Mark pointed to two wires on the engine. Callie glanced at them and shook her head, unsure what he was suggesting.

"They're corroded, and they came loose. I cleaned them and fastened them down, but in the spring remind me and I'll replace them, if you decide not to change them yourself."

"Thanks. I couldn't do it without your help." It was hard to admit that.

Mark grinned. "You're welcome. I helped Doug all the time. Besides, you have to clear away the snow to let the vets in. Seems like you might as well move them in, as often as we see them head your way."

Callie grimaced. "Har, har. The vets from PVS have been here too often this month. Heinz Kruger's bull bred my little heifers and now they're calving."

"How many are there?"

"I have twenty. So far, there have been eight calvings and six C-sections. My bill at PVS is insane. I refuse to think about how much I owe."

"That's bad luck, but those PVS vets are great." Mark waggled his eyebrows. "Is there one who's extra helpful?"

Callie shoved him with her shoulder and grinned. "What did you hear?"

He shrugged and kicked at imaginary debris with the toe of his boot. "This and that. Small town, you know."

Callie crossed her arms and squinted at him. "As revealing as always, Mark."

"Please, give me something to take home to Trace. She ordered me to find out what you were up to."

Callie grinned. "I'm attracted to Lauren Cornish, but she's difficult to understand. Sometimes she's interested in me and other times not. Not like I have time for that kind of thing anyway."

He tilted his head. "I heard she deserted her family in Ontario. Kids and all."

"She has a child? A partner? She said something about a daughter the other day, but I thought it was hypothetical."

"She has two kids."

Callie frowned. "Two? And she left them?"

"Maybe she's not so interesting anymore? You wouldn't want her to bail on you and Becky."

That was true, but it felt so judgmental. And if they stayed just friends, then her past didn't matter. "I prefer to give people the benefit of the doubt. I hope there'll be more to her story."

"The couple of times she was at our place she appeared to be a good person. We can't picture her abandoning kids. She's great with ours and teaches them something about animals each time she's there. Amanda has decided to be a veterinarian."

In his tender tone Callie heard pride and affection for his family. "Lauren seems nervous sometimes when she's near Becky. Like she's not sure how to act around her."

"Nervous near Becky or near you?" Mark nudged Callie with an elbow. "Do you make the vet nervous?"

"You're full of jokes today."

Mark hooked his thumbs under imaginary suspenders and strutted. "Yup, I'm a funny guy."

Callie swallowed and blurted her thoughts before she could lose her nerve. "I kissed her." She had also coaxed Lauren into her bed, but that was more than Mark needed to know.

Mark quit his goofy walk. "You what?"

Callie hid her face in her hands. "I lured her into my house for breakfast and kissed her."

"Way to go, Callie. She's been to your place so often she must be almost part of the family now."

Callie playfully punched Mark in the shoulder. "You've reached your quota, man. No more jokes."

"Trace and I are hoping for the best for you, but please, be careful. Maybe you should learn more about her, you know?"

Callie nodded. "I wouldn't become involved with a woman who abandoned her children. Couples break up, but you always care for your kids. If she just walked away, that's something I couldn't handle."

They fell silent for a few minutes while they straightened Doug's workbench and tools. "Weren't you dating a woman you met in the city? You brought her for a barbecue once," Mark said.

"She loathed the farm, and the smell nauseated her. She asked me why I didn't sell and live somewhere clean."

"What did you say?"

Callie frowned. "Poplarcreek is my home. It's a hard life, sure, but I love it here. This farm's also Becky's inheritance and I have a responsibility to guard it for her."

"Guard it from Kruger." Mark frowned and locked eyes with Callie. "Heinz pulled some shit and bugged Doug to sell, but Doug refused. Watch out for that family. They don't give up."

"What did they do?"

"Once Doug left to visit his sons and their families. He left me in charge. I got off the school bus one day and there's this big van in the yard. Surveyors. These two guys said Poplarcreek was for sale and they were told to take measurements."

"Heinz?"

"You bet. Heinz told Doug that it was a misunderstanding and that the men had come to the wrong farm."

"Liar."

"Absolutely."

"That explains the report I got this morning. Poplarcreek all marked out on a neat map and a purchase offer stuck in the middle."

"Man never quits. If you ever want me to talk to him I will. Heinz doesn't scare me."

"Thanks, Mark, but he's my problem and I have a plan." Callie considered telling him about the cattle theft and drug smuggling, but it wouldn't do to drag Mark and his family into the drama unless it was absolutely necessary. She'd let the police decide that one. "I'm always looking over my shoulder for Heinz." *And now Kyle.* She had told Becky never to go anywhere with the Krugers or ever get into their vehicles ever again. They were dangerous and to be avoided. Becky seemed to finally understand, and while Callie didn't want to scare her, Becky needed to be afraid of that family. "I'll protect Poplarcreek."

Mark grinned and gave her a one-armed hug around the shoulders. "I'm picturing your girl carrying on the family tradition of running Poplarcreek."

"Every chance she gets, Becky is in the barn with the animals. The trick is getting her to sit still long enough for homework. I was thinking of trying heavy duty tape." Callie helped Mark carry his tools to his truck. "Thanks for your help today. I haven't broken anything else, so today is a good day. Would you like lunch before you go?"

"Thanks, but if I head home now, I can join Trace and the baby for lunch."

Of course. He had people waiting for him. She tried not to let it get to her that her house was empty at the moment. After Mark left, Callie tidied the drive shed and put the rest of the tools away. Doug was a precise man, and every tool had its place. He never left trash on the floor and he always cleaned up any oil he spilled. She made sure to carry on that legacy.

While Callie cleaned, she reviewed her conversation with Mark. He was a reliable friend. Not a gossip. He had told her what he heard to be helpful. She liked Lauren and Becky liked Lauren. She refused to believe that Lauren had backed off because of the Krugers. Lauren had already proven that they didn't scare her. There had to be something more.

Callie frowned. She and Lauren had chatted a few times, but those meetings sometimes left Callie disappointed because she had revealed more than Lauren. Lauren could write her biography while she had nothing. She'd learned about Lauren's children from Mark.

Maybe Lauren had trust issues and was quiet to keep her private life private? But it was unnatural and unhealthy to be so closed off. Maybe Lauren needed somebody to talk to, to confide in? Callie would be that good friend because she cared and because Lauren had helped her so much. Callie nodded in determination. Lauren needed to open up and now was the time to coax her.

After lunch, Callie called PVS and caught Lauren between appointments. "Will you come to Poplarcreek for lunch one day? We need to talk."

"You're right, we do. There's something I want to tell you. I'm off this Wednesday and I'm headed to the city. Like to join me?"

She'd expected Lauren to turn her down flat, and the invitation was a nice surprise. She'd have two days to work out a plan to get Lauren to open up. "I'd love to come. I'll be ready by nine, but I need to be home by four to meet Becky's bus. If that messes up your plans, we can meet another time."

"Four is fine with me. In this weather, I avoid driving after dark. Hey, I'm planning to get sushi for lunch."

That sounded like a treat after so many basic home cooked meals, which was all she had time for since Martha left. "I love sushi. Ate it every week when I lived on the coast."

"On the way home, I promised to stop at a friend's place, to check on her horse. That okay with you?"

"As long as I'm home by four."

"It's a deal. My next appointment's here. See you at nine. Thanks, Callie."

"Bye, Lauren." Callie shook her head, unable to decipher what had just happened. Three days ago, Lauren wouldn't even accept lunch, and now she was inviting her for a road trip. Maybe Lauren had changed her mind? She did say she had something to tell her. Maybe Lauren would open up about her past? She'd sounded friendly, but her tone was firm, like there was an important reason to meet. Good for her. Good for them.

CHAPTER TWENTY

Callie leaned against the wall by her front window and watched for Lauren's truck. She blew on the glass and drew a heart in the moisture her breath left. It was minus thirty degrees Celsius outside, but the breeze had brushed the road clear of snow and the sun was shining. She felt her own mood start to lift. She was excited, like a little kid. The last time she'd been to Saskatoon had been a week after Valentine's Day when she and Rachel had run into Lauren at the Rainbow Club. It had been twenty-five days since she'd danced with Lauren, and six days since she'd kissed her. But who was counting?

At nine a.m. exactly, Lauren drove into Poplarcreek. Callie pulled on her coat, jogged to the truck, and climbed in. "Hi, Lauren. Beautiful day."

Lauren smiled. "Incredible."

Callie relished the quick full-body scan Lauren gave her when she climbed in. She'd put her hair up in her favorite 1950s style and wore a little makeup. She spent all her time in farm clothes, and it was nice to dress up and spend time on her makeup, especially when her efforts were so appreciated. She straightened the front of her dressy coat. She'd had it for years, but it was still in decent shape, and besides, it was blue and Martha promised it made her eyes pop.

As Lauren pulled away from the farm, a painful awkwardness floated between them. Callie struggled for something to say. There was a ton of serious conversation to have, but she didn't want to jump in right away. Right now, she wanted to enjoy the company of an attractive woman and have a pleasant adult conversation. She settled on a discussion of the weather, which when you depended on agricultural for a living, wasn't a throwaway conversation, but an item of extreme importance.

"I'm hoping for a milder winter this year," Callie said. "Last winter there was late snow and a cold snap in April. Some farmers lost a third of their new calves still in the pasture. We didn't lose any. Our cows brought their calves into the lean-to barn when the temperature dropped and before the snow was too deep for the calves to walk."

"Lucky. Animals are smart that way."

Callie adored Lauren's easy smile. Lauren slouched in her seat, the muscles of her shoulders relaxed. Lauren's hand rested on her knee as she steered with two fingers and whistled a tune Callie couldn't decipher. Callie itched to brush a hand down her soft cheek and smooth away the last of the Lauren's stress.

Lauren glanced at her expectantly and she realized she'd missed something. "Hmm?"

"I asked what you'd like to do today in the big city?"

Callie straightened in her seat. "Imagine us thinking Saskatoon is big. It's only two hundred and twenty thousand. Surrey is more than twice that. How big is Toronto?"

"The GTA, Greater Toronto Area, is over five and a half million. Too big for me. I prefer living in a town the size of Thresherton and having a city within an easy drive if I need a change or a little space."

"Space. I get that. In Saskatoon everybody doesn't know all my business. I'm looking forward to a little anonymity."

"So, what would you like to do today?"

"I always have errands. You?"

"I often wander through one of the malls. My real motivation for the trip is the sushi. The Thresherton Diner is okay, but I'm tired of sandwiches, lasagna, and burgers. The only other restaurants serve pizza or fried chicken."

"Do you cook for yourself?"

"Not well and not often. I buy frozen dinners. The organic kind from the market, and I eat a lot of tuna." Her expression turned sad. "Not much point in cooking when it's just you."

It was still too soon to delve into serious topics. "So, sushi's a treat. The mall's a good idea. I need new winter boots. I wear men's boots in the barn, but I can't find nice leather boots, in a women's size eleven in Thresherton. Apparently, there aren't a lot of women with big feet in our town." That was okay because she didn't have the money to spend on new boots. It was fun to look though. The boots she was wearing were out of fashion, but as long as they were dry, she'd be wearing them.

Lauren laughed. "Anything else? New clothes?"

"I have enough dressy clothes, and everything else I buy at the farm store."

"Do you own many dressy clothes?" Lauren asked.

"I have a few nice dresses and slacks. I don't go to the club often. That night at the rainbow club was my first night out in months, but you looked comfortable there." It wasn't subtle, but it worked.

"I did? Val dragged me. I don't go out often either."

They spent the morning roaming the mall and shopping for dress boots. Callie didn't find boots to buy, but Lauren purchased a pair of low-heeled black leather boots for herself.

Callie winked. "Nice boots. Very sexy."

As they walked, Callie linked her arm through Lauren's. Lauren's arm muscles tensed for a second and then relaxed. Callie relished the feel of Lauren so close. "Do we have time for the children's clothing store? I didn't plan to drag you there, but Becky's growing faster than I can buy new clothes for her." She always found money to spend on Becky. Her daughter came first.

"No problem. I understand. Even a nine-year-old is conscious of their appearance."

Callie glanced at Lauren and waited for her to elaborate. She wasn't sure how to broach the subject of Lauren's children. How did you bring up something like that without it feeling intrusive?

Callie paired tops and pants she knew Becky would like and then became playfully indecisive about her other choices, until

Lauren stepped in and helped her guess sizes and create options. Callie knew how to shop for Becky but hoped this shopping trip would coax Lauren into finally opening up about her children.

"You have a real eye for this, Lauren. Becky will love the clothes you picked out for her. The sizes look perfect."

Lauren winked. "You've discovered my hidden talent. Personal shopper for the preteen. Will the jeans suit her? I don't know her well, but at Becky's age I would've loved them."

"She'll love the metal studs. They're cool and a little dangerous. Thanks for talking me out of the skirt. It would've looked cute on her, but the last dress I bought for her collected dust in her closet for a year until I let her give it away."

"You know best, but from what I've seen, Becky's style isn't dresses and skirts."

Callie waited, but Lauren didn't elaborate. So much for the perfect opening to talk about her kids. She'd get her to talk later.

At half past one, with shopping and errands finished, they arrived at the sushi restaurant. They gorged themselves on fresh sashimi and sushi, discovering they both preferred the spicy rolls.

Lauren popped a spicy salmon roll in her mouth. "We should just order spicy rolls next time and skip the rest."

Callie cocked her head and smiled at Lauren.

"I don't want—I mean…Callie's a great name. Is it your first name? Is it short for another name? A nickname? Or is it a complete name? Are you named after a movie star?"

It was painful to watch Lauren's discomfort, and Callie rescued her. "It's short for Catherine Leigh. Catherine and Leigh are my grandmothers. My mother's also Catherine but goes by Cathy. Lauren's a classy name. Is it a family name?"

"I'm also named after a grandmother. I don't mind the name Lauren, but I wish it had better nicknames like Callie. Laur is harsh. I tried Ren for a while when I was younger and trying to be tough."

Callie snorted and then said, "Sorry."

Lauren shrugged. "Yeah, Ren and the tough act didn't last long. I know another woman called Lauren whose friends called her Elle. Most people call me Lauren or L.C."

"Why Elle?"

"For the letter L in Lauren." Lauren grimaced. "I bet that was the longest answer to the shortest question you've ever asked?"

Callie just laughed. It was good that Lauren was opening up a little. Maybe she could push a little now. "How did you end up in Saskatchewan?"

"I was looking for a complete change and wanted out of Toronto. I answered an advertisement for a mixed animal practitioner in Saskatchewan. As soon as Ian and Fiona hired me, I packed my trailer and moved to Thresherton."

"Do you like it here?"

"Great job, awesome people, and nice summers, but last winter the first snow arrived on September seventeenth. I remember because it was my parents' wedding anniversary. I was ready to flee back to Ontario where everyone was still wearing shorts."

"It snows only a little in Surrey, but it can be cold, sometimes below zero. It rains all winter. I like the snow better."

Lauren leaned forward and shuddered. "The worst eye-opener was Halloween last year. It was on a Saturday and I drove into Saskatoon to do my shopping. I was home by four p.m. and ready for the kids, but none showed up."

Callie smiled, anticipating Lauren's next words. Lauren was interesting and alluring in the green shirt and loose jeans. Callie enjoyed the grin and sparkle in Lauren's eyes, but how did they end up talking about the weather again? Was it going to take a crowbar to pry Lauren's story out of her?

"The next day at work I begged everyone to eat the candy I had left before I ate it myself. I asked Val why no kids came to my door." Lauren's demeanor was wide-eyed and innocent. "She told me the kids went out after lunch trick-or-treating because it's too cold to let them outside after dark. Who trick-or-treats at one in the afternoon?"

"Welcome to Saskatchewan, eh?"

Lauren laughed and ducked her head when the other diners focused on them. Her whole face and even her ears reddened.

Callie cupped Lauren's warm cheeks. "You need to quit blushing or you'll catch your hair on fire," she whispered.

"You're lucky you don't blush."

"Oh, I blush." Callie winked and lowered her hands.

Lauren smiled and bent forward. "I'd like to see that."

Callie enjoyed the light banter, and she knew a little more about Lauren now, though not what she was really hoping for. She had so many questions. The question about why a woman snuck out of your bed and ran off without a word was a conversation to have in private. Callie sighed. If she wanted to hear about Lauren's family, and why her kids didn't live with her, she'd clearly have to be more direct.

After lunch, they argued politely over the bill. "I should pay because you drove," Callie said.

"But I invited you. You bought last time. Lunch is my treat today."

Callie leaned back in her chair. She crossed her arms over her chest and lifted an eyebrow. "I pay my way and I expect to do my share. Please, don't assume I want somebody to look after me."

Lauren blinked and retreated. "You win. No offense meant." After Callie paid, they walked back through the mall.

"You heard anything more from Heinz or Kyle Kruger? I worry about you and Becky alone at Poplarcreek," Lauren said.

"People have offered to stay with us, but I like my independence." Callie wanted to scream as the dark cloud of Kruger settled over them. "Heinz phoned me Monday morning and said he was still working out how much he owed me for the two cows. Made some comment about impatient women who shouldn't be in business."

"And you said?"

"Told him I'd hired a lawyer to help us with the math." Callie laughed, but it hadn't been funny and Heinz's condescending attitude had struck a nerve.

"Good for you. What can I do to help?"

"I've got it covered." Callie stopped and squeezed Lauren's forearm. "Just be careful around them."

Lauren opened her mouth then closed it again.

"Lauren?"

"Nothing. Right. Watch out for the Krugers."

Callie frowned and let the strange exchange go. They exited the mall, hurried to Lauren's truck, and headed toward home.

Callie twisted in her seat to look at Lauren. There wasn't a lot of time left before they got back. There would be no more talk of the weather, cattle, or the Krugers. "Thanks for helping me find clothes for Becky. You have amazing taste." Callie waited for a response. "Lauren, will you tell me about yourself?"

"Now's the time," Lauren muttered.

Callie waited.

Lauren grimaced and shook her head. "You asked for it. The tragic saga of Lauren Cornish. T.J. and I met when we were students at the Ontario Veterinary College in Guelph, Ontario. T.J. is short for Tanya Jenkins. I'm not sure if it was love or lust at first sight. It no longer matters. Anyway, after graduation we moved to Toronto and worked every hour we could. After four years, we had a new house, a thriving practice with six office staff and technicians, and another veterinarian to share the work."

"Impressive. Why'd you break up?"

Lauren shrugged and stared out the windshield. "We stopped sharing the same dreams and everything kind of faded away. T.J. loved the noisy city, with its busy streets and millions of people. I wanted something else, and we'd drifted too far apart to find a compromise."

It was a common story, but Callie could see how sad it still made her. "It's hard when relationships fade away."

"In ten years, we went from meeting to married to divorced." Lauren shook her head. "Our kids are just starting to understand. Wish I did."

Callie held her breath, afraid the wrong words would spook Lauren and she'd stop sharing. "How old are they? And where are the children now?" This was the background Callie had been hoping for, but the sadness in Lauren's eyes made her wonder if she was prying where she shouldn't.

"In Ontario with T. J."

Callie waited for more. The only sound in the truck was the rattle of something in the back. Why was Lauren living so far from her children? Had she run away? Did she still see them? She almost asked, but given Lauren's pinched expression, she was hesitant to say anything more about it.

Lauren bit her lip. "I hope you don't despise me for living so far from them." She paused, then started talking again, her hands tight on the steering wheel. "William's eighteen and Samantha's twelve. When we met, William was six. T.J. had already divorced his father and she was pregnant by Sam's father. William's dad is a good guy and has always been active in his life. Sam's father wasn't around." Lauren cleared her throat. "I held Sam first. I caught her when she was born." Tears glistened in Lauren's eyes behind her sunglasses.

"Sweet." Callie smoothed her hand up and down Lauren's arm to comfort her.

"I loved that time in my life, but are you sure you want to hear more?"

"Tell me whatever you wish. No pressure."

"Life was great. I was a mom to those kids, and I love them. But eventually, T.J. and I had moved so far apart mentally and emotionally we couldn't find our way back. When the business was thriving, we escaped to Cuba for a week in the winter. It was a treat for the first two years, but later we had nothing to talk about except the house, the kids, and the business. It was like we weren't interested in each other as people anymore."

"That's sad."

"I was a mess physically and not happy in Toronto. I don't belong in the city. Never did. I should've told T.J. at the beginning, but I thought I could learn to like Toronto. The country and endless space suit me better." Lauren scanned the fields and nodded.

"When did you last see William and Sam?"

Lauren stared through the windshield and took several deep breaths. "Eighteen months ago." Callie gasped and Lauren glanced at her. "Not seeing them wasn't my idea, but after I moved out, they refused to see me. They said I abandoned T.J. and them. It's kind of dramatic, but I thought I deserved to be cut off. I thought they'd be better off without me, so I moved two provinces away."

"What will you do now?"

"Recently, I've been Skyping with Sam and she told me it was William's idea to cut me off. It was a cooperative divorce, but I still hurt T.J. He was pretty angry."

"I'm so sorry. How is he now?"

Lauren gave a watery smile. "I don't know if I'll ever reconnect with him. We've only spoken a few times in the last month, but Sam's considering visiting me this summer. T.J. and I are cordial. She's encouraging them to talk to me."

"I sure hope Sam visits."

"Me too. I miss her. It tore me apart when she and William discarded me. It makes me…"

Lauren's voice was toneless and filled with pain. Callie's heart ached for her. "It makes you?"

"Leery of loving another woman's children and risking the pain of that loss." Lauren sighed and shook her head. "I can't go through it again. My children barely talk to me, and all the pain I caused is something I live with every day. Relationships are hard enough, and I know that forever is just a word from romance novels. But add in kids, and you're asking for devastation."

Callie thought about that for a moment. "Even though Becky was born before I came into the picture, and I lost Liz shortly after, I wouldn't trade my little girl for anything. I'd risk a world of hurt for a child."

"You're braver."

"I don't know." Maybe she was braver and stronger. She wouldn't have run away from Becky if she and Liz divorced. Callie shook her head at the instant judgmental thoughts. How could she know? She'd never been where Lauren was. She agreed it would be devastating to be rejected by your own child.

Callie shifted to stare out the side window. If Lauren was terrified of another relationship with a woman who already had children, she didn't have to worry. And she didn't have to worry about Becky getting too attached to Lauren. She'd keep Becky at arm's length. The knowledge of all that distance between them made Callie's heart ache.

CHAPTER TWENTY-ONE

"Here we are." Lauren slowed and turned into a property with a small white house and green barn. As soon as the truck stopped at the barn, Callie unlatched her seat belt and slid close. She brushed a tear off Lauren's cheek and dropped a kiss in its place. "We can stop talking about your children for now. I never meant to upset you."

Lauren nodded and wiped her eyes with a tissue. She missed her children and confessing to Callie that Sam and William had once rejected her was painful. It must make her look like a horrible mother, to have moved so far away from her kids just because the relationship broke down. And when put simply, that's what it looked like. But it went deeper than that.

"My friend is at work. If I gave you rubber boots for the barn would you hold the mare's head for a few minutes?" Lauren regained her composure and confidence and jumped out of the truck. She was in medical mode and that calmed her. Emotions, family, and relationships were confusing. Medicine was not.

Callie followed. "Sure, but size eleven, remember?"

"I borrowed Ian's old boots. They're a little big for you, but if you shuffle, they'll stay on your feet."

Lauren slipped on a pair of coveralls and lifted her medical kit from the truck. They switched boots and entered the barn. Lauren dropped their dress boots in the tack room. "I'll leave our boots here to keep them warm."

She led the way into the horse barn. There were four box stalls, and she unlatched the first door on the right. The mare was a bay with a white blaze and about the friendliest horse Lauren had ever met. She caught the horse, led her into the aisle, and handed the lead to Callie.

Callie caressed the mare between her eyes until the mare's head drooped with pleasure. "Oh, you are a sweetheart."

Lauren's cheeks warmed at the soft words and she wished they were for her. She unwrapped the bandaged leg and glanced at Callie. "I'm surprised you don't have horses. You have the barn and pasture."

Callie's eyes clouded, and she shrugged.

Lauren had the urge to punch herself. What stupid words had escaped from her mouth this time? Callie looked as if she were a kid who had lost her grip on a balloon and was watching it drift away.

After a moment of silence while Lauren worked on the horse's leg, Callie said, "I love horses, but I never learned to ride. Duke and Jake, Doug's horses, lived at Poplarcreek when Becky and I moved there. They were Liz's horses when she was younger. Doug told us Jake was an amazing barrel racer and had a true competitive spirit."

"Where'd they go?"

"Jake broke his leg while out on pasture. I don't know what happened, but Doug found a ton of ATV tracks near Jake's body. We knew it was something terrifying because Duke ran home alone. The poor guy was white with sweat and in a panic, so we went searching for Jake. Becky and I stayed with Jake. We did our best to keep him quiet and comfortable while we waited for the vet. I took Becky home when Doug arrived with Ian. If Jake were younger, surgery might have been an option. But, well, you know…"

"Somebody chased him on an ATV? People can be such jerks." The mare flinched, startled by the angry tone of Lauren's voice. She switched her tone to soothing. "Sorry, girl. You're all right. Everything's okay now."

"After Jake died, Becky cried for days. Losing Liz and then losing Liz's horse crushed her. Living with Doug and hearing about the adventures of Liz and Jake helped bring Becky closer to a mother she was desperate to know, but never would."

Callie sniffled and Lauren's eyes burned with unshed tears. She wished she could bring Liz home to Callie and fix her little family. Callie was a strong woman, but Lauren sensed the loneliness in her voice.

Callie shook her head. "Jake's death was also hard on Duke. He stopped eating and lost fifty pounds, so Doug shipped him to live with his sister in Alberta. We visited her farm last summer." Callie focused a watery smile on Lauren. "Duke has new horse friends. He's gained his weight back and then some. He has a distinct belly now."

"I'm glad he's doing well." Lauren returned the mare to her box stall. It was a sad story, and yet another reminder of the fact that Liz's ghost was alive and well in Callie's life. She couldn't compete with a woman who wasn't even there.

"She's a sweet animal. How's she doing?"

"Healing well, and no infection. She'll have a jagged scar, but she'll be fine other than that. Let's go to the tack room and switch boots."

Callie held Lauren's hand as they walked, and she still looked lost in memories. "Becky loved both of the old horses. One day at dinner she said, 'Now Mama can ride Jake again because he's in heaven with her.' Doug disappeared into his office and closed the door." Callie ran a sleeve over her eyes. "A parent never expects to outlive their child."

"I can't imagine how that would feel and I don't want to try." Lauren shoved away the idea that if something happened to her kids, it would take her two days to get back to Ontario.

Callie squeezed Lauren's forearm. "I apologize for upsetting you earlier."

"You didn't upset me. It was good to talk about it." Lauren studied Callie. "But are you okay?"

Callie shrugged and busied herself with her boots, then she dug around in her pockets. "Why is there never a tissue when you need one?"

Lauren extracted a paper towel from her kit and handed it over with a shrug. "Will this work?"

Callie nodded and blew her nose. Then, with a deep breath, she squared her shoulders. "Nostalgic day for both of us."

"Yeah." Lauren stared at Callie and rubbed her palms nervously on her pants. Callie seemed like she needed a hug, but would she welcome one? There had been some great kissing a week ago, but then things had cooled considerably. She didn't know where they stood. Her indecisiveness crippled her, and she stood like a statue.

Callie stepped forward, slipped her arms around Lauren's neck, and rested her head on Lauren's shoulder.

Lauren froze, startled at first, but then relaxed. Callie was naturally more relaxed about affection and it felt like heaven to hold her. She returned the hug and ran her hands in a soothing fashion up and down Callie's back.

Callie broke the hug first and stepped back. "You give great hugs."

Lauren blushed as she struggled for something meaningful to say. Defeated by her waffling, she picked up her gear with one hand and took Callie's with the other and led them out of the barn. Every nerve in her body warred between the excitement of holding her and the peace of being held. Confused and frustrated, she loaded her gear and they headed for home.

It was a quiet trip back to Poplarcreek. The conversation had drained her. She'd revealed more to Callie than she had to Val. Callie was leaning against the door with her head on the headrest. Lauren admired her ability to relax. Then she leaned forward and looked again. Callie was asleep in the sun, her face sweet and tranquil.

Lauren turned the radio down and drove them to Poplarcreek. She wasn't the only one drained.

Twenty minutes later, Lauren rubbed Callie's arm gently. "Callie, you're home. Callie?"

Callie stirred and stretched. "Did I fall asleep? What a lump I am. Sorry."

"No problem. You obviously needed the nap."

"Thanks for a great day. Do you want to come in and have dinner with us? Becky will be home soon and will have a million questions for you about the animals."

"Thanks, but I should do laundry tonight." The lamest reason in the world was all her head could muster and the confused expression on Callie's face announced that she wasn't buying it. The second-best escape route was diversion. "Max is ready to come home."

"That's wonderful news." Callie nudged her with a shoulder. "Do you deliver?"

"Sure. I could do that."

Callie climbed out of the truck. "Then bring him Friday after work and have dinner with us."

Lauren could only nod. She'd been cleverly backed into a corner. Her brain fired off escape routes, but then she said, "Okay, thanks."

As she drove home Lauren searched for a way to decline the invitation. Tonight, her tired brain only wanted the peace of her house. But maybe she did want to go to Poplarcreek? She most definitely wanted to see Callie again. She had two days to settle down and slot Callie into the friend zone.

On Friday night Lauren pulled into Poplarcreek and parked. She petted Max, who was curled on the seat beside her. "You're home." She was still embarrassed by the amount of personal detail she'd revealed, but Callie hadn't seemed to judge her. The next ten minutes would tell her what Callie thought of her. She was prepared to leave Max and head immediately back to Thresherton if she wasn't welcome at Poplarcreek.

Lauren exited the truck, carried Max to the door, and set him down. She knocked, then opened Callie's door and entered the mudroom. She stuck her head into the kitchen. "Hello to the house. Anybody home?"

Callie rounded the corner into her kitchen and sashayed up to Lauren. Callie gave her a warm hug.

Lauren tucked a loose strand of hair behind Callie's ear. "I enjoyed that welcome. What if I leave, then come back, and we do it again?"

Callie replied in a sultry voice. "I can't guarantee the second welcome will be the same."

"Is there a chance it might be warmer?" Lauren grinned. It was nice to flirt with Callie even if it went no further. There was no doubt that Callie wanted her there.

Becky bounded into the room like a rabbit on caffeine. Callie lowered her voice and backed away. "You'll never know now."

Becky bounced on her toes beside Callie. "Do you have our new puppy, Lauren?"

Lauren glanced at Callie. Becky was excited, but she didn't have a puppy with her. Why hadn't Callie prepared Becky? Max had healed, but he wasn't pretty. The fur she'd shaved off for the surgery hadn't grown back.

Callie rested her hands on Becky's shoulders and Becky looked up. "Becky, honey, it's not a puppy. Lauren brought Max home. He's our dog now. He's not a puppy, but he's only two. I hope Max is a nice surprise."

Lauren led Max inside. "Rebecca Anderson, please meet Maximilian Anderson." Max gazed at Becky and sat, his wagging tail brushing the floor. After a few seconds of being ignored, Max quit wagging and plopped on his belly with a sigh.

Lauren, eyebrows raised, looked at Callie.

Callie grimaced and lifted her shoulder in a half shrug.

Becky glanced at Callie. "Max is our dog? For keeps?"

Callie nodded, looking a little worried. "Yes. Is it okay? Max, I mean? He needs a home. I know I said puppy…"

"I like Max. Hi, Max." Becky held out her hand for him to sniff. She stroked him, which started Max wagging again. "Come see your new bed, Max."

Lauren handed her a rawhide bone. "He had major surgery two weeks ago, so no running and no going upstairs, yet."

"Okay, Lauren. Mommy and I have a bed for him in the living room." Lauren unclipped the leash, and Max hopped after Becky.

He stepped normally on his back legs and then did a bounce to take the place of the missing front leg.

Lauren watched them. "Max is slow now, but in a month when he's stronger you'll not catch him."

"Thanks for taking such good care of him. I never imagined you'd have him at the clinic this long," Callie said.

"It was unfortunate we had to deal with an infection. It meant we had to keep him longer and delay today's homecoming." She spared Callie the details, but the infection was serious, and she had put a drain in. That meant another surgery and anesthetic. Val helped her one evening and Lauren paid the clinic for the supplies they used. She'd spent Callie's eight hundred dollars in the first week. But she didn't need to know any of that.

Lauren handed Callie a small bottle of pills. "These are his antibiotics for another week. He's lost weight, so feed him as much as he'll eat." Lauren set a small bag of dog food on Callie's floor. "I recommend feeding him puppy food. It'll have more calories and nutrition per cup than regular adult dog food. Please call me anytime if he has problems. I like that little dog."

Callie wrapped her arms around Lauren's neck. "Perfect." Then Callie bent her head and kissed her.

Lauren slid her arms around Callie's waist and deepened the kiss. In the back of her mind she worried that Becky would return and see them, but it felt as if a line of fire shot down her body and landed at the base of her stomach. The strange mixture of arousal and fear caused her stomach to flip, and not in a nice way. Why couldn't she relax and enjoy herself? When they broke apart, they stood staring into each other's eyes. Callie's eyes had turned darker than their usual blue. Callie was all arousal. No fear in her. They separated and Lauren could breathe again.

When Becky and Max returned, Callie focused on the dinner preparations. She'd prepared a wonderful chili and had baked fresh bread to go with it. It should have been a happy meal, but Lauren spent much of it in a state of conflict. She was attracted to Callie, and it petrified her that Callie was attracted to her. Becky was a great kid, and she was becoming attached to her, but she would only get her heart broken if it didn't work out between them. She'd already lost enough.

Being with Becky triggered memories and Lauren longed for her daughter. Becky had the same brown hair and brown eyes as Sam, and the same interest in everything to do with animals. In Toronto when Lauren returned to the clinic in the evening, Sam had often accompanied her. When he was younger, William had helped too.

Callie waved her hand in front of Lauren's face. "Hello, Lauren, are you there?"

Lauren shook her head to clear her thoughts and focused on Callie. "Pardon?"

"Becky asked for help with her biology homework."

"My project is on the cow. I have to report on their digestive system." Becky frowned at an escaping bean on her plate.

Lauren hesitated for a second. More time meant more connection.

Becky fiddled with her cutlery and in a small voice said, "It's okay if you're too busy."

Callie frowned at Lauren.

Lauren mustered her enthusiasm. There was no need to hurt her feelings. But maybe she needed to make herself a little more scarce in the future. She wasn't part of this family. "Sure, Becky, no problem. Where do you want to work?"

Becky bounced in her chair. "Upstairs, please."

"You two go ahead. I'll put the leftovers away and wash the dishes," Callie said.

Forty minutes later, Lauren left Becky to her project and walked downstairs. She found Callie reading in the living room, in front of an inviting wood fire. She hesitated in the doorway until Callie lowered her book and sent her a warm smile.

Callie patted the couch beside her. "Thanks for helping Becky."

"She's a great kid." Lauren plopped beside Callie.

"She's enthusiastic about this project. She likes anything to do with animals. May I call you next time she asks for help with her history or math homework?"

"Not my subjects, I'm afraid."

Callie was joking, but the thought of doing that kind of regular homework made Lauren feel panicky. "Becky showed me her drawings of you and the cattle. I could tell they were you."

"Correction. She likes art and anything to do with animals."

Lauren had difficulty concentrating. She thought if she focused on Callie's lips while she spoke, she could follow her words. It didn't help. At all.

Lauren said, "Becky's smart. She'll learn what she needs to and buckle down."

"I admire your confidence."

Lauren choked on her coffee and wiped her mouth. Callie thought she was confident? Boy, had Callie read her wrong.

"I never thanked you for helping a week ago when I told you about Kyle borrowing my trailer. Sorry. I should have done it sooner. You kept me sane that night." Callie nudged her with her shoulder. "Thanks for talking me out of taking an ax to my trailer. What a mess it would've been."

Lauren scrutinized Callie for a few seconds. Was she going to talk about how that night ended? Maybe Lauren staying and holding her had meant nothing to Callie. She had just been a stand-in for Liz. "No problem. On our last trip I filled our time talking about me." She stood and wandered to the bookshelf. She tipped her head and read a few titles as she browsed but absorbed nothing. "Do you remember what happened after we went to bed?"

Callie shot to her feet. "Did I do something that made you uncomfortable? I remember you holding me." Callie stepped closer. "I felt warm and safe in your arms."

Lauren bent and spoke while she petted Max. "You stirred in the morning and I kissed you. You pulled my hand over your breast." She straightened and jammed her hands in her pockets. "Then you said Liz's name. I thought at first you were awake, but you were asleep. Maybe you were dreaming of her?"

Callie shook her head. "I recall the cuddling, but nothing more." Callie dropped to the couch. "I remember hands on my breasts, but I thought it was a dream." Callie looked at Lauren. "It was nice."

"I won't be a stand-in for Liz, Callie."

"You can't expect me to control my subconscious. I don't remember saying her name, so I must've been asleep. I always felt safe with her, and that night I was scared. When I'm scared my mind turns to the person I love. The person who protects me." Callie's tone was neutral.

"She wasn't there. I was. And I can't compete with Liz. She was perfect." Lauren spoke louder than she intended as she forced the words past the lump in her throat.

"She was *not* perfect." Callie shrugged, her expression closed off. "I have no control over what I say in my sleep. Liz was always my protector. In my head, I don't need protection and I don't want it, but that night thoughts of her appeared. I'm sorry if I upset you."

"Thanks for helping me to understand." Lauren snatched her empty coffee mug off the table and carried it to the kitchen. Even when she was the one there, it had been thoughts of Liz that Callie turned to. "Anyway, getting late." She wrenched on her coat and shoved her feet into boots. "Thanks for dinner."

"Thank you for bringing Max home." They studied each other for several seconds until Callie leaned forward and kissed her on the cheek.

Lauren gave a quick wave and headed home. How could she compete with Liz's memory? Liz was confident, not an insecure chicken. And there was the obvious. She jabbed at her soft stomach and glanced at her round face in the rearview mirror. Liz had been a police officer, fit and strong.

Lauren struggled to tamp down her insecurities. She wanted to understand Callie, but it wasn't easy. Could she replace Liz? Part of her longed to flee, but Callie peppered her with invitations and little caresses she found difficult to resist. Besides her obvious beauty, Callie was warm and generous, and stronger than she gave herself credit for. Callie was irresistible and Lauren did not want to resist.

She slammed her hand on the stirring wheel. "I'm a waste of space. Useless. Useless to Callie, useless to my kids, and useless to myself." Maybe the solution was to move again. She liked Thresherton and PVS, but if her life here had become a train wreck she would do better to move on. She'd be running away, but staying to face life's difficulties was overrated. If she left it would solve everyone's problems. There'd have been less drama in her life if she'd left T.J. when she first wanted to, but instead, she'd hung on for years hoping life would improve.

And then there was Becky. So like Sam. She'd hurt Sam and William with the divorce and abandonment. And now they would spend thirty years in therapy talking about how bad a mother Lauren was. She shook her head. She should come with a warning label. *Beware. This woman will destroy you.* She wanted to be in love in a stable relationship, but she lacked the necessary skills. Her brain wasn't wired properly. It was time to accept the fact that she was a failure.

Lauren nodded. She'd stay away from Callie and if Callie objected, she'd give her T.J.'s number. One phone call would no doubt help Callie see she and Becky were better off without her. Better off with a strong woman like Liz or Mitch, not a wimp and a loser like her.

CHAPTER TWENTY-TWO

Callie served Lauren a cup of coffee. She had invited Lauren for afternoon coffee anytime she was in the area and had time to visit. The days were busy, and Callie looked forward to their time together as an oasis in the storm she perpetually lived in. Veterinary bills piled up, Becky needed things for school, the farm equipment needed updating, and the house was in desperate need of attention.

Kyle had stopped coming around, and she rarely saw the Krugers, but when she did, she didn't miss the vitriol in their eyes. Some days, it simply felt like too much. Her time with Lauren helped ground her and she was coming to depend on it, even though she'd sworn not to depend on anyone ever again. They hadn't talked any more about Lauren's concerns about Liz's memory, and they left the topic of Lauren's kids alone, too. It probably wasn't good there were things they were avoiding, but Callie was happy to enjoy the simplicity of what they had. For the moment. It had taken a bit of cajoling on her part to even get Lauren to come by, and she didn't want her to take off again.

Callie set a steaming mug of coffee in front of Lauren. "I have muffins too, if you want one. I hope you can come back for dinner tonight. We had fun on Friday." Callie laughed. "My kid was excited this morning. And that's unusual for a Monday. It's because her project on the cow's digestive system was finished and she was feeling good about it. Thanks for helping her."

"No problem."

Callie sat across from Lauren and focused on her. "She said the oddest thing. She said she would be a big girl from now on and do her projects on her own."

"That is odd."

"It is. Any idea why she would say that? Did you really not mind helping?"

Lauren sighed and pinched the bridge of her nose. "Callie, I can't do this."

"Do what? Have coffee and chat? Come back for dinner? It was fine on Friday night when you brought Max home. What's changed in three days?"

Lauren shrugged

"So not fine. Is it Liz again? And my saying her name in my sleep?"

Lauren shrugged.

Callie stared at Lauren in frustration. Was she supposed to guess? Was she supposed to list everything that wasn't perfect in her life and see if Lauren latched on to one item? She was a widow, with a child, she had a farm she could barely run, she had a debt load that was barely manageable. If Lauren wanted perfection she was at the wrong place. And perfect didn't exist. Not to mention, it wasn't like she was asking for a lifetime commitment. Would flirty friendship be so hard? "Is it Kruger? You're worried about him."

"Given everything Kyle's done it only makes sense.

"Kyle is a loser. I can't believe I gave him so much power over me."

"Scary loser."

"Scary? Did he come after you? If he hurt you, I'll—"

Lauren held up her hands. "Nothing happened. He just spooked me. Showed up at the clinic late at night pretending he had a calving, but there was no cow. Just his creepy behavior and threats."

"Threats? He threatened you? No way. Not again." She grabbed her phone. "I'm calling the police. We'll stop this now."

"I spoke to Mitch right after it happened. She said she'd talk to Kyle, but there's nothing to prove and Tommy was my only witness.

Kyle just said I should leave Thresherton or learn to shut up. I did neither. It's just that I felt a little exposed. I was alone and there was nobody waiting at home to miss me."

The loneliness in Lauren's voice tugged at Callie's heart. At Poplarcreek, she had no other adults to depend on, but with Becky, she was less lonely. The loneliness she couldn't solve, but she could help against the Krugers. "When was this?"

"Day after we went to the police?"

Callie paced her kitchen. "Why didn't you tell me?"

"What would you do? Besides, you have enough to worry about from them."

Callie dropped to her knees in front of Lauren and took her hands. "Do you think you don't matter? I care about you."

Lauren smiled at her.

"And Becky does too."

Lauren's smile slipped. She slowly withdrew her hands and looked away.

Callie grabbed Lauren's knees and gave them a shake. "Are you being weird because of Becky?" She ended on an incredulous squeak. "I thought you liked her?"

"Damn it. I do. Too much, but she's tied to you, and if we break up, then I lose her too. I know this. I've lived this." She dropped her face into her hands. "I wouldn't survive again," she muttered.

"What? Break up? How did you get there? A few meals and a few cups of coffee, combined with some fooling around, does not make a relationship." Just the notion that they were in a relationship made her twitch.

"I just meant if we were, or if we, you know. William barely speaks to me and Sam is just coming around, but it's like I have to start over with her."

Callie moved back to her chair. She needed some distance. She struggled to keep her tone neutral as Lauren crumbled before her eyes. "I'm sorry they hurt you and I believe you're a wonderful parent, even if you're not sure. But it's not our situation today. Don't plan our breakup before we're even a couple."

Lauren stood. "I should go. I'm making a mess of this."

"Don't run. Talk. Help me to understand where you're coming from. I got the impression Becky thinks you don't like her, and I'm confused."

"It's not like that."

"Then stay and say hi." Callie glanced at the clock. "She'll be home soon."

"Next time." Lauren pulled her coat on and stepped into her boots.

"This is so frustrating. I don't get it, but you should know, Becky comes first with me. Always has and always will. The health and happiness of my child is my priority." Callie shook her head to dismiss the conversation. If Lauren was conflicted about Becky, they had no future. And truthfully, getting involved this far had clearly been a huge mistake.

Without another word, Lauren left.

Callie poured their coffee down the drain. She was going to wash their dishes, but it was more likely she'd bounce the mugs of the wall if she picked them up. She pressed her temples. Lauren had some struggles with her children, but how did it come around to Becky?

Callie shook her head, yanked on a coat and boots, and jogged to the road. She greeted Becky when she exited the bus and walked her to the house. They hung their coats on hooks and kicked off boots.

Callie hugged her. "Would you like a hot chocolate?"

"Was I bad, Mommy?" Becky gazed at her feet.

Callie squatted in front of her. "No, honey, why?"

"I just saw Lauren's truck. She left so she wouldn't have to see me. She doesn't want to be *my* friend."

Callie caressed Becky's cheek. "Yes, she does."

"She drove right by. Didn't even wave."

Callie swallowed hard. Could Becky be right? "No, sweetie. She's your friend. I'm sure she just didn't see you. She left because we argued. We have to make up, but we're still friends."

Becky shrugged.

"Is something else bothering you?"

Becky dropped onto a chair. Max laid his head on her thigh and she petted him. Becky's words burst from her in a rush. "If you want me to go away, I'll go."

Callie kneeled beside Becky's chair with her hands pressed to her aching heart. "Oh, honey, why do you say that?"

"You can get rid of me. Give me away. Same as Mrs. Macpherson gave Max away. I don't make you happy."

"I love you. You're my daughter and my pal. The best thing in my life." Tears flowing down her face, Callie shook her head in horror at Becky's words. She yearned to hug Becky and promise it would be all right, but she hesitated because now was the time to listen.

"With Mama you laughed and smiled. When Mama died, you cried all the time and were no fun. Sometimes Grandma Wilkins had to make you eat."

"I'm so sorry."

"Then we moved to Saskatchewan and lived with Grandpa Anderson and you were fun again. We painted my room, went on hikes to the creek, and you taught me to play basketball. Then Grandpa died, and you cried again and didn't see me anymore."

"Oh, Becky, honey, I'm sorry." Callie grappled for words to reassure her. Becky's words stunned her. Had she been so blinded by grief she'd left her daughter alone in hers? "I was hurting and missing Grandpa and Mama. Just like you. I let myself get overwhelmed by that. But it doesn't mean I don't love you and you're the one thing that's always perfect in my life."

"When Lauren's here, you're happy." Becky glanced at Callie. "You sing and dance in the kitchen. You're dressing all pretty when you go to town. Lauren makes you happy. I don't." Becky spoke with a strangled cry as if she was tearing apart. "And Lauren was nice. She showed me how a calf was born and let me hold the kittens, but now she doesn't see me either. And I know she didn't want to help me with my project."

"Lauren likes you too. But sometimes she's confused, like when you can't decide if you want a Popsicle or ice cream." Okay, it was more serious than that, but how could she explain what she didn't understand? "Just because you pick a Popsicle, doesn't mean you don't like ice cream." She wanted to knock her head against the wall. She usually had no trouble communicating with Becky.

"Mommy, I don't understand. Am I ice cream or a Popsicle?"

"I'm just saying that Lauren likes you. Even if she sometimes acts funny, it's not because she doesn't like you."

Becky shrugged. "So, Lauren's mixed up?"

"Exactly." Callie wanted to cry with relief. Becky had summed them up in four words. "She's mixed up about her life. What she wants and what to do. And I'm mixed up, too. You're fine. You're awesome."

"Can I stay?" Becky asked in a small voice.

Callie hauled Becky off the chair and into her lap. She wrapped Becky in her arms and held her tight. They cried together as Callie rocked her. "Oh, Becky, I love you. You're my daughter and I want you with me always."

Later, Callie sat in her living room with her head cradled in her hands. Too upset to eat dinner, Becky had gone to bed. It took an hour of Callie reading to her before Becky fell asleep. Constant reassuring had only taken the edge off her anxiety. If her relationship with Lauren harmed Becky it was doomed. Her heart squeezed in pain at the thought of losing Lauren, but Becky was her priority. And clearly, she needed to show her just how important she was to her. She'd promised herself a relationship wouldn't get in her way, and she'd allowed what she had with Lauren to do just that.

It was time to step back and get the three of them on even footing. Her attraction to Lauren was strong, but it was a chemical thing and she would tamp it down. They had become friends and that was good enough. She'd not let it go further again. Especially not if it caused them all pain.

CHAPTER TWENTY-THREE

The day after her argument with Callie, Lauren shuffled through the clinic in a daze. She did her job but had no energy for small talk with clients or the endless chatting with the staff. When she could, she escaped into her office and hid. She only emerged to see patients.

As Lauren placed a cat in its cage, Val approached her. "Are you coming to my party this weekend?"

Lauren shrugged. "Sure, thanks."

"I invited Callie."

Lauren whirled. "Oh no. Why did you do that? We had a fight yesterday. Tell her not to come."

Val winced. "I didn't realize you two were on the outs. You didn't tell me."

"Now you know." She was being petulant but didn't care.

"I can't uninvite Callie. That would be rude and mean. If you have a problem being near her, stay home." Val smiled. "Besides, I like Callie. I want her to come to my party."

Lauren's face flushed with anger. "What do you mean?"

"Hold your horses there, L.C. I've got Christine." Val put her hands up with palms out and stepped back. "Gwen and Becky are friends and that's thrown Callie and me together. I'm not after Callie, but I guarantee others in the community will pursue her if you're out of the picture."

Lauren's fists balled at her sides. "Who?"

"Suzanne Mitchell, for one. You know, Mitch the super cop. She's been a friend of Callie's and Becky's since they all lived in British Columbia."

"Yeah, I've met Mitch. You ever date her?"

"No way. She towers over me. My face is level with her boobs." Val laughed. "I like butch, but she's too intense. Also, she doesn't like to dance, and I do."

Lauren's shoulders drooped as she changed from angry to despondent. She felt as if she was drowning and land was out of reach. "I've met Mitch. Do you think Callie prefers ultra butches with flat stomachs?" Lauren straightened her top and splayed her fingers over her soft middle. "Yeah, probably."

Val's expression was sympathetic. "Are you comparing yourself to Mitch or Liz?"

"Both." Fear sabotaged Lauren's resolve and crushed her confidence.

"What are you afraid of?" Val asked.

"I wish I knew. I'm all twisted in knots. Is it possible to be afraid of being happy?"

"Is it Becky?"

Lauren sighed. "Imagine if Gwen told you to go away, forever. Imagine how devastating that would feel."

"That doesn't make sense. Are you talking about Callie, Sam, Becky, or Gwen? Have you considered discussing your situation with a therapist? I'll give you the phone number of mine. I spent hours talking to her when my ex-girlfriend dumped me and moved to Vancouver." Val scribbled a number down and handed the scrap of paper to Lauren. "Call her."

Lauren shuffled her feet. "I can handle it on my own."

"You only think you can. If you blow it with Callie because you're scared of whatever, then you're not handling it." Val put air quotes around the last two words.

"I'll think about it. Maybe you're right. I've been pretty out of it today, I'm sorry." Val was right. Lauren was messing up everywhere. Her new start here was turning into a muddy pool.

Lauren looked up and frowned at Janice's smirking face.

Janice leaned against the doorjamb. "Poplarcreek is calling for help, again. That woman must have PVS on speed dial." Janice snickered. "Surprise, surprise. She's having another calving problem."

"Can't Ian or Fiona go?" Val asked.

"Nope. I sent Ian to Kruger Farm and Fiona to Starview."

Janice walked away before Lauren could respond. "How much do you think she heard?"

"Nothing," Val said.

"What if she tells people I'm chasing a client or behaving unprofessionally? What if clients don't want to see me anymore? They could insist on seeing only Ian or Fiona. I'd have to move again. I've worked so hard to build a good reputation in Thresherton. I need this job and my career." Some days it felt like PVS was the only solid, reliable thing she had left. As if she were clinging to the edge of precipice and being a veterinarian was the rope that kept her from falling. It was irrelevant that she'd considered moving only the day before. She didn't want to *have* to.

"Whoa, L.C. Don't panic." Val tapped the paper with the phone number that was clutched in Lauren's hand. "Therapist. Call her. Today."

Lauren nodded, but right now her problems didn't matter. The animals needed help. Lauren changed her clothes, fetched her kits, and trudged to her truck. She yanked the door open, tossed her kits in the back, and climbed inside. Her hands trembled on the steering wheel.

Thirty minutes later, Lauren arrived at Poplarcreek. "Hello, Mrs. Anderson. How are you doing today? Beautiful sunny weather."

Callie crossed her arms and shifted her weight to one hip. "What's this, Lauren? Why the stupid perky voice and the Mrs. Anderson shit?"

"What's wrong with the way I'm talking?" Lauren attempted to sound neutral as she busied herself with her equipment to avoid eye contact.

"You're being phony, and it doesn't suit you."

Lauren shrugged. "What do you mean? I'm being professional and detached."

"Detached? Is that how you want it?" Callie's voice caught as she spoke.

Arms loose at her sides and palms out, Lauren faced Callie. "I don't know what to do or what to say. Every time I open my mouth, I say something wrong." When they had fought, Callie had summarized what they had as "a few dates and some fooling around." Now Callie was criticizing her for being detached. Which was it?

Callie glared at Lauren for a few seconds. "You're right. Forget it. Let's start over. Welcome to my farm, Dr. Cornish. Lovely weather we're having, but still cool. Please, follow me to the barn, to help my heifer, her—" Callie sighed, her eyes closed.

Lauren longed to wipe the pain from Callie's expression. But that wouldn't help them move forward. "Pardon? I couldn't hear your last sentence. What's been happening?"

Callie studied Lauren and spoke louder than necessary. "Her calf is stuck, and I can't fix it." After her outburst, Callie dropped her face into her hands. When Lauren tentatively touched Callie's shoulder, she shrugged her off. Callie wiped her eyes on her sleeve and stalked toward the barn.

Lauren followed, shaking her head. "Messed up again," she muttered.

In the barn, Callie fetched the light, rope and buckets of water while Lauren organized her equipment. "What's been happening? What have you tried?"

"Well, Dr. Cornish, I found two legs, but no head and I can't pull it out."

Callie's sharp tone sliced through Lauren and she winced. "Back legs?"

"No, both front. Forget the lesson. Just pull the calf out and go away." Callie stormed from the barn.

The heifer was lying in the straw. Lauren washed her hands, slid on an OB glove, and reached inside the heifer. Callie was right, it was two front legs and one calf, but its nose had caught on the pelvis. Lauren's blood pressure shot up a notch. After a struggle, she slipped the head into position. Lauren grasped the calf's front feet and heaved, but it didn't come. She searched for Callie to help, but she was gone. Lauren ran to her truck and fetched the calving jack. This was the reason it was a mistake to become involved with clients. With anyone, really. Lauren assembled her calving jack while she muttered to herself.

"What's that?"

Lauren glimpsed Callie hovering over her. "A calving jack, or calf jack. A tool to help pull out a big calf when you're alone."

"Oh?" Curiosity crept into Callie's voice.

Lauren worked fast and described what she was doing, more out of habit than because she wanted any conversation. "The jack has a U-shaped piece attached on the end of a long metal pole, with a winch on the pole. First, I loop the chains on its legs." Lauren slipped the chains into place. "The trick is to put the U-shaped end around the back end of the cow." She demonstrated. "Then attach the calving chains to the winch and winch the calf out by pumping this handle."

Callie hovered above Lauren. "As easy as that?"

"Sometimes I have to winch quickly to get the calf out fast. Today is one of those days. This calf is in distress." Lauren winched, pumping as fast as she could. "In a normal birth, when the cow pushes, I winch. When she stops, I stop. That keeps the calving more natural and reduces the risk of damage to the cow and calf."

After a minute, the calf slid onto the straw with a whoosh. Lauren examined it and removed the chains. She shook her head and sat back on her heels. Instead of white or beige, its fur was stained yellow. "Damn."

Callie kneeled and rubbed the calf. Then she stuck a piece of straw in its nose to stimulate it to sneeze and clear its nose.

"Don't bother," Lauren said. "It won't help. He didn't make it. Poor thing."

Callie rubbed frantically. "Do something. Give him a shot of stimulant."

"It won't help. I'm sorry. He's dead and has been for a while."

Tears gathered in Callie's eyes as she focused on Lauren. "What happened? Why?"

Lauren needed to tell the truth, even if it made things worse between them. "Well, maybe…"

"Maybe?"

"His head was caught on the heifer's pelvis and she couldn't push him out."

"But you fixed it."

"How long was she calving?"

Callie shrugged. "I didn't realize she was ready. When I found her in the paddock, she was already straining." Her eyes went wide as she stared at Lauren. "Did I wait too long to call you? I screwed around too long trying to pull the calf myself, didn't I?"

That was probably the case, but there was no need to rub it in. "I'm not sure it would've helped if you'd called as soon as you found her. You did your best."

Callie stroked the calf's neck. Tears slipped down her cheeks and landed on its damp fur. "I should've stayed with you to help instead of sulking."

"It wouldn't have made any difference. He was already dead when I arrived," Lauren said.

"It's all my fault. I'm hopeless." Callie jumped to her feet and plunged her dirty hands into the bucket of hot water. She snatched the brush floating in the bucket and scrubbed her hands until they were red. Then she wiped her wet hands on her jacket as she paced. "Why did you tell me to deliver my own calves? I should never have tried. Now the calf is dead. Heinz Kruger's right. I can't do this."

Lauren pushed off the ground as if she were a hundred years old. She washed her hands, scrubbing gently, and dried them on an old towel. Then she stepped to one side as Callie paced. "Don't blame yourself. We can't tell when she started. The calf may already have been dead when you found her."

"But we don't know."

"No, we don't, and we can't know. This kind of thing happens, Callie."

Callie turned her back to Lauren and covered her face with her hands. "I'm so stupid. I shouldn't have tried."

"Please don't beat yourself up. It was bad luck. That's all."

"That was the last of my heifers to calve. Will the older cows need help?"

"Some may."

Callie whirled and pointed at Lauren. "Then I'm calling you if I see any problems."

"Okay, but you *can* do it. I know you can, and Heinz is a jerk. He's not right about anything. Please don't listen to him."

Callie swiped at her cheeks and shook her head.

Lauren stepped toward Callie, but her arms hung at her sides. They weighed a thousand pounds and she couldn't lift them. If she touched Callie would she brush her off again? She longed to hold Callie and kiss the tears from her eyes. Lauren understood the self-loathing and despair that swarmed a person when an animal died. The dead calf had shaken Callie's confidence, but she had to attempt a calving again or she would never recover.

Callie's eyes bored into Lauren's face as if searching for something. Then Callie's shoulders slumped, and she studied the ground. "If the cows don't need help, I guess I won't see you anymore?"

Too scared to speak and too scared to move, Lauren did nothing.

Callie scrutinized her for a few more seconds. Then she turned and sprinted from the barn.

Lauren dragged the dead calf out of the pen. She cleaned her equipment and stowed it in her kit. Disappointed and feeling inadequate, she carried her calving kits to the truck and packed them away. She washed her boots, dumped the dirty water, and tossed her bucket and brush with more force than necessary into the truck. She scanned the farmyard for Callie but couldn't find her. Not sure if she was relieved or disappointed, Lauren hauled herself into her truck and drove off.

Callie's voice and posture had screamed defeat, and Lauren had yearned to say something meaningful about the dead calf. And about their fight. Their ridiculous fight. Callie was better off without her. Everyone was better off without her. Callie had enough stress in her life she didn't need a friend or whatever they were to complicate it. Callie needed strong and steady. Not weak and waffling.

And what did she need? Lauren needed peace and stability. She was connecting with Sam and William again and needed to concentrate on the hurt she'd caused them. And she needed to stay away from Poplarcreek to avoid hurting Becky. Lauren nodded. The best place for her was a thousand kilometers from Poplarcreek.

Chapter Twenty-four

L auren? Lauren, are you there?" Ian waved a hand in front of her face.

"Did you say something?" She couldn't concentrate. It had been two days since she'd delivered the dead calf at Poplarcreek. She'd picked up the phone a dozen times to call Callie and chickened out. Every time the front door of the clinic opened, she listened for a certain voice.

"I said I need you to go to Kruger Farm. Heinz called and his most valuable bull has sliced his shoulder open. Sorry to send you, but he's demanding a veterinarian this morning. Fiona is off today, and Janice says my schedule is full."

"How badly injured is the bull?"

"Janice said it's a deep wound. Be prepared to suture him."

"I'll go, but Heinz doesn't let me near his bulls. He only trusts you."

"True, but he wants you today. Bulldozer's a valuable animal."

Lauren swallowed with difficulty, and every drop of moisture vanished from her throat. The Krugers had gone largely silent since the police had started nosing around, but the last thing she wanted to do was go to their farm, where she'd be alone with them.

She hadn't told Ian and Fiona about the altercation at the clinic with Kyle and Tommy. About how Kyle had lured her to the clinic and threatened her. She should have done it right away, but she worried Ian would take the Krugers' side. He wouldn't do that, or would he? Kruger Farm was a big client and Ian had known Heinz for over twenty years. What if he saw it as only a misunderstanding? She *was* the outsider after all. But it was broad daylight and there were other people around. There was nothing to fear.

Lauren sighed. How could she explain her spinning thoughts to Ian without looking like the wimp she was? "Bulldozer?"

"He's their biggest bull."

"Would it be too much to hope the dozer part of his name is because he's a sleepy little guy?" Lauren crossed her fingers and prayed.

Ian chuckled. "He weighs twenty-five hundred pounds. They called him Bulldozer because he flattens anything in his path."

"Okay." Lauren squared her shoulders. She wasn't afraid of bulls. Proper facilities would keep her safe. It was Heinz and Kyle Kruger who unnerved her.

"You'll be fine. They have an adjustable squeeze chute, big enough for bulls."

Lauren had used the squeeze at Kruger Farm at an earlier visit for some cows. The chute resembled a cage of solid steel bars designed to hold cattle. Heinz's headgate was top quality and opened far enough to let an animal's head through before closing to encircle their neck. The headgate wasn't tight around their neck, but it restrained the animal and kept it from moving more than a step in any direction. The steel bars along the side of the chute protected Lauren if the animal kicked.

"No problem, Ian." Determination pumped through her veins as Lauren packed her gear and switched her lab coat for coveralls and boots. When she arrived at Kruger Farm, Kyle and Tommy were waiting for her. Tommy stood with his arms at his sides and the same inscrutable expression on his face as always. Since Tommy's wife left him and had taken their three children, she'd heard that Tommy only spoke when he had to.

Kyle lounged against the farm gate with one foot on the bottom rung and smoked a cigarette. Lauren parked, collected her medical kit, and walked toward the brothers. Kyle was five feet eight inches of grease, dirt, and yellow teeth. He made her skin crawl.

"How ya doing today, Doc?" Kyle spat into the dirt.

Lauren walked toward the big squeeze chute. "Good, thanks. I'm here to see Bulldozer."

"Wrong way, Doc." Kyle snickered. "Chute's broke, but we got Bulldozer locked in his pen."

Lauren skidded to a halt and squinted skyward for five seconds. She took a deep breath, determined not to show any fear. "No problem. Let's go."

They had locked Bulldozer in the headgate located in the corner of his pen. His pen led to a barn with a door to allow them to move the bull inside without handling the dangerous animal. The headgate prevented Bulldozer from escaping, but there was no other protection for Lauren if he kicked out. She glanced at the laceration on the bull's shoulder. Could she treat it and keep out of the way of its hooves?

She stuffed gauze and a bottle of iodine in her pocket and entered the pen, staying as close to the bull's head and shoulders as possible. "It's not too bad." Lauren cleaned the wound, unable to hide the relief in her voice. "It's just a deep scratch. It'll heal well, if you keep it clean. No need for sutures."

"Bulldozer's a good bull. He gave Callie those free calves her heifers are having. Those should be mine," Kyle whined.

Lauren scrutinized the huge bull. The poor heifers wouldn't have been half his size when he jumped on their backs and bred them. No wonder there were so many dystocias at Poplarcreek. She continued to clean the wound, relieved that Kyle wasn't standing behind her for once. But that in itself was strange. Kyle was fussing near Bulldozer's head and telling him he was a good bull. Maybe he cared about his animals? He certainly didn't give a shit about people.

A second later, Lauren was in midair. She flew ten feet backward until her back smashed into the barn. The impact knocked the breath from her, and dazed, she slid down the wall into the dirty snow. When her vision cleared, she gasped at the sight of Bulldozer lumbering toward her.

The bull lowered his massive head and pressed down against her chest as if he intended to grind her into the ground. Lauren couldn't do anything to prevent him from crushing her. Too stunned to scream or cry, she waited, expecting something to break inside. But then Bulldozer raised his head and sauntered off to the corner of his pen to munch on a bale of hay. He acted as if he'd swatted an annoying fly.

The men charged into the pen, with Tommy dragging Kyle by the arm. Kyle tiptoed between Lauren and bull. "Hurry, bro, before he sees us," Kyle muttered between clenched teeth.

Strong arms lifted Lauren and carried her from the pen. Tommy looked as if he might cry. Perplexed and disoriented, Lauren wondered why. She was the one flattened. She deserved to cry, and as soon as she could, she would, but right now her chest wouldn't move. Every breath was agony. Tommy lowered Lauren gently to a bench and kneeled to peer into her face.

Kyle slunk toward them. "What a hit. You're lucky he's got no horns." He didn't look in the least concerned, and there was no question that the look he gave her was a reminder of his earlier threats.

"Kyle, shut up and go away." Tommy's voice was full of anger and a hint of danger. Kyle held up his hands and scurried away. Tommy focused on Lauren. "Are you all right, Lauren? Can you speak? Your back's bleeding."

Lauren shifted an inch and gasped in pain. "A nail or something sharp stuck me when I hit the barn. I think it cut my back when I slid down the wall." Her words emerged as a croak. Every word and every breath were painful. "It's probably what cut Bulldozer. Fix it so he isn't hurt again." It was ironic that she wanted to protect the health of the animal that attacked her.

"Do you want an ambulance?"

"No, thanks. It'd take them thirty minutes, and I don't think anything's broken. I'm only bruised. Help me to my truck?" She would have insisted on an ambulance for anybody else, but she refused to wait. All she wanted was to escape from Kruger Farm.

Tommy helped Lauren to her feet and half carried her to her truck. She spread a pair of clean coveralls on the back of her seat to keep the blood off it and crawled into the cab. Her back and chest ached, but her head was clear.

Tommy said, "Sorry about that, Lauren." Then gave her one last concerned glance and shut her door.

While Tommy collected her equipment and stowed it in her truck, Lauren called PVS and explained the bull had knocked her to the ground. She told them Bulldozer would be okay and promised she was only sore and winded and would go home for the rest of the day. Tommy, his hands stuffed in his pockets, stood there watching her drive away. She watched in her rearview until she turned onto the road, but there was no sign of Kyle.

At home, Lauren swallowed a couple ibuprofen. She stripped off her clothes and staggered into the shower. Her back stung, and pink water swirled around her feet. Peering at the water was a mistake as it nauseated and disoriented her. She steadied herself against the wall of the shower until her head cleared. Bulldozer's attack was mild compared to what it could have been.

It was always a danger treating an animal that size without it in a chute. Had Kyle let Bulldozer out of the headgate on purpose? There was no way to know, but she wouldn't have put it past him. One second, she was treating the animal, the next, his massive head was slamming into her chest. She dried off and crawled into bed.

As her eyes fluttered closed, a small warm body stretched along her legs. "Hey, Digi. Hey, big guy, stay off my back, please." When she slept on her stomach, Digit often curled between her shoulder blades to sleep. Today, he didn't. It was as if he sensed she was sore.

Lauren woke to concerned blue eyes gazing into hers and a hand stroking her face. "Lauren, Lauren, wake up, baby."

Baby. She called me baby. Lauren pressed her cheek into Callie's warm palm and closed her eyes. She longed to slide closer to Callie's heat and the comfort of her.

"Get her to sit on the side of the bed."

The deep booming voice shattered the fantasy, and Lauren shot awake as the male voice invaded her bedroom. She half rose and jerked toward the voice, causing a shooting pain to slice from her neck to her lower back. With a groan of agony, she collapsed on the bed. She took a second to focus. It was the local doctor in her room, with Callie beside him.

"I can get up." She cleared her throat and blushed. "I can get up, but I'm not wearing anything."

"Get her a towel or something, Callie. Lauren, hold it in front of you and sit so I can examine you."

When he left the room, Callie passed Lauren a robe. Lauren held it in front of her and sat on the edge of the bed, groaning with every movement.

When the doctor returned, he examined her back and neck, and listened to her lungs. With the robe lowered a few inches, he listened to her chest and inspected her arms. "You should go to the hospital."

"I'm just sore."

He probed her ribs. "Nothing broken. Lie on your stomach."

She turned over and winced when he started dabbing at her back. "That stings."

"I'm cleaning the wound and then I'll bandage it."

"Thanks," Lauren said.

"There. That's done. Callie, can I talk to you?" he said.

Callie bent until her eyes were on level with Lauren's. "I'm going to talk to the doctor and come right back. Okay if I stay for a bit?"

"I don't want to be annoying."

Callie ran her fingertips over Lauren's cheek. "You're not annoying."

"I'm surprised to see you."

"Val called me. She couldn't get away from the clinic and was worried about you. She told me where you hide your spare key."

"Thanks, Callie."

Callie straightened and pointed at Lauren. "Now stay right there. Back soon."

"I've nowhere to go." Her body was one giant ache. All she wanted to do was sleep. She'd planned to stay away from Callie, but for some reason, Callie was there, and as she drifted off again, the thought that Callie was nearby helped soothe some of the pain.

CHAPTER TWENTY-FIVE

The doctor motioned Callie to follow him into the kitchen. "No broken bones. Her ribs are okay, I think. A nasty gash, but not deep enough to require stitches. Her thick winter clothing must have protected her. She should bend as little as possible for the next three days. No showers until then. Keep her wound dry. Here's a prescription for antibiotics. Watch her, Callie. If she has *any* problems breathing, or the pain worsens, take her to the hospital. I'd send her now, just to be certain about those ribs, but she's stubborn."

Callie had been surprised not only when Val rang to tell her about the attack, but when Tommy had as well. If anything, he'd sounded more upset than Val, and though she wasn't certain what he meant by, "He shouldn't have done it," she had a pretty good idea it wasn't a total accident. "I'll look after her."

After the doctor left, Callie entered Lauren's bedroom. She was lying on her stomach with a twelve-inch bandage stretching down the middle of her back, between her neck and waist.

Callie had turned her back when Lauren sat up, but not before she'd glimpsed Lauren's large, firm breasts and delicate pink nipples. *Quit ogling her. She needs help, not lusting after.*

Callie sighed. Lauren's shoulders were finely muscled and her arms strong. She tilted her head and grinned at the abundance of freckles on Lauren's shoulders. How long would it take her to kiss them one by one?

When Lauren shivered Callie snapped out of her reverie. She tucked the sheets and the comforter over Lauren, caressing her shoulders as she did. Lauren moaned softly in response to her fleeting touch.

When Callie opened the bedroom door, a gangly orange cat bolted into the room. It jumped on the bed and stretched along the side of Lauren's legs as if it belonged there. Callie closed the door, leaving a gap to allow the cat to leave when it was ready.

Callie tiptoed back to the kitchen and stared out the window. Lauren was injured and could have been killed. Callie frowned. Val's garbled and evasive explanation about not leaving the patients at PVS hadn't rung true. Was Val trying to push her and Lauren together? Lauren wouldn't have asked for Callie's help. It had to be Val. Callie shook her head. It didn't matter. Lauren was her friend and she needed help. That was enough for now, and it had to be enough when there was nothing else.

Callie explored the little house. This was her first visit, and she surveyed the rooms with interest. There were two bedrooms with the bathroom between them. The second bedroom had a desk, a rowing machine, and hand weights set at forty-five pounds. Lauren's kitchen was small, with a two-seat table tucked into one corner. The living room led off the kitchen. There was room for a couch, armchair, television, stereo, and bookcase. It was cozy and warm, and it fit Lauren perfectly.

Callie expected a bookcase packed with veterinary textbooks and medical journals. She grinned as she perused Lauren's extensive collection of lesbian romance novels. On the third shelf, there were books written by or about famous women, including Jane Goodall, Birute Galdikas, and Dian Fossey. Callie perused a shelf with an atlas and books on history. A woman's book collection was a window into her personality, or so she'd heard it said.

Callie had never read *Gorillas in the Mist.* She lifted it off the shelf and set it on the coffee table for later. The romance novels were tempting, but Dian Fossey's book was educational and she needed to be smarter. Besides, she didn't need some sweet romance reminding her of everything her life was lacking.

She studied Lauren's veterinary degree hanging on the wall. It was a reminder of one of their differences. Below her, tucked into one corner of the couch was another orange cat. It was mature, but no bigger than the first one. Callie stroked it and her reward was a delicate purr. The cat raised its head and curved its neck for more contact with her hand.

While Lauren slept, Callie cleaned the house. Lauren had said she could stay, and that meant making herself useful. She tossed a load of smelly work clothes in a basket and put it in the basement. Then she washed the dishes. She hunted in Lauren's kitchen for something to serve for lunch. The freezer held many individual meat pies and stuffed chicken breasts from the local farm store. Ketchup, mayonnaise, a jar of natural peanut butter, two apples, and a bag of mini carrots summarized the contents of the refrigerator. In the cupboard, she discovered a loaf of fresh bread and twenty cans of tuna. She found no oil, salt, sugar, butter, or spices.

When she had finished her chores, Callie curled on the couch with the little cat and phoned PVS.

"Prairie Veterinary Services, Val speaking. How may I help you?"

"It's Callie."

"How is she?"

"Sore, but asleep. The doctor didn't send her to the hospital, and she didn't need stitches."

"I was worried."

"What about tonight? She shouldn't be left alone."

"Can you take her home with you?"

Callie grinned and scratched the little cat under the chin. "Thought you might suggest that." No doubt about it, Val was matchmaking. "Can you keep Becky for the night? I want to be able to run Lauren into the hospital if she starts feeling worse and I can't leave Becky alone. I'll drop some clothes off later for her."

"No problem. Gwen and Becky are great pals. Pajamas aren't an issue, but I don't have any jeans to fit Becky. What if I washed hers tonight and loaned her a clean shirt for school? Save you a trip back into town."

"Awesome. Thanks, Val."

"No problem. I've got to go. Take care of Lauren."

"I will." Because that's what friends did. Even after a stupid fight. She picked up the book and flipped to the first page. After twenty pages of gorillas, her eyes slid to Lauren's collection of lesbian romances. Lauren was tough on the outside but had a soft heart. She saw it in Lauren's eyes when she patted the heifers before surgery and said, "Sorry, girl, I'll finish as soon as I can."

Callie lifted the cat off her lap and rose to her feet. They might not belong together, but Lauren was special, and she'd look after her. She had just finished preparing lunch when she heard footsteps in the bedroom. She knocked on Lauren's bedroom door.

The movement inside ceased, and a hesitant voice responded. "Hello? Who's there?"

"It's Callie. May I come in? Can I help?"

"Just a second."

Callie winced as Lauren groaned and shuffled around the bedroom. When Lauren yelped, Callie opened the door and rushed into the room. Lauren stood by the closet, her eyes full of pain. She was wearing a pair of loose sweatpants with the matching sweatshirt held in front of her chest. Callie gasped when she saw large areas of purple bruising on Lauren's bare shoulders. She hadn't noticed them when the doctor had been there, but they were certainly visible now.

"I can't get the top on by myself. It hurts too much to lift my arms." A tear slid down Lauren's cheek.

Callie's eyes watered in sympathy. The vulnerability in Lauren's eyes was heartbreaking. "Let me help, please." She took hold of the sweatshirt and gave it a little tug, but Lauren didn't let go.

"Um, I'm not wearing anything."

Callie struggled to keep her features neutral. A joke about roasting marshmallows on Lauren's cheeks would be unkind given the circumstances. "What if I keep my eyes closed?"

"I'm not sure."

Callie closed her eyes and stuck out her hand. When the sweatshirt landed in her hand, her mouth went dry. Lauren was half-naked in front of her. She squeezed her eyes shut against temptation and, heart hammering, set to work. After a few minutes of attempting to slip the sweatshirt on Lauren, without touching her breasts, Callie abandoned the task and turned her back. "Do you have something with a zipper or buttons?"

"Oh, good idea. In the closet." Ten minutes later, they had Lauren in a cotton button-down shirt and a fleece jacket that zipped up the front. Lauren hobbled into the kitchen and sank into a chair. Callie had prepared a tuna sandwich with apple slices and carrots on the side. "Thanks for your help today," Lauren mumbled before biting into the sandwich.

Callie spotted a pair of heavy socks protruding from Lauren's jacket pocket. She plucked the socks from the pocket and slipped them on Lauren's feet. The doctor had said Lauren shouldn't do any bending for a few days, but Callie wasn't sure how she'd manage that on her own. When she straightened, Callie noticed Lauren had quit eating and her head was hanging.

"I appreciate your help, but I don't deserve it after everything that's happened." Lauren's voice trailed off as she twisted to face the wall.

Callie caressed Lauren's cheek. "Lauren, look at me. I want to help you, and I hurt as much as you do about our argument." Lauren opened her mouth, but Callie silenced her with her finger pressed to Lauren's lips. "Eat your lunch and rest. Then we'll talk."

Lauren smiled and resumed eating her sandwich.

To lighten the mood, Callie pointed to the other cat sitting beside Lauren's feet. "Your cats are cute."

"Thanks. I adopted the little female, Elsa, when she came into the clinic as a stray." Lauren winced as she gestured over her shoulder. "That's her on the couch." She grinned down at the other cat. "This big guy with the crooked tail is Digit. He must have broken his tail when he was a tiny kitten and it healed at an odd angle." At the sound of his name, Digit leaped into Lauren's lap for a cuddle and kisses.

"Digit was my first friend in Saskatchewan. I adopted him from a farm when he was about six weeks old. I was there to treat a cow, and I found this little guy."

"Was he starving?"

"He was a fat, well-fed kitten, but too tiny to be on his own. I asked the farmer if I could have him. He looked at me as if I had two heads and said, 'Can you have him? I have another thirty in the barn you can have.'"

Callie laughed.

"Digit followed me from barn to barn, crawling in and out of mud puddles. He meowed the entire time, and he's not stopped since. I never meant to adopt a kitten, but he picked me."

"So, you rescue animals?"

"Most vets have homes full of abandoned or damaged pets. I'm just starting my collection." Lauren laughed softly.

"And Max would have been one?"

"Yes, but I'm glad you have him."

"He follows Becky everywhere. She loves him."

When she finished lunch, Lauren gingerly crawled into bed and Digit followed.

Callie put the food away and washed the lunch dishes. Then she slipped out to fill Lauren's prescription and collect first aid supplies to change the bandage. Callie had animals to feed, and she needed to get home. When she returned from shopping, she woke Lauren. "Sorry to wake you, but you have to come home with me."

"You've done too much for me already."

"I promised the doctor and Val I'd look after you, and you're not all right on your own. I want to help, but I need to be home to see to my animals." Lauren had every right to say no, but she did need watching and Callie hoped she'd come back with her. She enjoyed caring for people. "If you close your eyes and really think about how you're feeling, you'll know I'm right."

Lauren sighed and closed her eyes. "Okay, I surrender. Thank you."

Callie changed the cat litter tray and filled an extra bowl of water and dry cat food. She packed a bag for Lauren, grabbed Lauren's laptop, and set them by the door. Then she maneuvered Lauren into a heavy coat and scooped up Digit and Elsa so Lauren could kiss them on the head. She helped Lauren into the Poplarcreek pickup truck, collected Lauren's bags, and they drove to Callie's farm.

Chapter Twenty-six

There was a moment of awkwardness when they entered the farmhouse. Callie flashed to their last conversation in her kitchen and winced. She carried Lauren's bags upstairs and settled her in the spare room with water, ibuprofen, and her antibiotics.

Lauren chuckled when Callie placed the white speaker beside her bed.

"Don't mock me," Callie said. "A baby monitor is more useful than a bell, and cell phone signals are unreliable. The tower's too far away. Talk into the monitor if you need anything. I'll carry my end with me. And don't you dare go downstairs on your own."

"Yes, ma'am."

Callie had a busy late afternoon. There were pens to clean and cattle to feed, and she wanted to try to get it done before dark. Her youngest heifers didn't produce enough milk, so she supplemented the calves with milk replacer. She was bottle-feeding each calf one to two times a day. Two calves had scour, and she checked for dehydration the way Lauren taught her. They would be all right for now with electrolytes and a dose of antibiotics.

When she returned, she heard Lauren's slow steps in the upstairs hallway and bounded upstairs two steps at a time. When she saw Lauren was okay and had only gotten up to use the bathroom, Callie jumped into the shower. After a long soak, she pulled her wet hair into a ponytail, dressed in clean clothes, and returned to the kitchen to prepare dinner.

She tucked the phone against her cheek as she worked and phoned Val's house to speak with Becky.

"Hi, Mommy."

"Hi, honey, how are you? Having fun?"

"Gwen and I just finished homework. Val said we could watch some cartoons before bed."

"That sounds like fun. Do you understand why you're staying with Val and Gwen?"

"Lauren is with you."

Callie winced. That didn't sound good. "Lauren was hurt today at work and I need to keep an eye on her. It's no fun here tonight. More fun at Val's."

"Can I come home tomorrow?"

Becky's hesitant question tore at her heart. "Yes, honey. Yes, and I'm going to miss you tonight. In fact, I miss you already. What if I come there and watch cartoons with you?" If Becky was upset again, she'd go to her. No questions asked.

"You would? But what about Lauren? Val said you can't leave her in case she needs help."

"That's true. What should I do?"

"You stay with Lauren. I'll stay here tonight and come home tomorrow."

The tentativeness left Becky's voice and the power returned. Callie smiled. Becky not only looked like Liz more each day, she sometimes sounded like her. "Okay. Thanks, honey. I love you. Big hugs."

"I love you too, Mommy."

Callie woke Lauren with a gentle caress on her cheek. "Hungry?"

Lauren leaned into her palm and sighed. "Yes, thanks."

Callie placed a small table beside the bed and set dinner on it.

Lauren sat up and grimaced as she swung her legs over the edge of the bed. "I feel like I've been sleeping all day. Antibiotics do that to me."

Callie flinched as pain washed over Lauren's face. "It hurts you to move even an inch."

"It does, but I'm starving and dinner smells delicious."

"Good." Callie pulled a chair to the other side of the table and they ate.

"How were things in the barn?" Lauren asked.

"The last heifer to have surgery is doing well. The calves are good, but I need four hands to feed them all. I was feeding two and another one was butting against my backside."

Lauren burst into laughter. Then she wrapped her arms around herself. "Don't make me laugh, it hurts."

Callie grinned. "I didn't make you do anything. Tiny calves are ganging up on me and this you apparently find funny."

"Your gang of calves."

"So, are we going to talk about what happened?"

"When?"

"What do you mean when? Today. At Kruger Farm. Did something else happen?"

"I've been lying here thinking of little else. I'm almost certain Kyle opened Bulldozer's headgate. He was fussing around Bulldozer's head while I worked. I'm pretty sure Tommy was as surprised as I was when the bull escaped and flattened me."

"Tommy called me afterward and said, 'he shouldn't have done it.' He meant Kyle. He must have seen him let the bull go."

"That's confirmation, but it won't be enough for the police and I'll bet Tommy won't tell them."

Callie clasped Lauren's hands between hers. "The Krugers are after you too. You have to stay away from them."

"They're clients. It's hard to do."

"But you could have been killed." Callie shivered as a chill crept down her back. The Krugers had shifted from letters and threats to attempted murder. Was this all so they could get their hands on Poplarcreek? Hurting Lauren wouldn't get them the farm. Was there something else? Was it the stolen cattle or drug smuggling? How could she stop it? There had to be a way to protect Becky, Lauren, and herself.

"I was thinking about the night Kyle pretended to have a calving and lured me back to the clinic. Tommy showed up after Kyle and

I think sort of blocked Kyle from being meaner. I'm not sure, but I was scared. I never thought Kyle would actually do anything. Today proves how wrong I was. I'll call Mitch and tell her about the bull. Maybe it's all related."

Callie stood and paced the bedroom. "You must *not* go to Kruger Farm again or see them alone." She stopped in front of Lauren. "Promise me. Promise or I'll never be able to sleep again for worrying about you."

"I think I may safely promise you never to return to Kruger Farm. I'll tell Ian and Fiona the whole story if I have to."

Callie dropped into a chair. "I want to hug you, but you look so sore."

"Rain check?"

Callie smiled. "Deal."

After dinner, Callie cleared the dishes and carried them downstairs. She set the kitchen to rights and phoned Becky again just to say good night. Then she pulled on a heavy jacket and boots and jogged to the barn for the evening check on her animals.

When Callie returned to the house, she climbed the stairs to her bedroom. She changed into blue fleece sleep pants, a matching top, and heavy socks. She turned in front of her full-length mirror and winced at her outfit. It wasn't sexy but was typical winter pajamas in Saskatchewan. She'd freeze in a nightdress, and besides, it wasn't that kind of sleepover. Callie tiptoed down the hall and halted at the door to the guest room. She ached to spend more time with Lauren but had no wish to be a pest, and she suspected Lauren had fallen asleep after dinner. Should she leave or should she knock?

"Come in, Callie."

The low timbre of Lauren's voice skittered up Callie's spine and stole her breath. She perched on the uncomfortable decorative antique chair beside Lauren's bed. Dinner had been innocuous, but a late evening visit at bedtime gave the room a charged atmosphere, ratcheting up the heat and intimacy level. She tried not to let her eyes roam, but she noticed Lauren breathing faster than normal. "Are you in pain? Can I get you anything?"

"How about the license plate of the truck that ran me over? The truth is, I'm doing better, thanks, Cals. Everything all right in the barn? I wouldn't be much use to you tonight if there was trouble."

"Everything's good." Callie yawned and leaned forward, resting her elbows on her knees and her chin in her hand. Her head was spinning. *Cals.* No one had used that nickname before, and she liked it. The word was warm and intimate coming from Lauren. "The heifers have finished calving. I only have the cows left, so that's a bonus." Callie squeezed her words out around another larger yawn.

Lauren rested her hand on Callie's knee. "Tired?"

Callie rolled her shoulders and stretched. "I'm exhausted. How about you?"

"I'm beat. I just took two ibuprofen and my antibiotics. When those kick in, I'll sleep." Lauren squeezed Callie's knee. "I love chatting with you, but aren't you uncomfortable in that chair?"

"I am, and I need to sleep too." She was drained from the stress of the day and needed to get to bed, but she was drawn to Lauren. Callie sat quietly and held Lauren's hand. It was as if by touching her she could keep her safe. While they held hands, the pills took effect. Lauren's eyes drifted closed and popped open again several times. Callie watched Lauren struggle against sleep and caressed her cheek. "Relax, baby. Go to sleep."

"Thanks, Cals. Thanks for everything." Lauren smiled and her eyes closed.

Callie placed a light kiss on Lauren's cheek. "Night Lauren." She tucked the comforter over Lauren and tiptoed from the room.

The next morning, Callie brought breakfast to Lauren's room. She had been awake for hours and had eaten breakfast already. She set the food on Lauren's table and left Lauren to eat when she woke up. Later, water running in the bathroom signaled Lauren was awake. Callie collected the bandaging supplies and brought them to the guest room. "Good morning. I have to change your dressing."

Lauren grimaced and swiveled to unbutton her shirt with her back to Callie. After removing her shirt, she lay on her stomach.

Callie shook her head. Why was Lauren still shy after everything they had done? She placed the chair beside the bed and sat. "Sorry, the doctor told me to remove the bandage slowly." The muscles of Lauren's shoulders bunched and twitched as Callie removed the bandage as gently as she could. When she finished Lauren sighed and relaxed.

Lauren glanced over her shoulder. "How's it look?"

"The cut is swollen and red, but clean."

"It itches."

"Lucky you can't reach it, or I'd have to fasten one of those plastic cone collars on you."

Lauren giggled.

Callie dabbed antibiotic ointment on the wound and bandaged it. She spent more time smoothing the edges of the bandage than was necessary. The swell of Lauren's breasts was visible where she lay on them and it unnerved her. When she finished with the bandage, she drew the sheets to cover Lauren. "Sleep now." She placed a tender kiss on each bruised shoulder and tiptoed from the room.

In the afternoon, Callie brought Lauren lunch in her room. At some point Lauren had risen and put her top on. They sat on either side of the small table the way they had the first night. When they finished, Callie set the dishes and table aside. Lauren lay on her side in bed and pulled the covers over herself. Callie dropped into her chair and sat hunched with her elbows on her knees while she scrutinized Lauren's face. "We have to talk."

The color drained from Lauren's face.

"Becky will be home today, and she needs to be comfortable in her own home. She feels like you've been avoiding her. That true?"

"Is she upset?"

"She's been through a lot and worries about losing people. Can you just be her friend? Like you are with Gwen?"

Lauren nodded. "I'd like to."

"Thanks. Her happiness is my priority."

Lauren looked up at her and held her gaze. "Of course."

At four p.m. Callie met Becky at the bus and walked her into the house. They removed boots and coats and Callie motioned for Becky to sit with her at the table.

Becky gazed at Callie. "Where's Max? He always meets me when I get home."

"He's upstairs keeping watch over Lauren. She's staying with us for a few more days."

"Why?" The child's voice betrayed her trepidation.

"She's too sore to be on her own. Thank you for staying with Val last night while I looked after her." Callie kissed the top of Becky's head and gave her a one-armed hug. "I'm glad you're home. Max and I missed you."

"I like being home, Mommy."

Callie kissed Becky's cheek. "Lauren needs lots of rest, so we have to be quiet upstairs. She's in the spare room and you may visit her if you wish."

Becky shrugged and played with the zipper of her hoodie, zipping it up and down nervously.

"Sweetie, Lauren has been behaving strangely the last little while, but it'll be better now. I promise."

Becky swung her legs and repeatedly hit the legs of her chair with her heels. "If Max is with her, I guess it's okay."

"I'm going to make dinner now. Would you like to help?" She didn't want to pressure Becky into visiting Lauren, and she wanted to spend more time with her. She'd missed her.

Becky brightened. "Can I?"

"I'd love the help. Grab a chair and sit at the table." Callie gathered her supplies. "Tonight, you're going to learn how to peel potatoes. It's where everyone starts in the kitchen."

Callie watched her work and couldn't resist dropping kisses on her head. Becky concentrated intently on her project. She was very thorough and got all the peel but dug a little deep and peeled off half the potato. Callie grinned as she neatly scraped three potatoes to Becky's one. They didn't need two pounds of potatoes and they'd be eating them all week.

She was still worried about Becky and Lauren. She'd never send Lauren home injured, but their friendship had no chance of going further if Becky was unhappy. Callie shook her head. And no chance if Lauren was unhappy. She liked Lauren and it was too bad if their budding friendship imploded, but Becky was her priority, always.

CHAPTER TWENTY-SEVEN

Lauren lay in bed on her stomach with Max curled on the carpet near her. Max always followed Becky around the house and property, and when she was at school, he followed Callie. Callie had told Max it was his job to stay with her, and he hadn't left her side.

She tried to concentrate on her audiobook, but her mind kept wandering to Callie, Becky, and the Krugers. The Krugers were dangerous and had proven it yesterday. But why had Kyle let Bulldozer go? Was he trying to cover something else up? She and Callie had told the police everything. If she were dead, she couldn't testify at trial, but the police had her statement. It didn't make sense, but then how did any of the harassment of Callie make sense. She discarded her musings when Callie appeared.

"Hey, Lauren. I have dinner for you." Callie dragged a bigger table and another chair into the bedroom. She struggled from bed and hobbled to a chair. It was painful, but she needed to move before she stiffened further. Becky and Callie sat in the other chairs and Max's bowl also landed in her room for dinner.

"How was your day?" Lauren asked Becky.

"Okay."

"How did your project on the cow's digestive system go?"

"Okay." She played with her food, pushing it around in circles.

"What are you working on now?"

Becky shrugged.

Lauren asked a few more questions and Becky answered in quiet monosyllables, never lifting her eyes from her plate. *I'm such a jerk.* She wouldn't give up, though.

"How're your calves? Your mom says you're feeding them after school." She noticed Callie was staying quiet, no doubt to give her and Becky a chance to reconnect.

Becky brightened, always ready to talk about her animals. "While I was feeding Bolt, Rhino sucked the tail of my coat. He made it all wet and slobbery."

Lauren chuckled and smiled when Becky glanced up. "I guess Rhino was hungry too."

"Yeah." Becky grinned. "I fed him next."

"Max looks good. He's gained weight."

"We feed him three times a day. He gobbles up the puppy food and walks faster now."

"Well done." Lauren smiled at Becky. "Want to watch a movie with me tonight? We can watch it on my laptop, since I can't really move around much. You pick."

Becky looked at Callie.

Callie laid a hand on Becky's shoulder. "After homework."

After dinner and homework, Becky brought a movie to Lauren's room. They talked for a while and Lauren told Becky about T.J., William, and Sam. Becky asked many questions about Sam. Lauren apologized for being distant and told Becky she liked her, and she'd never do anything to come between Becky and her mom. When Becky was satisfied with Lauren's explanation, she started the movie.

At Lauren's invitation, Becky crawled into the bed and curled at her side. They laughed and cheered through the movie. Lauren gazed down at Becky and was thankful Becky had forgiven her. She'd missed the energy and exuberance of a child.

❖

As Lauren rose from her bathtub after a hot soak, her phone rang. *Damn it.* She wasn't on call and ached to put on soft pajamas and relax in front of a movie. It had been a long day at work even though Ian had put her on light duties. Her wound itched, and she was sore, but she had returned to work on Monday after four days of pampering at Poplarcreek. Callie invited her to stay longer but had driven Lauren home when she insisted. It was sweet of Callie, but she needed to get back to her own life, her own routine. Things were okay between them. Not flirty and easy like they had been, but gentle and even, like the friends they were.

Lauren sighed as she answered the phone. "Dr. Cornish speaking."

"Hi, Lauren. I'm having trouble with another calving. Can you help me, please?"

Lauren hesitated for a second. Callie had phoned her at home instead of going through the clinic answering service. This was Callie calling her good friend, not her veterinarian. Lauren had Val's friendship and now Callie's and it was awesome. "Sure, Callie. On my way." Friends helped friends and she'd go to Poplarcreek even if she had to crawl.

Lauren arrived at Poplarcreek an hour later. Callie met her at the barn door. "Sorry for the terrible drive."

"No problem." It was a thirty-minute drive to Poplarcreek, but it took an hour in the driving snow. Lauren's back and shoulders burned after the long drive. She had slipped off the road twice, but with the four-wheel drive, she didn't get stuck. "What's been happening?"

"I've found two front legs and the nose, but when I heave on the legs, it doesn't come. It's not a big calf. Its legs are skinny. I was hoping to handle the calvings now that the heifers are done, but I can't handle this one and I'm scared it's taking too long."

"I agree they're front legs." *Please, be a calving, not another C-section.* Lauren washed the cow as usual and tugged on an OB glove. She kneeled and reached inside the animal. It felt good to stretch her shoulders, but her back screamed. "You have two front legs, but they're not part of the same calf." Lauren watched the confused expression on Callie's face transform into understanding.

"Twins?"

"Two calves for you tonight, my friend. I love calving twins. The puzzle of sorting out the legs of each calf and choosing which to deliver first. Twins are small and easy to pull out, so there's no need for a C-section or even calving chains. We have enough time with this calving. Do you want to feel inside?"

Callie squinted at Lauren.

"I promise there's enough time. The calves are all right."

"Okay, I'll try." Callie slipped on an OB glove and kneeled beside Lauren. Her forehead creased in concentration, Callie groped inside to find what Lauren described.

Lauren sat back on her heels and admired Callie as she worked. *How does she manage to look so gorgeous in insulated coveralls and a worn orange wool cap?* Lauren sighed. It was the glow and energy radiating from Callie's body. It was as if Callie were magnetic and drew her in.

After a minute, Callie relaxed and grinned at Lauren. "So cool." Callie shifted, prepared to remove her arm.

Lauren stopped her with a hand on her shoulder. "While you're in there, do you want to pull the calves out?"

Callie nodded. "All right, but you stay right there." Callie pointed with her chin to the other side of the cow.

"Deal." Lauren sighed in relief. Her back was more painful than she had realized. It was a mistake to respond to Callie's emergency call because she wasn't ready, but she couldn't resist answering Callie's request for help. If it had been a C-section, she would have called Ian.

"How do I start? With the calf whose head I'm touching?"

"That's what I would do." Callie impressed Lauren in so many ways. She was smart, eager to learn, and dove in there. She wasn't afraid of anything. The dead calf hadn't destroyed Callie's confidence, which was what Lauren had been worried about.

"Got it."

Lauren stood and pulled on the legs of the first calf in one steady motion. It was a small calf and slid out with room to spare, past Callie who leaned out of the way. "I'll clean this calf. You grab the second one." Lauren flipped the calf on its chest, wiped its face, and tickled the inside of its nose with a piece of straw. When the calf was snorting and blinking, Lauren focused on Callie.

A minute later, Callie popped the second calf out and worked away on it as she often had in the past. "Two healthy calves. My lucky night."

It was a pleasure seeing confidence return to Callie's eyes. "You were incredible. I hope you're proud of yourself."

Callie did a little happy dance. "To think only a few months ago I thought the stork brought calves." Callie nudged Lauren with an elbow. "Oh, what the heck." Callie grabbed Lauren's face and placed noisy comical kisses on each of her cheeks. "Thanks, teach."

Lauren gasped as the abrupt movement jarred her back.

Callie's hand flew to cover her mouth as she stepped back. "Oh, Lauren. I'm sorry. I wasn't thinking. You're not ready to be calving cows again. Why are you here? I can't believe I was so stupid. I had trouble and I panicked, and I instantly went to you." Callie clasped Lauren's hands and stared into her eyes. "Are you all right? Did I hurt you?"

Lauren couldn't stifle the groan of pain. "Fine, Cals. Just sore."

Callie insisted on doing the entire cleanup and stowed Lauren's equipment in her truck. Then Callie grasped her hand and led her into the house. In the mudroom, Callie shook wet flakes off her coat and hung it up. "The snow's coming in sideways."

"I should go now before the weather worsens."

"I don't think it could be worse." Her arms crossed over her chest, Callie scrutinized Lauren until she squirmed. "It's not safe to drive. If you become lost or stuck, you might freeze to death or get frostbite. The roads are deserted this time of night. If you skidded off the road nobody would find you until spring. I shouldn't have called you out, but I did, and now I'm responsible for you. Please stay. I've plenty of room."

It wouldn't hurt to get warm, at least. The shivers were making her back hurt. They toed off their boots and Lauren hung up her coat. They set their gloves and hats near the radiator, and their boots upside down on the boot warmer.

In the kitchen, Lauren headed to the window and studied the storm. The snow slammed against the glass and a cold draft leaked around the window latch. She could no longer see her truck or Callie's barn. She would prefer not to drive home in this weather but regretted imposing on Callie yet again.

"You're not considering leaving, are you?"

"No, you're right. Visibility is nonexistent." Lauren continued to peer into the storm. "It reminds me of the snowstorm in *The Painted Door*."

Callie moved behind Lauren and placed her hands on the Lauren's hips, careful not to touch Lauren's back. "Sinclair Ross helped the reader see the harshness and loneliness of a winter storm on the prairies. I see the beauty and the magnificence of nature in a storm. As long as the people I love are safe, and I don't have to drive in it." Callie kissed Lauren on the back of the head.

The people I love? Love? The word made Lauren both tingle with delight and quake with terror. She stuffed her feelings deep and reentered the conversation. "I see the beauty you mention, but the cold and loneliness were in the heart of a wife dissatisfied with her life." Touched by the affection in the small kisses, Lauren twisted to grin at Callie.

Callie bestowed the next kisses on Lauren's lips before she returned to the dinner preparations. "Don't you think part of the failure between husband and wife was his decision to work fifteen hours a day? He ignored her request for him to spend more time with her."

Lauren tilted her head, thinking. "There was a lack of communication and one partner made all the decisions. It was wrong then and would be wrong now. How can one person believe they're so smart their decisions must always be best?" She walked toward Callie. "Can I help with dinner?"

Callie continued to chop vegetables for their meal, her expression contemplative. "You've worked enough tonight. Why don't you rest in front of the fireplace?"

Lauren accepted the invitation and strolled into the living room. She studied the stack of logs beside the fireplace. She'd love a wood fire but wasn't sure she had the energy to build it. She riffled through a stack of papers sitting on top of the logs.

"Those are all from Heinz."

"Sorry, I wasn't snooping. I was going to build a fire and they were just sitting here."

Callie took the stack. "They're various surveys, letters, and offers from Heinz to buy Poplarcreek." Callie held up a paper. "See this one? It's a listing for a berry farm for sale in British Columbia. Think Heinz is hinting?" Callie laughed. "I use them as fire starter. It's very satisfying." Callie kneeled and built the fire.

Lauren watched the papers catch fire. She almost suggested Callie was destroying evidence she might need later, but she tamped the idea down and settled on minding her own business, for once. Lauren stretched out on the couch. Callie spread a blanket over her and perched on the edge of the armchair.

"I see that look on your face. Those papers are all photocopies. A couple are legitimate offers for Poplarcreek. It's astonishing how little Heinz thinks he needs to pay me. Anyway, my lawyer says they won't help us against the Krugers. The big deal is the drug smuggling, and apparently, the police have another video of Kyle at the border, which they only paid attention to thanks to us reporting what we did. I'm hoping the Krugers have more to worry about than continuing to hassle me."

"I still worry about you and Becky."

"And we worry about you. Enough Kruger talk. Let's have a peaceful evening." Callie stood. "I'll leave you alone. Rest now."

Lauren woke with a start when Callie kissed her. She blushed, embarrassed at being caught napping. She cupped Callie's face in her hands and kissed her soft, parted lips. "How long was I asleep?"

Callie was leaning over Lauren, her arms braced on the edge of the couch. "About thirty minutes." Callie straightened and held out her hand. "You looked relaxed and peaceful. It was a shame to wake you, but I couldn't let your dinner get cold."

Lauren took Callie's hand so she could stand and then stretched one sore muscle at a time. Becky was already seated at the kitchen table and Lauren gave her shoulder a squeeze.

"Anybody interested in going to a horse show in Saskatoon next weekend?" Lauren asked.

Becky bounced in her seat "Is it the same one Gwen's going to?"

"It is."

"Mommy, can we go, please?"

Callie gave Becky a one-armed hug. "Sure, we can go. How about we take Lauren to dinner afterward?"

"Is Sam coming?"

"Sam? I—she…" Lauren went cold. What was she doing? She wasn't part of the Anderson family and needed to remember that. Her children were three thousand kilometers away.

Callie said, "Sweetie. Sam's in Ontario, but maybe when she visits next, we can take her."

"Cool."

Lauren smiled at Callie with gratitude. "Anything's possible. Sam's thinking about visiting me next summer." Maybe the two families could do something together.

"Does Sam like cattle?" Becky asked.

"Not sure she's seen many."

Becky puffed out her chest. "I'll show her Poplarcreek and the calves. Mommy, can I see the twins after dinner?"

"It's too cold. I'll show you in the morning," Lauren said and then paused with her fork halfway to her mouth. "Sorry, Callie." There she was thinking she was a parent again.

One eyebrow raised, Callie focused on Lauren. "Sort of automatic for you? This parenting thing."

"Sorry. Becky, it's up to your mom when you see the twins."

After a beat, Callie leaned over and kissed Becky on the top of the head. "Yes, Lauren will show you the new calves in the morning but only if you get out of bed right away. You're not missing the bus just to look at the twins."

"Okay, Mommy. Thanks, Lauren. Yippee!"

After dinner, Lauren did the dishes while Callie checked on her animals. When Callie returned, they climbed the stairs to bed. At the top, they hesitated until Lauren headed toward the spare room after giving Callie a quick kiss on the cheek.

Lauren lay awake thinking about Callie. She ached to go to her, and the invitation had been there in Callie's eyes, but she was too sore, and sex would be disappointing. It was still excruciating to raise her arms to undress, let alone do anything romantic.

In the morning, Callie prepared breakfast. They ate in companionable silence and lingered over coffee. Then Callie loped upstairs to wake Becky for school.

"Knock, knock."

Lauren glanced up from her coffee and spied Mitch in the mudroom. *Damn it. Way to wreck a great morning. Officer Butch and Bossy has arrived.* "Callie's upstairs getting Becky ready for school. She called me last night to help with a calving." Lauren blushed. Why did she feel the need to defend her presence? Did Mitch drop by often? They'd never crossed paths, and with all the time Lauren spent at Poplarcreek, it seemed unlikely. It made her feel a little better.

"Hello, Dr. Cornish." Mitch poured herself a coffee. "You arrived the night before and are still here at breakfast?" Suspicion marred Mitch's handsome features. "I hope you're not charging her by the hour."

Lauren noticed the formal address and followed suit. "Hilarious, Officer Mitchell, but don't give up your day job."

"Oh burn. So, why *are* you still here?"

"I thought you had me figured out. You're not much of a detective." Mitch glowered at her. Had she pushed the cop too far? "I was snowed in. Satisfied?"

"Why are you here? I mean in Saskatchewan. You ditched your wife and children in Ontario."

It was Lauren's turn to glower. "Didn't realize gossip was part of your job."

Mitch shrugged. "You're not good enough for her. She deserves better."

"Not good enough?" Lauren asked.

"You clearly can't or won't protect her. When I told you to come stay with her after you reported all this shit to the police, you told me to do it instead. She's here alone way too often, and you're not doing shit to keep her and Becky safe." Mitch scowled. "You can't even protect yourself. I warn you to watch your back and you go to Kruger Farm and pick a fight with a bull. You're lucky to be alive."

"Well, my matador skills *are* rusty."

"She thinks you're funny, but you're a smartass. Callie deserves better than a woman who would abandon her family and run away." Mitch's nose crinkled as if there were a bad smell in the room. "When was the last time you saw your kids? Do you ever send your ex-wife money? Your eyes just filled with guilt, Cornish. More than a smartass, you're a wimp. Liz was worth ten of you."

"You don't know what you're talking about, Mitchell. And none of this is any of your business." Lauren gulped her coffee. Instead of child support, she had given T.J. her share of the house and business. Sam and William were teenagers, not babies, but she didn't need to share that information. Lauren lashed out, stung by the suggestion she was worthless beside Callie's late wife. It might not have hurt so much if she hadn't already been wondering if it were true. "Maybe you get paid to sit in people's kitchens and gossip, but I don't. See you around."

Without saying bye to Callie, Lauren waded through the snow to her truck and took her time getting to the main road. Was there truth to Mitch's words? How did her relationship with her ex and kids become village gossip? Her stomach clenched uncomfortably. Was this how she appeared to the rest of the town? Clearly, Liz had been something special around here, and yeah, Lauren couldn't be any more different. And yeah, maybe it was true that Callie would be safer with Mitch. But did Callie have to go back to what she'd been with before? Said who? Lauren sighed. There didn't seem to be any way forward when it came to whatever she had with Callie.

It was a busy day and Lauren concentrated on her patients. After the last client left, her mind slid to the morning and her breakfast conversation. Lauren groaned and her cheeks grew warm with shame at having run off without showing Becky the new calves. She'd broken a promise and that wasn't what friends did.

After dinner, Lauren called Callie. "I apologize for leaving without thanking you for breakfast."

"Did you have an emergency?"

"No."

"Why did you go?"

"I left because Mitch was there," Lauren said.

"Why? Mitch and I are just friends."

"I don't get the impression she thinks the two of you are just friends. And she made it pretty clear I wasn't welcome there."

"More than friends? I don't believe it. I haven't given her any encouragement." Callie's tone was clipped, and her irritation was evident.

Lauren cringed inwardly. Mitchell had just been protective. Rude yes, but protective, and Callie and Becky needed that. "May I talk to Becky, please? I shouldn't have bolted, but it didn't feel right to stay."

"You promised you'd show Becky the twins. I took her, but you should've done it. Not okay, Lauren."

"I know and I'm sorry. May I please speak with her?"

Callie relented and let Lauren speak with Becky. Lauren apologized to Becky for leaving and Becky forgave her. Lauren had no reason Becky would understand. How could she explain to a nine-year-old child that her insecurities had sent her running from Poplarcreek again?

Chapter Twenty-eight

Spill, Callie. How are you and the delicious Dr. Cornish doing? The last time I saw you was the women's dance the week after Valentine's Day and tomorrow is April Fool's day."
Rachel scowled slightly.

Callie laughed. "That's very precise, Rach."

"Precise records and dates are my job. Now quit stalling and spill already."

Callie shrugged and inspected her coffee cup as if it was the most interesting dish she had ever seen. "It's been a busy calving season." It was Wednesday, Lauren's day off, and Callie had driven to the city with her. They had separate things to do but had agreed to meet for lunch. It was domestic and couple-like, and she loved it, even if they were still in uncharted territory.

Rachel squinted at Callie. "Busy with the vet season?"

"That too, Rach. That too."

Rachel leaned toward her. "Is she good to you? Does she look after you?"

"I did a calving on Monday night with only a little coaching. It was twins. A year ago, I never dreamed I'd be able to do it." Callie squared her shoulders. If one more person suggested she needed someone to make decisions she'd scream. "I don't need looking after."

"I hear Lauren does, though, and I demand details. Where is she today? I thought she was with you?"

"There's a half-day lecture at the vet college. She'll meet us afterward."

"So, you're with me this morning?"

"I am. Now quit teasing and put me to work." Callie grinned to take the sting out of her words.

"Suits me. I don't work until three today. We'll spend the morning at the women's shelter."

"You've been volunteering there for a year. Good for you."

"Who knew my job in medical records at the hospital would be excellent training for organizing the shelter records."

Callie accompanied Rachel to the shelter. They organized files, did the shelter's bookkeeping, and helped the residents with personal tasks.

Later, Callie stopped in the common room for another cup of coffee and glanced at the small family sitting at a table. The children were asleep or coloring. The woman was trying to breast feed while she flipped through a government form.

"Can I help?" Callie asked. "Like a cup of coffee?" The woman looked up. It was Heather Kruger, Tommy's wife, but gone was the round face and sunny smile from the previous year. "Heather?"

"Oh, right, Callie. Hi." Heather ducked her head and focused on her baby.

Callie slid into the chair beside her. "Can I help?"

Heather shrugged.

"How are you? I see you've had the baby."

"Yes. That's four girls for me. And the answer to your first question is not so great." Heather waved the documents around in frustration. "I need to apply for more aid, but I might as well be reading the French version of these government forms for all I understand. Why do they make it so difficult? I swear they take four paragraphs for what could be said in one line."

"I recognize that form. Want some help?" Callie was careful to offer help and push gently. In Heather's place women felt as if they had very little control in life and she wouldn't want to take any more of it.

"Thanks, Callie."

Callie smoothed out the crumpled papers and started at the top. She filled in the information Heather gave her. "You see much of Tommy?"

Heather shook her head. "He's stopped calling. He still emails begging me to move back to Kruger Farm, but I can't live with Heinz and Kyle again."

"I hear that."

"Poplarcreek will be nice. We'll get settled this summer and be ready when my oldest starts kindergarten in September."

Callie went cold. "Poplarcreek?"

"When you sell. Tommy emailed me yesterday and said Heinz is buying your farm and plans to give us the house." Heather laid her hand on Callie's. "You okay? I'll take care of it, I promise. You and Becky can visit if you want."

Callie carefully laid the pen on the table. She successfully suppressed the urge to stab the table with it. "But I'm *not* selling. I've turned down every offer from Heinz." Heather's face fell and Callie was sorry about that, but if Heinz and Tommy were lying to Heather she needed to know now.

"Mommy, are you okay?"

"Yes, honey. Take your sisters and get some juice. Rachel's put some cookies out."

"Okay, Mommy."

Callie smiled as she watched the three little girls toddle away holding hands.

Heather leaned forward. "He said you're moving home to British Columbia and happy to sell." She frowned. "So, Tommy was lying? Lying to me? I don't understand. It's not like him."

"I'll bet Heinz is lying to Tommy. I'll bet he needs Tommy to stay and work for him. Few people in town will and the farm's too much for Kyle to manage alone."

"That figures. My husband's a gentle man, and I love that, but I wish he'd just punch his father in the face and come back to me."

"I hope he breaks away before Heinz and Kyle drag him down with them." While they finished the forms, Callie told Heather all the things Heinz and Kyle had been up to. It was her right to know, and the only way she'd keep her little girls safe.

An hour later, Heather gathered her girls and headed for the door. She squeezed Callie's hand. "Thanks, Callie, and don't sell to Heinz. Keep Poplarcreek for Becky, but please stay safe. My girls and I will find something on our own."

Callie handed Heather's baby to her. She'd been cuddling her while Heather wrangled the other three into snowsuits. "Thanks, and you take care." After a warm hug Heather left.

Rachel joined Callie at the front window, and they watched Heather load her four girls into a rusty van. Rachel pointed. "Another reason to stay in the city. She's my age and has four children already. Four!"

"There are big families in Saskatoon, too, Rach." Callie waved as Heather drove off. Helping Heather and the other women was rewarding work and made Callie remember how lucky she was to have the farm, no matter how much work it was.

Rachel glanced at her watch. "Let's go have a coffee while we wait for Lauren."

"Good idea."

They drove to their favorite bistro and picked a table at the window. They sipped their coffees while they discussed Becky, and Callie's farm and all the work.

"If it ever gets too much for you, sell and move to the city. Move in with me. It would be fun, you, me, and Becky."

Even Rachel was trying to tell her what to do. It was unbelievable. "It's a generous offer, but if I ever leave Poplarcreek, Becky and I are headed west and we're not stopping until we get to my parents' berry farm. Besides, we might cramp your style. Get in your way."

"Not a chance," Rachel said.

Callie considered telling Rachel about the latest from the Krugers, but she was tired. Tired of Heinz Kruger and his nonsense consuming so much of her life. Besides, Rachel would just tell her, again, to sell Poplarcreek or find somebody to protect her. Instead Callie chose to just smile and listen as Rachel described the man she was pursuing before she switched to quizzing her about Lauren.

"Who was Lauren's date at the club that night?" Rachel waved her hands in front of her. "Nina?"

"Tina." Callie leaned back in her chair and crossed her arms. "Lauren told me Tina was twenty-three, drunk, and that was the first time she'd ever met her, and the last."

Eyebrows raised, Rachel mirrored Callie's posture. "Not the impression Tina gave. She led you to believe she and Lauren had hooked up." Rachel tapped an index finger on the table. "Why didn't Lauren set you straight, so to speak, that night?"

Callie laughed and leaned toward Rachel. "She told me she tried but was so flabbergasted at what Tina said that by the time she could form a sentence I had vanished."

"Okay, but what was she doing with Tina after that?"

"Lauren dragged Tina to the restroom because Tina was going to be sick." Callie whispered to keep from bothering the other diners. "Nothing else happened."

Rachel laughed. "Hilarious. You were miffed and scampered off into the night."

"True story. Turns out, Lauren hasn't had many girlfriends. She doesn't jump into bed with women."

"She's older and should be more experienced than you. A woman of the world." Rachel laughed. "What a difference. You had loads of girlfriends in high school and college before you met Liz."

"Not loads." Callie grinned. "It just took me a long time to find Liz. She was my one serious love, and I had her for such a short time."

Rachel took Callie's hands. "Ah, Callie."

"Lauren had tears in her eyes after I told her what happened to Liz." Callie let go of Rachel's hands and dug in her purse for a tissue. "It was sweet."

"She sounds nice, but aren't you worried Lauren has ties to Ontario? What about her family there?"

"When Lauren divorced her wife, their children cut her off. She still loves them. Having her children reject her was agony, but they're reconnecting, and she hopes her daughter will come to Saskatchewan in the summer."

"And have you slept with Lauren?"

Callie shrugged and traced the pattern in the tablecloth with a finger. "There's a mutual attraction, but we're going slow. Not pushing our relationship too far or too fast."

Rachel smirked. "So, how hard is the going slow part for you?"

Callie shook her head. "I have the urge to tear Lauren's clothes off every time I'm near her."

Rachel winked. "Keep going."

"A big bull knocked Lauren down and she stayed with me for a few days. It was wonderful having her close and helping her for a change, but I didn't sleep much picturing her in a bed ten feet down the hall."

"Is she okay now?"

"Bruised, but no broken bones. But it took a toll, for sure. There she is. My vet's here." Callie tipped her head toward Lauren, who was standing at the entrance to the restaurant.

Rachel winked at Callie. "She's as cute as I remember, but *my vet* sounds possessive."

"You know, Rach, I am possessive, and I think I'm falling for her."

Lauren removed her coat and scanned the tables in the restaurant, searching for them. Callie raised her hand and waved. Lauren raised one finger, pointed toward the restroom, and disappeared.

Rachel waggled her eyebrows at Callie. "You're feeling possessive or feeling as if you want her to possess you?"

"Both. She's amazing." It was true. Despite their differences and everything that still lay between them, Lauren was a wonderful person.

Lauren wended her way to their table. She bent to give Callie a light peck on the lips and said hello to Rachel.

They had a nice lunch chatting about family and work. After lunch, Lauren said, "I parked my truck two blocks away. It's freezing outside. Callie, would you like to wait here? I'll fetch my truck and come back for you."

"Thanks." Callie would've walked to the truck, but Lauren was giving her a few minutes alone with Rachel. Once again, it was thoughtful, and not controlling.

"Bye, Rachel." Lauren tried to shake Rachel's hand good-bye, but Rachel hugged her instead. Lauren left looking a little bewildered.

"Well?" Callie had watched Rachel scrutinize Lauren as if she were assessing her for worthiness.

"Lauren's interesting, friendly, and hilarious. Points to her for being polite to the waitstaff. Too many people aren't. I love that she held your hand whenever she could. She also listens to you and appeared interested in your opinions. And she makes you laugh."

"You like her?"

Rachel tilted her head. "I've only known you a few years and you're the happiest I've ever seen you. And I love seeing you cherished and respected. Hang on to her."

"Thanks. I am happy, for the most part." Callie hugged Rachel and kissed her on the cheek.

"Does Lauren have a single brother or sister?" Rachel asked.

"Either is fine. I'm not fussy."

Callie smiled as she waited just inside for Lauren to pick her up. It felt good to have a partner sitting beside her, out in public with friends. It felt so normal, so easy. She could get used to that.

CHAPTER TWENTY-NINE

On Thursday, Callie arrived at PVS to pay her bill and buy more medication for the calves. Wednesday had been a nice day out with Rachel and Lauren, but the reality of farming was back. As she headed to the front counter, she scanned the clinic for Lauren. Callie stopped at the counter in front of a woman who was busy tapping away on the computer.

"Hi, I'm Janice. May I help you?"

"I'm Callie Anderson and I own Poplarcreek Farm."

"Right, Poplarcreek. Nice to meet you." They shook hands and Janice laughed.

Callie's eyebrows winged up. "Is something funny?"

"No, no, not at all. What can I do for you?"

Callie grimaced. "I should pay my bill, or at least part of it."

"I'll print it for you." A minute later, Janice handed Callie a copy of her bill and excused herself to answer the phone.

Callie gaped at the amount she owed and collapsed into a chair in the waiting room to catch her breath. The many C-sections and calvings added up to a huge bill. She could have used the four thousand dollars Kyle stole from her, but Heinz hadn't paid her yet. She would probably have to go to court to get her money, but the thought of dealing with them at all made her stomach roil. When Janice returned, Callie dug out her credit card to pay her bill.

"The veterinarians have been busy at Poplarcreek. Dr. Cornish gave you a break, so that'll help." Janice snickered. "Lucky you."

"Pardon? A break?" Callie resented the sly look on the other woman's face. What game was she playing?

"See this line? A C-section listed as no charge. You got it for free." Janice smirked. "I guess it pays to be dating a veterinarian."

Lauren exited her office and smiled at Callie. "Hello. I thought I heard you."

Callie frowned. "Did you give me a free C-section?"

Lauren stepped back and blinked. "I told Ian every tenth heifer C-section or calving should be free. That's all it is."

Callie struggled to maintain a neutral tone. "May I speak with you in private, please, Dr. Cornish?"

"Certainly." Lauren led Callie to the exam room. After closing the door Lauren spread her arms and stepped toward Callie.

Callie crossed her arms, shifted her weight to one hip, and glared at Lauren. "Why did you deduct a C-section from my bill? I didn't ask you to do that," she whispered.

"I wanted to give you a break." Lauren glanced toward the closed door as if assessing for escape routes from a dangerous animal.

"Don't patronize me and don't make decisions about my finances." There was steel in her voice when Callie spoke. "I appreciate you were trying to help, but I don't need charity." She stalked from the exam room and handed over her credit card. "Janice, please have the missing C-section added to my bill. I'll come back and pay."

Janice glanced at Lauren. At Lauren's nod Janice said, "I'll do it. Thank you, Mrs. Adelson."

"My name is Anderson." Callie turned toward the front door.

Janice spoke in an unnecessarily loud voice. "Do I add last week's calving too, Dr. Cornish?"

Callie whirled and her eyes burned into Lauren. Her body was rigid with indignation. "Yes, add it, please." Then she stormed from the clinic.

Lauren followed Callie to her car. "Why are you being this way?"

"I don't expect you to pay my bills. I don't expect you to look after me. My whole life everyone else's been telling me what to do. At Poplarcreek, I make the decisions. I pay the bills and for the first time, I'm in charge. I manage my farm and my family, and I like it that way."

Lauren gave a little bow. "My apologies for trying to help."

Callie took a deep breath to steady herself. "I don't need help. Please, put the C-section and twin calving on my bill."

"You got it, lady." Lauren raised her voice. "I'll add the C-section, but not the twin calving. I helped you with the calving as a friend and on my own time. I only coached, but don't worry, I'll add the ten dollars for the supplies we used. I wouldn't want to offend you some more by trying to make things a little easier."

Callie stepped back, shocked at the sarcasm. She had never seen Lauren this angry. It was more than anger. Hurt swam in Lauren's eyes. "Fine. Thank you."

"Out of curiosity, do you expect a bill for the calving lessons I've given you? If you do, please, tell me how much to add to your bill. But first, deduct the amount I owe you for various meals and a hundred cups of coffee. Oh, and what's the going rate for home nursing care? I stayed with you for four days."

"Add the C-section and leave off the twin calving. As for the other items, I'm not a hotel, restaurant, or nursing home. I helped you because I care about you."

"Exactly!" Lauren yelled. "That's all I was trying to do!"

Callie's shoulders slumped. "You're not listening. This situation is different." She held her palms up, pleading for understanding. "I was a kid when I married Liz. I loved her, but she made *all* our decisions. For the first time in my life I'm making important decisions for myself and I like it. It's not just about the money. You did it without even asking me. Can you understand that?" Callie ended on a defeated note. The fight had gone from her. She longed to crawl into bed and burrow under the covers.

Lauren shivered and tugged her lab coat closed against the cold day. "I thought we were building something, and that means we help each other. Giving you a break on your bill isn't controlling you. It's just…helping."

"You're not listening, and you don't understand me." Callie shook her head. "I've changed my mind. And the horse show on Saturday isn't such a good idea. Becky is becoming fond of you and I don't want her hurt if you quit coming to the farm." She'd be crushed if Lauren vanished from her life. "I want a relationship, but I can't give up control again." A sharp pain settled in Callie's heart at the idea she was chasing Lauren away.

"I hurt your pride and now we're over?"

"I need to think."

"As you wish." Lauren dug through her wallet and extracted the tickets. "Here, you have them and go alone or give them away." Lauren shoved the tickets to the show at Callie. "You can invite Mitch."

Callie snatched the tickets and tried to hand them back. "Why don't you use them?"

"Val and Gwen already have tickets and I've nobody else to invite. Anyway, I'm freezing. Enjoy your very controlled, independent life." Lauren shot the last comment over her shoulder as she whirled and jogged into the clinic.

As she drove home, Callie reflected on how angry she and Lauren had been. They had argued over putting a price on helping each other. And as far as Callie was concerned, if Lauren made financial decisions about Poplarcreek, without talking to her first, the price was too high.

Callie drove faster while her irritation level spiked and her tires skidded at each turn. "Slow down, stupid. Wrecking your truck won't help." Taking her own advice, she slowed to a less reckless speed and paid attention to the winter roads. "Shit, shit, shit."

Callie drove home at a calmer pace. Maybe Lauren meant well, but it was high-handed of her to meddle in her finances. She thought Lauren understood her by now, but obviously not. When the fight was less raw, she'd try again to make Lauren understand. Maybe.

❖

Lauren stomped into her office and slammed the door while muttering under her breath. "You help somebody, and they always turn on you. Never mind, it's better this way. And how embarrassing to have that infuriating woman yell at me in front of everyone. I won't put up with it. She's ungrateful, unreasonable, and irrational. Life was better before I met her."

She collapsed into her office chair and allowed her forehead to crack against the edge of her desk as her head dropped. Life *wasn't* better before Callie. It was stable and predictable, but boring and lonely. Had she overstepped? "Damn it." Lauren glanced up and found Janice smirking at her. The smirk changed to a neutral expression in a flash. Had she imagined it? And why did Janice always seem to be lurking? "Yes, Janice?"

"Minnie said the dentistry's ready and are you coming, or do you want her to do it?"

"I'll go." Lauren sighed and trudged into the treatment room. She didn't mind cleaning a pet's teeth. Perhaps staring into a slobbery mouth smelling of dog butt and day-old dog food would help her put Callie out of her mind. Minnie had Bucky anesthetized and the dentistry equipment ready for her. "Thanks, Minnie." Lauren set to work cleaning the dog's teeth.

Thirty minutes later, Val peeked over her shoulder. "His teeth look good. Are you done soon? Mr. Pips is here."

"Remind me, Mr. Pips's pet is a…gerbil?"

Val shook her head. "Not even close, L.C. Mr. Pips is a cat. Velma Peters is his owner."

"Right, yes. I forgot."

Val studied Lauren. "It's not like you to forget a pet's name."

Lauren shrugged. She was lucky to remember her own name. It took all her effort to block out Callie's disappointed expression and concentrate on the dog.

After Lauren had vaccinated the cat, she joined Val for lunch in the PVS staff room. They took turns reheating their lunches and then sat.

Val grinned. "What were you doing to that poor dog? Did he have any teeth left?"

"A few at the back. Buggy will be eating soft food for life, but when his mouth heals, he's going to be so happy."

"His name was Bucky."

"Right, Bucky."

"So, Lauren..." Val managed to stretch her name into four syllables.

Lauren focused on the ceiling. She sensed an interrogation in her near future. "Yes, Val?"

Val tipped her head to the side and studied her. "How's Callie these days? Are you two ready to venture into public? I'm meeting friends at the Rainbow Club this weekend. You two are welcome to join us."

Lauren glared at her square cardboard dish of bland microwave pasta. "Yeah, maybe."

"What's going on?"

Lauren raised her head and grimaced.

Val squeezed Lauren's arm. "Ah, Lauren. What did you do?"

Lauren bristled. "Why do you assume I did something?"

Val smiled, and her left eyebrow arched as she studied Lauren.

Lauren sighed. "I gave Callie a break on her bill. I pretended we had a deal on C-sections and didn't charge her for one. She was angry and yelled at me. I yelled back and now she's off *thinking*." Lauren put air quotes around the last two words and then snugged her lab coat closed for protection against the memory.

"You were being nice, and she got all uppity?"

Lauren smiled. "Right. I knew you'd understand."

"She's ungrateful. I mean, if you give her money she should accept with gratitude, right?"

Lauren squirmed in her seat. "Well, no. It wasn't like that."

"It wasn't? If you pay a bill for her without asking, she should shut up and be grateful. Women, eh?" Val leaned back in her chair, her eyebrows raised.

Lauren sputtered as her emotions darted between annoyance and shame. "You don't understand. It wasn't like that."

"What was it like?" Val whispered.

Lauren held her head in her hands. "I was being nice. Who gets mad when somebody gives them a deal or just does something to help them out? I'm confused. I thought we were in a relationship, of some sort, and that means we help each other. It's not like there were strings attached or anything."

"Did you step in and take charge, or did you offer first?" Val motioned at her with her fork. "She wants to be her own woman for the first time in her life. Someone making decisions for her, about anything, is going to piss her off."

"Okay, maybe I should've asked her, but doesn't everyone want to be taken care of, sometimes?"

"How much of your money did you spend on Max?"

"I don't know. About four hundred. Callie's money lasted a week and Fiona told me to ask Callie for more or pay for it myself."

"Does Callie know about the four hundred?"

Lauren whirled to face Val. "No, and you must never tell her, or I'll be in worse trouble."

"I'll keep your secret. But if you know it will piss her off, you shouldn't have done it."

"And what was I supposed to do? Ask her for more money that she doesn't have? She looked after me after the bull bashed me and I hoped to repay her by giving her a C-section for free."

"Tell me you didn't say that to her?" Val gaped at Lauren. "Did you really say you were repaying her for looking after you?"

Lauren glared at her unappetizing lunch and stirred it with violence into a disgusting puree. "Yes, in a way."

"There you go. Reimbursing her for helping you when she did it because she cares about you was mistake number two."

"I always looked after T.J. and she never freaked out about it like this."

"Callie's not T.J. How do you feel when you're with Callie?"

"I like her. More than I ever planned to or wanted to, but the last thing I said to her was, 'Enjoy your very controlled life.' What do I do now?"

"It wouldn't hurt to be honest and apologize. Some women would appreciate a gesture like flowers, but I'm not sure about Callie. She's more straightforward. Like you."

"You think I was wrong?"

Val sighed. "I know you, and I know you were trying to be helpful, but based on her anger your approach wasn't okay."

"Thanks, Val. I'll consider it, but I think this separation is for the best. Don't roll your eyes at me. Maybe Callie and I should keep our interactions professional." Lauren tossed the remains of her uneaten lunch in the trash and fled from the room.

For the rest of lunch, Lauren hid in her office and pretended to read a veterinary journal, but even the article on pneumonia in calves couldn't hold her interest. All she could think about was Callie and how Callie didn't understand her need to help, to feel useful to her. Lauren sighed. Callie was gone and she couldn't decide if that was a good thing. If Callie and Becky were gone from her life, at least her heart wouldn't be at risk again. But that line was getting old, and it wasn't a good excuse anymore. What the hell was she supposed to do now?

As Lauren drove home from work, she examined the argument from Callie's point of view. Where Lauren thought she was being helpful, Callie saw it as interfering and controlling. Lauren sighed. She didn't want a professional relationship with Callie. She wanted more. "Damn it." Callie mesmerized her. Lauren was hooked but filled with conflicting emotions.

There were no ethical rules preventing veterinarians from becoming involved with clients, but it had created an awkward situation. They lived in a small town, and there weren't enough vets to go around, let alone to always send someone other than Lauren to Poplarcreek. Why could life never be simple? If she admired a woman, and they were both single, why not date? Was she ready for another relationship? Lauren wanted a peaceful life but when she was within ten feet of Callie, her peace drained away. Did she want Callie or peace? Was she ready to risk her heart on another family? The answer to the big questions didn't come to her. But apologizing was a must.

After dinner, Lauren wrote a letter to Callie. She explained what she did and why and apologized for overstepping. She wrote how much she respected Callie and thanked her for the excellent help after the bull attack. After several drafts and multiple rewrites, it was ready. At the end of the letter, she begged for an opportunity to meet and talk things out. At one in the morning, she drove the thirty minutes to Poplarcreek and put the letter in Callie's mailbox before she could chicken out.

On her way home, Lauren noticed yard lights on at Kruger Farm and saw a big stock trailer heading down the laneway. It was an odd time to deliver cattle, but who knew what went on over there these days. She just wanted to stay away from them. As she drove on, she forgot the trailer and her thoughts returned to Callie. Maybe it was time to risk her heart again. Callie was worth it.

CHAPTER THIRTY

A nd I got a ninety-five on my science project. My teacher said it was one of the best she'd ever seen," Sam said.

"Good for you, honey. I'm proud of you. Oh, here's Digit," Lauren said. It had been four days since the fight with Callie and she'd heard nothing from her. It was a blow to think she'd ruined that burgeoning relationship, but she was Skyping regularly with Sam and sometimes William, and that helped remind her she wasn't a complete failure at relationships.

"Hi, Digit." Digit stood on Lauren's computer and put his nose to the screen when Sam talked to him.

"He thinks you're here. I better pet him." She stroked his fur and felt calmer, the way she always did when he was on her lap.

"I get to meet him in person this summer. And Elsa. Bet she'll cuddle with me."

"I bet she will." Lauren cleared her throat. "Is William home tonight?"

"Sorry, Mom. I told him you wanted to talk, but he went out with his friends."

"I miss him. Please tell him I love him." She was trying to reconnect with William, but he was often too busy to speak with her. She tried to take it in stride and remember he was eighteen, almost a man, but it hurt.

"I will, but he knows that."

"Thanks, Sammy." Lauren sniffled and glanced around the room desperate to change the topic. "The color you picked for your room looks great." She'd channeled her nervous energy about

Callie into spending her weekend painting the spare room for Sam. "Do you want to pick your own furniture when you come in the summer?"

"Yes please, thanks, Mom."

They chatted for twenty minutes about school, Toronto, and Sam's friends and then Lauren asked, "Do you like cattle?"

"Cattle?"

"My friends have a farm with some beef cattle, and they offered to show you around."

"Your friends?"

"Callie and her daughter, Becky. They own Poplarcreek. Becky is about your age."

"Sounds cool. It's been fun, Mom, but I have a pile of homework."

"Okay, Sam. I love you."

"Love you too, Mom, bye."

Lauren stared at the blank screen for a moment. T.J. encouraged the increasingly frequent conversations and Lauren ensured they didn't interfere with Sam's schedule. She'd said Callie was a friend, but was she more? She couldn't figure it out. With a deep sigh, she set Digit on the floor and headed to her room to change into workout gear. It was time for some physical activity to blunt her anxiety about Callie.

Forty minutes later, Lauren dropped the weights on their cradle and collapsed on the bench in her home gym. "Enough." She plucked at the white tank top glued to her chest with sweat. Her shoulders and arms ached. She had spent too much time on her biceps and shoulders. She would pay for it tomorrow and perhaps the next day. Her exercise goal wasn't big muscles, but to increase stamina and muscle strength in her arms, shoulders, back, and legs. Working with farm animals could be hard on the body, and staying in shape was an important part of preventing injuries.

She jabbed at her still soft stomach. Exercise was also about getting fitter although she'd never measure up physically to Mitch. "And why am I even trying?" She hadn't had a flat stomach since she was a child. It was more important to be healthy than thin.

Lauren gazed at Digit, curled in a ball on her office chair. He followed her from room to room through the small house. "Well, sir, do I stop or keep going? Exercise is better than eating, but the chocolate peanut butter ice cream in the freezer is calling me. Big mistake to buy that, eh?" Digit peered at Lauren and she was sure he understood. "I dropped the letter off, but she hasn't answered. What do I do, Digi?"

Bang, bang, bang.

"What the?" Lauren jumped to her feet. Digit leaped off the chair and darted under her desk.

Bang, bang, bang.

Lauren crept to her back door and parted the curtains an inch. Callie was standing outside with her arms crossed and her weight on one hip. The scowl on Callie's face was frightening, and Lauren considered hiding under the desk with Digit.

"I can see you. Open up."

Lauren stood to one side as Callie burst through the door, kicked off her boots, and stormed into the kitchen.

"I found your note. I've been driving around trying to decide whether to come here. Becky's done with her painting class in thirty minutes."

Callie sucked in a deep breath. Lauren's skin tingled as Callie scanned her body.

"Go put something on or I'll grab at you, and I came to talk, not ravish you." Callie whirled and stomped into the living room.

Lauren obediently ducked into her bedroom. She stripped off the wet top and pulled on a hoodie, but she had no clean sweatpants. Lauren jogged into her living room and hunted for somewhere to sit in sweaty shorts. She dropped to the floor across from the couch and sat with her legs crossed.

Callie yanked off her coat and tossed it on the armchair. Then she perched on the edge of the couch and regarded her in silence for a few moments. "I'm confused. Do I give off a needy, pathetic vibe? Is that why you paid my bill? I appreciate your help and support, but if you think I expect you to pay my bills, you don't understand me."

"I thought I was helping. Honestly, Callie, I was just being nice."

Callie sighed. "I know, Lauren."

Elsa crept from behind the furniture and Digit tiptoed into the room. The cats peered at Callie with trepidation and slunk toward Lauren. Digit crawled into her lap and curled into a contented ball as she petted him. Elsa posed, sitting with her tail wrapped around her feet, keeping her distance.

"I prepared a speech about independence, interference, and respect." Callie pointed to Lauren's lap. "But all I want right now is to be Digit."

Lauren blinked in surprise at the comment and smiled. "You're more like Elsa. She comes close enough for contact but makes me work for it. She's sometimes friendly and sometimes hisses at me."

Callie shrugged and her shoulders slumped as she glanced away.

Lauren's smile dissolved. *Stupid joke. Well done, Cornish.* "I overstepped. I shouldn't have adjusted your bill and I apologize."

Callie locked eyes with Lauren. "Do you think we can forgive each other as easily as that?"

Lauren's voice was strong, and she spoke with no hesitation. "I hope so. I messed up and I'm sorry. I promise I'll be more careful, because I want a future with you. I don't want to fight anymore."

"I don't either. I'm sorry I yelled at you. I admit I might be a little oversensitive about certain things, but I can't help it." Callie abandoned the couch and kneeled in front of Lauren. She cupped Lauren's face in her hands and kissed her. The cats disappeared as Callie crawled into Lauren's lap.

They continued to kiss as their breathing accelerated, and they explored each other with their hands at a frantic pace. They shifted until Lauren was on the bottom with Callie on top. Callie buried a hand in the sweaty hair on the nape of Lauren's neck and kissed her. Lauren slipped her hands under Callie's sweater and caressed the warm, smooth flesh of her back and the sides of her breasts.

Callie straddled Lauren's leg and pressed down. "Lauren, please."

"I can feel how hot you are against my leg."

Callie moaned as Lauren flipped her over. She slipped her hand under the front of Callie's top to stroke warm breasts. "I want to taste you." She slid the sweater and bra up Callie's chest and found Callie's nipples. Callie bucked and moaned at the contact as Lauren gave equal attention to both breasts.

Lauren fingered the button on Callie's jeans and stared into blue eyes for an answer to her unspoken question.

"Oh, yes. Hurry, please."

The request sent Lauren into action. She popped the button of Callie's jeans and opened the zipper. She slid her fingers across soft, warm skin pulling a gasp and an urgent moan from Callie. Callie trembled as Lauren caressed her abdomen and slid her hand into her panties.

She moved her fingers achingly slowly over Callie's center until they were inside her, surrounded in wet and warmth. Callie trembled and her back arched at the intimate contact. Lauren thrust and increased her speed as Callie directed her.

"I can't wait. Now, baby," Callie said.

Lauren slipped from the warmth bringing Callie's wetness with her. She rubbed and circled Callie's clit carrying Callie higher until she crashed. She held Callie until the trembling stopped and peppered her face with warm kisses. "You're incredible, Cals."

Callie kissed Lauren and cupped her between her legs. "I wish we had more time."

Lauren snatched two pillows off the couch, and they lay on the floor. They gazed into each other's eyes as they kissed and promised more. When it was time, Lauren helped Callie to her feet and into her coat. Callie pressed her body against Lauren's. Then she rested her head on Lauren's shoulder and sighed when Lauren embraced her. "Thank you."

Callie stepped back and Lauren grinned at the dreamy expression on Callie's face and her drooping eyelids. "You're so beautiful," Lauren said.

"I hope I'm safe to drive. I'm a little distracted." Callie giggled. "Becky has a birthday party and sleepover at a friend's on Friday. Come for dinner?"

"I'd like that. I'm not working this weekend." Lauren rejoiced at the invitation. "Thank you for giving me another chance."

"A date then. I'll see you on Friday."

Callie leaned in for a deep, demanding kiss. Lauren's heart swelled and her legs turned to rubber, and then Callie pulled away, her beautiful eyes intense, before she loped down the stairs and back to her truck.

Lauren closed the door behind Callie and then flopped onto her living room floor. What had just happened? It wasn't the way she'd imagined their first time, but Callie had approved. She'd loved taking care of her and the quiet moan when Callie came still excited her.

Lauren frowned. Aside from being beautiful and sexy, above all else, Callie was generous and kind. She had given Lauren another chance, and Lauren finally understood how Callie felt.

Lauren stood and stripped off her clothes as she headed to the shower. Callie had a right to control over her farm bills. She would be more careful in the future. Lauren grinned. And there did seem to be a future for them. Or, at least an actual date.

Friday night, Lauren dressed with care. Digit was available to consult, but she ordered him to stay away from her black pants. Black clothes were a disaster in a house with orange cats. It didn't matter how often she vacuumed there was always hair. After dressing, she would risk sitting nowhere and would be out the door a second later.

Lauren gathered her packages, jumped into her truck, and headed to Poplarcreek. Her stomach fluttered. All week, she had waited for this evening with a mixture of anticipation and trepidation.

At a quarter after six, she arrived at Poplarcreek and knocked. She entered the mudroom and discarded her outdoor clothing. She ignored the sudden overpowering sense of disquiet washing through her. *You will enjoy this evening, Lauren Louise Cornish. You will not say or do anything stupid.* The past needed to stay where it belonged so she could get a glimpse of her future.

CHAPTER THIRTY-ONE

"Hello to the house," Lauren called.

Callie stuck her head out of her bedroom. "I'll be right down." She pirouetted in front of the mirror and inspected her outfit. She was wearing a loose royal blue sweater dress with black leggings. Her hair was off her neck in a knot and she wore a little makeup. "Simple, yet sexy," she whispered to her reflection. She slipped on shoes and sashayed downstairs and into Lauren's open arms. "Hey, you." She caressed Lauren's shoulders and kissed her. When their mouths broke apart, they held each other in a loose embrace and grinned.

"Dinner's almost ready. The corkscrew is in the drawer by the stove."

"Smells delicious." Lauren rummaged through the mishmash of implements in the drawer and emerged with the corkscrew.

Callie put the bottle of wine Lauren brought in the refrigerator and passed her the bottle she had chilling. Lauren opened the wine and filled the two wineglasses Callie passed her.

Callie accepted a glass of wine and winked. "Thanks for the gift, but I find a toothbrush is all I require." She pointed to the package Lauren brought.

Lauren grinned and shrugged. "Then I'll give it to Max." An instant later, Max hopped forward. He was a polite pup and had waited for Lauren to notice him. Lauren carried the rawhide bone into the living room and Max followed.

When dinner was ready, Callie and Lauren sat across the kitchen table from each other. Callie had rearranged the dishes and cutlery on her table three times. She wanted to sit where she could both see and touch Lauren. She'd made salmon filets with herbs and lemon, wild rice, spinach salad, and squash from her summer garden.

Callie struggled to focus on Lauren's face, but she had little control over her desires. Her eyes strayed down Lauren's body and then returned to Lauren's eyes. She couldn't help it. Lauren wore simple black dress pants, with a blue dress shirt under a dark-green fleece vest. She looked gorgeous.

Lauren sipped the wine. "I hope the wine I brought is drinkable. I purchased what they recommended in the liquor store."

Callie smiled. "I did the same thing." There was no pretense with Lauren. She was thoughtful and didn't try to impress. Another woman might have overspent on the wine or repeated words the salesperson told her to sound smart.

Lauren grabbed the bag she'd left hanging on the chair beside her. "I saw this in the city on Wednesday." Lauren shrugged. "It was on sale and I thought Becky might like it."

Callie accepted the light khaki vest and held it up. "She'll love all the pockets. There's room for her camera, extra batteries, a notebook, and her pocketknife, plus whatever interesting bits of nature she collects on her hikes."

"I hope you don't mind that I bought it. I don't mean to imply you can't afford it. Am I meddling again? I am, aren't I? I apologize. Do you want me to return it? I will if you want."

"It's all right, Lauren. It's a gift. I understand." She kissed Lauren on the cheek. She adored Lauren for thinking of Becky and spending time with her, and she didn't want to seem ungrateful.

"I often took Samantha clothes shopping. My daughter prefers dresses and frills. We had fun mother and daughter trips to the mall, then I bought us lunch or dinner. On the days when we had more time, we'd see a show or go to the ballet. Sam enjoyed *Jersey Boys* though most of their songs were older than me. I'm being boring, but I miss her." Sadness and hurt crept into Lauren's eyes.

Callie cupped Lauren's cheek. "Honey, I enjoy listening to stories about your children. And for the record, you never bore me."

Lauren sniffled. "Thanks."

"How are Sam and William?"

Lauren brightened. "Sam's coming this summer, but if I want to see William, I'm going to have to fly home. He's still not there yet."

Callie concentrated on her plate as she pushed food around. Lauren had called Ontario home. She needed to ask the question keeping her awake at nights. She had tried to ask before but hadn't been strong enough to hear the answer. Callie wasn't sure she was ready yet, but she had to know. "Do you ever think of moving back to Toronto?"

"I'll never live in Toronto again, but west of Toronto, near Stratford or London would be all right."

As Lauren's words sliced into her, Callie jumped to her feet and busied herself collecting their dirty dishes. She couldn't make eye contact as she stacked the dishes on the counter. *What did you expect her to say? I want to live in Thresherton forever?*

Lauren scooted in behind Callie and slid her arms around her waist. "I just realized how that sounded, and what you were really asking. I'm not going anywhere. Saskatchewan and Thresherton are home now, and I'm happy. I enjoy being with you and I want to see where we can go with this. I'm even considering talking to Ian and Fiona about buying into PVS as a partner."

Callie smiled, relieved at the clarification. "Thanks for telling me." She motioned for Lauren to sit at the breakfast bar while she finished clearing the dishes. Once the dirty dishes were stacked for another day, she slipped around the bar until she stood in front of Lauren. She would worry about the future another time.

Callie slid her hands along the inside of Lauren's thighs, Lauren gasped and crushed her mouth to Callie's. Callie stepped back and tugged Lauren's hand. "Come to bed with me."

"Is that it? Is that all you're going to say? What about sweeping me off my feet?"

Lauren joked, but Callie detected a note of panic in her voice. "You're a farm animal veterinarian and slop through straw and manure all day. I need to sweep up after you, not sweep you off your feet." She tugged on Lauren's hand. "Please, baby, I want you."

"I'm crazy attracted to you, but I'm petrified. You're the first woman I've been with in four years."

"Four years? But weren't you—" *Still married?* Callie finished the sentence in her head. She had heard of lesbian relationships where couples stayed together for years after their sex life died.

Lauren laughed softly. "Val says that makes me a virgin again."

"Intriguing." Callie laughed. "It'll be fine. Like riding a bicycle."

"Don't say that, I'll panic." Lauren blinked and raised her hands in mock terror. "I was on a bike last summer for the first time in seven years. There was a helmet, elbow pads, and knee pads. I squeezed into tight biking shorts with a padded ass and a crotch that clung unbecomingly."

"Sexy. Thanks for the image."

Lauren continued, the words tumbling from her lips. "I'm not kidding. I wobbled along the path and almost killed another cyclist. There were lots of bruises and blood, and I had to concentrate to keep from crying."

"Oh no." Callie covered her mouth and her body shook with laughter.

Lauren waved her hands in front of her. "If sex after four years of celibacy is like riding a bicycle, sex is way too dangerous."

"Well, it could be dangerous." Callie let her eyes roam Lauren's body. "Let's see how it goes this time." Callie scanned Lauren's pale face. "Do you want to make love? No pressure."

"I do, but I'm still worried I'll faint."

Callie sighed with exasperation. "Do you always joke when you're nervous?"

"Yes, but I also tell jokes when I'm bored, diffusing conflict, or trying to be funny. You won't find a pattern."

Tired of the banter, Callie pulled Lauren into a hard kiss. "Shut up, Lauren."

"Make me."

Callie smiled as she unzipped Lauren's vest. She gripped the edges of Lauren's shirt and yanked it open. The sounds of tearing cloth and bits of plastic raining down on the kitchen floor sidetracked their passion.

Lauren laughed until she gasped for breath. "No snaps on this shirt, Wonder Woman."

"Sorry," Callie mumbled. "I thought there were."

Lauren tilted Callie's head up and kissed her. Their lips brushed in a soft, sensual joining.

Callie broke away and stooped to gather buttons and pieces of buttons. "Maybe I can fix it."

Lauren snorted. "Now you do need to sweep up after me."

Callie focused on Lauren and smiled. Lauren lounged against the counter with her shirt hanging open, allowing a glimpse of gorgeous breasts spilling from a simple black bra. Callie loved breasts. Her own were too small, but Lauren's were beautiful.

Callie discarded the buttons and pressed her body against Lauren's. She yanked her shirt open wide and kissed the tops of Lauren's breasts, caressing her nipples through the fabric of her bra.

By the time they landed in Callie's bedroom, Lauren's nervousness had evaporated and Callie's confidence had returned. She finished removing Lauren's shirt and bra, then perched on the edge of the bed, pulled Lauren closer, and feasted her eyes and then lips on her full breasts.

"Wait, Callie." Lauren dragged Callie to her feet and removed her sweater dress and bra.

Callie undid Lauren's pants and pushed down both pants and panties until Lauren stepped out of them. She kissed Lauren's breasts and slipped her hand between her legs. "So wet."

Lauren stood with legs apart. "I can't stand any longer. I need you on top of me."

Callie paused for half a beat, excited by the unfamiliar request. Lauren was struggling for air and shaking with desire. Callie yanked the covers out of the way and Lauren lay on her back. "Lights on or off?"

"On please, always. I can't imagine not looking into your eyes."

Callie switched on the reading lamp beside her bed and draped a red scarf over the shade to dim the harsh light. She peeled off her leggings and panties and slid into bed. Lauren spread her legs in invitation as Callie settled on top.

"Are you okay?" Callie kissed Lauren's face and neck. She never realized how much she would love leading or how sexy Lauren's surrender would be.

"Oh yes, Cals." Lauren breathed the words.

Cals. There it was again. The nickname no one else had ever used. "What do you want me to do for you, baby?"

"I want to feel you inside me."

"You're in a hurry." Callie entered Lauren slowly. "You're so ready."

"Wet for you since I arrived tonight." Lauren mumbled something else Callie couldn't decipher as she raised her knees to take her deeper. When Lauren asked for more, Callie increased to three fingers as she pumped faster. Lauren's eyes snapped shut, and she moaned with each thrust. Callie followed her hands with her mouth and scooted lower. She licked and circled, but Lauren was close and came with a quiet groan.

Callie kept licking and kissing until Lauren nudged her head away. "Come here." Lauren spoke her breath coming in small gasps.

Callie kissed flushed skin as she crawled up Lauren's body and drew her against her.

"Incredible," Lauren said.

"My pleasure." Callie stroked Lauren's back. She winced as she traced the new scar tracking down the middle of her back.

After a few minutes, Lauren rose on one elbow to caress and kiss Callie's skin. Since Lauren had recovered, Callie became demanding. "On top."

Lauren slipped between Callie's legs and lowered herself until their breasts touched. Full breasts swept along Callie's body, leaving goose bumps in their wake and fulfilling her fantasy.

"I prefer to take my time, but I aim to please. Tell me what you want, Cals."

"You."

That was enough for Lauren as she kissed Callie's palms and the insides of her wrists. Then she flicked her tongue against Callie's earlobe until she writhed underneath her.

When Callie could wait no longer, she pushed against the top of Lauren's head and Lauren shifted lower, where Callie hungered for her. Lauren draped Callie's legs over her shoulders and slid her hands under Callie's ass. She drove her tongue deep inside, and they moaned in unison at the contact. Lauren replaced her tongue with one, and then two fingers.

"Now, now, baby," Callie said.

Lauren thrust her fingers in and out. Then Lauren shifted to Callie's clit and licked and rubbed with her lips while she thrust. Callie gripped the bed and threw herself repeatedly against Lauren's fingers. After a minute of frantic movement, she stilled, tensed, and came with a series of moans. Lauren kissed her thighs and belly until Callie tugged on Lauren's shoulders to bring her to lie face-to-face.

"I want your weight on top of me," Callie said.

"I'm too heavy."

"You aren't. Please." Callie orgasmed again under the weight of Lauren's body and from the pressure of her thigh. Lauren slid off and Callie burrowed into Lauren's chest. She kissed each breast once and promised to return for seconds.

Callie woke in the quiet room and glanced beside her. It had taken forever to coax Lauren into bed and now she was here. Callie was warm and content and ached to crawl on top of Lauren and make love to her again. It was a struggle to drag herself from bed.

Lauren yawned. "Where're you going, Cals?"

"The barn. Go back to sleep."

Lauren glanced at the clock. "At midnight? You expecting a calving?"

Callie dug in her dresser for jeans and a sweater. "I always check on my animals after dinner. Tonight, I was too busy."

"Can I come?" Lauren leaped out of bed and searched the floor for her slacks.

"You already did." Callie giggled when Lauren blushed.

Lauren squeezed into one of Callie's sweaters and frowned as she tugged at the tight garment. Callie enjoyed the way the sweater clung to Lauren's curves and accentuated her generous breasts. She held Lauren's hands and kissed her on the nose. "It's a perfect fit."

They held hands as they walked to the barn. Lauren topped up the hay for the cows and Callie checked on the calves. Satisfied the animals were well, they returned to the house.

Callie pulled dishes from the cupboard. "The fire is ready to go, and the matches are on the bookshelf. I'll be right in."

Ten minutes later, Callie entered the living room with a tray holding two cups, a small pitcher of cream, a sugar bowl, two huge slices of pie, and a carafe of coffee. "I never fed you dessert." She set the tray down and handed a plate of pie to Lauren.

Lauren forked a piece of pie into her mouth. She chewed slowly and squinted at Callie. "This is delicious. Is it blueberry?"

"It's not all blueberry. It's a berry mix. Wilkins family secret recipe." Callie dropped into the couch beside Lauren. "My parents shipped me buckets of fresh and frozen berries last season."

After finishing the pie, Callie stretched out against Lauren. They lounged in contented silence as they drank coffee and stared into the fire. Callie sighed and relived every step of the perfect evening in her mind. Then Lauren began to laugh.

Callie sat up. "What is it?" She winced. "Did I do something wrong?"

Lauren smiled and stroked Callie's face. "You're incredible, but I liked that shirt."

"Oh you." Callie playfully slapped Lauren on the shoulder. "I'm sorry I destroyed your shirt, but it was sexy."

Lauren attempted a serious expression, but still ended up smiling. "Careful. I have a limited wardrobe of nice clothes."

Callie pressed closer. When she slid her hands under Lauren's sweater and demanded more, they rose to their feet. She set the screen in front of the dying fire and took Lauren's hand to lead her upstairs. Invigorated by a nap and boosted with a feed of sugar, they made love again. The future might be murky, but this moment was as perfect as it could be.

CHAPTER THIRTY-TWO

"Pineapple does too go on pizza," Gwen said and emphasized her point by poking Becky in the ribs.

Becky tickled Gwen. "Does not, and stop poking me. Pineapple's a dessert."

"Stop it, you two." Callie grinned at the two kids. Ever since meeting Heather Kruger's girls she'd been wishing Becky had a sister. Now she did, almost. They'd met Val and Gwen after school on Tuesday for dinner, but a last-minute emergency had prevented Lauren from joining them. Callie hugged herself. The weekend of lovemaking had been amazing, and she wanted to spend many more with her.

"I thought we solved this by getting pineapple on only one side?" Val asked. "Besides, Gwen, we can't help it if the Andersons are *limited* in their pizza topping choices."

"Ha, you think so?" Callie smiled at Val. She wondered where she and Lauren would end up, but thanks to Lauren's introduction, she had a new friend in Val. A local lesbian, a single mom, and a smart independent woman.

"Oh no." Val tipped her head toward the door of the pizza restaurant.

Callie turned in time to see Heinz Kruger lumber in. She turned her back while he placed his order. She could feel his mean little eyes burning into her back, but she plastered on a smile. She was fed up with the Krugers spoiling her fun.

A few minutes later, Callie jumped as Val tipped Callie's plate and slid her nearly untouched dinner into the empty pizza box without so much as a word of warning. She gave Callie a quick warning look before turning to the girls with a reassuring smile. "Okay, girls. Time for home. Popcorn and cartoons?" Val asked as she picked up the box with Callie's pizza and the box with the small pizza they'd purchased for Lauren.

"Yahoo." Gwen and Becky tossed on their coats and charged outside. Val followed, and then Callie saw what had caused Val to move so quickly.

"Hello, Catherine," Heinz said from his position against the counter. "You have a nice evening? You and your pervert girlfriend?"

Callie ignored him, but she burned with anger as she walked to Val's car. Now he was making comments about Val, too. Enough was enough. She paused with her hand on the handle of Val's car, then turned back to face the restaurant.

The car window slid down. "Get in, please, Callie. Don't do it."

"I'll just be a minute. Stay here and watch my back."

"He's dangerous."

Callie ignored the sound advice and stormed back into the restaurant. A quick glance told her she and Heinz were the only customers.

"Forget something, Catherine?"

She stood with her back straight and her hands relaxed at her sides. "Heinz, I've had enough." Her resolve never faltered as she looked Heinz in the eyes. "You and Kyle have been threatening my family and trying to intimidate me for too long. I want you to stop."

Heinz laughed. "What are you talking about, Catherine?" He lowered himself into a chair and looked at her quizzically.

"Quit the games. I'm talking about using my trailer to smuggle stolen cattle and drugs. I'm talking about the harassment and pretending to kidnap Becky. I'm talking about telling Heather she'd be moving to Poplarcreek because I was selling it. You're also trying to get money from me because your bull crashed through my fence and bred my heifers. I'm talking about the leaflets, the letters, the threats. Oh, and, Heinz, I did the math. It took six weeks for all my heifers to calve. Didn't you notice your bull missing for six weeks, Heinz? Didn't you need Bulldozer, Heinz?"

He shrugged. "Well, Doug had crappy fences."

"Stop right there." Callie glared at him. "Doug and I were mending fences when he died. Even if the fence of the heifer paddock broke that still doesn't explain how your bull was in there for six weeks." She waited for Heinz to say something and then continued. "Oh, and if it broke, why didn't the heifers escape?"

Heinz laced his hands behind his head and stretched his legs out but didn't say anything.

"Based on the calving date of the first heifer, your bull got in with my heifers about the time Doug died. Curious coincidence."

Heinz's face turned purple, and he opened his mouth as if to say something but closed it again.

"You can't explain that can you, Heinz? I'm tired of your games and the bullshit you've pulled on Lauren."

"Dr. Cornish? What does she have to do with anything?" He looked genuinely confused.

"Kyle lured her to the clinic after dark and suggested she should stay out of his way or he'd assault her." Callie glowered at the man. "Later, your bull attacked her when he was let out of the headgate."

Heinz shrugged. "It happens."

"You're attacking her to scare her into keeping quiet. She's not scared of you and neither am I."

Heinz was fast for a large man. He stood and stepped toward Callie. "You look scared now."

"I'm not scared, Heinz. I'm pissed off. You might have scared me before, but not now. I'm tired of your shit. You need to quit before you kill somebody. You'll never own my farm."

Heinz snarled at her, looking like the dangerous animal he was. "You better be careful. Don't tell me what to do. I'm the one in control."

"Wrong again, Heinz. You were in control because I let you walk all over me." Callie's voice emerged as a growl. "But we're done with that. You've no power over me. Back off and leave my family alone."

"Or else, Catherine?" Heinz stepped closer to Callie and pointed a finger at her, almost touching the tip of her nose. "*You* better back off."

Callie recalled the rumors of spousal and child abuse, and it occurred to her Heinz might hit her. Still, she didn't step back. She refused to let him intimidate her anymore. "You leave my farm alone and you leave my family alone and that includes Lauren. And you better quit sending letters and emails. I'm done with you, and I'll make myself a nuisance at the police station if you don't leave me alone. I'm sure you get my meaning."

His face was red with anger and his voice was low and menacing. "You better be careful, girlie."

"I'm not a girlie, and you're a pathetic, greedy old man and I'm done with being bullied." Heinz's face darkened, and she feared he might have a heart attack. Not that it would be the worst outcome.

Heinz moved so close his hot, fetid breath hit her face. "You better watch your back, bitch. Nobody threatens me, and it's time you moved back to British Columbia."

Callie's nose wrinkled as she detected the unpleasant smell of whisky and cigarettes. She had said what she needed to. She stomped from the restaurant, working hard to keep from running to Val's car as his evil stare stabbed her in the back.

When they arrived a Poplarcreek, Becky jumped out and charged toward the porch. "Knapsack," Callie called. Becky ran back, grabbed her bag, and loped toward the door. "Homework and then bed."

"Yes, Mom."

Callie ran her hand along the side of Lauren's truck as she walked past. It was nice to arrive home to a warm, bright house and the music with a fast beat that sailed out to greet her.

Lauren greeted her at the door and accepted the pizza boxes and a quick kiss. "Becky's upstairs. Thanks for the pizza. Join me? I just got home, and I lit the fire."

Callie slipped out of her boots and coat and entered her kitchen. She took the pizza from Lauren and set it on the table. Then she hugged her hard. Lauren had called Poplarcreek home.

"Callie? You okay?"

Callie headed into the living room and sank into the couch. "We ran into Heinz at dinner."

"Are you okay?"

Callie nodded. "I yelled at him." Pride settled around her as if it were a protective cloak. She had faced Heinz. Confronted her bully. He would have to leave Lauren alone. Warmth and love penetrated all the cells of Callie's body. Lauren was special, smart, and kind. Insecure sometimes, but who wasn't?

Lauren sat on the couch. "What happened?" Her voice resonated with concern.

"Can we not talk about it right now? I just want to...be." Lauren stroked her hair and tucked a blanket around her. Warm, safe, and cared for, Callie allowed her eyes to drift shut.

Later, Callie sat up and rubbed her eyes. She had fallen asleep and Lauren had held her. "How long was I out?"

"About twenty minutes. Feel better?" Lauren asked.

Callie kissed Lauren on the tip of the nose. "Yes, thanks." The adrenaline had worn off and she felt drained.

"What happened with Heinz? Did you do something crazy?"

She locked eyes with Lauren. "I ordered him to leave us all alone. I'm tired of Heinz and Kyle harassing us, and I let him know it. I warned him I'd go back to the police."

Lauren held Callie's hand. "You're brave, but it wasn't safe. What happens if they retaliate?"

"It was time for me to stand up to him."

Lauren leaned back and gazed at Callie. "Did you really yell at him?" Lauren chuckled. "I bet few people yell at Heinz Kruger. I'm impressed." Lauren cupped her hands around her mouth imitating a megaphone. "Callie faces down the bully and wins."

"I care about you. And I want to keep you safe." Callie clasped Lauren's hand and held it to her lips. "I won't have you injured again. I'll fight all the Heinz Krugers in the world to keep you safe."

❖

Two days after the confrontation with Heinz, Callie spotted Kyle in the Thresherton hardware store. He made a shooting motion at her with his hand and smirked. She locked eyes with him for a few seconds, then shook her head, and continued shopping. She'd stood up to Heinz and she could handle Kyle.

While she crouched by a bin of electrical receptacles, selecting white GFCI ones for the bathrooms, he snuck close, loomed over her, and whispered in her ear. "You should've been more careful, you dumb bitch. Yelling at my old man was stupid."

"Go away, Kyle."

"You'll be sorry, girlie. You and your bitch girlfriend. Just like Doug's stupid old horse."

Her stomach lurched. "Horse? That was you? You chased Jake?"

"Now *you're* gonna wish you'd kept your fucking mouth shut." He backed away, his eyes hard and cold.

She'd stood up to both Heinz and Kyle, but it was hard to ignore the new threat. Her stomach roiled. Kyle had chased poor old Jake to his death. Callie abandoned her shopping and hurried from the store. She nearly turned back to confront him, but she was worried about Kyle's threat to hurt Lauren.

Callie groaned as she got into her truck. It was getting tedious calling Mitch with each new incident with the Krugers, but Mitch wanted everything documented. She'd call her from home, but when would the harassment end? When one of them was dead?

She called Lauren's phone and left a message. "Hi, it's Callie. I'm in Thresherton and headed home now. If you're near Poplarcreek at lunchtime, drop in and I'll feed you. It would be nice to see you." If she could see Lauren, she would know she was safe.

Callie pulled out of town into a snowstorm. The snow had started after she left home in the morning. But now strong winds whipped the snow into a white cloud, reducing visibility to twenty feet. It was nothing she hadn't driven in before, but she kept her eyes locked on the road as she drove. She didn't want to slip into the ditch.

Twenty minutes into her trip, a huge truck pulled up behind her, riding her bumper. Callie peered through the flurries of snow to see more details. The truck was big and green or black. Her heart began to race as she thought of Kyle's threat.

The truck jerked out from behind her and into the oncoming lane. It was a pickup truck, a size larger than hers. She slowed to let it by, but it veered toward her. She swerved to avoid a collision, and her right front tire hit a patch of ice. Callie bounced off the door of her cab as her truck slued off the road. She screamed as it flipped and slid down the hill of the river valley, metal grinding until it burrowed nose first into an enormous snowdrift.

Callie hung from the seat in a sling made by her seat belt. Disorientated and dizzy, she tried to slow her breathing and get control. She swung her body until she could grab the steering wheel and while holding on, opened her seat belt and dropped onto her hands and knees in the broken windshield glass and snow covering the inside of her truck.

She was shaken and bruised but had no broken bones. All she saw through her windows was the hardpacked white of the snowdrift the truck had lodged in. She dug at the snow through her side window and then through the smashed windshield. It would have been easier to chip through cement. The weight of the truck had packed the snow and her only digging tools were a hand-held snow scraper and a travel mug lid.

Callie stopped digging to review her options. She considered conserving her energy and waiting for rescue, but that was a gamble she was unwilling to take. It wasn't her style to wait for rescue or to let others look after her, and besides, only her neighbors used the road she was on. Waiting to be rescued was too big a gamble. She had to do something before the falling snow buried her truck, with her in it.

Callie squeezed under the headrest of her seat and struggled to open the rear window. As she pushed at the closed window, she tamped down her desperation and concentrated on a logical plan of escape. She pushed and heaved, then she lay on her back and kicked at it. The window slid open four inches before it jammed. The impact of the crash had bent the window frame, and it was stuck.

If she didn't escape, she would die of hypothermia. Any trapped heat had vanished when the windows broke. Callie punched in the emergency number on her cell phone. *No signal. No surprise. And no chance.* Her calm slipped and panic built. "No, no, no. Please, no. Please God, no."

Callie cried in frustration but resumed digging through the snow blocking the driver's window. As she sweated from the exertion of digging, she cooled to a dangerous degree.

Shivering, she remembered her emergency kit, with flares and a flashlight. It also included insulated snow pants and thermal shirts. Callie managed to yank it out from under the passenger seat, and by contorting herself, she pried off her boots and wriggled into the snow pants. She stuck the foil thermal packets into each of her boots. It would help, but only for so long.

Callie's best chance appeared to be the rear window. She repeatedly slammed the heel of her boot at the window. "Shit, shit, shit," she yelled. She searched for something to break it with, but it was safety glass and difficult to smash. Logic and common sense deserted her, and she pressed her face to the narrow opening and screamed for help until she was hoarse. She shivered as her words echoed in her snow tomb. Exhausted from her exertions, she rested and munched on a chocolate bar she found in her purse. She had lost track of how long she had been trying to escape. Even in her warmer clothes, her feet and backside were numb.

Her gloves were light driving gloves and when she removed them to eat, her hands cooled until her fingers were stiff when she wiggled them. She longed to unzip her coat and warm her fingers against her body, but she needed to keep her core warm to survive. She would live without a few fingers.

After a while, Callie became more peaceful and ceased shivering. She smiled as much as her cold facial muscles allowed. "The chocolate bar is warming me," she mumbled as she dug through her purse for a bottle of water. She dumped her purse and pawed through the contents, searching for the water.

She unscrewed the bottle, but her fingers wouldn't cooperate to lift it to her lips. The bottle slipped from her grasp and emptied as it rolled away. She burst into tears. Her brain was foggy, and she couldn't concentrate on her task. Callie slumped against the seat.

"Sorry for leaving you an orphan, Becky." Becky would have no parents. Her worst fear for her daughter was to lose another person she loved and now it had happened. She shouldn't have to lose two mothers. Callie hugged herself and imagined hugging her daughter. She pictured Becky's first few wobbly steps as she walked from her arms across the room and into Liz's strong hands. Liz was gone too. "I failed, Liz. I should have looked after Becky and now she's alone. I'm so sorry."

The vision of Liz faded, and Lauren slid into view. Callie saw her smiles, her warm lips, and an ocean of caring and respect in her eyes. She could almost feel Lauren close to her. The feeling of lying curled in Lauren's arms while they slept and then waking to make love again. There would be no future for them after all. Even if she crawled out of all the worries that made her hold back, it was too late. The Krugers had won

"Stay safe, Lauren. Look after Becky. She needs you." Callie couldn't protect Lauren and Becky from the Krugers. She couldn't even protect herself. What a waste of time. She'd fought everyone for control over her life and she'd lost that too.

Callie curled into a ball, drifting in and out of sleep. As the cold settled deep into her bones, her brain became more muddled and a curtain of grayness dropped across her mind. She removed her hat and unzipped her jacket. "Odd, I'm warmer now." Then she let herself go. Sleep was peaceful.

CHAPTER THIRTY-THREE

Lauren drove along the road to Poplarcreek to meet Callie for lunch. It was snowing but was no worse than the weather she had driven in a hundred times already this winter. It was a rare treat on a busy day to have lunch with Callie.

Engrossed in her daydreams, Lauren almost missed the tracks that veered off the road and were nearly covered in fresh snow. She turned her truck, careful to keep her wheels on the road, and drove back. She flipped on her hazard lights and jumped out to scan the river valley. The snow still fell and would cover everything soon. She was about to turn away when she spotted the tailgate of a vehicle protruding from a snowdrift part way down the hill. The license plate read POPCRK. Her stomach clenched in fear.

Lauren's immediate instinct was to throw herself down the hill and get to Callie as fast as possible, but her emergency training helped her keep a cool head. She snatched her cell phone from the cab of the truck, but the signal was weak. Twice she telephoned the clinic, but following a period of static, the calls dropped. Callie's message at ten thirty said she was on her way home. Ninety minutes ago. Way too long in this cold. She searched the slope for footprints. There were none. Had the falling snow buried Callie's footprints? Had Callie escaped or was she still in her truck?

"Callie!" she shouted. "Can you hear me?" There was no answer. She grabbed the ropes and halters from her med kit, tied them end-to-end and then tied one end to her bumper. She looped the other end over her shoulder and clipped on the snowshoes she sometimes had to use to get to animals in the field.

Snowshoes weren't great on steep hills and Lauren was clumsy. Halfway down, she tripped and slid the rest of the way. She stopped when she slammed into the tailgate of the truck. The impact knocked the breath out of her for a few seconds.

Lauren ducked under the tailgate and dug through to the window at the back of the cab. It was open four inches and Callie lay slumped inside. "Callie? Callie, wake up, love." When there was no answer, Lauren stared hard to see if she was still breathing. Her chest was barely moving. "Callie, love, please wake up." She struggled to open the window. The adrenaline of terror propelled her to fight until it opened another two inches, wide enough to reach through. Pressing until her body was flat against the glass of the rear window, she could touch Callie's leg. Her leg was ice cold. "Please, Cals, please wake up." She grasped Callie's pants leg and shook it with fierce determination, as tears of frustration seared their way down her freezing face.

When there was no response, Lauren removed her arm and crumbled. Callie was cold and unresponsive, but she couldn't be dead. Lauren scrambled on hands and knees from under the truck. "Hang on, Cals, I'll be back."

Lauren searched for any useful items thrown from the truck bed when Callie crashed. All she found were empty feedbags and a few wisps of straw. Pulling hand over hand on her rope, she climbed the hill. When she reached the road, she sank to her knees on the ground. Her lungs burned from the deep breaths of the cold air she inhaled.

She forced herself to her feet and stumbled to the cab to try her cell phone again. Still no signal. She considered going for help, but terror at the possibility she would be too late to save Callie stopped her. The falling snow could obliterate the truck's tracks before she returned with help and she might not find the exact spot where Callie skidded off the road.

In desperation, Lauren dug through her veterinary equipment. Discarding useless items, she searched and prayed for something useful. She stuffed tools for working with horseshoes in her pockets. Lauren could use her truck to rescue Callie, but if she drove down the hill, she would be stuck. Still, she could rescue Callie and keep her warm until the truck ran out of gas. They would freeze to death wrapped in each other's arms. Not a good option either.

Lauren pounced on her calving jack. "This might work." She slung the calving jack over her shoulder and jammed the calving chains in a pocket. She charged down the hill and slipped again. This time when she crashed into the truck, the impact cut her forehead above her left eye. Her warm blood, as if it were a line of fire, burned its way down her frozen face. She held a handful of snow to the gash until the blood slowed to a trickle and then crawled to the back window.

Lauren fastened one end of a calving chain around the horseshoe puller and the other to the winch. She stuck the puller thorough the opening in the window of the cab and turned the tool forty-five degrees, as if turning a key in a lock. She positioned one side of the U-shaped end of the calving-jack above the window and the other below and winched. An instant later, the chains slipped and pinched Lauren's finger between sharp metal. "Damn it, Damn it."

Lauren wiggled her finger. It didn't appear broken, but it was numb with cold and she couldn't be sure. The muscles of her face felt paralyzed with cold and when she touched her cheek, she discovered a streak of frozen blood running from forehead to chin. *Enough fussing. Back to work.*

Lauren's thick gloves prevented her from manipulating small objects, so she had removed them. Her numb fingers fumbled with the calving chains. She tried to grab them and whimpered when her frozen fingers wouldn't cooperate. Lauren stuffed the fingers of her left hand into her mouth to warm them and switched them with the fingers of her right hand. The temporary warming gave her enough dexterity to hook the chains to the winch again. She winched keeping her speed slow and steady.

Again, the horseshoe puller slipped, and she fell backward. She repositioned the tool, hooked the calving chains on, and continued winching. The next time the tool slipped it fell from the chains onto the ceiling of the cab. She stuck her arm inside and reached for it, but it was too far. Calm abandoned her. She removed her arm and pounded at the window in fury. "Damn it, Damn it, Damn it. Stupid crappy window. Callie, wake up and help me. Callie, please." Callie didn't so much as stir.

Lauren cursed winter and her clumsiness until she collapsed panting. "Well done, stupid. That was a waste of energy." Her hands would be bruised and sore when they thawed, but at least they were warmer now.

Lauren searched her pockets for the hoof rasp. She attached the chains and positioned the rasp through the window. Holding the chains to keep the rasp in place, she hooked them to the winch. She braced her feet on either side of the window and pumped the winch handle. She strained, pumping it until her shoulders and arms neared exhaustion, and the pole started to bend.

Panting, Lauren paused with her head hanging while she struggled to drag air into her lungs. She no longer had enough strength to pump. "Stupid winch. Stupid window. And stupid winter. One more time or she'll die."

Lauren grabbed the handle and pumped. This would be her last effort. She would have no more strength to continue and too little energy to pull herself up the hill. She would stay with Callie and in the spring, somebody would find them. "I tried, Cals. Sorry, love. I won't leave you." She pumped the winch one more time and shouted when the window broke apart, throwing her on top of the metal winch. Her brain registered pain, but she blocked it as a surge of relief swept through her.

Lauren crawled to the opening. "Callie? Callie? Wake up." There was no response. In her bulky clothes, Lauren didn't fit through the window, so she shed her winter parka before wedging herself into the cab. She cupped Callie's face, and it was as if she held a bucket of ice.

Elation filled her when she located a jugular pulse and discovered Callie still breathing. Callie was feminine and curved in all the best places, but farming was hard work and Callie was solid muscle. At this angle, Lauren couldn't lift her. She retrieved the calving chains and wrapped them under Callie's armpits. Then she squeezed through the window, repositioned the calving jack, and careful of Callie's head, winched with her last ounce of determination.

When Callie passed through the window, she dropped into the snow, and the impact woke her. She struggled against Lauren's hands and cursed incoherently.

Callie was alive. Lauren cradled her in her arms, rocking Callie and kissing the top of her head. "You're alive. You're alive."

"Lauren? Are you real?" Callie slurred her words.

"Yes, Cals. I'll haul you up the hill to my truck soon. Are you hurt anywhere?" Lauren skimmed hands over Callie's body examining her for blood, broken bones, or tears in her clothing.

"All right, but dizzy." Callie rose as far as her knees. She vomited and would have fallen into it, but Lauren caught her and yanked her away in time.

"That was sexy," Lauren said. She was ecstatic to have Callie alive and didn't care if she sounded foolish.

"Gross," Callie mumbled before fainting in Lauren's arms.

Lauren held her for a few minutes and kissed her soft blond hair. Lauren's muscles screamed and her chest hurt from the deep breaths of chilled air. Her bones were lead and her muscles refused to obey her. She rocked Callie in her arms. She had to get them somewhere warm, but she longed to rest and to close her eyes for a few seconds.

Lauren jerked awake. How long had she slept? It could mean death for them both if it happened again. She concentrated on her hands and struggled to straighten her frozen fingers and let go of Callie. She lowered her to the ground. Lauren shivered and her teeth chattered as she pulled her coat back on. The coat was freezing, but better than nothing. She sucked on her fingers until they thawed enough that she could zip her coat. Then she yanked on her gloves and turned her attention to Callie.

Still unconscious, it was clear Callie couldn't climb the hill. Lauren looped one end of the rope around Callie's body under her arms. She crawled from under the truck until she could stand. Then she dragged Callie out and got her into position.

Lauren stumbled up the slope, convinced it was higher and steeper than when she climbed it the first time. She untied the rope from the back of her truck and dropped it through a loop on her bumper.

Lauren's shoulders throbbed as she hauled Callie up the hill. Fortunately, Callie's coat slid well over the snow.

Lauren finally dragged Callie onto the road. She gazed down at her and fought against the exhaustion that tempted her to lie beside Callie. It would be a fatal mistake. She rolled her shoulders and stooped to grab Callie under her arms. She half carried and half pushed her into the cab of her truck. She removed Callie's damp coat and boots, then she wrapped her coat and a blanket around her and shoved spare boots on her feet. She got into the driver's seat, shaking and exhausted, but determined this wasn't the end of them. She cranked the truck's heater and whipped along the snowy roads to the hospital.

Lauren delivered Callie, unconscious and freezing, to the emergency entrance at the hospital. She kissed Callie on the forehead and the doctors took Callie in right away. Lauren staggered into the waiting room and accepted the warm blanket the nurse handed her. With shaking hands, she pulled out her phone and dialed.

"Prairie Veterinary Services. This is Val. How—"

"It's Lauren. I'm with Callie. Her truck went off the road."

"Oh no! Is she hurt?"

Lauren swallowed her tears. "I don't know. We're at the hospital. There's no blood that I saw. But she was unconscious and so cold."

"You stay with her. Want me to get Becky after school?"

"Please."

"Just a second."

Lauren touched her forehead and studied the blood on her hand with curiosity. Her head didn't hurt.

"Ian said take all the time you need. He'll cover your calls. Want me to call Mark?"

"Why Mark?"

"Are you okay? You sound like you're in shock. I know Mark sometimes watches Callie's cattle."

"Good idea. Thanks, Val."

"Take care of Callie and find a doctor for yourself. And keep me informed, okay?"

Lauren slid the phone into her pocket. When summoned, she followed a nurse into a room to be examined and to have her forehead sutured. Afterward, they gave her another warm blanket and hot soup, which helped her thaw enough to focus. "Can I see her?"

"Soon," the nurse said. "She's in X-ray."

Lauren lingered in a state of fear for forty minutes until the nurse updated her on Callie's condition and permitted her to enter Callie's room. Callie was in bed, curled in a ball and wrapped in blankets. She shivered and her teeth chattered so much that "Lauren," was all she could squeeze out as her eyes misted with gratitude.

Lauren pulled a chair close to Callie's bed. She didn't care who saw her hold Callie's cold hand to her lips. She didn't care who saw her tears of relief.

"You'll be all right, Cals. Maybe a wicked cold, but they told me your fingers and toes are okay and no broken bones."

"It hurts." Tears welled in Callie's eyes.

Lauren kissed her forehead. "You're thawing out. If the pins and needles hurt too much, I'll request painkillers."

"No." Callie shook her head. "It's okay." She brushed a shaking finger underneath the line of fresh sutures on Lauren's forehead. Then she smoothed her hand down the side of Lauren's face and along her cheekbone to her chin. An instant later, Callie was sobbing. "I almost died. Becky would've been an orphan."

Lauren carefully scooped Callie into her arms. "But you didn't die. You're too tough to let a little snow stop you."

"Becky needs me."

"Damn right she does. But I've called Val, so you can relax. She'll take care of Becky, and Mark will check on your farm. Your job is to get warm."

Callie smiled. "Bossy woman."

Lauren winked. "Sometimes. When I think I can get away with it." She remained by Callie's bed while she warmed and slipped in and out of consciousness. She drew Callie's hand to her lips and lay beside her on the bed. When Callie shivered, she held her tight against her chest. "What would I have done if I'd lost you?" Fear sliced through her. Callie meant everything to her, and she believed it deep in her soul.

While Lauren cradled Callie in her arms, Callie mumbled in her sleep, "Oh, Lauren." Overjoyed to hear her name, Lauren wasn't sure whether to weep, sing, or cry.

Later, Lauren woke to soft kisses on her forehead and opened her eyes to find Callie smiling at her.

"Hi," Callie said.

Humor illuminated the laughing blue eyes, a clear sign Callie was feeling better. Lauren tilted her head and kissed Callie's lips with all the love she could convey. Callie's lips were warm, and she only shivered a little. "You're awake."

Lauren fetched the nurse and with her help, they maneuvered Callie into the bathroom and then back into bed. Lauren tucked Callie in with a kiss. The nurse disappeared, and ten minutes later, returned with a tray of food she handed to Lauren.

"Cals, I have a bowl of thick hot soup. Let's see what you can get down."

Lauren helped Callie sit up and propped a pillow behind her. Callie cradled the bowl and spooned the warm liquid into her mouth. "Amazing." Callie gripped the spoon, but it tapped against the side of the bowl as her hand shook. Her hand shook so much that the spoon was only half-full by the time it reached her mouth.

"Let me." Lauren lifted the bowl from Callie's hands and fed her. "What happened, Cals? Did you go into a skid?"

Callie shook head. "Forced off the road. Kyle, I think. What an asshole."

"I'm going to call Mitchell." She didn't care who she had to go to for help. Callie could have died, and Lauren's heart would have gone with her. Lauren wasn't a violent woman, but if Kyle had appeared in that room at that second, she'd have throttled him.

When the bowl was empty, Callie slept, and Lauren phoned the RCMP. Mitch had already heard about the accident and was waiting until the doctors said Callie was strong enough to interview. She was interested in the suggestion that Kyle had forced Callie off the road, and her tone had changed from professional to mercenary. Lauren grinned as she ended the call. She was sure Mitch would help her throttle Kyle.

When she woke again, Callie asked Lauren to explain her rescue. After the story, Callie hugged her tightly. "Thank you for saving me." As the nurse entered the room, Callie turned to the nurse and laughed. "My veterinarian calved my truck and delivered me." Callie squeezed Lauren's hand and smiled at her. "I'm reborn, but thanks for not sticking straw up my nose."

The nurse donned a polite smile, and Lauren knew the nurse assumed Callie was still disoriented from the hypothermia.

Lauren left Callie to sleep and phoned Val with an update. Then she paced the halls of the hospital as she struggled to control her temper. The woman and child she loved were in danger from creeps and assholes. Maybe this time the police would put an end to the harassment. If they didn't, she'd find a way. It might cost her job or her license to practice. She didn't care. For a long time, she'd thought her career was all she needed. What a fool she'd been. She needed friends and family, and most of all, Callie.

CHAPTER THIRTY-FOUR

Two nights after Callie's truck crashed, Lauren was still staying at Poplarcreek. She'd taken Friday off work and said she would stay all weekend, but she wasn't going anywhere. She'd be at Poplarcreek every night until Kyle and Heinz were in jail. After the accident, Callie had called her parents and Martha had offered to come back to Saskatchewan, but Callie had said she was in good hands. Lauren was sleeping in the spare room and looking after Callie and Becky. When they finished dinner, they curled on the couch, Callie in Lauren's arms and Becky in Callie's, and watched an animated movie. After Becky went to bed, Callie and Lauren sprawled on the living room couch and watched a lesbian movie.

Lauren caressed Callie's arm. Callie was doing better. Her movements were still a little slow and stiff, but she no longer lowered herself to a chair as if she were a hundred years old. The large bruises on Callie's back were deep purple. Miraculously, Callie had escaped serious injury, but her truck was scrap metal. The Thresherton Garage had winched the truck up the hill. Before disposing of the truck, the men had carefully collected the contents of Callie's purse and delivered it to Poplarcreek.

With a bit of coaching from Mark, and with Becky's help, Lauren had taken over checking on Callie's cattle. At least she didn't have to subject Callie to her cooking. Five families couldn't have eaten all the food friends and neighbors dropped off. Lauren had repackaged some of the casseroles, labeled them, and wedged them into Callie's big freezer. She'd grown used to the surprised looks when townsfolk found her at Callie's house. She was too happy Callie was okay to care if the whole world knew they were together.

Lauren sighed, a deep sigh filled with thoughts of Callie. She tried to tamp down her worry. Kyle had probably tried to kill Callie. Poplarcreek wasn't worth her life. She longed to protect them, but the itchy scar down the middle of her back was a reminder that she couldn't even protect herself.

Their goal was to collect evidence against Heinz and Kyle. Since their first visit to the police, she and Callie had reported every incident with the Krugers to the RCMP and Callie had handed over all the letters and emails from Heinz going back to before Christmas. Mitch had even arranged for a recorder to be attached to Callie's home phone to catch any more phone calls from Heinz.

Lauren dropped a kiss into Callie's hair. Callie lounged on the couch with her head nestled against Lauren's shoulder while they watched the movie. When the movie ended, she sat up and stretched. "Thanks. Funny movie. I can't believe I've never seen it. It was sweet." Callie leaned in for a kiss. "And sexy," she whispered against Lauren's lips.

They lingered over the next kiss and as the heat built, Lauren's head swam. She spoke when she could assemble words into a coherent sentence. "How're you feeling?"

Callie yawned. "I'm full of yawns. I've had a long day of lazing on the couch."

"Why don't you relax some more? It's not like there's anywhere you need to be." And if she was right there in Lauren's arms, she knew Callie was safe.

"Okay." Callie lay her head in Lauren's lap. Then Callie kicked off her shoes and brought her long legs onto the couch.

"Here, try this." Lauren positioned a small throw pillow beneath Callie's head. She gazed down at the beautiful woman in her lap, amazed that she'd grown so comfortable with the idea of having someone in her life again.

Callie yawned again. "Thanks. I'm too comfortable. I'm liable to fall asleep on you."

"Go ahead. I love holding you while you sleep. But I can keep you awake, too." Lauren caressed her cheek and her finger feathered along the line of Callie's jaw to caress soft lips that parted when touched. Callie's pink lips, already flushed with blood, became darker. *She does blush.*

Callie sighed and her eyes fluttered closed.

Lauren smoothed her left hand in lazy circles on Callie's stomach. Then she slid her left hand under Callie's sweater and upward to cup Callie's right breast. Her explorations paused. "You're not wearing a bra."

Callie smiled. "I don't need to. You C-cup women don't understand, I suppose? And besides I've been on the couch all day while you and Becky pampered me." Callie put her hand on Lauren's hand and shifted it over her breast. "Don't stop."

Lauren smiled as she swept her hand along Callie's chest, skimming her nipples, teasing them as she brushed past. Under her palm, Callie's heart raced. Lauren rolled each nipple between her fingers. "Tell me," she said softly. There was no response. "Tell me, Cals."

"Tell you what?"

"Are you too sore? Should I stop?" Lauren whispered.

Callie gasped as Lauren pinched her nipple. "Don't you dare stop."

"Then tell me what you want. I'll do anything."

There was a wicked set to the curve of Callie's mouth. "Anything?"

Lauren grinned. "Try me."

"Pull my nipples harder."

Lauren tugged on each nipple and increased the pressure when Callie moaned. Her right hand continued its gentle exploration, and she traced the edge of Callie's ear and down her neck to a pounding pulse. Callie turned her head and sucked two of Lauren's fingers into her mouth. "Oh, Callie." Lauren gasped in pleasure.

Callie struggled to sit up. "Wait." Callie crawled off the couch and locked the living room door. It wouldn't be good to have Becky walking in on them.

Lauren waited in anticipation for her orders. Her skin and lap were cold without Callie's presence. Callie positioned herself in front of Lauren's knees. Lauren splayed her hands on Callie's flaring hips and round ass and drew her close. She lifted Callie's sweater and planted a series of kisses on her flat stomach. "You're athlete fit, Cals. I can feel every muscle and you taste like heaven."

Callie leaned on Lauren's shoulders and propelled her deeper into the couch. Then she tore off her sweater and straddled Lauren's lap. Lauren accepted the invitation and kissed the breasts on a level with her mouth. She traced the junction of Callie's breasts and rib cage with her tongue and licked her nipple. Callie moaned and arched her back. Lauren sucked and nibbled and strove to elicit deeper moans. As she explored Callie's chest, she clasped Callie's ass with her hands and squeezed. She rubbed her hands up and down Callie's thighs. "Let me up for a second."

Callie blinked, slid off Lauren's lap, and stood weaving.

Lauren rose to her feet and cupped Callie's face to kiss her. Then she removed her own sweater and spread it on the couch. She skimmed Callie's jeans and panties down her legs and maneuvered Callie until she sat on top of the sweater. She kneeled in front of Callie and caressed her trembling thighs. "I've been fantasizing about doing this."

Callie couldn't speak but bobbed her head and spread her knees.

Lauren slid her arms and shoulders under Callie's long legs before lowering her mouth to her center. She avoided Callie's clit so she could delay the orgasm and have time to explore. She kissed and licked the inside of Callie's thighs, tracing the delectable flesh from one side to the other. Lauren skimmed her tongue across Callie's sensitive center as she passed by. Then she blew over where she had licked.

Callie growled in frustration. "Now. Please, baby."

Lauren ignored the request and continued to tease. So much for doing what she was told. Callie placed a hand at the apex of her legs to circle and rub herself. Lauren kept licking and kissing but watched from the corner of her eye. When Callie's speed increased, Lauren said, "Stop. That's my job." She followed her command by nipping at Callie's hand with her teeth until Callie removed it. Callie was open wide and exposed. She drank in Callie's sweet smell and dipped her tongue to flick at her pulsing clit.

Callie's body jerked once. "More, more." Callie's head rolled back and forth where it lay on the couch.

Lauren obliged, licking and sucking harder. Callie's excitement tightened around the two fingers Lauren slipped inside her. She moved faster and faster with hand and tongue as she sensed Callie's passion build. Callie stiffened and orgasmed. Soft gasps emerged in time to contractions as Callie held Lauren's fingers inside.

Lauren slowed, though her fingers remained buried inside as she bestowed a series of small kisses along Callie's thighs, labia, and stomach. When she sensed Callie relax, she withdrew and rose on her knees to gaze into satisfied blue eyes, hooded by drooping eyelids.

Callie shifted to perch on the edge of the couch and wrapped her arms and legs around Lauren as the soft aftershocks of the orgasm continued.

Lauren held Callie close. "I could do this for a week and never tire of pleasing you." She enjoyed Callie's orgasms more when Callie yelled her pleasure, but it wasn't possible with Becky one floor above them.

Callie peeled off Lauren's bra and tossed it on the floor. She pushed Lauren back on her heels. Then Callie lowered herself over Lauren's lap. Lauren took the hint and slid two fingers inside Callie. While Lauren thrust, and rubbed her thumb against Callie's clit, Callie rode her fingers.

Callie looped her arms around Lauren's neck and their breasts rubbed together with each thrust. Then Callie pressed down hard and climaxed again, this one stronger than the first. Head thrown back, Callie bit her lip to muffle her scream of satisfaction.

Callie sagged in Lauren's arms and they rested with their foreheads pressed together. "I hope my legs will hold me." Callie grabbed Lauren's hand and struggled to stand. "I've got plans for you. I want you upstairs, now."

"My pleasure." Lauren followed Callie toward the door. She stopped for a second to scoop their clothes off the floor and hand them to Callie. Then she positioned the screen in front of the glowing embers in the fireplace and accompanied Callie upstairs. They made love again before falling asleep under a thick comforter. They slept naked in each other's arms, legs entangled, and skin touching everywhere possible.

The next morning, they snuggled in bed. Callie lay with her head on Lauren's shoulder and caressed Lauren's hand where it lay on Callie's chest. "I guess we should get up."

"When you're ready," Lauren said.

There was a quiet knock at the door. "Mommy, may I come in and visit, please?"

"Um no, sorry, honey." Callie sputtered the sentence. She popped to a seated position and met Lauren's smile with her own. "How about I get dressed and we make blueberry pancakes? We still have some of the berries Grandma sent us."

"Yay, pancakes for breakfast. Can I flip them?"

"Yes, honey." Callie sprang from bed and rummaged in her dresser for clean clothes.

"Do you like blueberry pancakes, too, Lauren?"

Callie whirled, clothing clutched to her chest, and gaped at Lauren.

Lauren mouthed, "Busted." She smiled and pulled the blanket over her chest, just in case Becky came in. "Yes, thank you, Becky. Yummy." Becky must have assumed Lauren had spent the night in Callie's room. Kids were way too smart, sometimes.

"Okay, Lauren and Mommy. I'll go get dressed."

Lauren listened to Becky skip along the hall accompanied by Max's hopping gate.

Callie stroked Lauren's face. "I love having you here, but I should've talked to Becky before you stayed the night with me, when she was home. I don't want her confused"

With her fingertip, Lauren traced lazy patterns on Callie's bare back. "She didn't sound upset."

"Let's hope not. I'll shower, dress, and head downstairs. Join us when you're ready."

Eyes wide, Lauren did her best at an innocent expression. "Should I wash your back?"

Callie shot to her feet and waggled her finger at Lauren. "You stay put. If we go in there together, we'll never get to breakfast."

Satisfied, Lauren snuggled under the covers while Callie walked down the hall to shower. Life was good. She had slept with Callie in her arms and now there would be a big family breakfast. She was ecstatic, but still scared. She had been here before and lost it all.

❖

"Those were awesome pancakes, kiddo," Lauren said as she carried their dirty dishes to the sink.

"You liked the raspberry ones best. You ate four," Becky said as she helped clear the table.

"Busted. I like blueberry, too. Callie, you stay put and rest. Becky cooked so I'm in charge of dishes." Lauren hugged Becky and kissed the top of the head. Becky grinned up at her, and Lauren knew she was part of the family. The thought was far less frightening than it had been.

Lauren did the dishes while Callie sipped her coffee. It had been an awesome breakfast and Becky had run upstairs to play afterward. It felt wonderfully domestic and her soul was at ease. Her phone buzzed and she wiped her hands and pulled it from her pocket.

"Do you have to go?" Callie asked.

"No. Ian's covering for the weekend. That's Tommy. He wants to see us. What do you think?" Lauren tapped at the phone, disliking the Kruger name on the screen.

"I'm curious about why and I don't think he's the problem. I say let him come now, so we can get it over with. But he must come alone."

"Agreed." Lauren responded to the text and continued with the dishes. She put on another pot of coffee and sat with Callie to wait. Ten minutes later, a truck arrived followed by a knock on Callie's door. Lauren gave Callie a reassuring squeeze when she felt her tense and rose to let Tommy in. He kicked off his boots in the mudroom, hesitated in the kitchen doorway and then sat across from Callie at the table.

Tommy sat with his head hanging and didn't touch the coffee or muffins Lauren placed in front of him. "Tommy? You said you had something to tell us?"

"This has to stop." Tommy hesitated and then his words poured out. "I can't be part of this anymore. I know my father and brother have been hassling you, but I don't want them to go to jail."

Lauren frowned. "But it's likely they will, given everything they're into. And now with Callie's crash—"

"She would've died if you hadn't found her." Tommy straightened and his eyes met Lauren's. "And that's not right." He took a deep breath. "It was Kyle and it wasn't an accident. It was my dad's idea. If you died the farm would probably be auctioned and then he could get it for almost nothing." Tommy's head dropped and his shoulders sagged.

Callie slammed her hand on the table. "I knew it. I saw a black pickup truck."

Tommy raised his head. "I want my family back, and I want to escape from my father and brother. Will you help me?"

Lauren leaned toward him. "Tell the truth. Tell it to the RCMP or to a lawyer first, but you *must* tell the truth or Callie and Becky will continue to be in danger. Confessing is the path to peace and your way back to life. Back to your wife and children. Nobody should ever give up on a chance to reunite with their family." She would've crawled through broken glass to reconnect with Sam and William.

"I will. I'll make this right. I'll go right now." Tommy wiped the tears from his cheeks. Then he left.

That evening, Tommy phoned Poplarcreek and told Lauren and Callie that he'd gone straight to the RCMP detachment. "I told them I needed to keep my father and brother from hurting anyone. They interviewed me for four hours and I told them everything I knew. They know about the stolen cattle, and I told them about Kyle threatening Lauren that night at PVS, and how my dad wants Callie's farm at any cost. And I told them how Kyle let Bulldozer go, hoping he'd crush Lauren so she couldn't tell the police anything else. And how he ran you off the road, Callie. I'm really sorry about all this, you guys. I'll make sure nothing else happens."

After answering all their questions, Tommy hung up.

"Wow," Lauren said. "I can't believe it's over."

"Don't be too sure. I'll believe it when Heinz and Kyle are in prison."

Lauren pulled her close and rested her cheek against Callie's soft hair. "I'll feel better when that happens too." She shifted and kissed Callie gently. "So, what are we going to do when we're not running from crazy people?"

Callie took her hand and pulled her toward the stairs. "I have some ideas on that."

Chapter Thirty-Five

On Saturday night, Callie dropped Becky and Max at Val's house. Gwen and Becky were becoming inseparable and she was happy for them. Callie hummed as she drove the short distance from Val's house to Lauren's. Mitch had called the day after Tommy's confession to say that Heinz and Kyle had been arrested, and between Callie and Lauren's evidence as well as Tommy's, they wouldn't be getting out any time soon. The border authorities had tracked down the people Kyle had met with after crossing the border, and it had exposed a drug ring they'd known little about. The laundry list of charges meant neither Kruger would be getting out for a very long time. She shook her head to push the Krugers aside and enjoy her weekend.

She was excited because she was spending Saturday night and most of Sunday alone with Lauren. The calvings were done at Poplarcreek and she'd done the last two by herself. Two months ago, she would never have imagined she could do it. Her animals were happy and healthy, except one of her cows who had a foot abscess that wasn't healing. She had booked Ian after lunch on Monday to examine the animal. She had considered asking Lauren, but Lauren would want to do the work for free and that wasn't okay with Callie. But Lauren had understood that boundary and acquiesced with grace.

Callie sighed. She had relatively little farm work until spring seeding. All she had to do was tune up her farm machinery and wait for the ground to thaw. It was late April, and the temperature bounced between minus five and plus five degrees Celsius. She scanned the lawns and driveways as she headed to Lauren's. The snow was melting, and it was still light out at six p.m. Callie grinned and switched to singing. Spring was on the way.

Lauren was cooking and had warned her not to expect much in the kitchen. "I can cook a few meals that wouldn't kill anyone, but I'm not a fancy cook. Dinner will be edible, but every dish is less than four ingredients."

Callie grinned at the pronouncement that any dish with over four ingredients was considered too complicated.

Callie parked her SUV and plugged it into Lauren's garage. She walked along the side of the house and as she passed the kitchen window, glanced in. Lauren lay face down on the floor with Digit curled in a ball in the middle of her back. A sharp pain stabbed Callie in the chest, and she dropped her suitcase and sprinted to Lauren's back door. Discovering the door was unlocked, she rushed inside and dropped to her knees beside Lauren. "Honey, are you all right? Baby?" Her voiced trembled as she shook her.

Lauren rolled slowly onto her back and Digit jumped off. Lauren grinned up at Callie.

"Are you okay?" Callie ran her hands along Lauren's body, hunting for injuries.

"Hello tall, blond, and beautiful." Lauren winked. "What a nice way to wake up. I love getting felt up. Carry on, please."

Callie's brow furrowed as she stared down. "Are you hurt? Why are you on the floor?"

Lauren sat up. "It was a long day. I did two C-sections and three calvings and I was too tired to stand in the shower. I was napping until I had the energy to shower and change." Lauren shifted to her knees and kissed Callie. "I'm too smelly to lie in my bed or on the couch, so I lay on the floor." Lauren stood and reached down a hand to bring Callie to her feet. "Are you all right?"

Callie wrapped her arms around Lauren's neck, dragging her close into a crushing embrace. She shook as the burst of adrenaline drained away. She was on edge and constantly checking over her shoulder for the next attack by a Kruger.

"Cals, are you all right?"

Callie stepped from the embrace. Her eyes stung with unshed tears. "I saw you on the floor and it scared me. I thought Kruger had hurt you again."

Lauren caressed Callie's face with the back of her hand. "That's all done now. Heinz and Kyle have been arrested." After a beat, Lauren squirmed. "You're kind of crushing me."

Callie released Lauren and kissed her on the lips. She scanned the kitchen and forced herself to relax. "Your kitchen smells nice."

"I popped a chicken in the oven before my floor nap, but I'm ready for a shower now."

Lauren disappeared into the bathroom and Callie collected her bag from the path where she dropped it. She wiped her wet footprints off the kitchen floor and waited for Lauren in the living room. Digit joined her on the couch for a cuddle.

Fifteen minutes later, Lauren returned in jeans and a tight sweater. Callie swallowed and scanned Lauren. Dinner first. Then other activities. "Can I help with anything?"

"No thanks. I've got it." Lauren uncorked the wine and passed Callie a glass. Then Lauren set the table beginning with an elegant white tablecloth and ending with candles. When dinner was ready, they sat to eat and chatted about the minutia of their day.

Thirty minutes later, Callie wiped her mouth with a cloth napkin. "Dinner's delicious. You should cook more often."

"Even I can't screw up a roast chicken with apple and raisin stuffing. I'm particularly proud that the baked potatoes and cooked carrots were ready at the same time. It never happens. Often one is mush and the other raw."

When the meal ended, they cleared up the leftovers and washed the dishes. After Lauren popped the final clean dish in the cupboard, she turned to Callie. "Would you like to watch a movie?"

Callie still simmered from the last time they made love. They had been planning to make love last night, but Lauren had to leave to do an emergency C-section on a dog. An occupational hazard for a veterinarian. It had taken a long time for Callie to fall asleep alone.

Callie tapped her bottom lip with an index finger as she pretended to consider the movie idea. "No, thanks."

Lauren waggled her eyebrows. "Cards? Monopoly? Want to see photographs of my trip to Peru?"

Callie sidled toward Lauren's bedroom and crooked a finger over her shoulder.

❖

In the morning, Callie woke cozy and content in Lauren's arms as Lauren bestowed warm kisses on her nape and shoulders. No place in the world was better than lying on her side with Lauren curled around her. Callie struggled to recall the last time she'd felt this content and she knew she never had. Her marriage had been wonderful, and she'd never forget Liz, but what she had with Lauren was something else, something beyond special, and she treasured everything she brought to her life.

Lauren slid out of bed and reached for her robe. "Coffee?"

Callie squinted up at Lauren. Callie wasn't a morning person and discovering Lauren was had annoyed her. She rolled her head on the pillow and stuck out her tongue at Lauren.

Lauren chuckled and stepped back. "Don't stick that out unless you intend to use it."

Callie pawed at Lauren's leg. "Come back to bed and I'll be happy to demonstrate."

"Our brunch reservation is for eleven, or would you prefer to stay home? I know better than to make decisions without consulting you."

"Switch it to one and get back in here."

Lauren giggled as she grabbed her phone. "Yes, ma'am."

After the call, Lauren dropped her robe and pinned Callie to the bed. "Ever spend a whole day in bed where you only get up to make a sandwich or let the dog out?"

Callie pulled Lauren's face down and kissed her soundly.

Two hours later, Lauren got up. "I'm starving"

"Okay, I'm up." Callie dragged herself from bed as if she were a kid on the first day of school after a summer of playing outside all day.

They showered, dressed, and headed out for the three-course brunch at a country restaurant in the next town.

"I'd like to pay," Callie said. "You made dinner."

"Please, the weekend is my treat for us. A celebration of the end of calving season."

Callie grinned and kissed Lauren's cheek. "Okay and thank you." Callie relented and agreed to let Lauren pay. She had learned the difference between being cared for and controlled, and although she might still get stressed about it once in a while, she knew she'd grown thanks to Lauren's sweet patience.

On the way back to Lauren's, Callie watched out the windows and shivered when a black pickup truck passed them.

Lauren took her hand. "You still having nightmares about being buried in snow?"

Callie grimaced. "Not when you're holding me." And that had been all week. Nearly every night since the accident she'd been safe and warm in Lauren's arms.

Callie traced the edges of Lauren's palms. She admired Lauren's strong, deft hands and long fingers. Lauren's hands, body, and the way her muscles danced along her bare arms while she performed surgery had mesmerized Callie from the first day she'd met her.

As planned, Lauren pulled over at a park on the way home. "I'm too full for a long hike, but it's a beautiful day." After a short walk into the woods, Lauren spread a tarp in the sun, at the base of a tree and motioned for Callie to lie between her legs.

"Do you think Heinz and Kyle are really done hassling us?" Callie asked as she leaned back against Lauren.

"You still worry about them."

"It's hard not to. I feel as if I've been on guard for months."

"Cals, we beat them, with Tommy's help. I'm not looking forward to the trial, but they won't be bothering us anymore."

Callie slid closer to Lauren and Lauren wrapped her arms around her. "That's a relief. I want to thank you for everything you did for us."

"I care about you and Becky."

"And we care about you. Hey, I should call and check on Becky. Want to join me?"

"I'd like that." Lauren sighed. "Some days I can't believe we're together. I'm still astonished that I was able to emerge from my cocoon of insecurity and fear long enough to find you and Becky."

Callie sat up and kissed Lauren on the lips. "I'm glad you did. You're a warm, beautiful woman and shouldn't stay cut off from people. Do you still think you're a stand-in for Liz?"

Lauren locked eyes with Callie. "No, I don't."

"Good. There'll always be a place in my heart for Liz, but I'm ready to be in love again." Lauren blushed and smiled. Liz never blushed. Where Liz was abrupt and tough, Lauren was gentle. Except for both being honorable with a strong commitment to work, Callie couldn't imagine two more different women.

Callie settled again and leaned back against Lauren. "Let's call my kid." Callie put her phone on speaker and held it between them.

"Hi, Mommy."

"Hi, honey, I'm here with Lauren. Are you having fun?"

"We made our own pizzas last night. Val showed us how to roll the dough and everything. Now I can make us pizza at home."

"With pineapple?" Lauren asked.

Becky laughed. "Only on yours. Gwen said you have a dog surgery on Monday, and she gets to watch."

"Would you like to come too?"

"I'm not in the way?"

"Never, kiddo. I like your company and you're a lot of fun. Besides, I'm going to be an owner soon, so I get to decide who visits."

"Awesome. You're fun too. I have to go now. We're taking Max for a walk."

"Bye, honey. See you at dinnertime. Love you," Callie said.

"Love you too, Mommy and Lauren."

Callie smiled. Becky has said she loved Lauren as if it were the most natural thing to say. Callie swiveled to rest on one hip and brushed a tear off Lauren's cheek. "You okay?"

Lauren sniffled. "I'm touched. Becky's an amazing kid. And I can't wait until the summer when Sam's here. I want her to meet you both."

"How's it going with Sam?"

"Awesome. She texts all the time and we talk almost every day. Sometimes for only a few minutes, but it's like I'm there in the room with her." Lauren shrugged. "I've had a couple of short conversations with William, but he's eighteen and over needing a second mom." She grinned. "But I'm not giving up. He's kind of stuck with me."

"Wonderful. I'd love to meet Sam, and William if that happens. So, what's this about you being an owner at PVS?"

"Ian wants to retire in a couple of years. So, I'm buying in. It will take a while to pay it off, but I'm ready to be a practice owner again."

"And stay in Thresherton."

"You'll have to decide if Poplarcreek wants the family rate at PVS."

Callie slapped her playfully and grinned. Then she stared into the woods and reflected on their conversation. Now was the time to say what had been building in her heart. What had been there for a while, but she hadn't been ready to acknowledge. She took Lauren's hand in hers. "Lauren, I love you."

Lauren gaped. "Oh, I—oh."

Callie nodded and Lauren blushed. Callie tucked her bottom lip between her teeth and waited. And waited. "You don't—"

Lauren launched herself at Callie and knocked her to the ground. Callie landed flat on her back in the snow with Lauren on top. "I love you too." Lauren kissed her hard.

Callie rolled Lauren onto her back, pinned her in place, and claimed her mouth. They kissed for a few minutes, and Callie searched her eyes for any doubts. "I love you. You're kind and generous, and you've had my back since I first met you. I'm stronger with you, and braver."

"You were always strong. You never gave up and I'm impressed."

"You're strong too."

"I don't know if that's true, but I know I'm ready to be in love. Ready for a relationship with you. I came to Saskatchewan for a peaceful life all alone, but when I'm within ten feet of you, I feel anything but peaceful and I love not being alone."

Callie laughed. "Peaceful isn't a word to describe life at Poplarcreek, but I want you to join my family. Share our lives." She had yearned for somebody to share her life with and longed for somebody to cuddle with on the couch and hold in bed every night. She'd just lost her way. Now, somehow, she knew they'd be just fine.

"I'd love to. I love you, Cals. I never want to be anywhere but with you," Lauren said.

"And I love you." Callie bent and kissed Lauren only stopping when Lauren shivered. Callie nibbled Lauren's bottom lip. "You turned on?"

"Yes, but I'm getting cold. The snow is soaking through my clothes."

Callie climbed off Lauren and helped her off the ground. She did her best to brush the debris off, paying particular attention to doing a thorough job of brushing Lauren's backside clean. "Don't want the seat of your truck to get dirty."

"Good story, but how is squeezing my butt a technique for removing dirt?"

"Come on, you."

They returned to the truck and headed back to Lauren's. Their lovemaking was unhurried as they shared the love in their hearts and took their time over each other's bodies. Lauren fell asleep curled in Callie's arms. Callie watched long, dark eyelashes flutter as Lauren slept, and was content in the knowledge that love meant forever.

About the Author

Nancy Wheelton graduated over twenty years ago from the Ontario Veterinary College in Guelph, Ontario. She spent the first few years after graduation working in a mixed animal practice in a small town in the province of Saskatchewan. Then she settled in the Great Lakes region of Ontario, where she is a practicing veterinarian.

When Nancy's not kayaking, photographing wildlife, or working on her beach house, she enjoys the crashing waves and sunsets while writing. Please visit her at Nancywheelton.com.

Books Available from Bold Strokes Books

All the Paths to You by Morgan Lee Miller. High school sweethearts Quinn Hughes and Kennedy Reed reconnect five years after they break up and realize that their chemistry is all but over. (978-1-63555-662-9)

Arrested Pleasures by Nanisi Barrett D'Arnuck. When charged with a crime she didn't commit Katherine Lowe faces the question: Which is harder, going to prison or falling in love? (978-1-63555-684-1)

Bonded Love by Renee Roman. Carpenter Blaze Carter suffers an injury that shatters her dreams, and ER nurse Trinity Greene hopes to show her that sometimes hope is worth fighting for. (978-1-63555-530-1)

Convergence by Jane C. Esther. With life as they know it on the line, can Aerin McLeary and Olivia Ando's love survive an otherworldly threat to humankind? (978-1-63555-488-5)

Coyote Blues by Karen F. Williams. Riley Dawson, psychotherapist and shape-shifter, has her world turned upside down when Fiona Bell, her one true love, returns. (978-1-63555-558-5)

Drawn by Carsen Taite. Will the clues lead Detective Claire Hanlon to the killer terrorizing Dallas, or will she merely lose her heart to person of interest, urban artist Riley Flynn? (978-1-63555-644-5)

Every Summer Day by Lee Patton. Meant to celebrate every summer day, Luke's journal instead chronicles a love affair as fast-moving and possibly as fatal as his brother's brain tumor. (978-1-63555-706-0)

Lucky by Kris Bryant. Was Serena Evans's luck really about winning the lottery, or is she about to get even luckier in love? (978-1-63555-510-3)

The Last Days of Autumn by Donna K. Ford. Autumn and Caroline question the fairness of life, the cruelty of loss, and what it means to love as they navigate the complicated minefield of relationships, grief, and life-altering illness. (978-1-63555-672-8)

Three Alarm Response by Erin Dutton. In the midst of tragedy, can these first responders find love and healing? Three stories of courage, bravery, and passion. (978-1-63555-592-9)

Veterinary Partner by Nancy Wheelton. Callie and Lauren are determined to keep their hearts safe but find that taking a chance on love is the safest option of all. (978-1-63555-666-7)

Everyday People by Louis Barr. When film star Diana Danning hires private eye Clint Steele to find her son, Clint turns to his former West Point barracks mate, and ex-buddy with benefits, Mars Hauser to lend his cyber espionage and digital black ops skills to the case. (978-1-63555-698-8)

Forging a Desire Line by Mary P. Burns. When Charley's ex-wife, Tricia, is diagnosed with inoperable cancer, the private duty nurse Tricia hires turns out to be the handsome and aloof Joanna, who ignites something inside Charley she isn't ready to face. (978-1-63555-665-0)

Love on the Night Shift by Radclyffe. Between ruling the night shift in the ER at the Rivers and raising her teenage daughter, Blaise Richilieu has all the drama she needs in her life, until a dashing young attending appears on the scene and relentlessly pursues her. (978-1-63555-668-1)

Olivia's Awakening by Ronica Black. When the daring and dangerously gorgeous Eve Monroe is hired to get Olivia Savage into shape, a fierce passion ignites, causing both to question everything they've ever known about love. (978-1-63555-613-1)

The Duchess and the Dreamer by Jenny Frame. Clementine Fitzroy has lost her faith and love of life. Can dreamer Evan Fox make her believe in life and dream again? (978-1-63555-601-8)

The Road Home by Erin Zak. Hollywood actress Gwendolyn Carter is about to discover that losing someone you love sometimes means gaining someone to fall for. (978-1-63555-633-9)

Waiting for You by Elle Spencer. When passionate past-life lovers meet again in the present day, one remembers it vividly and the other isn't so sure. (978-1-63555-635-3)

While My Heart Beats by Erin McKenzie. Can a love born amidst the horrors of the Great War survive? (978-1-63555-589-9)

Face the Music by Ali Vali. Sweet music is the last thing that happens when Nashville music producer Mason Liner, and daughter of country royalty Victoria Roddy are thrown together in an effort to save country star Sophie Roddy's career. (978-1-63555-532-5)

Flavor of the Month by Georgia Beers. What happens when baker Charlie and chef Emma realize their differing paths have led them right back to each other? (978-1-63555-616-2)

Mending Fences by Angie Williams. Rancher Bobbie Del Rey and veterinarian Grace Hammond are about to discover if heartbreaks of the past can ever truly be mended. (978-1-63555-708-4)

Silk and Leather: Lesbian Erotica with an Edge edited by Victoria Villasenor. This collection of stories by award winning authors offers fantasies as soft as silk and tough as leather. The only question is: How far will you go to make your deepest desires come true? (978-1-63555-587-5)

The Last Place You Look by Aurora Rey. Dumped by her wife and looking for anything but love, Julia Pierce retreats to her hometown, only to rediscover high school friend Taylor Winslow, who's secretly crushed on her for years. (978-1-63555-574-5)

The Mortician's Daughter by Nan Higgins. A singer on the verge of stardom discovers she must give up her dreams to live a life in service to ghosts. (978-1-63555-594-3)

The Real Thing by Laney Webber. When passion flares between actress Virginia Green and masseuse Allison McDonald, can they be sure it's the real thing? (978-1-63555-478-6)

What the Heart Remembers Most by M. Ullrich. For college sweethearts Jax Levine and Gretchen Mills, could an accident be the second chance neither knew they wanted? (978-1-63555-401-4)

White Horse Point by Andrews & Austin. Mystery writer Taylor James finds herself falling for the mysterious woman on White Horse Point who lives alone, protecting a secret she can't share about a murderer who walks among them. (978-1-63555-695-7)

Femme Tales by Anne Shade. Six women find themselves in their own real-life fairy tales when true love finds them in the most unexpected ways. (978-1-63555-657-5)

Jellicle Girl by Stevie Mikayne. One dark summer night, Beth and Jackie go out to the canoe dock. Two years later, Beth is still carrying the weight of what happened to Jackie. (978-1-63555-691-9)

Le Berceau by Julius Eks. If only Ben could tear his heart in two, then he wouldn't have to choose between the love of his life and the most beautiful boy he has ever seen. (978-1-63555-688-9)

My Date with a Wendigo by Genevieve McCluer. Elizabeth Rosseau finds her long lost love and the secret community of fiends she's now a part of. (978-1-63555-679-7)

On the Run by Charlotte Greene. Even when they're cute blondes, it's stupid to pick up hitchhikers, especially when they've just broken out of prison, but doing so is about to change Gwen's life forever. (978-1-63555-682-7)

Perfect Timing by Dena Blake. The choice between love and family has never been so difficult, and Lynn's and Maggie's different visions of the future may end their romance before it's begun. (978-1-63555-466-3)

The Mail Order Bride by R Kent. When a mail order bride is thrust on Austin, he must choose between the bride he never wanted or the dream he lives for. (978-1-63555-678-0)

Through Love's Eyes by C.A. Popovich. When fate reunites Brittany Yardin and Amy Jansons, can they move beyond the pain of their past to find love? (978-1-63555-629-2)

To the Moon and Back by Melissa Brayden. Film actress Carly Daniel thinks that stage work is boring and unexciting, but when she accepts a lead role in a new play, stage manager Lauren Prescott tests both her heart and her ability to share the limelight. (978-1-63555-618-6)

Tokyo Love by Diana Jean. When Kathleen Schmitt is given the opportunity to be on the cutting edge of AI technology, she never thought a failed robotic love companion would bring her closer to her neighbor, Yuriko Velucci, and finding love in unexpected places. (978-1-63555-681-0)

Brooklyn Summer by Maggie Cummings. When opposites attract, can a summer of passion and adventure lead to a lifetime of love? (978-1-63555-578-3)

City Kitty and Country Mouse by Alyssa Linn Palmer. Pulled in two different directions, can a city kitty and country mouse fall in love and make it work? (978-1-63555-553-0)

Elimination by Jackie D. When a dangerous homegrown terrorist seeks refuge with the Russian mafia, the team will be put to the ultimate test. (978-1-63555-570-7)

In the Shadow of Darkness by Nicole Stiling. Angeline Vallencourt is a reluctant vampire who must decide what she wants more—obscurity, revenge, or the woman who makes her feel alive. (978-1-63555-624-7)

On Second Thought by C. Spencer. Madisen is falling hard for Rae. Even single life and co-parenting are beginning to click. At least, that is, until her ex-wife begins to have second thoughts. (978-1-63555-415-1)

Out of Practice by Carsen Taite. When attorney Abby Keane discovers the wedding blogger tormenting her client is the woman she had a passionate, anonymous vacation fling with, sparks and subpoenas fly. Legal Affairs: one law firm, three best friends, three chances to fall in love. (978-1-63555-359-8)

Providence by Leigh Hays. With every click of the shutter, photographer Rebekiah Kearns finds it harder and harder to keep Lindsey Blackwell in focus without getting too close. (978-1-63555-620-9)

Taking a Shot at Love by KC Richardson. When academic and athletic worlds collide, will English professor Celeste Bouchard and basketball coach Lisa Tobias ignore their attraction to achieve their professional goals? (978-1-63555-549-3)